Praise for *A True Impediment*

An impressive feat, an Oxbridge life of the mind and a very painful, complex, and moving love story, lived through with the help of literature. The meticulous academic's pace of life, the art, the music, the beautiful trips, made such an important backdrop to the story. . . Beautiful, complex work . . . This could be the next Oxbridge love story . . . Alan's inner life [is rendered] with such precision and delicacy.

Carmen Bugan, author of *Burying the Typewriter*

A TRUE IMPEDIMENT

S. J. Christie

Grosvenor House
Publishing Limited

The right of S. J. Christie to be identified as the author of this
work has been asserted in accordance with Section 78
of the Copyright, Designs and Patents Act 1988

The book cover is copyright to Tim Barber
Cover Design by Tim Barber

This book is published by
Grosvenor House Publishing Ltd
Link House
140 The Broadway, Tolworth, Surrey, KT6 7HT.
www.grosvenorhousepublishing.co.uk

A CIP record for this book
is available from the British Library

ISBN 978-1-83975-890-4

For H

Let me not to the marriage of true minds
Admit impediments; love is not love
Which alters when it alteration finds,
Or bends with the remover to remove.
O no, it is an ever-fixèd mark
That looks on tempests and is never shaken;
It is the star to every wandering bark,
Whose worth's unknown, although his height be taken.
Love's not Time's fool, though rosy lips and cheeks
Within his bending sickle's compass come;
Love alters not with his brief hours and weeks,
But bears it out even to the edge of doom.
If this be error and upon me proved,
I never writ, nor no man ever loved.

PROLOGUE

24.vii.1996

My dear Charlotte,

I was so very sorry to hear that you have been laid low by this tiresome illness, and may have to rest for some time. I do hope you are not feeling too wretched?

I wish I could come and see you, but I gather that visitors are rather strictly rationed at the moment, and I am off next Friday for a three-week symposium in Heidelberg (Crusades and Crusaders in Mediaeval Literature. Lewis Friedman's paper looks interesting: I might see if I can get you a copy).

Perhaps I could drop in on my way home through London? Or will you be recovering here in the country with your grandparents? Your uncle says there will be plenty of things in the garden, later on, which would welcome the not-too-strenuous attention of a convalescent gardener.

At the moment, however, your appetite for new reading-matter will surely be stronger than ever. Do you remember the conversation we had one evening about how much one could read in a day? It was while you were staying here for your first year in the sixth form, while your parents were abroad with the British Council, and the three of us used to sit up over the supper table, debating the significance of various historical events, and the merits of various historians. I expressed some scepticism about your claim that since you had arrived you had read all the books in the bookcase on the landing – and I had to make a very contrite apology when you showed me beyond doubt that it was true!

Now your uncle has suggested, and – after a good deal of thought – I have agreed, that you might like to read the enclosed account. You mustn't think of starting it before you feel strong enough for a fairly substantial read, but then perhaps it may help you through some of those long hours before you can start living life again with all your usual energy. And I know you can be trusted to read it with an open mind, to check your impressions of the people involved against your own, first-hand experience, and to use your discretion in how far you mention any of it outside your own family. I hope you will find it interesting, and may perhaps feel that, as a document of human affection, it has some worth.

Looking through the pages last night, however, I realised with some surprise what a different world we were living in when these events began. Well, that was more than twenty years before you were born, so perhaps I should have expected it. But I wonder how that world will seem to you? As an historian, you will probably be less surprised, and find those years – in the 1950s, '60s and early '70s – less puzzlingly unfamiliar than many of your contemporaries would. But perhaps, as you read, you may still find yourself wondering, 'Why didn't he send an email? – or leave a message on the answer-phone?', or even 'How could anyone keep house in the country without a car? – or a fridge? – or electricity?'

I think it was you who once complained that a large proportion of adult conversation could be reduced to the single statement that 'inflation is now at x per cent a year'. Will you find it startling, all the same, that forty years ago ten shillings (fifty pence) an hour was a fair rate for coaching a twelve-year-old? Or that ten years later twenty-five pounds was a serious loan which a professional man might find it difficult to spare? You will have to read pounds for shillings – or multiply by twenty – to get a rough idea of what any sum was worth to us at the time.

One thing that I think anyone in your generation will find it hard to believe, or even to imagine, is what life could be like only thirty years ago for a homosexual man.

Many otherwise kind and broad-minded people found the idea of any homosexual relationship horrifying; and male homosexuality was illegal, and punishable by imprisonment. (A curious cure for a man's tendency to form close relationships with other men.) It was only in 1967 that the law was changed to allow sexual acts between two men who were both over twenty-one. And even since then, it has been only through the courage of a few people, in openly challenging the prejudices of the majority, that public opinion has gradually – very gradually – begun to swing round towards the more sensible and kindly views which are beginning to prevail today.

Well, I must take this to the post. I wish I could bring it myself, and we could go on with the conversation we've been having, on and off, ever since Bridget and Charles used to bring you to the cottage for tea and Happy Families.

Let me know when this arrives, and later, perhaps, what you think of it. But please don't feel you must write at length. Save your strength for getting better.

With love to you all,
Yours affectionately,
Alan

CHAPTER 1

2nd June, 1969

I love the house when it is still and sunny like this. I lie in bed five minutes longer than I should, and then come down and make breakfast, with the motes rising and falling over the pots of bulbs by the sink. If it's still not very late, I can have a second cup of coffee before quarter past eight. I can shave and do the chores without hurry, with an unimportant sort of satisfaction, while my mind turns and settles towards work. And by nine o'clock there is no company or sound, no bacon-rind un-thrown-away, or blanket untucked, to hold me back from the desk and the notebooks and the pile of paper.

Even now, there is just a very little reluctance, a thin layer of dread, as well as the exhilaration of having nothing – almost nothing – between me and work. To find it so often so unreasonably difficult, to fail yet again to catch the necessary word, to let the sentences lock themselves yet again into ugly contortions: why should a straightforward piece of literary criticism demand such expense of effort?

There was a time when I could hardly bear to give it, when anything was enough to keep me from starting – straightening the books on the tables, sorting out the coats behind the kitchen door. Sometimes I did not start until nearly twelve o'clock. But I did start, thank heavens. I managed to start, every day, and even, occasionally, to get some real work done. Otherwise I should not be sitting in the sun and stillness of the living-room now. I should have become like Oblomov, with nothing to get out of bed for; or I should not be here at all.

The first two hours' work of the morning usually begin slowly, but once I have warmed up it is the best time of all. The sentences start to come, the ideas and words running through me

1

like physical force. At eleven o'clock I have coffee. I walk in the garden or, if it's cold, sit by the fire. For fifteen minutes I indulge my mind, let it swing to where, in some sense, it has been straining since I woke. I used to think it would be possible to keep it in check completely. When I first started to work full hours again, to get up in time (or nearly so), to take back control of the day, I would make extreme efforts to direct my thoughts to places without risk. Music was dangerous: the swelling and twisting of emotion would leave the stuff of the music – the notes, harmonies, patterns – and take off, then settle, half un-noticed, where I would most have it avoid. When it stayed too long – when my disregard became too deliberate, and I had to wrench my attention back with half-genuine reproach – then it seemed necessary to find some way to annul this slackening of resolution, some difficult thing to make myself do. But there was nothing so difficult as the continuous effort in which I had just failed. To switch off the gramophone, to go on working after supper, to get up early, fill in my income-tax forms before breakfast – all seemed like the pains of courtly love: glorious with the reflected glory of their object.

Now I need only deflect the swerves of my thought until the next day's grace: it is almost always completely possible to wait for eighteen hours or less. If it seems particularly difficult some evening, then that is an evening for reading something tough and exact, like Auden.

The second half of the morning goes more quickly than the first. By quarter past one I feel I have only just started again, but the casserole is ready in the slow oven. If I am within reach of some satisfactory stopping-place, or on the point of getting down an elusive sentence, I bring my lunch to the desk. But writing straight on into the afternoon won't work (except as a last resort, to meet a deadline); it hardly ever worked, even as an expedient, to make up time lost, or simply to fill my mind. Now that work is again my wholest pleasure, my obsessive, strenuous joy, it is still necessary to blot it and leave it, shut the notebooks, push the edges of the paper level, have lunch and go out, not much after two o' clock.

On Wednesdays I go considerably earlier. I have lunch at a quarter to twelve, as soon as Mrs Weaver arrives to do the cleaning. It is not easy to justify paying someone to do the part of one's own work that one most dislikes. To say that she wants the money and I want the time is not enough: any bone-idle Edwardian gentleman, any exploiter of sweated labour, could have said the same. If I had to clean other people's houses for a living (or part of a living), I imagine that the best I could hope would be to do it in my own way: to leave the sitting-room door open and go in and out; to sing if I wanted to sing. So I do not try to work after Mrs Weaver has arrived, and I go out as soon as I have had lunch. I should like to have enough strength of concentration, enough control over my own irritability, to resist this erosion of the day (or most of it). As it is – or until I can change it – it seems better to accept the inability and lose the time than to risk losing my temper.

I come back in time to make a pot of tea for us both, and hear as much as she wants to tell me about her two daughters and, from time to time, her husband. This is clearly as important to her as the money. When she needs to talk about her husband, she usually misses the five o'clock bus and I drive her home.

It takes a few hundred yards, on the other afternoons, to shake off the last tentacles of the desire to go on writing, to put down just one more paragraph. Out across the rough ground at the back, and up the lane to the top, and by the time I can see across the fields, and must make the choice which way to go, I am clear of the close detail, the obsession with time and progress, and my mind lies open, free and well-breathed, to turn over a single problem easily, or to move in parallel with the stretching of my body, over the bent, wet grass along the headland, the suck of mud by the gate. Wet days are almost better than fine ones: there are fewer people about. Enclosed in a circle of rain, defended from the chance of meeting, the slight, ineradicable wince of shyness which even the friendliest neighbour produces, privacy and happiness intensify, uninterrupted. But even the worst days – the gritty, rainless days in the beginning of December or the middle of March, with a blank sky and a grating wind – even these days are good, especially since I have bought a sheepskin jacket, cheap, by post.

When I get home, I rake up the fire and make tea, with toast, or sometimes, on Thursdays when I've done the shopping, with crumpets. Between tea and supper there are three hours more for work. Occasionally I can go straight on from where I left off in the morning, but more often it is reading and making notes, or consolidating work – re-reading and crossing out. If I am very sleepy, after a windy walk or an exceptional struggle in the morning, it has to be putting in footnotes, or typing up the earlier part, but only when I'm sure I'm not fit for anything else.

Supper is always soup or eggs, with bread and cheese. I eat a lot of cheese. Then I read, or listen to music, or, if absolutely necessary, write letters or mend my clothes, until bedtime. I find that after an unsatisfactory day, when nothing has gone right, and I have written two paragraphs in four hours and crossed one of them out, I tend to sit up late, reading last Sunday's papers. But this is no solution to the day's failure. If the record reduces itself to meaningless jigging, the poem to savourless obscurity, then the *Observer's* gossip column is not going to salvage the day. There is only one positive action – indeed, only one positive pleasure – left for such an evening, though it needs, in such a mood, some strength of mind to take it: sleep. To go to bed early seems like a deprivation of the first full liberty of the day. But then, next morning may be clear and free, words moving with precision, dancing with energy, mind warmed and exulting with exercise, the passage of power.

And once the decision is made, and followed, it is, in fact, a large sensual joy to lie warm in the darkness, with no haste to sleep, and turn one's thoughts almost anywhere one will – anywhere at all, in the end, since no-one is responsible for his thoughts' bent at the very edge of sleep.

CHAPTER 2

It would not have been possible before the age of thirty. It would have been terrible to be young, to think the end of a year beyond the horizon, next week an intolerable oppression of delay. It was only possible after the beginning of middle age, with its level prospect, its relentless patience.

I have been in love for seven or eight years now, I suppose. It is hard to tell when I first knew it, though I remember very exactly when I first conceded the knowledge to myself. It was a few minutes after nine o'clock in the evening, a little less than seven years ago, at the end of June. I had been looking for Sam, a friend's dog, who was staying with me while the friend went abroad. I have never much liked dogs; and that afternoon, when Sam disappeared into a wood more than an hour's walk from home, I disliked them more than ever.

A sweaty three-quarters of an hour in the brambles of the wood, calling and whistling with no result, made me angry enough, and thirsty enough, to decide that the dog could find his own way home. By the time I had got back, washed the scratches on my hands, and made a pot of tea to drink while I wrote, I was over an hour late in starting work. My irritation lessened the usefulness of the time that was left, and my inability to stop worrying about Sam increased my irritation. I realised that my friend was coming to fetch him at the weekend.

I had meant to work late and have supper when I'd finished, but in the end I gave up at half-past seven, put some antiseptic on my hands, took a torch, thick gloves and Sam's lead, and started to walk back towards the wood. About halfway there, I left the road and went across the fields to a farm, in case he had gone there after the poultry. There were no signs of pursuit or destruction in the farmyard, but I went on beyond the farmhouse, in the diminishing light, and Sam came up from a hedge to meet me. I supposed that I ought to beat him with his lead, but I have always disliked the dog-lovers' assumption of unlimited right to organise and punish, their serious pleasure in discipline. And he seemed extraordinarily pleased to see me.

I said, 'Sam, you're a bloody nuisance, and you'll be lucky if you get any supper,' and put his lead on his collar.

He stayed close by my leg, and I looked at him and realised that it was intolerable that he was going away, that his friendliness and unselfconsciousness and grace were admirable and lovely, and that after Sunday I should be without them. I felt extremely lonely. I needed to talk to someone, to take some warmth of human company into the hollow evening, the empty region of days. It was absurd, especially for me, to feel like this about a dog. I thought that I could talk to Ben; it was the sort of thing one could tell Ben.

The house would not be much out of my way, if we went home across the fields. I walked there quickly, and when I was near enough to see that his light was on, I began to feel a strong, warming happiness at the thought of talking to him, drinking a cup of his coffee, looking at his ridiculous posters.

The happiness spread, illuminating the grey air over the hedges, and the dark, layered fur of Sam's back and head. It rose inside me, pressing against my lungs, until, stopping by the wall at the side of the yard, seeing the ends of straw round my feet and, across the yard, Ben's curtains unevenly drawn, the light coming through where they didn't touch, I realised why this happiness was so great; why, therefore, it would have to remain unfulfilled.

I felt no anxiety, and certainly no unhappiness, only a blunt, thudding shock and a remote recognition that this might cause pain, later on. Then I could feel only elation: the abandon and truth of saying without evasion, 'I am in love with him'; the joy of taking Ben into a particular and acknowledged place in my mind; of knowing and possessing him in this way, though he might never know it, and never be possessed.

After some time, Sam began to grow restless, his guilty deference wearing off. I did not want Ben to come out. I wanted to contain my joy, and I knew that I could not hope to do this if I saw him now. For the rest of that evening I could keep it entire, unfragmented by questions of acknowledgement or response.

I walked through the yard quietly and went home across the fields with Sam. And as soon as we had both had supper, I went to bed, slowly, rejoicing in my still unthreatened love. Before I slept, I began to tell over all the occasions of our meeting, and in my sleep I hoped for unattainable happiness.

CHAPTER 3

It was nearly nine years before that, when I had first come to the cottage. I was working on the edition of *Piers Plowman*. I did not know how long my research grant would last, and the couple of hundred pounds left to me with the cottage was all I had to live on otherwise. If I was to do the edition as I wanted to do it – as it deserved to be done – it would take another year at least, or even two. Money and time were stretched tight. I had not yet discovered my own limits of energy and concentration, and I worked most of the time I was awake, emerging once a week for shopping, like an owl into the morning.

There is a proportion of semi-mechanical work in all editing, otherwise I could not have gone on so long. As it was, I had two or three times had to surrender to migraine and lie for twenty-four hours in the dark. The day after such a migraine was a sort of holiday. I would get up late and take time to do small, neglected jobs in the house and garden, putting out empty milk bottles, or picking up windfall apples, with the cautious ease of relief from pain.

It was on a morning of this kind that Ruth Grayson came to the gate with one of her children. She and her husband were almost the only neighbours I knew. Told of my arrival by a cousin of theirs who had been my colleague, they had duly asked me to dinner; then, on discovering my solitary housekeeping, to supper on Saturday night a couple of times. I was grateful for this friendliness, and for the occasional provision of evenings of general conversation and untinned food. But the prospect of yet another invitation was only uneasily welcome. I could not afford the time. I ought to refuse; or, if I accepted, I ought to ask them back. I did not know how to do either, and I could not cook.

Ruth called, copied by the little boy who stood beside her.

'Alan. Are you there?'

'Are you there?'

I went towards the gate from the sprawl of brambles I had been cutting back at the end of the garden.

'Hello, Ruth.'

'Hello.'

'Hello,' said the little boy.

There was a pause and I said, untruthfully, 'I meant to write – to say thank you. I did enjoy Saturday evening.'

'Oh. Yes,' said Ruth. 'Alan, could you possibly give us a lift into Bramston?'

'I'd love to,' I said, also untruthfully, and added, 'but I haven't got a car.'

'Oh. Oh, I see. I'm sorry. Oh, God.'

'Is it something – ? Yours isn't working?'

'James has taken it over to Harchester. He won't be back till this evening.'

'After the shops have shut?'

'It's Bridget. The school's just telephoned. She's had an accident in the playground.'

'Oh dear. Can't they send her home?'

'They're taking her to the hospital. They think... they may have to operate.' She dropped her head quickly.

I tried to think of something to say. 'It's a good hospital, isn't it? A very good one. She'll be all right there.'

'Yes. I expect so. But I want to be with her.'

I hadn't understood that. Tears were running down Ruth's face.

'Taxi?'

'I've tried. Can't get an answer.'

'I've got a bicycle,' I said helplessly.

'Have you? Can I borrow it?'

'Of course, if you want to.'

'Can I come on the carrier?' said the child.

Ruth and I looked at each other.

'There's no-one at home to leave him with,' she said.

'I can go on the carrier.'

'I've got to be very quick, Marky.'

9

'I don't expect it would bear you,' I said.

'I'm very heavy,' he answered with satisfaction.

'Would he be all right staying here?' I asked.

'Alan, could he? You wouldn't mind? Your work – ?'

'No. That's all right. If he wouldn't mind. Only you'll have to tell me... what he likes to eat, and so forth. I haven't had a lot to – ?'

'Anything,' said Ruth. 'Can you show me where the bicycle is?' And then, pushing it to the gate, 'He'll tell you. He's very sensible for a four-year-old.'

Mark helped me pick up the windfalls. I showed him how to turn them over with his foot before he touched them, in case there was a wasp inside. He did this well, and rather silently, only saying occasionally, 'This one's a very big one,' or, addressing the wasps, 'Out you come. Out you come.'

At eleven o'clock I made coffee and gave him some milk.

'What's for lunch?'

'What do you like having for lunch?'

'Potatoes. And meat.'

It was the day before I went shopping. I looked at the tins in the cupboard.

'Do you like baked beans?'

'Yes.'

'I was going to burn the brambles,' I said. 'We could make a bonfire and cook the potatoes in it to have with the beans. Would you like that?'

We had lunch sitting on the grass, digging the potatoes out of their skins with spoons, and adding baked beans from the tin. When we had finished, I took the spoons and mugs indoors to wash up. Coming outside again, I saw Mark standing beside one of the trees, crying.

'What's the matter, Mark?'

'I want Mummy.'

The grass steamed, and a patch of his shorts was wet.

'It doesn't matter.' I helped him take them off. 'Will you be warm enough, running around in your shirt? Or shall I lend you something?'

'Your trousers would be too big,' he said.

'Yes. But you could wear one of my shirts.'

'It's all right.'

So he ran about on the grass, naked from the waist down, while I sat in a deckchair and wrote letters.

After about half an hour, he said, 'Have you got any books?'

'Yes. I've got quite a lot.'

'Can I have one of them to read?'

'Can you read?'

'I can if someone tells me what the words are.'

With some searching, I found an illustrated life of Napoleon and a book of photographs of local churches. I took them outside, with a blanket for Mark to sit on. He liked the life of Napoleon best, and when I had given him a paraphrased and translated account of each picture, he said he would read it to himself. Ten minutes later he was asleep, the blanket half wrapped over him, the fingers of one hand stroking the binding along the edge. I brought out a writing-board, and my collation of the texts of Passus IV, and started to work on the notes.

It went well, and Mark slept until after four o'clock. Then I was aware of him humming to himself and moving his finger about on one of the pictures.

I said, 'You've had a good sleep.' He looked up, and nodded, and went on humming.

Someone said 'Mark' from the gate, and he pushed back the blanket with his feet and ran across the book and over the grass. A boy, about five or six years older, was standing by the gate. He said again, 'Mark' and then, 'What've you done with your shorts?' and held out his hands. Mark caught them, and was lifted by them, then jumped so that his bare legs were round the boy's waist.

I put my writing-board on the grass and got up.

'Are you Mark's brother?'

'Yes. Mum's sent me to fetch him.'

'How's your sister?'

'She's OK. She's at home.'

'She didn't have to have... to stay at the hospital?'

11

'No. They thought she might have to have an operation, but she didn't. She got a bone in her arm broken, though.'

'But they let her go home?'

'Yes. They put it in plaster, and she came home in an ambulance.'

'Oh, I am glad. Do tell your mother how glad I am.'

The elder boy stooped, and put Mark back on the ground.

'Yes. Get your shorts, Marky. I've got to take you home.'

I fetched the shorts and underpants from under the tree. They were still damp.

'I'm afraid I should have dried them or something.'

'He can borrow my anorak.'

He took off his faded, buff-coloured jacket, and put it on Mark, zipping it up in front.

'It looks like an overcoat on you.'

Mark started to dance, jumping from one bent leg to the other, waving the cuffs, which came a long way beyond his hands.

His brother looked at me. I smiled and, abandoning responsibility, he smiled too.

'Would he like – some milk or something? Before you go? Would you?'

'No, it's all right, thanks.'

'I'd like some orange,' said Mark.

'I haven't any orange-juice, but I have got some milk.'

The sun had become very hot. They drank the milk, standing by the gate, and handed me their mugs.

'Thank you very much,' said the older boy. He took his brother's hand and turned him towards me. 'Marky – ?'

'Thank you for having me.'

They went out through the gate and down the lane, Mark doing three steps, in the sandy earth, to his brother's two.

CHAPTER 4

Physically I could – and can – remember it with a closeness that stops the breath in my throat, making me giddy. But looking back to what I felt then, nearly sixteen years ago, setting aside, or trying to set aside, the swelling and breaking of love which the memory starts in me now – flooded as it has become by all the other rememberings and by present knowledge – I can remember only an unaccustomed lightness and content, and a sort of contagion of gentleness from Ben's holding of his brother. And I remember I worked on at Passus IV until late in the evening, with an ease I had not expected on the day after a migraine.

Even to remember that would be too much – much too much, for many reasons – if it were not for the present unplanned hiatus in the progression of the week's work. Until the Press send back my typescript and their comments, work on *Mediaeval Narrative Technique* is neither finished nor continuable; and until I am free of it, I can do nothing else. I cannot even begin to sort out and consider the ideas about French and Italian influences before Chaucer, which were starting up so vigorously and insistently towards the end of *Narrative Technique*.

As soon as this Monday's post was empty, I knew it was not safe: this vacuum, this large, indifferent force of emptiness, pulling into the centre everything that must be kept on the periphery – and the weightiest, of course, most powerfully. I had thought I had left enough still to do: references to check which would take at least a fortnight; final revision of the bibliography; the list of abbreviations; the acknowledgements. They could hardly keep the typescript longer than three weeks.

And, in fact, there was still enough to do at the beginning of the fourth week – enough to suppress all but the lightest, subversive tremor of expectancy. It was not finished until Wednesday evening. On Thursday I took the day off and drove into Harchester to buy a new piece of carpet for the spare room. On Friday morning I telephoned Brian Robson to ask him what had happened to the typescript. His secretary said he had had to go to New York unexpectedly for a couple of weeks. She was sure he would let me have the typescript soon. She thought he had taken it with him.

I worked in the garden for the rest of that day, and all the next; there was a lot of weeding to do, some planting, which I had postponed, and the lawn to be cut. By the time I went to bed on Saturday, I was in the state of glowing, self-righteous, physical weariness in which all moral effort seems possible.

On Sunday I went for a very long walk, coming back while it was getting dark. I was in the prickly, shivering state between chill and sunburn which I remembered from summer holiday evenings as a boy, and I began to despair of going on indefinitely. Unless the typescript came next day (and I didn't see how it could), there would be very little more that I could oppose to the perpetual, gentle siege of my mind.

I put on a sweater, and had a glass of sherry before supper, in spite of being alone. But the alcohol only added irresponsibility to my apprehension: I could find other things to do, very probably; if not, would the harm be so great?

I woke next day with a headache, and spent the morning bruising and muddling the ideas, which had been so fresh and urgent, on the French and Italian influences. After tea, I even took out the verse translation of the Cycle, but it was no more effective than it has ever been in defending my mind against serious distraction. Creation – even of this modest, ancillary sort – demands an easiness, a lowering of one's guard, which I could not afford. By the end of the evening I was pulled, to the point of physical trembling, between the unacceptable alternatives of the impossible, continuing effort, the too-welcome surrender, and the temporary respite, the unstable comfort, of self-pity. To the last I did give way for a time, waiting to go to sleep.

About half-past two in the morning, I woke out of some sort of half-sleeping, endlessly revolving confusion of thought. I got up and drank some water, then went across the passage into the bathroom, and looked at the trees standing in the field beyond the rough ground at the back of the house.

I set it out as clearly as I could, in words. To let myself start thinking about Ben, to give my thoughts liberty to frequent him, now, with nothing else to take a comparable share of their time or their intensity: it would not merely be a reneging of my serious decision, a breaking of the benign pattern so strenuously and painfully built up; it would infect all my consciousness of him, and thence, in any future meeting, our apprehension of each other, our mutual behaviour. I knew, too nearly, how the channels of thought, too much used and all in one direction, brim over and spread – when the force is too great to be stemmed – into a marsh of prurient, egotistical imagining; how the image of the beloved becomes endlessly more false, more contrived merely for such indulgence, until even the achievement of so much longing, the occasion of meeting, if there were ever to be one, would produce, instead of joy, a hot, stiff consciousness of everything imagined – in the end even a turning from the incongruity, the awkwardness of reality, back to the consoling malleability of invention: 'Zum Eckel find' ich immer nur mich.'

I cannot – could not – do this to the only thing I possess which is valuable not relatively, nor indeed reciprocally, but absolutely; which is complete in itself, like the oval stone, lying on the papers in front of me, or, heavily, in my hand.

If it was impossible – and I must think it was – to keep my mind away from Ben until the typescript should come back, I had to find some way to hold this thought in control: to give it firmness and intent and limitation, even to keep it within the proper pattern of the day.

Then I thought, with clarity and relief, that I should write about it. I should write an account of our whole acquaintance, and I should honour Ben by writing it with the full rigour of my faculties, as carefully, as truthfully, as if I could show it to him when it is finished.

On the whole, it would give me great joy. I could not pretend that it wouldn't; though, when I had taken the decision, I was

15

aware only of exhaustion and the cold air beyond the window, round the shapes of the trees. I went back to the warmth of my bed and an annihilating load of sleep.

In the morning, not too long after nine, I started to write this; the room was still and full of sun. Before I went back to the beginning, to remembering the first, innocent, undeliberate occasions of meeting, I thought I should set down the pattern of my days, as it is now (and as I am determined it shall remain), and then the moment, seven or eight years ago, when I realised that I had passed a turning point – that, irresistibly and irreversibly, the direction of my life had changed.

I have been writing for just over a week now, every morning. It is slower, more difficult to get right than I had expected. I don't use the evenings, too; the mornings are enough. And if I take the time between tea and supper for various outstanding chores – sorting out the attic, unblocking the drain, lagging the pipes – or for extra cooking to get several weeks' food ready in the freezer, then when I start work again, I should be able to make up at least a large part of the time I am losing. And unless the Press are going to be unusually difficult, *Narrative Technique* should be finished off before the end of July. I had hoped for June, but July will do, or even August, as long as all the libraries aren't shut.

Two weeks in Florence – three, if the royalties from *Gower* are as good as last year's – a working holiday: the Pitti and the Uffizi and the Tuscan countryside, and lots of reading on the *dolce stil nuovo*. And then the autumn, clear for work. I can take the key round to the Graysons before I leave, and say goodbye.

CHAPTER 5

I must have worked on at full stretch at Passus IV and V that first autumn at the cottage. I can remember only a rage of exactness, straining continually against the necessity for speed; the perpetual sting of tiredness in my head and back; and the blur of everything beyond the focus of the words and the writing-table – cut apart, very rarely, by a swathe of clarity. I remember seeing some dahlias, shaggy and brilliant, when I was walking to the post; and I remember, though more remotely, being irritated at an interruption to the morning's work. A child had knocked at the door. There was bright light behind him from the sky.

I said, 'Hello?'

He seemed uncertain, and then handed me a box.

'Yes?'

'These are for you, from my mother.'

My eyes started to manage the glare, and took on the longer focus.

'You're Mark's brother.'

'Yes. Mum sent me with these. She wanted to thank you very much for looking after Mark, and being so kind. And for letting her have the bike; I forgot to say. And she hopes Mr Chinnery brought it back safe.'

'Oh, that's all right. Yes, he did. How's your sister?'

'All right. It hurts a bit sometimes, but it's OK. She's probably going to have the plaster off next week.'

'That's excellent. I'm so glad. Would you like to come in?'

'No, thank you. It's all right. They're eggs. Ours.'

'Fresh eggs? Marvellous. Will you thank your mother very much?'

I tried to illustrate my gratitude by looking into the box, but it was tied round several times.

'It's not a very good box. You ought to undo it rather carefully.'

'You'd better come in and help me,' I said, 'and have some elevenses. I was just going to make some coffee.'

'All right. Yes please.'

There were two-and-a-half-dozen eggs in the box. The boy unpacked them into a bowl, while I made coffee for myself and, by his own choice, for him. We drank it at the kitchen table, or rather, I drank mine and watched him looking helplessly at his cup after a first mouthful, until I realised that he needed some sugar, but did not like to ask for it. Looking for a packet of sugar, I found some chocolate, too, in the back of the cupboard. We divided the bar, and he drank his sugared coffee and told me about his family.

His name was Ben, and he was the eldest of the three. Bridget and he went to the same school, and she was eight – two years younger than he was. He disapproved of the children in her class who had not stopped her going to the top of the slide in the playground, especially as she wore glasses and was bad at heights. He and a friend had gone to the head master about it, and now the top of the slide had been more safely railed.

'That was a good thing to do,' I said. 'And she'll be all right?'

'Yes. But she might have fallen on her head, though. They thought she had.'

Mark would go to school next summer.

'But I'll only be there with him one term.'

'You'll see him settled in?'

'Yes. Yes, I'll do that. Still – .'

'You're going on to a bigger school?'

'When I'm eleven. Depending where I get in.'

'I see. Some more coffee?'

'No, thank you. But it was very nice.'

He stood up, and then, wondering how to take his leave, said, 'You've got a lovely garden.'

We walked through it to see the only patch which could justify his politeness, where the sun had brought various dark, bright flowers above the level of the grass. He fetched his bicycle from the lane, and asked if he might lift it into the field through a gap in my hedge.

'It's quicker over the stubble. Only, with the eggs, I had to come by the road.'

While he was manoeuvring his bicycle, he was able to say goodbye.

CHAPTER 6

I don't remember seeing much of the Graysons' children for
some time after that. A glimpse in the back of their mother's
car on a wet day in Bramston; illicit scurrying in the background of
a supper-party: were these in that first year, or were they later, their
dates sunk irrecoverably into the deposit of anonymous days?

The next time I was fully aware of any of them – of Ben –
must have been at Christmas the following year. That was to have
been my first Christmas alone at the cottage: I had been away the
year before. I had not thought much about celebration – had done
nothing, in fact, beyond opening various Christmas cards and
standing them in odd, clear spaces in the living room, – too late, or
too poor, or too indifferent to answer them. Then Ruth, meeting
me in the grocer's ten days before Christmas, discovered that I
should be alone, and asked me to spend the day with them. And
I realised that I was, after all, glad: glad to have a part in the
necessary rites, as long as they were organised by someone else.

On Christmas Eve, I realised that that part nevertheless
included providing presents. I finished Envy's speech in Passus V
that morning, and my bicycle had to be fetched from the repair
shop, so I took the afternoon off and walked into Bramston.
There was still frost along one side of the plough ridges, and the
sky was reddening at the edge before I was into the town.

I had almost no idea what to buy, but the odd little man with
dyed hair at the stationer's gave me sensible advice about children's
paperback books, with an eagerness that suggested it was not
often asked. I bought a white cyclamen in a pot as well, and an
almost respectable bottle of wine, without exceeding the extra
thirty shillings I had drawn, and rode home as it was getting dark,
the parcels in my basket producing a curious cheerfulness.

It was a good Christmas. I walked over the fields to the
Graysons' in the morning, in a whitish mist; the sun came out as

20

I arrived, giving the baubles on their Christmas tree a paler, day-light shine.

The children were in high spirits, and Ruth had cooked a magnificent lunch. James told me long afterwards that they had been astonished by how much I ate. The rich weight of food sobered even the children for a short time, but their excitement returned as we walked in the lanes, and was jumping and crackling between them like electricity before we went back to the house for tea and present-giving. My presents for them were adequately successful, as far as I can remember, and there were presents for me, which I had forgotten to expect: some thoughtful household gadget from Ruth and James – an oven-proof casserole? a whistling kettle? – and little things the children had made: a cardboard bookmark, labelled 'Book Mark'; a pencil with a loop of tape attached to it by a sealing-wax knob; and a paper-weight, an oval stone lacquered in patterns of blue and grey and green. My clearest memories are of Ben, kneeling among torn wrapping paper and gilded string, turning his mother's cyclamen, in its pot, round and round in his hands; and of Mark unwrapping a miniature guardsman's uniform in the brown light under the branches of the tree, incredulous delight spreading silently across his face.

CHAPTER 7

By that new year, I had almost finished the text and notes of *Piers Plowman*; only the preface and the glossary remained before it was ready for the press. I knew that I had done it properly, and that neither time nor money was going to run out before I had completed it. New ideas were beginning to quicken – a feeling that I had something to say about Chaucer's earlier poetry; a strong inclination to do some full-scale criticism.

My grant had ended the summer before, but I had enough left to live on till June. I did not know what I should do after that, unless the money from *Piers Plowman* was unexpectedly good. Meanwhile, the slackening of pressure, the beginning of new excitement, were enough.

I went to the cinema in Bramston, once for the rare occasion of seeing a good film, and then another time to see a marvellously bad one. In February, while I was waiting for the proofs, I bought a cookery book and began to discover what to do with fresh meat and vegetables, and tried to bake some bread. I cut back the hedge and cleared the brambles from quite a large patch of the garden.

If they had asked me four months later, I should have refused. Those first months of Chaucer, nothing could have made me undertake extra work, even for an hour a week. But it was only the middle of February when James met me in the public library and asked me if I knew Latin.

'Adequately. I'm not a classic.'

He did not think that would matter. Ben had been offered a place, in the second year, at Harchester Grammar School. He had just failed the entrance exam the year before, but had been kept on the waiting list. Now there would be a space for him in September, but the class would have done a year of Latin.

'And we were just wondering – . Or perhaps you know someone else? You'd have to let us know how much you usually charge.'

I had the time; I did not refuse. And I did not – I knew I must not – demur about the money. Ten shillings an hour was a fair rate; and ten shillings a week, with the royalties, might spin my savings out well into the autumn.

'You sure that's enough?' said James. 'It'll be worth more than that for us, not having to pay the school fees. And giving Ben a bit of a chance. This little school at Birdbrook we found for him, I don't think they've really taught him anything there. Except football. He's never said anything, but I don't think it's done much for him, really. You know?'

In the end, when the Grammar School had sent the textbooks, we decided that once a week would not be enough. Ben was to come on Tuesdays and Fridays, after school, for an hour. And though I told him it wasn't customary, James insisted on adding something for time spent in preparation, so it would be twenty-five shillings a week.

I took a little trouble over the first lesson, but within ten minutes I knew it had been misdirected. It is not possible – or at least, it is not easy – to teach Latin to someone wholly ignorant of formal grammar.

'You must tell me,' I said, after my third unsuccessful explanation of the functions of the nominative and the accusative, 'you must tell me if I say something you don't understand, – use a word you don't know.'

'I'm sorry,' he said, 'but I don't *know* what I don't know.'

'Do you know the difference between a subject and an object?'

'Not really. Well – not at all.'

I managed to avoid asking why he hadn't said so at first, set aside my parti-coloured tables of the first declension, and started to illustrate this difference in any way I could devise. I drew pin-figure men eating circular cakes, beating pin-figure dogs, building schematic houses. Ben took the point quickly: when I asked him for a sentence with 'the man' as the object, he drew a benign Labrador threatening a cowering pin-man with a stick.

'The dog beats the man,' he said. 'And serve him right.'

So I added eyes and teeth to one of my cakes, and Ben drew the head and legs of an Edward Lear man, drooping from either side. The lesson became slightly hilarious. I had noticed before, occasionally, in university teaching, how laughter can fix understanding, establishing it as memory.

Ben began to draw currants on the cake. It was after five o'clock.

'Have you had any tea?'

'Well, no. I came straight from school. The bus goes past the bottom of your lane.'

I should have thought of it before.

'Are you hungry?'

'Well, yes, a bit.'

He ate four slices of bread and butter and jam, and a number of ginger biscuits, and drank all the milk I had. I made myself a cup of tea, and we talked about Latin derivatives in English.

I had the kettle boiling next time, and tea ready on the table; it seemed justifiable to spend two shillings of James's money on chocolate cake. After tea, we tackled the genitive, dative, and ablative, which Ben understood much more quickly. I wondered whether it was increasing familiarity with the grammatical idea, or the effect of the cake. It could have been rather that teaching at this pace was less tedious than I had expected.

He found the whole notion very interesting, and even anticipated my revised plan by several weeks, trying to work out for himself the functions of subject and object in a passive sentence.

Looking back, it is difficult to believe that the lessons could have been so peaceful, so entirely without the tensing of particular joy or disappointment, without more than the mildest anticipation: a change in the pace of the week's work; an hour, twice, of justifiable company; the minor pleasures of breaking off for a meal, of lighting the sitting-room fire, even of chocolate cake. Is happiness unregarded still happiness?

I did find that I took pleasure in setting out the comprehensive symmetry of the language, in beginning to make it clear, stage by stage; and in a sort of innocent un-defensiveness and quickness in Ben's response, whether he found a point easy or difficult, quite without the idle watchfulness of too many of my university pupils, regarding Chaucer and Langland and Gower (whatever they would say in their essays) either as a prize crossword puzzle or as a chore.

I gave him homework, I remember, and we would correct it together, immediately after tea. His hand-writing was large and rather untidy.

Sometimes his bus arrived before I had got the tea ready, and then he would make toast at the fire, or go into the garden until the kettle boiled. One evening in March, he came back into the kitchen almost immediately.

'Did you know you'd got some crocuses coming up?'

'Have I?'

'And I think some daffodils.'

'Splendid.'

'Would you like to come and see?'

We went to a patch in the angle of the hedge. There was a tangle of grass pulled back from the few smooth, small, vertical blades. Ben squatted and pulled back more of the grass.

'There's another,' he said, with affection, with tentative possessiveness. 'There's probably quite a lot under here, if you cleared it.'

He spent more of his time in the garden after that, sometimes staying on after the lesson into the lightening evenings. I tried to remember to notice what he had done, and he tried not to show what he thought of my neglect of such a garden. By May, he had found some of the best things: the peony by the corner of the house, the clematis – still very short then, the scyllas and the lily of the valley under the trees.

We finished the grammar-school work by the middle of June: all the declensions, all the regular, active, indicative verbs, and a good many of the simpler rules of syntax. Ben had worked very well. I asked him if he wanted to stop coming now. He said he'd still like to come on Fridays, if he could; his form would be going swimming on Tuesdays, after half-term.

I agreed to this. *Chaucer's Earlier Poems* was underway by now, but there was not much more preparation to do for Ben. Several of the last Fridays were hot, and we walked over to the church and read the Latin on the gravestones and memorial tablets, or worked outside in the garden, reading a book of Mediaeval legends of the saints – my seventeenth-century edition, with the woodcuts. He liked these – the saints who befriended lions, or spoke to seals, or had their shoes eaten by mice – much better than the pieces of simplified Caesar which the text-book provided at this stage.

I bought strawberries for tea on the last Friday, and Ben arrived carrying, carefully, a flat, square packet. He gave me first a cheque from his father, and then the packet.

'From you?'

'Yes.'

There was a gramophone record inside it. I didn't know how to thank him properly. It was a large present, I thought, for someone of his age. I said what I could.

'You have got a record-player?'

'Well – .' No lie would be convincing. I looked at his face, and turned the record over in my hands. 'I had a letter from my publishers two or three days ago. They've had a lot of advance orders for the book I've been doing – *Piers Plowman*. It's going to sell much better than they thought.'

He said politely, deliberately, 'So you'll make a lot of money?'

'More than I've had before, anyway. And one of the first things I'm going to buy – something I've been wanting to buy for a long time – is a gramophone; the sort that works on a battery. So you couldn't have given me anything better. Especially Bach.'

His face widened with pleasure, and his narrow shoulders.

'If you want to hear it before that, you could bring it when you come to supper.'

I thought of giving him the book of legends – writing his name in it, and the date. But to do it while he was there would be too obviously reciprocal, and there seemed no other opportunity. And I was rather fond of that edition, I suppose, even then.

CHAPTER 8

I should know, now, how to hoard and increase it, the small, inevitable intimacy of such teaching. Even six or seven years later, I should have known, with the sharp-eyed opportunism of love, how to nurture it, to take each occasion to keep it alive and growing, give it no time to dwindle back into slight acquaintance. To have wasted so much, so many opportunities, taken their profusion so fecklessly for granted... But perhaps – surely – it was better like that: the serenity and unselfconsciousness of those meetings a better ground for later growth and burgeoning. And if I could have foreseen that growth, the changes it would produce in Ben and therefore in myself, I doubt if it would have been tolerable: to have carried for those extra years, even in prospect, the too-frequent burden of homosexual love – tenderness too great to be laid on so tender an object; the choice between unremitting restraint and crude, ruinous exploitation of trust and unformed judgement. (And yet people supposed that such love would be too easy, if it were unrestricted by the law.)

I went to America the following summer. *Piers Plowman* had had reviews beyond my expectation, especially in the quarterlies; and as well as being chosen as an exam-text by several universities, and possibly by a school board, it produced an invitation to lecture at Brandeis for a year. *Chaucer* was planned by then, the bulk of the reading done, and the first half-dozen chapters more or less written. It looked as if the lecturing would leave me time to finish the first draft, at least, while I was over there. I should also be able to get down to Washington before the term started, to look at their Caxton *Canterbury Tales* and various other early editions, in the Folger Library. I was hoping to find confirmation of a new hypothesis about *The Parlement of Foules* – the first major, original idea, as it turned out, which I was able to prove definitively from primary sources.

27

I said goodbye to the Graysons when I left in June. They came in for a drink, and we talked of the children's exams, and the problems of James's business. Ben wasn't there, I think; he was off somewhere with a group from the school. I sent a postcard from New York – to him, or perhaps to all the children – and he replied some weeks later with one of Harchester market square, written in the careful, diminished hand he must have adopted at his new school. I found it a few years ago among my papers from Brandeis, and put it in my desk:

'Thank you for the postcard of Battery Park and the Skyline. New York must be terrific. I'm glad you had a good journey. We are all fine. Dad has started market-gardening and we're going to have to live on tomatoes if the glut goes on. Bridget's started her first term at the Girls' Grammar, which she likes. Marky has been lent a pony. It is like him: small and round and black-haired. [Then, written round the edge] I am doing Greek this term. Love from us all. Ben.'

I must have put it away quite soon, among my letters. The ink is still bright and black.

It was very hot in Brandeis, however interesting and vigorous, with the academic year just ending. Washington was even hotter. I worked as late as I could at the Folger, and had difficulty in getting to sleep in the little room at the hotel, where the air-conditioner had broken down. I dreamt a lot, I remember, when I did fall asleep.

The heat slackened a few weeks after I got back to Massachusetts, and the autumn was magnificent: clear, and brilliant with turned leaves, and full of the disarming American immediacy of friendship and communication. My lecturing went pretty well, to my relief, in spite of my being four years out of practice. I took a couple of seminars as well, and I liked a good many of my students.

I lodged with a young professor on the English faculty, and his wife who was doing a Ph.D. in Medicine. Saul Heyman was from New York, where his parents kept a radio-shop. Marcia was from a high-born, Christianized family of Connecticut Jews who could not quite approve of Saul. These two admitted me at once to their friendship, and the three of us – or often more – would sit over the dinner table in the evening and talk. They were both vehemently anti-Republican, and rather less vehemently pro-Democrat, and much involved with support for integration movements in the South. Lewis, one of Saul's post-graduate students, often came in after dinner – a tall, narrow, Jewish boy, with a small, neat head and fiercely pacific opinions. He was intelligent, and much less naive than many of the post-graduates. I got on well with him; we talked about his subject, which was pre-Elizabethan drama.

One evening, when Marcia didn't feel well and Saul had taken her to lie down, Lewis told me that he was in love with Marcia. He also told me that he thought she was pregnant, and that the idea of her carrying Saul's child seemed to make his desolation final. When he bowed his head onto the back of the sofa, I put my arm along his shoulders, and felt a quick, surprising pulse of sexual interest. I fetched him a drink, and sat down on another chair and tried to listen, to let him feel able to talk. My own reaction I dismissed without difficulty.

After the short break for Easter and Passover, I realised that I was going to have to work very hard to get the first draft of *Chaucer's Earlier Poems* completed by the summer. Living with such congenial company in the house, it had been much more difficult to work regularly on anything beyond the immediate necessities of the week. I did not regret it – both intellectually and humanly, it had been worth an even greater loss of time – but I started to work late at night, when the air was cooler, and the house and the street were quiet.

By the end of May the heat was building up, and I began to dream again, in the hot early mornings. I dreamt that Lewis came into my room, worrying that he could not understand some lines in *The Boke of the Duchesse*. I asked him to sit down and started to help him, but every time we had finished the passage, he would realise it had been the wrong one, and begin searching through the book again. In the end, he went away and I lay in bed, saying to myself, 'It was no dreme: I lay brode waking.' Then Ben came in, and said, 'It's all right. He doesn't really like Chaucer. It was only a dream.' He sat down on the end of my bed, where I had pushed the blankets back. I said, 'That wasn't Chaucer; it was Wyatt,' and Ben said, 'I know,' and I woke in a state of great happiness.

CHAPTER 9

I finished the first draft of *Chaucer's Earlier Poems* in time to take an excellent three weeks in California before I left. I was back in England by the end of July, and after two more months on the revision, working fairly fast, it was all done, and I began to be consciously aware of being home again. The absence of fourteen months made it seem very solidly and completely home now; I felt the cottage and the garden benign and welcoming, and almost formidably private. The individual rooms somehow failed my anticipation, though. As I worked on the revision, there was sometimes an unease, at the edges of my mind, about the grey, cluttered emptiness of the living-room.

Early in October, as soon as the typescript was posted, this uneasiness gathered into a strong, unfamiliar itch to tidy, to start sorting out the accumulated, toppling piles on the three or four packing-cases along the sitting-room wall: letters, envelopes, papers, reviews, and also, as I found later, biscuit packets, shopping lists, and dirty saucers.

I did not do it at once. I took, deliberately, one whole, long day walking to the river, and for a good way upstream, eating in a pub at midday. Then there were several days' worth of letters to be written – chiefly to America – and bills to be paid, and short, tedious, urgent chores to be dispatched, before I could begin the tidying.

By the time I had finished – and it took much longer than I had expected – there was a thick, spreading outline of dust and scraps round the packing-cases. I had to leave this till the next morning, but that was so fresh and fine that I pulled, first the cases and, in the end, all the furniture out into the garden, to clean the room completely.

The paint was patched and knocked and yellowish. My desire for order spread. I turned out the kitchen, too, and the bedroom, and the little room at the head of the stairs, which had been stacked with books since I arrived. I bought whitewash in the town, as well as a more effective broom and mop, and whitewashed each room when it was clean, before putting the furniture back. The effect seemed to me magnificent, though the furniture, even re-arranged, now looked rather inadequate. I had time to consider this before the proofs were returned, and even to start making lists.

When the proofs were corrected, I calculated margins of time and money as narrowly as I could, and spent a little of my fee from Brandeis on an extra set of bookshelves and a hearth-rug. I put up the 'easily-assembled' bookshelves, with great difficulty, in the living room, and spent two satisfying evenings arranging all the extra books. Then I asked James and Ruth to dinner.

This was partly to thank them for an introduction to friends on the West Coast; partly to obviate – while free time and energy lasted – my mild but continuing guilt about my social debt to them; and partly, no doubt, from pride in the new state of the living room.

It was a good evening. I cooked a chicken dish I had learnt from Marcia, and we talked of America, and of local gossip, and of house-keeping as well – no longer restrained by my indifference or their tact. Their admiration for my reforms seemed genuine, and Ruth, in her equal, unofficious way, offered me some spare curtains for the living-room window (the blue ones that I have across the back door now, in the winter). James told me where one could buy, very cheaply, a reliable refrigerator which worked on bottled gas. I had not realised that that might save me so much money and time. Later that autumn, the BBC asked me to do a series of talks on the *Canterbury Tales*, and I was able to afford the fridge.

It must have been about then that I knew that I was going to be all right; that I could make enough money to stay here and write, and would not have to look for another job. It seemed then that no relief could have been larger. I felt it increasingly throughout the early part of the next year: the expanding of time, the release from absolute stringency in the apportioning of money and attention. I began to take a couple of hours, walking or gardening, in the afternoon. I slept better and had fewer migraines. In March, when it became clear that *Chaucer's Earlier Poems* would have to be reprinted before the end of the year, I put down the deposit for a telephone. Then I was able to ring up professional friends, occasionally, when I wanted a second opinion on a crux in the *Confessio Amantis* (I had started re-reading Gower intensively). The renewed contacts gave me unexpected pleasure.

One or two friends came down for the day. I began to notice weekends again – to feel them distinguishing the weeks – and I would spend Friday afternoon cooking lunch or supper in advance. A past colleague introduced me to some of the English department at the New University on the other side of Harchester, and I was invited now and then to take part in seminars, or to lecture to undergraduate societies. I had time to accept, and time to take pleasure in it, to do it satisfactorily.

In April, Douglas Renishaw rang up from London. He had come south for the Easter vacation, and asked if he could have a couple of nights with me. I had not yet found a real direction in Gower, so I asked Douglas for the following week, abandoned the *Confessio Amantis* without great reluctance, and began to furnish the little room at the head of the stairs. The living-room divan just fitted through the door (the firewood man gave me a hand to get it up the stairs), and there was still space for a small chest-of-drawers and a chair. I hung a red bedspread over the curtain-rail, put coat-hangers on the back of the door and books on a stool by the bed, and felt a ridiculous pride of possession in my spare room. It left very little to sit on downstairs.

It was bitter Easter weather. Douglas and I had some excellent walks – wintry and companionable – and were asked to dine with the Graysons. One of the other guests fell out at the last minute, and Ben came in in his place. He came into the drawing-room as we were finishing our drinks, looking taller than I had realised he would, clean and breathless.

I had not yet seen very much of him since my return from the States. I think that even then there may have been a deposit of hope at the bottom of my mind – an unacknowledged sediment of general, un-urgent expectancy, which I preferred to leave unstirred by any specific anticipation. Now he came over to talk to me, and I felt his shyness very suddenly and sharply: his own diffidence, mixed with the awkwardness of a former pupil – the working intimacy dispersed, the greater equality not yet assumed.

He sat across the corner of the table from me at dinner, isolated between two conversing pairs, drinking his wine warily. We managed a general conversation for a time, at that end, and he told us about a holiday they had had in Brittany. He had walked on the empty shore of a bay in the early morning, and found shells embedded in the sand; and it had begun to rain. I cannot remember why he told us this – the point of his story – but I remember the white width of the bay, and the rain against his shirt.

'Who was the boy?' Douglas asked as we walked home, the night suddenly mild.

'James's son – James's and Ruth's.'

I was holding a field-gate open; I looked back and saw rectangular light come and go at the doorway.

'Sorry. Didn't I introduce you?'

'It didn't matter. I could have guessed.'

'It was at the last minute, to square the numbers.'

'He managed very well.'

'Yes. Difficult at that age.'

'"In standing water between boy and man."'

'Cesario?'

'If you like. Viola.'

Douglas had brought a puppy with him, a young black Labrador who ran riot in the garden. We found him sleeping close to the door when we got in, and Douglas picked him up like a child, and carried him, still sleeping, to his box in the kitchen.

CHAPTER 10

It must have been in May, I suppose – it was certainly the same year – when Ben came over to the cottage late in the evening. I saw the lamp flame shrink and stretch with the opening of the front door, and heard him calling uncertainly:

'Mr Pearce?'

'Yes? Hello?'

'May I come in?'

'Of course.'

I found him in the hall. 'Come in.'

'I'm sorry to bother you.'

'That's all right.'

He came back through the sitting-room door with me.

'Come and sit down.'

He sat down in the armchair, saw my book and writing-board beside it, and got up again.

'I'm sorry. That's your chair. You were working.'

'It doesn't matter.'

He sat on the upright chair at the other side of the hearth. I took my own chair again, moving the board.

'How are you?'

'I'm all right,' Ben said; and then, 'It's just, I don't know what to do.'

'Is something the matter?'

'Someone keeps ringing up.'

'Oh?'

'And saying – sort of odd things.'

'I should just ignore it. Put the telephone down. Or don't answer it.'

'I can't not answer it, because it might be my parents.'

'You're on your own?'

'They're away till tomorrow evening.'

35

'Ah.'

'And Mark and Bridgie are being dropped home tonight. I hoped it'd stop – the telephoning. They've been with friends. I hoped it would stop before they got back.'

'How long has it been going on?'

'Since about Friday evening, when I got back. I've been staying with a friend, too. It's been half-term. But there's school again tomorrow.'

'Yes?'

'And they're getting back about half-past ten. And I didn't know what I ought to do.'

'Yes, I see. What sort of things does this person say?'

'Oh... I don't know.'

'It's not just a wrong number?'

'No.' Ben moved in his chair. 'He asks if my father's there, or my mother. And then – he's got a sort of funny voice – he says, "Are you all by yourself in the house?" And I say, "Not really", or something. And he says, "Have you got a little brother? Or a little sister? Isn't that nice?" And then he goes on about – do I look after them well, and he hopes I look after them well – and then... oh, sort of sex and things. I didn't really mind. I just used to put the telephone down, like you said. And I'd said I didn't mind being on my own for a couple of nights, and I could water the tomatoes. Only this evening, I didn't know what to do when Marky got home. And Bridget. I know it's silly, but I sort of – don't like having them there, and this person keeping on ringing up. Only I didn't want to talk about it with them there – I mean, to Edna or anyone – their friends' mother who's dropping them back. And they'll be pleased to see me, and I don't know how I could get to talk to her alone. I don't know her very well, anyway. So I thought I'd come and ask you. Only, I'm sorry...'

I looked across at him, embarrassment and relief hot and pale in his face.

'You were perfectly right to come.'

He leaned back. 'What do you think I ought to do?'

I looked at the time. 'I think we ought to ring up the people the children are staying with, and ask if they can keep them one more night.'

'Oh. Yes.'

'They won't have started yet, will they?'

'Ten past nine? I shouldn't think so.'

After a moment, I asked, 'Would you like me to do the telephoning?'

'Could you?' He gave me the number.

I came back twenty minutes later. He was sitting on the hearth, fiddling with the fire, and looking at the *Confessio Amantis* with the other hand.

'All right?'

'Yes, it's all right. I spoke to Mrs Wylie, and she's going to keep them. Bridget can borrow some school uniform from her daughter, for tomorrow.'

'Oh, good. Good. But she won't tell them, will she? Marky?'

'No. She said she'd invent something dull and convincing about the car. She said it wouldn't be difficult: Mark was nearly asleep on his feet already.'

'Larking about with Adam till midnight every night, I expect.'

'And I rang the exchange.'

'What did they say?'

'What they always say: "Just a moment, sir. I'll give you malicious calls."'

It made him laugh. I had arranged with the exchange to intercept calls to his house, and to transfer his parents to my number if they should ring. I had also rung the police, though I did not say so to Ben.

We sat and drank coffee, and I put another log on the fire. Then at ten o'clock Ben stood up, putting his cup down on the hearth.

'I don't think my parents'll ring later than this. Thank you very much.'

'Wouldn't you like to stay the night?'

'No. No, really. It's all right.'

'I don't think it'll be much fun, will it, going back into the empty house?'

'I don't mind. Honestly.'

37

'Honestly or not, I really don't think you should. It's silly to take chances. It might have been more sensible to come earlier – or to ring up.'

'I couldn't find your number. And it seemed silly to be coming at all.'

'Directory Enquiries would have had my number, if it's not in the book yet.'

I wrote the number on a scrap of paper, and handed it to Ben, who stood, folding it round his fingers. 'If you go, I think I ought to come with you.'

He looked up, then down, embarrassed. Then he asked, 'Which would be more nuisance for you?'

'Going back with you, unquestionably.'

'I'd have to get up very early, that's the only thing. My stuff for school is all at home.'

'I've got an alarm clock. That's all right.'

'It's awfully kind of you. Please don't worry about... I can sleep on the floor, or anything.'

'You can sleep in the spare room.'

Shortly after he had gone up, I went to show him how to turn out his lamp. He was already asleep, in his shirt, face down, the lamp still fully bright. I moved it away from the bed, turned it down, and blew it out.

In the morning, we had breakfast before seven o'clock. Ben was pink from sleep, and happy about his family's return. He drank several cups of coffee and told me about his work at school. They were to have exams the following week: his revising work at half-term had gone well, and he felt more confident than he had expected.

It was still early when he left, in the grey, gleaming air, taking his bicycle through the hedge and skirting the fields by the headlands, round the edge of the new, short wheat. I walked round the garden before I went back into the house, and found that the lily of the valley was coming out. When I went indoors, there seemed to be a lot of space – time and house were free and empty. The *Confessio Amantis* was still on the floor, open near the end. (Could I really have overlooked it the night before?) I lifted it onto my desk, and read:

Whil there is oyle forto fyre
The lampe is lyhtly set afyre,
And is fulhard er it be queynt.

I decided, thinking about it for two or three days after the event,
that I ought to tell James about the anonymous telephone calls,
but that it would be right to tell Ben first of my intention. If I was
to trespass further on his independence, I would only do so openly.
As it was not a discussion that I felt I could manage well on the
telephone, I fetched my jacket to walk over to their house. Just
then, James came through the gate and towards the door – friendly
and uneasy, and talking about the warm afternoon and their trip
to Scotland for a friend's wedding. When we had gone indoors, he
said that he had come to thank me for helping Ben while they had
been away.

'He's just told us. He didn't say anything before. Ruth thought
there was something, but he didn't say anything; not until last
night, when the younger ones had gone up. It was very good of
you.'

I said I was glad that Ben had come – had felt he could come,
that I had been there. I hoped I had not taken it too seriously, or
imposed my authority too much.

'He didn't think so.'

'It's difficult to know…'

'It's always difficult,' said James. 'When you're a parent, you
worry all the time. Are you fussing over them too much? Are you
taking risks, being irresponsible?'

'How can one ever get it right?'

'You can't. Not all the time; you can't hope to. But you did,
this time. Just right, according to Ben.'

I liked James: his stiff, ingenuous kindness, and stiff, sandy
hair.

'I'm usually here,' I said. 'If he – any of them – if they need
somebody, they can always come, or telephone. I gave Ben my
number.'

It was some time before my offer was taken up.

CHAPTER 11

I am fond of Gower. He seemed stolid after Chaucer, and there were several months when work was heavy on the hand, before I could begin to feel his strength and solidity, to delight in them continuously, throughout his long-windedness. I learnt a lot from work on that book, though it was not as successful as the other two.

The summer of the next year was unusually long and hot. The first draft of Gower was done by late August, and I knew that the revision was not going to be difficult. I let it go slowly, and took long afternoons walking over the stubble-fields, crossing rows of stooks and bales, to the river. A little way downstream there is a pool, deep enough for swimming, and even, in one place, for diving. I would stay there until I was cold, then put on my clothes again, on my damp body, and walk home feeling still cool in the strong, late sun, still smelling the damp, earthy, river-weed smell of the banks. There were men working, always, in one or two of the fields, and we would shout acknowledgement and civility as I went past the tractor. But there was no-one near the river. I swam alone and unwatched, though there was a path reaped and trodden through the nettles above the bank.

It was still hot late into September, and I still swam more days than not. Once, rather late at the river, after four o'clock, I heard children talking upstream, walking towards me. I had no bathing trunks with me. I stopped undressing, and sat on the bank, and waited below the tall, heavy weeds, until they should go past.

They came over the top of the far bank, Bridget and Mark, moving awkwardly on the steepness, among the nettles, down to the mud of the edge.

Mark said, 'I thought he'd bashed the nettles down,' and took off his shirt and shorts, and dipped his hands in the water.

'Don't go in,' said Bridget. 'Don't till Ben comes.' She unbuttoned her dress, too, and took it off, and folded her glasses inside the stuff. She put the bundle higher up, where there was some grass, and went to the edge, in her bathing-suit, and put one of her feet in the water. She looked very young and thin. Mark stood up in his trunks and held his arms above his head, as if he would dive.

'Don't.'

'If you're going to, I'm going to.'

'I can swim – ' said Bridget.

'So can I swim.'

' – but I can't swim well enough to pull you out. Wait. You said you would.'

He swayed and balanced on his toes, putting his head down, looking round under his armpit at Bridget. She said nothing more. Mark sat down and picked a dock-leaf, rubbed it on his legs and dropped it into the water.

'Why did you come up that side?' said Ben, above me, and a little down-stream. 'Isn't it very nettly?'

'I thought you'd bashed them down,' said Mark, shouting.

'This side. I said come this side: don't cross at the bridge.'

'We thought you said do.'

'Never mind. I'll come over.'

There was nothing for a moment. Then Ben stood over the deeper part, waited, and dived, breaking the brown, cold, moving water, which closed over him and then let him through, and up, among the travelling rings of his own making. I picked up my shirt, and saw the water running down over his face from his darkened hair.

I stood up and walked round the curve of the bank, without their seeing me, without their calling to me.

From the empty field at the top, I once looked back, hearing Mark calling from the near shore, 'Show me how, Ben. Show me how to dive.'

He was standing above the deep water, and Ben pulled himself up to join him. They stood together, then Ben crouched and Mark copied him, crouching too. They both dived, Mark after Ben. And I went home over the reaped, whitened fields, without seeing them come up through the water, one after the other, or at the same moment, together.

CHAPTER 12

In the end, I had to work very hard on Gower, doing almost the whole revision in five weeks, ignoring the garden and the countryside, under the astonishing October sun, until I had finished at the beginning of November, when the river was again too cold for swimming.

I had had a letter from Douglas Renishaw just before the university term began. He was staying in one of the great houses, near Repton, and had found a manuscript in the library which he thought I ought to see. As far as he could tell, it was an unfamiliar contemporary version of one of the cycles of Mystery Plays, but he did not know enough to identify the cycle. I telephoned him that night, and he read me parts of the manuscript. None of them had any close counterpart that I could remember in any of the extant cycles. I took some passages down over the telephone, and spent the next day confirming my impression that this was not an undiscovered version: it was an undiscovered cycle.

I rang Douglas again, as soon as I was reasonably sure, and urged him to get immediate permission from the family for an edition.

'I want you to do the edition,' he said.

I refused, with shame at his formidable generosity; shame that I had not kept the ravening scholar's envy out of my voice.

'That's absurd,' said Douglas, with his light, obstinate Edinburgh intonation. 'You identified it. I merely found the pieces of parchment.'

'But still, it's your find.'

'But still, this has got to be a proper edition. What do I know about contemporary parallels, and topical references and so forth? I could offer it to Archie Tanner, I suppose.'

'Don't do that.'

'Well, if you don't want to do it – '

'Of course I want to do it. You know that. And rather than let Tanner loose on it.... But I still think you ought to do it.'

'It's just not my field.'

'It must overlap a good deal.'

'Well,' he said, rather less inflexibly, 'overlap... If you wanted any help with the philology.... It seemed to me there were some very interesting North Midland variants: one or two Norse borrowings, even, which must be nearly unique at that date.'

So we did the edition together: Renishaw and Pearce. I went up to Derbyshire as soon as I had got Gower off to the Press, and Douglas joined me at weekends; then, after Christmas, for a whole sabbatical term. We had six months altogether before the owner was to shut up the house and go abroad: six fierce, gloriously single-minded months to make the transcription and all the notes we should need.

The owner was afraid – I thought with reason, though Douglas did not – that photocopying would damage the manuscript, so the whole transcription had to be done by hand, and checked, and discussed, and rechecked for any possible variant readings, before we left.

It is a magnificent manuscript: better preserved than almost any of the others, full of original material, and with a vitality, and a skill in disposing comedy and tragedy, which I still find extraordinary and moving. We started early each day, and worked on it until we were dizzy, only occasionally collecting Douglas's young dog from his companions in the stables to walk in the rich, bare Derbyshire countryside, without a break in our discussions.

I learnt a lot about Midland dialects, and Douglas said he learnt a lot about the other cycles. (The relationship to the Coventry Cycle, in particular, is interesting.) We quarried each other's knowledge relentlessly, and produced a body of notes so thick, even in its preliminary form, that we doubted that we could persuade the Press to publish it all. We disagreed violently, but almost never with animosity, and never with any dissipation of our energy.

The transcript was finished by the middle of May, soon after Douglas's summer term had started, and we took a few days at Whitsun in the Western Isles. We walked on the hills in strange,

fine weather, and saw seals bobbing off the Atlantic shores –
weaving and tumbling – and sometimes talked of other things
beside the Cycle. I remember our sense of relief, and a whole,
uncomplicated happiness.

When Whitsun was over, and we had both gone home –
Douglas to his teaching, and I to clear up after my tenants – we
began the slow, exact, satisfying grind of preparing the text. The
Press had agreed to publish whenever we were ready (though I still
foresaw a battle about the extent of the notes). They realised that
this would not be for some years, and had more or less promised
us an advance. It was restful to be working on something of
which the shape was already so closely defined, and to be doing it
without haste.

CHAPTER 13

It was a wet, cold summer. Things in the garden blossomed early or not at all. The wheat was laid, sodden swathes of it, flat against the ground. I met Ben, walking one day by the edge of a wood. It was beginning to rain. We stood and talked, and he walked a little distance with me, until our ways divided. He told me he had been in France, returning the visit of the French boy who had stayed with him in the Easter holidays. Afterwards, he had walked on his own, along the course of the Loire. He had come back the week before to work on a farm nearby, helping with the harvest, to pay for his holiday; but if it didn't stop raining, there would be no time to earn anything before the school term began.

The rain did stop the following week, and the crops began to steam in the sun, and dry, and lift a little. I went to drink sherry one evening with a lecturer from the New University, and found Ruth and James there. I had not seen much of them since my return from Derbyshire, and we talked together for some time. They had had a hard-working summer; James had taken on more land for the market garden earlier in the year. But it had done well, in spite of the rain, and they were borrowing a cottage in Norfolk for two weeks of family holiday before school began. They were leaving on Saturday.

'It looks as if you might even get some sun,' I said.

'Such luck!' said Ruth. 'Only not for Ben. He's missed his chance of harvest money, I'm afraid. Mr Bracknell doesn't think he can start cutting before Monday.'

'And Ben doesn't want to stay behind?'

'Well, I think he does,' said James. 'Only there won't be anybody at home. He can manage on his own, normally, but they work them damned hard, harvesting: off at six, back after it's dark. Ruth thinks there ought to be someone there for him when he gets back, have his supper ready and so on.'

'You think so, too,' said Ruth.

'I expect you're right,' I said. 'Both of you. Still, he'll enjoy Norfolk, I imagine.'

'Yes. Oh, yes. Being near the sea. But I think he'd rather be independent, all the same.'

'He can probably get something at the Post Office, over Christmas,' said James.

'Or if it would be any help,' I said, 'he could stay with me.'

Ben telephoned that evening to thank me and accept. His parents had demurred only shortly, politely, about the intrusion, the interruption to my work: explicitly about the extra cooking being too much for me; implicitly, perhaps, about it's not being enough for Ben. Ben demurred hardly at all. I heard his voice with pleasure.

After we had finished talking and I had put down the receiver, I felt a sort of ease, a superfluity of physical wellbeing, as on coming into a warm room, or waking after an extra hour of sleep.

Ben came on Saturday evening with a bicycle and a knapsack. He brought a large cold chicken, too, in a carrier bag. We had supper in the garden, and talked there until after it was dark. He had grown more than two years, I thought, since he had stayed with me last: he was a good deal older, more unexpected, less anxious. We talked about Verlaine, whom he had started reading at school, and Wordsworth, whom he very mistakenly disliked. And we argued with no more than a minimum of deference on his part, and of conscious restraint on mine. Then he admitted that he had not read *The Prelude*, and admitted it with such embarrassment, such youthful certainty of my astonishment, such absolute surrender of his position, that I felt my mind contract and tilt, and then return to a new balance.

It was late when we went to bed, and Ben slept late next morning, coming down into the kitchen after ten, apologetically. He would have to be up at five-thirty next morning, so I lit the boiler in the afternoon, and after supper I broke off our talk before nine o'clock, and said that I thought there would be enough hot water for a bath. He took the hint, and got up, and carried a tray in across the grass, still arguing, defending Day Lewis, with his head turned back towards me, away from the direction of his feet.

I saw him off next morning, gave him the sandwiches and chicken leg I had cut for him the night before, and watched him push his bicycle onto the slope of the lane, jumping on as it started to move downhill, faster.

I had a long day ahead of me for work. I watched the last of the sun-rise, and made a half-resolution to get up more often at this clean, private, peerless time. I had two more cups of coffee with a good conscience, and started work by seven, working with a vigour and serenity which lasted all day.

Ben came back about eight in the evening, his clothes dusty with straw, and the skin of his face and hands stretched and browned. I had made some of his chicken into a pie, and it was ready, hot, in the oven. He had three helpings, and while I was taking the empty dish and the plates to the sink, he fell asleep in his chair. I spoke to him without waking him, and then put my hand on his arm, and, when he still slept, held both his arms, through the folded stuff of his shirt, and pulled him up, and brought him across the kitchen and almost to the foot of the stairs, before he woke enough to go up to bed.

Next morning it was much hotter. After Ben had left, I settled less easily to work. I began to make mistakes as the heat thickened, and then to check obsessively for mistakes I had not made. I had finished so little by lunch-time that I took some work out into the garden, with a sandwich, and did another couple of hours before stopping for the afternoon. Then I went indoors to get into cooler clothes for walking to the river, and lay down on my bed and went to sleep.

I woke a little before six – before Ben returned, at least. The air was still very hot, and I should have liked to go down to the river now, but it was much too late. I splashed myself with cold water, put on a clean shirt, and laid the table, before I started work. Ben had slept early last night, while I made sandwiches, and he was very much younger than I; such comparisons, in any case, were absurd.

He came back late – I did quite a lot of work, in the end – wide awake and rejoicing in the heat of the day's sun. They would save much more than they had hoped, if the weather held. And if it looked like breaking, they would use the headlights of the tractors, and work on till ten or eleven every night.

We had a cheerful supper. Ben was in high spirits, charged with energy by the sun, and I think also elated by his own energy – by feeling it now adequate and growing and subject to his intention. There was some joke about the straw-bales – I have forgotten it now, but we laughed about it immoderately, tilting our chairs back while the laughter expanded, and elaborating the joke, and laughing again.

Ben went to bed after we had cleared away. I sat up for an hour or two answering letters, and then sewing on buttons while I listened to Haydn, with the gramophone turned low so that it should not keep him awake.

When I did go to bed, I could not sleep immediately. Some time after midnight, I got up and went to get a glass of water. I found Ben in the bathroom.

'I'm sorry.'

'It's all right.'

'I thought you'd be asleep long ago,' I said.

'Yes, I know. It's just, it's hard to get to sleep. My back seems to be sore.'

'You've pulled a muscle or something?'

'I think I must have caught the sun a bit.'

He would burn easily, with his stone-fair hair.

'Do you want me to have a look at it?'

'Could you?'

We went into my room, and I lit the lamp. He took off the jacket of his pyjamas and leant forward, turned from the lamp. The expanse of his back was a sharp, light red, looking bruised and muddy at the edges. Only his waist, as he bent, was still pale, and a short triangle where the hair had lain below his neck.

'You were working with your shirt off?'

'Yes. When it got so hot.'

'It does look burnt. Is it the first time this year?'

'I suppose so. Yes. There hasn't been much sun till now.'

'And then you stay in the sun for ten or twelve hours without a shirt.'

'I know. It was very stupid of me.'

'Still, you must get some sleep. What do you usually do for sunburn?'

'My mother has cold-cream and stuff.'

I looked in my top drawer: aspirins, sticking plaster, some penicillin which should have been thrown away, a thermometer.

'What about butter?' I asked.

'Wouldn't that be a waste?'

'I don't suppose it costs more than cold cream. But I think you should probably have something antiseptic. Wait a minute.'

I took the lamp to the bathroom. The tenants had left various half-used medicaments in the cupboard over the basin, and I found among them a bottle of 'soothing, antiseptic lotion'. I took it back to my room, and started to tip some into my hand.

'It's very runny. You'd better lie down.' He hesitated. 'Lie on the bed.'

He lay down, and I put the open bottle by the lamp and laid my free hand on his back.

I could feel the heat flaring and stinging. Ben shivered.

'That hurt?'

'Just cold.'

I began to smear the lotion on with the other hand. Ben started.

'All right?'

'All right. It just stings a bit.'

'It'll probably help in a minute or two.'

'Mm.'

I went on smearing in the lotion, since there was nothing else I could do, spreading it up and over the points of his shoulders.

'My God!'

'I'm afraid they are very burnt. How is it further down?'

'Easing off.'

'Then this shouldn't be long.'

'No.'

I talked at random as I worked, and as he lay there with his head on his arms. I talked about the modern cult of sunbathing, I think – the very recent distinction between a brown skin and a sunburnt one; the sunburnt sicklemen, all the sunburnt sailors and gypsies in second-rate fiction, well into the middle of the nineteenth century, who were surely brown, rather than red. It must have been the industrial revolution, taking the poor in from the fields to the factories, getting the rich to the Mediterranean by train, that made a white skin a sign of poverty, a brown one a prize instead of a misfortune.

'And a red one?'

'Perhaps that would have been a prize, too, if it didn't have so many other drawbacks.'

He laughed. 'Ouch.'

'You still have to be careful in the States. There's the same modern snobbery there about sunbathing, only if you say someone's brown, he may take it as a reference to his ancestry rather than his holiday.'

'That wouldn't have so much snob-value.'

'No.'

'What do you say, then?'

'You say he has a wonderful tan.' He laughed again. 'Is it any better?'

'Yes.' He moved his shoulders. 'Yes, much, really. That's marvellous. Thank you so much.'

He lay a moment longer, and then sat up. I handed him his pyjama jacket from the foot of the bed, and he put it on cautiously.

'I am sorry to be such a nuisance.'

'That's all right. Will you be in a fit state to go to work tomorrow?'

'Oh, lord yes. I'm sure I will. But don't bother to get up early – please. I'll do my own breakfast.'

'All right, I'll see. Wear a shirt, anyway.'

'Yes.'

I gave him the aspirins, in case he should need them later on, and we said goodnight. He went back to his room, and I got into bed, and lay for a long time without sleeping.

CHAPTER 14

That was harder than it would have been now. It took me so much by surprise, invaded my state of mind so completely unopposed – that shivering and disquiet of my whole skin, that local and specific longing – that I had no way of dealing with it, of keeping it in its proper place among the elements of my affection.

I want to go to bed with Ben, still – of course I do – but not chiefly, now, for the slaking of that need, nor even for the complete nearness to his body, for the delight in it, for once and at last unrestrained; rather for corroboration of what I have so long longed, and at one time, occasionally, even hoped, to be true: for acknowledgement of the true and final character of our love. So that now I can hold that physical and particular hunger in isolation, as I can hold a moderate, or even a considerable pain in a tooth or a knee, while I am working – can keep it not annulled, but separate, unable to overwhelm my mind. In that way, I can always – almost always – cope with it. But then I had no way, except not to recognise it – that, and to be very bad-tempered.

I did not sleep till nearly four, when the light was beginning; I woke at five-thirty, at the alarm. Ben looked sleepy, but unjustifiably well and refreshed. I put some more lotion on his back, and made the coffee, then went back to bed, leaving him to get his own sandwiches.

'And for God's sake keep your shirt on,' I said again, unnecessarily. I slept deeply after I had heard him shut the front door.

I recovered my temper after a short but productive morning's work, and swam in the afternoon. The deep water slackened my pre-occupations – conscious and unconscious – and as I dressed I felt my ease returned. But the vigour and equilibrium of my body, after swimming, turned all in one direction as I walked home. And by the time Ben came back, I was ready to be irritated by almost anything he could do.

I found reasons to lose my temper three times while we were having supper and clearing it away. After the third time, I apologized.

Ben said, 'It's all right. I expect you're tired.'

And for the rest of the evening we talked as we had not talked before – easily, as well as with equality; without wariness, or the social need to fill up silences.

While I was getting ready for bed, Ben knocked at my door and asked to borrow the alarm-clock. I heard him go in the morning, and thought of our conversation the night before, then fell asleep again.

I suppose it must have been then that Ben began to be a fixed point in the landscape of my mind, to provide a direction in which I knew I could choose to turn for argument or company or, sometimes, agreement; a destination for a discovery or a joke. He had not yet begun to dominate the whole field of my vision, to determine proportion and perspective even on the opposite horizon, even when I was looking most resolutely another way.

For the rest of that week, and throughout the next one, we gave each other increasing freedom of our thoughts – gradually expanding the limits of what was too trivial, or too private, or too inconsequent to say to one another. The fine weather continued, with the forecast set fair. As Bracknell grew less worried about saving his wheat, Ben stopped work earlier, and was often home by seven. I broke off for a moment at half-past six to put the supper in the oven, and then I would begin to expect his company, to anticipate – through the last stretch of footnotes and alternative readings – the quickening and warmth of the evening: Ben's large appetite for my cooking, our small news, jokes, considerations – with the hot food, and the reddish, growing light from the lamp – all chequering the surface of an ease almost as complete as the ease of solitude.

Postcards came from Norfolk one morning – one for me, from James and Ruth, and three for Ben. I put them by his place at supper, and he passed them to me when he had read them, which made me glad to have resisted my curiosity until then.

Darling Ben, It's lovely here, and we all miss you very much. But I hope you are having the same grand weather, and making stacks of money. The cottage is cosy, tho' small. Swimming excellent: B is surfing, and teaching M. M & Dad make fortifications and waterworks on the sand. M & I are getting brown – B & Dad rather burnt! Hope to have a day in Norwich soon, and perh. also a trip to a C 14 castle nearby. Love and thanks to Alan. If you are half as hungry as the other two, he's got his work cut out. See you on Saturday week.

Best love, Mum [secunda manu] and Dad

Dear Ben, I really wish you were here, but the Wilkinsons say maybe we can have the cottage again next year, so you can come then. The beach is lovely – huge stretch of pale sand – and very empty – (except prob. on Sats. so we are going to Norwich that day) – shells & seals & lots of birds and super surfing. v.b.l. Bridget

Dear Ben. I can surf. We haven't seen this castle yet. It is super here. We saw some seals through the glasses & stalked them, & I got so close that one of them splashed me when he dived. Love from Mark

I found the cards, two or three summers later, under the paper in a drawer in the spare room, and felt again – more consciously then – a stab of vicarious delight, and an ache of exclusion. I should have given them back.

On Sunday, Ben did not have to be at work until nine. I took extra trouble with the supper for Saturday night, and opened some beer. Afterwards, we bicycled to the cinema, coming back late, through the dark, the beams of our lights swinging and crossing, unsteady with laughter.

Until the last morning, I did not get up again to make Ben's breakfast, though I would leave his sandwiches ready, and I usually heard him go. Equanimity returned with adequate sleep, and work went fast and well. Having no lectures to write and no pupils to supervise, I had reckoned to do two pages to Douglas's one. I did much more than that, in those ten days.

The following Saturday, I woke when Ben got up. His family were to return that evening, and he was to go home. I went downstairs in my pyjamas, and fried bacon and eggs, in a half-humorous marking of the occasion. He came back briefly after work to collect his knapsack. I gave him a glass of sherry, and his ease started to recede before his embarrassment at having to thank me, in set terms, for my hospitality. Mine receded, too, and left, when he had gone, only emptiness and discontent, and a disinclination for work. I took an unnecessary time clearing away the sherry, and found enough busy-work in the kitchen to last until supper. Nothing seemed to be in the right place – I was corroded with impatience and irritation which could have no object but myself.

It took me two or three days to start working right through the proper hours again, without finding reasons for doing something else. For the first time, I wished that my present work had a less predictable track, and a nearer end. Struggling to navigate a path through a tangle of new ideas, against a financial deadline, would have been easier than keeping a steady pace through this prosperous, horizonless region of textual criticism, and would have taken up my whole mind, filling the recurring spaces in the passage of the day.

Some loneliness was inevitable after two weeks of company. I had only to work for the gaps to close over.

Then Ben arrived at the end of the week, at teatime, with a present from his parents (a book of Cotman landscapes from the Norwich museum). We made tea, and sat and talked as easily as we had ever done. He made the toast, and gave me one of the shells Mark had brought him from the shore. I should have taken account of my joy; the continuity had not been broken.

CHAPTER 15

B ut I took account of nothing that would disturb my content. Work went ahead briskly and accurately. On Saturdays, sometimes, and occasionally in the evenings, Ben would come in to talk or to borrow books. He was doing French and English and history for the Advanced Level exams the following summer, and we talked of his work, among other things. I did not count on his coming, or even calculate the days between one visit and the next (the minimum possible, the maximum foreseeable); each time he came was a bonus, not planned and not specifically expected, and yet altering all the days to either side of it with a pervading happiness of possibility.

Only some subterranean caution, I think, as well as absorption in work, made me limit my part in inviting his company – making my walk only occasionally by way of his parents' house, telephoning the family only when it was a practical necessity, waiting, for the most part, on his decision.

I did begin to find myself planning rather less narrowly for the week's house-keeping, reckoning to have something over, even the day before I did the shopping – some of the good coffee, enough biscuits, enough butter. And without a conscious decision, I let Ben's company come into the special category of allowable intermissions in working hours – those that could not be avoided, like the telephone, or the firewood lorry, or the men who were putting in the Aga.

He would always ask, 'I'm not interrupting your work, am I?'

And I would answer, with no shame, 'Not a bit. Come in,' and look at the clock, stack my papers, and disregard the time until he had gone.

One evening in March, he told me that he was worried about his revision for the approaching exams, and I began to help him plan his time in the holidays, dividing up the work between the available days. He asked me how many hours I thought he should work every day. (It had not occurred to him before that this should be a conscious decision: until now, he said, he had just gone on until he had to stop – or could bear it no longer.)

'That's up to you. People vary.'

'But roughly?'

'Well, I certainly shouldn't try to do more than eight.'

'Is that enough?'

'It's quite a lot, for intensive work. I think you'll find you get more done, working for seven or eight hours – really working – and then taking the rest of the time right off. If you try to do much more, the last few hours won't be proper work, and you'll exhaust yourself as well.'

'Seven then. Or eight.'

'And I should break it up. What I do, for instance, is four hours in the morning, with a quarter of an hour in the middle for a cup of coffee; the afternoon completely free; and then three hours more between tea and supper.'

'And you really stick to that?'

'I really stick to that.'

He looked at the clock. 'But I asked... You should have... I *am* interrupting you.'

'Not really. I'd come to a good stopping place – a sticking point, in fact. Something I had to think about before I could go on.'

'All those other times...'

'It didn't matter. I can always make the time up afterwards.'

'But you should have *said*.'

'I would have said, if I'd wanted to. And I will. It really doesn't matter. Do come – you can always come – when you like.'

He didn't come again during working hours. Occasionally I would find him waiting by the door when I came back from a walk, on an afternoon when he didn't have to play games at school, and we'd have a cup of tea together. More often, he would come in after supper, and sit and talk by the fire until I had to send him home to bed.

He was working very steadily, and apparently with confidence. I only felt that I must not let him shorten his sleep. At Easter, when he went to France again for a couple of weeks, there was no great distress in being without his visits. My walks were longer; I did less in the garden (there was less to do with the bulbs coming out, and the weeds not yet rife); and I listened to more music in the evenings. There were some things I thought Ben might like – some early Britten, Orff's *Carmina Burana*.

He came to see me soon after the end of his holidays, on a Saturday afternoon, when I was pulling up the first weeds of the summer. He said that he was fine, that he had enjoyed France and managed to do quite a lot of work, and that it felt strange to be speaking English again. He helped me finish weeding a bed, and then we went in and made tea. I put on a record when we had finished, and watched him as he listened, following the words on the back of the cover. He sat as if he was tired.

At the end of the first side, I asked, 'Can you follow the Latin?', and he said, 'More or less,' and I turned the record over without our saying anything more.

When it had finished, I said, 'Did anything happen in France?'

He looked at the other side of the cover, and said, 'How do you mean?'

I was not sure what I had meant; I had not known I was going to ask the question.

'I don't know. I thought you looked a bit tired. A bit... as if... I just wondered if everything was all right; if anything had gone wrong.'

'No. No, nothing. No, it was all fine. The food was fabulous.'

I knew, at least, that I should not try to force his confidence; but I had not realised how much I should have liked to be given it.

I walked back with him across the fields. When we came out onto the road, near their house, we met Mark and Bridget bicycling, reddened with wind and the early summer sun. Bridget got off and walked beside us, pushing her bicycle. We had been talking about the mores of French families, and she joined in, diffidently and rather amusingly, telling us of the importance of gloves in the household where she had been staying. When the twelve- and thirteen-year-old daughters were running out of the house, she said, putting on their jackets and pushing back their hair, Madame would call, 'Eloise? T'as tes gants? Geneviève?' And each child would pull a pair of gloves, or a single one, from her pocket, wave it at her mother, and push it back. Then they could leave, their respectability ritually ensured. Bridget had grown, her features finer and more angular, with flat planes to her cheeks.

Mark rode round us in circles, wobbling as the circles grew smaller. Then Ben got onto Bridget's bicycle, and rode in counter-circles, feinting at his brother as they passed, until Mark turned and chased him, and they went wildly down the road, shouting.

He was to do his A-level exams four or five weeks later. I saw him less often during those weeks, which was as I expected. When I did see him, he was unrelaxed and absent, his hair dull and unkempt. I was careful not to ask too much about his work. The weekend before his first paper, I consulted his parents and persuaded him to take a whole day off.

I had offered to re-deliver a friend's car, left for repair in Bramston. I took Ben with me, and we walked back nearly ten miles along the river: through rain in the morning, putting up a heron to labour off over the grey, soaked meadows; then going in sudden sunlight along the top of the bank, looking down twenty feet to the river-cutting, the short field grass by our feet winking and steaming as the quick heat intensified. We opened our jackets, and Ben took off his wet, heavy shoes and hung them on his belt by the joined laces.

About midday, we found a way down to the side of the river, and sat in the shade of the bank, eating our sandwiches, talking sometimes, with no feeling of separateness. Ben's nervousness about the exams, my indecision about mentioning them, his trouble in France, were not solved – we did not speak of them – but they were no longer between us. We felt easy without explanation, and leant back on the crumbling earth of the bank, and watched the variously hurrying water.

I heard from Ruth on the telephone that the exams were over, that they had gone – as far as she could tell – all right; but I did not see Ben again until a couple of weeks later.

CHAPTER 16

He was at the far side of a room full of people, standing against a drawn-back curtain, beside the window. I had not expected to see him, to find him part of an adult, university party. When I knew he was there, I did not go to speak to him immediately. I met several friends and talked with them, and with some students I knew from seminars. Then, when I was nearer the window, he came over to me, laughing and excited. He was buoyant with the release from exams, and drank quickly and absentmindedly whatever was put into his glass.

I said, 'I didn't expect to see you here.'

'I came with some friends of Michael's. Michael Frewin. His brother's at school with me.'

'How are you?'

'Fine. Absolutely fine.'

'Exams over?'

'Exams over.'

The cocktail, going round in a jug, was strong, and the party was getting noisier.

'Your parents here?'

'No, I came on my own.'

We smiled at each other, unable to think of anything else sufficiently trivial to shout.

Someone filled up our glasses.

'Lovely,' said Ben.

'But strong.'

'Is it?'

'Stronger than it tastes, I should think. Quite a bit of vodka in it.'

'Oh dear.' He looked into his glass.

'You've been here before?' I asked.

'The university? No. It's just, I know some people who are here.'

'George Frewin's pupils?'

'I think so. Some of them anyway.'

His hair was clean, and he was very tidily dressed in a suit and a tie; he held both hands round his glass.

Two undergraduates came up to us. He introduced me to one – the other I knew already – but we talked for only three or four minutes before George Frewin took me away to meet a visiting professor who was lecturing at the summer school, and I did not see Ben again before the end of the party.

I had supper with George and his wife and various other guests, and caught the last bus. When I had walked back across the fields from the bus stop, I found Ben waiting for me by the door.

'Hello. I didn't expect to see you here.'

'I know. I'm sorry. So sorry. Can I stay with you, Alan?'

'If you like. Is something the matter?'

'I can't go home. Not tonight. I'll have to stay here – here or something. I think I must have had too much to drink.'

'Come in.'

I opened the door. When I had lit a lamp in the sitting room, I looked at Ben. He was sweating, and his eyes were unsteady and reddish.

'Well, I think you have had too much to drink. But why can't you go home?'

'I couldn't. My father... I can't go.'

'Will he be so horrified? Have a chair. He's seen young men drunk before, hasn't he? You'll be past the worst, anyway, by the time you're home. He may be annoyed, I suppose, but I shouldn't think he'll disinherit you.'

Ben did not answer.

'It's not as if you did this very often?'

'No,' he said, still standing. 'No, I've never done it before, but I – '

I didn't hear the last words. 'What?'

'I... had the car.'

'You *drove* here?'

'Yes.'

'From the university?'

'Yes.'

'As drunk as this?'

'Yes. Or more, a bit.'

'How long have you been here?'

'An hour. Two hours. An hour. I don't know.'

'So, you drove when you were considerably worse than you are now?'

He said nothing. I got up out of my chair.

Then he said, 'I did drive very slowly.'

'That's not the point, as you very well know.'

Ben was silent.

'You ought to be ashamed of yourself. I might have some respect left for you if I thought you were ashamed of yourself, and not just frightened of getting into trouble.'

He could give only an inaudible reply.

'All right. You can stay the night if you want to. I'm not surprised you don't want to see James. But it makes no difference, really, where you stay, or what you tell your father. The fact is that you drove a car when you'd had too much to drink. And that means that you took the risk of killing someone.'

'Oh, God!'

'Well, didn't you?'

'No – I mean, yes – but I didn't think I really would.'

'I should think about it now.'

He stood in the doorway, looking down, not moving, while I waited for his answer.

'Yes,' he said eventually.

We were both silent, then I asked, 'Why didn't you take the bus?'

'I couldn't.'

'What?'

He said again, his face hot, 'I couldn't.'

'Why couldn't you?'

'I had to get away then – couldn't wait. I really couldn't.'

'Why not?'

He wouldn't answer directly, but said, 'Do you mind if I go to bed?'

'All right.'

As he went out, he asked, 'Do you think you could – could you possibly – ring my parents?'

'To say you're here for the night?'

'Yes. In case they worry.'

I went into the passage after him, and he turned round.

'So that's your idea of being a responsible son. You start worrying about their feelings now. And want me to ring up and tell lies for you.'

He started to answer, but I interrupted. 'Oh, go to bed. I can't take any more of this tonight.'

I did ring James, though, and gave some non-committal and more-or-less factual account of having met Ben at the party and asked him to stay the night. He said they wouldn't need the car until mid-morning.

I woke Ben at eight next morning, and told him I was making some coffee.

'None for me, thank you,' he said, when he came down and into the kitchen.

'You'd better have some. You've got to get the car home.'

He put his forehead into his hand, and said, 'My God. I am sorry.'

'What makes you think being sorry is enough?'

He sat down, and then got up again, and was violently sick into the sink. He waited some minutes, leaning on the draining board, then washed out the sink and rinsed his mouth. Then he said, 'I don't think it's enough. I know it's not.'

He sat down again by the cup of coffee I had poured out for him. I drank my own, and neither of us said anything. After about ten minutes he picked up the cooled cup, tasted the coffee unsuccessfully, and said, 'I'd better go.'

The car was parked a little way down the lane. From the doorway, I saw him put his key in the lock and then sit down on the grass at the side of the lane, and rub his hands over his face. After several minutes, I went down to him. He began to pull up bits of grass, and said, without looking at me, 'I know it doesn't make it any better, but I really am most terribly sorry. And I swear I won't do it again.'

I sat down on the grass beside him. He was nearly in tears.

'The trouble is, yesterday morning you would have said you'd never do it at all.'

'I know.'

He pulled up some more blades of grass, and then took his driving licence out of a pocket in his good suit, turned it over in his hand, and put it on the grass between us. We were both silent. After some minutes more, he asked, 'Did you tell my parents?'

'No.'

He did not answer.

'It was the first time you've been drunk?' I asked eventually.

He blew his nose, and said, 'Yes.'

'Did you mix your drinks?'

'Mix them?'

'Did you stick to one kind?'

'Well. I had some sherry to start with, I suppose – and then Julian gave me a gin and tonic – I think it must have been rather strong. And there was that stuff in a jug.'

'Oh, Christ! Ben! Well, you were going to do it once, I suppose. But now you know how much it takes, and what it feels like – then and later – '

'Don't do it again.'

'I don't think I was going to say that. That's up to you. I find people who are drunk tedious and disgusting, and you certainly no exception. But if you want to get drunk – and you will, if you mix your drinks like that – it's not my business to stop you. I don't think it's my business to tell your parents either. Only you *must* give someone else your car keys before you start.'

'Yes. OK. I will.' He tipped the pieces of grass out of his hand. 'I'd better go and tell my father. The car'll be all right there, will it, until he can come and get it? Could you keep that for me?'

I picked up the licence. It looked very new.

He started to get up. 'Christ!'

'How do you feel?'

'Pretty awful.'

'I'll get some more coffee.'

I brought out fresh cups for both of us, and he drank his.

'If you go on feeling like that, I should get some Alka-Seltzer,' I said. 'From a chemist.'

He said goodbye then, went through the hedge and across the field. It was about five past nine.

CHAPTER 17

I wanted to put my hand on his arm; he looked so physically and morally wretched; I knew so well that his behaviour had been out of character, the result of judgement obscured, and not of callous irresponsibility. He could have slept in the car, left his parents to worry, and gone home next morning as if nothing much had happened. Or he could have taken the bus home, endured a much less severe telling-off, from James, and offered to go back and fetch the car early next morning.

I had been too angry in the evening to care very much about his reasons for ignoring that obviously sensible solution; now I began to wonder if he had been telling me the whole truth – if there was something he did not want to say. It was not like Ben to be evasive. He had been characteristically – even courageously – candid about everything else that had happened that evening, telling me without prevarication what he had done, when he must have known that I should be very angry (though he appeared to be less afraid of my anger than of James's. I was glad of that, on the whole). He had taken my reproof without trying to excuse the inexcusable: I had never seen a young man so unevasively ashamed. And he had left me the firmest pledge he could find that he would not do it again.

But I had decided – I suppose rightly – that I must do nothing to obscure the enormity of what he had done. I must not blunt any of his misery, or let him absolve himself too easily with apologies. The horror of what might have happened – to others and, though I did not say so, still more appallingly to him – had supplied enough fear to keep my anger going until now. I had not let him sleep off his hangover, or found him my Alka-Seltzer, or offered to drive him home. When he was leaning against the sink, shivering and wiping his mouth, I had sat still instead of getting up to put an arm round him and bring him back to the table to sit down.

I should have liked to alleviate his wretchedness before he left, at least; to suggest, if not to say, that I accepted his apologies, that I knew how these things could happen.

My restraint had held, but what I had not allowed for was the current generated between my own opposing feelings. Watching him cross the far hedge and go down into the next field, out of sight; walking back up the lane, with fear and anger slackened and restraint no longer necessary; seeing the gathered surface of his first cup of coffee, on the kitchen table, I found myself taken, held, shaking with an urgent, continuing pulse of restless excitement and longing. It did not replace my other feelings for Ben – the feelings from which it flowed: fright, disapproval, compassion, and a physical longing to comfort him. But it shook and confused them beyond distinction or control.

It possessed me all day and far into the succeeding week – a craving which seemed at the time preferable to any other having, an alien, inescapable exhilaration, running over me, as close as cold water, bleaching the colour from all other forms of joy. It was only when Ben's letter had arrived, and I had to answer it, that I began to make the first grating efforts of dry will to throw off this possession.

The letter came on Wednesday morning. It was written with the unnatural neatness and fluency of a third or fourth fair copy (except that the first 'M' seemed to me to be a converted 'A').

Sunday, 24*th* July

Dear Mr Pearce,

I am writing to apologise for the way I behaved on Friday night, although I know it doesn't make any difference to what I did, or what I might have done. Whenever I think about that (which is most of the time), I feel sick and ashamed and absolutely terrified. There is no excuse that I can give; everything you said was true, and you could have said a lot more. I am very, very sorry indeed. I will never do such a thing again.

Thank you for letting me stay the night, and I'm sorry to have bothered you with that on top of everything else. My father said I had abused your friendship, as well as his trust, and had no right to expect any more of either. So I don't expect you to answer this, or even to accept my apology. But not to send it would make everything even worse.

Please keep my licence as long as you think fit.

I couldn't say any of what I meant on Saturday morning.

Ben

I wrote back:

27.vii.1961

Dear Ben,

Thank you for your letter. I am glad you have told your father. I will keep your driving licence for you as you suggest.

Of course I accept your apologies. I think the whole incident should now be, perhaps not forgotten, but closed. I hope you will come in some afternoon for a cup of tea.

Yours ever,

Alan

Our next meeting was necessarily delayed, and necessarily embarrassing. I wanted to see Ben again soon, to get over the first awkwardness quickly and to repair any breach he felt he had made. But I thought that I should wait until he was ready to see me again.

This was difficult, feeling that each day he put off coming was likely to add to his dread of coming at all. In the end, I allowed myself a time-limit: if I had not seen him by the end of August, I would make an excuse to visit James. But then he came – just after the middle of August and with his own excuse: a book, quite forgotten, that I had lent his father two years before.

'How good of you to bring it back,' I said. 'Have you got time for some tea?'

'I was really just passing the end of your lane.'

'Yes. But the kettle's on. Have a cup before you go on.'

We drank our tea and talked, Ben answering quickly, looking into his cup. I asked him about leaving school. His headmaster had advised him to try for Oxford or Cambridge in the winter. He told me this, when it came up, with pleasure, offering it to me.

By the time he got up to go – at five-fifteen, punctiliously – he had recovered his countenance enough to forget that he was supposed to be in the middle of a walk, and also to ask me to sherry with his parents the following Sunday morning, adding, with a fleeting, experimental glance, 'Or gin and tonic. But no vodka.'

I had become aware by now that there was a sexual strand in my feelings for him. I had not been able to ignore it – or some of its implications about my own nature – through the five or six days which had followed that Saturday morning; nor in the weeks after that, with the less alien, more manageable longing – growing and blossoming, steadily and painfully and familiarly, with the renewed and unfulfilled hope of every evening – for the delight of his company, his simple proximity.

Now, looking at me quickly, half-ashamed but half-laughing, testing the minefield of our embarrassment, he was at his most gentle and alive. And yet desire was not my predominant feeling, but relief – gratitude that our meeting was so familiar, and happily ordinary.

CHAPTER 18

I could not, as I have said, avoid some conclusions about my own nature. But it was not for want of trying. I could not fully accept them either. As I emerged from the first cascade of unfamiliar emotion, shaking my head clear of the submerging force, struggling to recover my orientation, I realised that what I needed most was exacting honesty. But I did not achieve it.

I was clearly capable of erotic feeling towards someone of my own sex. But I had read enough lay-man's psychology to know that this was not uncommon, and not conclusive. Many people – perhaps even most people – have some tendencies generally associated with the other sex. The entirely 'male' man and the entirely 'female' woman are rare. They seem to be particularly rare among academic and artistic people: if the arts have anything to do with humanity, or human emotion, it must be an advantage to an artist, or a scholar, or a critic, to have some intuitive understanding of both halves of the human race. (The philistine world recognises this, in a hostile way, with its caricatures of the female artist or academic as 'mannish', badly dressed and heavy-footed, and the male artist as a limp-wristed effeminate.)

I knew, too, that some of these secondary tendencies, including the erotic ones, could predominate temporarily in certain circumstances: that growing children, for example, are often first attracted to the more familiar sex; that there are homosexual attachments in prisons and boarding-schools between people who will prefer heterosexual ones again when they are free.

I could remember many friends, but few loves, since my childhood. Before I reached puberty, and especially after my mother died, I was finding my most profound excitement in reading, and in 'the earth and common face of Nature'. (Reading *Tintern Abbey* for the first time gave me the same astonished lurch of joy that an adolescent feels on discovering a first like-minded friend.) I should have approved, later on, if I had known it, of the definition of an intellectual as someone who has discovered something more exciting than sex. (The non-intellectual world has its parody of this, too.)

I wanted to go to university; the army was, in principle, only a temporary interruption, though in 1943 I realised that it might be a final one. I worked very hard in the Intelligence Corps, and was frequently very frightened, and in the snatches of time that remained I learnt Low German and Old Norse. The ugliness of the sexual encounters available made me prefer scholarship and (occasionally) alcohol as recreation. I did drink too much from time to time, though not when it would spoil my work. (I thought then, as I think now, that the war was one which had to be won.)

The university was an extraordinary liberation. I read as if I had been starving. I found friends, too, and some girls among them, though not among the most important. As we read and talked together, and drank coffee, and went to the cinema, I felt sometimes a sort of general exultation in the nature of our company – that we were whole and young, still, and jubilant with the absurd irresponsibility of our practical lives, the unlimited demands, when we cared to answer them, of the intellectual universe. It was an exultation which I sometimes took from physical forms – from bravery of gesture and brightness of skin. But I could not, or did not, remember feeling it more particularly about the young men.

Honest remembering is very difficult, especially with an unwelcome fact, lying on the far, blurring edge of memory. It was important then for me, looking back to undergraduate days, to find no early points of homosexual inclination, stirring and showing, confirming their profounder roots. And inadequate honesty then has finally obscured memory. I really do not know, now, how much, and towards whom, I felt, as a very young man. I think it likely that some deeper, ineradicable roots of longing were quickened, subterraneously at least, below the appearing shoots of energy and gaiety and mutual delight. But as I looked back, I was content to recollect those shoots alone as the original, innocent burgeoning of my present emotions.

70

I had worked hard and lived alone for more than eight years, containing my life, by the necessity of my choice, within straitening limits. Now that my work was secure and prospering, I could sleep longer and eat better; I had more time; and my mind could range more often and further beyond my work. It was not astonishing that part of my superfluous energy, physical and spiritual, should run over into a relationship which engaged imagination and memory as well as ordinary affection. It was not astonishing; it was not really even disquieting. If I was careful – and of course I should be careful – to put no burden of unsought closeness or unacceptable emotion on Ben; if I remained (and why should I not remain?) within the boundaries of our present relationship – the growing equality of mind and friendship, the accepted gradation of responsibility and experience; if I held even my protectiveness within the limits of real necessity – then I could do him no harm, and myself no disgrace.

Sunday was three days from now, and there was no real reason why I should refuse the invitation.

CHAPTER 19

Ben was not there when I arrived. It had not occurred to me as a possibility. I said to James, 'Bridget is looking pretty. Is Mark here?'

'I hope so. Do you like lemon with it? He's been fishing, so he may be late, or not fit to be seen.'

He took me across the room to meet some people. I drank gin and tonic and talked with them, feeling slightly dizzy. At ten to one, I left, letting myself out by the back door. The prospect of returning over the fields brought back the brightness and serenity of my walk there earlier; the gathering happiness of the morning while I had bathed and shaved and breakfasted; the warmth of expectation which had lined the past three days. The day was left now without focus; the gin and tonic turned in my head.

Ben was in the yard, washing paintbrushes in a jar.

'Hello.'

'Oh, hello.'

'I thought I'd see you indoors.'

'Yes. Well – no. I'm not... At the moment I'm... I thought I'd get on with some paint-stripping.'

'Yes, I see. What are you stripping?'

'My new room. Like to have a look?'

One of the outbuildings which stood round the yard joined the house at a right-angle near the back door.

'It used to be where we kept the cultivator and the extra cloches and things. But I didn't have room for my books, and I've had to move in with Mark when anyone comes to stay. So they thought now I'm going to college – trying to – we could put up a shed for the cultivator, and I could have this.'

I looked in through the door. It was empty – swept but grimy. Sugar-soap and paint-stripper stood by a step ladder near the wall.

'You've just started?'

'They only told me about it on Friday. It was a surprise – a prize, really, for getting through A-levels.'

'You've heard?'

'That morning.'

'And – ?'

'I got an A and two Bs.'

'Oh, Ben! Well done!' I felt extraordinary relief and pleasure; more than I had ever felt for university pupils, and with less reference to myself; more whole-heartedly, more nearly, I suppose, as a parent might, than I had expected to feel even about Ben.

'Which was the A?'

'History.'

'I am delighted.' I took his arm, without forethought, as he stood inside the door. 'All that hard work.'

'I know.'

'And now you're set for Cambridge.'

'Or Oxford.'

'Or Oxford.'

We leaned on the windowsill and discussed Oxford, and talked of his plans; then he showed me what he was going to do with the room – the wiring, the painting, the cupboards, how he would put up bookshelves, where the desk and the bed were to be.

Mark came into the doorway with dry, pale mud halfway up his legs.

'Mum said to tell you, lunch.'

'Tell her... tell her Alan's here.'

Mark turned in the doorway and shouted, 'Mum. Ben says Alan's here.'

'I could have done that,' said Ben, and took Mark's shoulders and moved him out of the way. Then he went across the corner of the yard and through the back door of the house, and almost immediately Ruth came out with him.

'I'm sorry,' I said. 'I'm disgracefully late. I started to go nearly an hour ago.'

She asked me to stay to lunch.

73

In the afternoon I helped Ben, stripping the paint. He worked very thoroughly, though he said he was in a hurry, going back over his missed corners and mine.

'I want to start painting as soon as they get the wiring in. Then I can leave it drying and move in when we get back from Norfolk.'

The steady, strenuous, manual work continued my sense of sober usefulness and level affection. While I was finishing the window frames, Ben measured and marked the places for electric points, and drew out on the floor the dimensions of a cupboard. I watched him lay the yard-rule along the wall and into the corner, and his absorbed, deliberate movements, so sharply remembered now, made me feel then only an increase of our serene, common satisfaction.

We went on until it was getting dark – Bridget brought us mugs of tea – and Ben walked with me to the road, and as far as the gate into the fields.

CHAPTER 20

He wrote to me when he was in Norfolk. I was extraordinarily pleased to get the letter. Seeing, again, no postcard on the floor below the letter-box, I had picked the envelope up without interest or recognition. But when I had turned it over, I weighed it in my hand, and read over the postmark, and his writing of my address, a second time, before putting it beside my plate and opening my other letters. When I had poured out a cup of coffee, I opened the letter and read it.

I wish that I had it now. I have kept everything I have had from Ben, except this – the first long letter he ever wrote to me, full of interest and some affection, confiding and intelligent. I lost it – I don't know how, and I spent three-quarters of a working day, several years later, looking for it. I remember that he admitted how much he wanted to go to Oxford, and how much, though he knew it was rash, he was hoping; that he gave me a long account of what he was reading; and that he ended:

'It is lovely here – wide and empty – with the thin sea running in over the shore. I wish you could come and see it all. Yours affectionately, Ben'

We were both busy in the autumn. He was working for the College Entrance papers in November, and I was involved in the production of a series of mystery plays on the wireless for the BBC. I had been asked, originally, to be a literary consultant, meeting in London once or twice and then giving advice on the telephone. But when I realised how little the producers knew of their subject, and when I discovered what they were planning to do with that little, I could not preserve the detachment, or the economy of time, on which I had resolved.

I had to explain the basic principles of speaking Middle English verse; to dissuade them from having the comic scenes played in music-hall Cockney accents; to show them something of the material they were neglecting. By this time, I was going to London once a week or more. When they suggested that I should collaborate fully on the script and in the production, and use some episodes from the new Cycle, it seemed illogical to refuse. As soon as the last play was done, at Easter, I told Douglas, I should be working on our edition full-time, once more.

Then the Press gave us a deadline: they wanted to bring out one section of the Cycle, at least, to coincide with the productions on the wireless. Could we have a section ready by Christmas, or at latest by the New Year?

'That will teach you to get involved in showbusiness,' said Douglas. 'What are we going to do about it?'

'I don't quite know. How busy are you?'

'Very. Examining candidates for entrance, amongst other things.'

'Oh, my God.'

'Why does it have to be New Year?'

'They want to have a pretty paperback out by Easter.'

'Book-of-the-film? Coloured pictures and the rest of it?'

'That sort of thing. Typical academic publishers: secret hankering after mass sales.'

We were both silent.

'As long as we're taking our full time on the real edition,' he said then, 'I suppose we could just fudge this one together and let it go? We could do an erratum-slip later, if necessary.'

'No.'

'No.'

'I can work on the train.'

I did; and on the platform, and in the coffee break at rehearsals, and after supper when I got back. Douglas carried bunches of index-cards in his pockets, and worked at them when candidates came late for interview. By December 17th – I remember the date – my part was done, and I had typed up the fair copy and sent it to Douglas for revision. His was to come to me before the end of the year.

Next morning it was very cold. I got up late and had breakfast by the Aga. The house was dusty, and there were two-and-a-half weeks' unanswered letters on my desk. I could not get warm. I put on another pullover and a coat, and went for a walk in the still, black morning. The road-metal stung my feet, until I had gone some way, and so did the plough; past noon, when I turned into a wood, the leaves slid, glazed and rigid, under my soles. There was no shadow in the wood – the sun was not visible in the white, close sky.

The marshy ground in the middle was hard; on the far side of it, a man stood with his back to me, leaning with his shoulder against a branch that hung, half-torn, from the trunk to the earth. I began to cross the stiff, roughened ground, then stopped, seeing that Ben was the young man. I stood and waited, suspended between my felt breath and his deeper, visible breathing.

In the end, he shifted the position of his shoulders, turning to put his arm against the wood. To give him warning, before he might turn again and see that I was there, I said his name. And then, as there was no change or reaction, unless perhaps in his breathing, I repeated it.

Then he did turn.

'Alan?' He was wearing no jacket.

'Ben? Aren't you cold?'

I finished crossing to where he stood.

'Not really. I don't know.'

After a few more blank exchanges, I asked, 'Which way are you going?'

'That way. Probably.'

'All right.'

We started together. I saw him shivering as we crossed the ditch out of the wood, and offered him one of my pullovers. He said, 'Alan, I've failed Oxford,' and burst into tears.

'Come on,' I said. 'Come on. It's too cold to stay here.'

I took my coat off and put it round him. Holding the sleeve apart from the body, freeing the passage for his arm, I think it likely that I first fully loved him. If, with my present consciousness, I could stand beside my past mind, there, outside the wood,

I think that beyond the wretchedness and the desire for consolation (made by sympathy concentric and co-incident with Ben's own), I should see an unrecognised firmament of happiness.

We were both very cold when we got home: I from walking slowly without a coat; Ben, I think, from interior misery.

I lit the fire in the sitting-room and brought some food for both of us in there. When we had finished, I tidied the room and sorted out my desk, in order that Ben should not feel it necessary to talk. When I had dealt with all the bills and shorter letters, and started on the longer ones, he began to rearrange the fire, then said, 'What the hell am I going to do now?'

I brought my letter over to the hearth, and asked him, while finishing it, 'What are the alternatives?'

'Nothing much. It's all just a waste.'

He told me how good his hopes had been, how well the interview had seemed to go. He had looked forward to his parents' pleasure.

'You did work hard. You deserved to hope. And that can't really be lost, you know. All that history under your belt, and a good mind – the beginnings of a trained mind: acquiring those can't have been a waste. And it won't be, unless you let it. You mustn't feel too discouraged, either – certainly not disgraced. There are so many candidates for every place. You should have seen some of the paragons we had to turn away when I was examining: four As at A-level, head prefects, captains of cricket – we just hadn't room.' He laughed.

'Well, where else is there?' I asked.

'Oh, one of the provincial universities, I suppose. But I don't know if I want to. I might just go and pick fruit in France or something.'

'By all means pick fruit in France. But not for the rest of your life. And I shouldn't despise provincial universities. It isn't wise, or accurate, to think all the alternatives are inferior – or even provincial. What about London? Edinburgh? Trinity, Dublin?'

'I know. I didn't mean it snobbishly.'

'And Wessex has a first-rate history department.'

'Do they?'

'And there's the New University here.'

'Oh, I don't know.'

'Too near home, perhaps. You don't have to decide now, anyway. But do decide *not* to decide. Don't give up or do anything silly.'

'I feel like doing something silly.'

'Of course you do. Only let it be short-term silliness. Get drunk – without your car keys – or put five pounds and your passport in your pocket and take the ferry from Harwich. But don't withdraw any applications, and don't tear up any notes.'

He looked up, and then down.

'Ben. Promise not to.'

'All right.'

'It's nearly three. I must get some wood chopped before it's dark. Would you have time to help me?'

After we'd chopped it, we made a large high tea and blazed up the fire with wood-chips. Later, we did a General Knowledge quiz from one of the Sunday papers, taking it less and less seriously, making deliberately absurd guesses where we were ignorant.

It was after ten when he got up to go.

'I'll walk you back.'

'Don't. It's late. And I'm cheerful now. You do do a lot for me, Alan.'

'Not so much that I wouldn't do more.'

As he was going out, I said, 'Have you thought of Cambridge?' He stopped so still that I wished I had left it alone.

He said in a moment, 'Not really.'

'Well, it's a possibility. Think about it tomorrow. Not tonight. I might look in, in the afternoon.'

'Do. I shan't be out.'

CHAPTER 21

So I began to go regularly to see him in his room at the side of the yard. There was no need, practical or social, to make all my visits to the whole family. James and Ruth were as much concerned, in some ways, as I was; in some ways, being parents, perhaps more. Now and then I would look in at the house as well, or Ruth would see me in the yard, from the kitchen window, and ask me to come in. She would consult me, unhappily, about Ben's state of mind. I had, perhaps, helped him in his first, undefended misery, but the despondency and aimlessness to which this was giving place were more serious, we both thought, though less painful.

'I didn't know he'd take it so hard,' Ruth would say again, pouring out tea at the kitchen table. 'I didn't know he'd mind so much.'

'Do you think he knew?'

'If he'd told us, perhaps we shouldn't have let him take it?'

'But you wouldn't have wanted to stop him? In the end, you'd have wanted him to risk it, wouldn't you?'

'It's something to do with himself – as if it would have made him sure. He's had the hardest row to hoe, in some ways. Bridgie's cleverer, really, and Mark can get away with anything.'

'And more difficult, perhaps, to be the eldest?'

'Much more. He minds more – for us as well as himself. He's very *kind*.'

'I can imagine that.'

'Not so much for the success – just that he would have had something to go on, that there was somewhere that thought he was really worth having.'

'He is enormously worth having, Ruth. You mustn't let him think he's not. He's got a good mind – possibly even a very good mind. He's got a real feeling for history, and he's learnt how to work. You can't ask for much more.'

'Will you tell him that, Alan?'

'I have. More than once.'

'I thought he might believe you. Mothers aren't credible about that sort of thing.' She dropped her head into her hands, and didn't say any more.

'What does James think about it?'

'He doesn't think it's doing Ben any good, sitting about brooding. He thinks he must start *doing* something.'

'He's right.'

'Yes. But in a way it gets us no further. If there was anything he *wanted* to do – it's because there isn't anything, now, that he's so wretched.'

'I know. No *raison d'être*. It's an intolerable feeling: it seems to wither everything else, too – self-respect; even ordinary little pleasures: a fine morning, a plant coming out in the garden.'

'*Yes*,' said Ruth. 'Yes. I didn't know you'd know that, Alan.'

'Have you seen the report, yet, from the college?'

'I didn't know there was one.'

'Their report on his papers. I think it's usual. The school should have it by now.'

It seemed best that I should show him the report, and discuss it with him. I dreaded this, and made several disingenuous plans, in case it was damagingly severe. In fact, it was encouraging. The college said clearly that they had liked him, and wished they had room to take him. Several of his papers had been good, but his French translation, and answers on economic history, had been inaccurate, and pulled him down. The school had enclosed a note, reminding him that the teachers who had coached him for Oxford entrance were ready to help him again if he decided to try for admission to Cambridge.

I took the report across to his room late one morning. I knocked and went in, and saw him lying across his unmade bed, drawing on a newspaper which lay on the floor. He was filling in the loops in the letters of a headline.

He reversed the newspaper and got up quickly. He had not shaved.

He talked while he took my coat, embarrassed by his own idleness and the state of his room, yet pleased – to see me, perhaps; perhaps just to have something to do.

'Alan. Good. You're not usually so early. Have a chair. Let me move those. Are you warm enough? What about some coffee?'

I sat by the fire, and he took the kettle to refill. When he thought I wasn't looking, he pulled the bed together, flattening the cover over it.

While we were drinking our coffee, I gave him the report; he read it, and thanked me, and gave it back.

'So you really ought to try for Cambridge.'

'No, Alan.'

'Why not?'

'I don't want to.'

'That's not an ultimate reason.'

'It feels like one.'

'You know what I mean. Why don't you want to?'

He hesitated, and then said, 'I suppose I'm tired of working hard and doing badly.'

'But you *didn't* do badly.'

'Of failing, then.'

I began to look through the report again.

'I'd rather go and do harvesting in a kibbutz.'

'Oh, Ben, don't be histrionic. The two things are not mutually exclusive. Even in Israel, the harvest won't be over by the end of January.' He did not answer. 'If you're determined on mortification, you can read this paragraph again, and see where you did do less well. A bit more French and economic history, now, and you can get into Cambridge first, and join the Foreign Legion afterwards.'

He laughed mildly, looked at the fire, and put down his cup. Then he said, 'Anyway, I can't work any more.'

That was something in which I did know how to help him. I knew in theory – if not yet fully in practice – what it was to be unable to make oneself settle to work, finding necessary and unnecessary things to do all through the morning, until it was too late to start.

82

I thought about it, hesitated, changed my mind twice, and then asked, 'Do you want to come and work with me? I've got a lot to do; we needn't interrupt each other. If you came at nine, we could start together.'

It might set a pattern again for his day. He would have to get up in good time (and after the second day, when I let him know that he had kept me waiting, he was very punctual); working in the same room, he could not get up from his desk and wander about without disturbing me; and I judged that he would be reluctant to be seen reading the newspaper or drawing in the margins of his notes.

He was reluctant, too, to break the silence which I very deliberately maintained, except when we broke off for coffee at eleven o'clock. Then Ben, with my encouragement, did feel free to bring up anything puzzling, or unusually interesting, that he had found in his work. On the strict understanding that I was not an historian, I would do what I could to suggest solutions to the problems, or further directions for a particular interest. After two hours more, he went home for lunch, with a good morning's work behind him, and time in the afternoon for any help his teachers could give him.

I was delighted to see him making such good use of the time. I had put a table for him in the corner by the window. Looking round only a little, I could watch him settling down to work, and working, as the days went by, with increasing vigour and unselfconsciousness. The same was not true of me. I knew that my concentration was important to his work, as well as to my own, but sustaining it, which had hardly ever been difficult before, was at first almost impossible.

I did achieve it in the end. After ten days, I had almost forgotten him while I worked. Not entirely: even at the height of concentration, I was aware of Ben working behind me and to the left – a sort of vibration at the bottom of my mind, like a tremolo on the low strings in an orchestra. It did not, finally, break the concentration; it made, rather, a quick tension which was very good for my work. I was properly tired when we stopped – tired, excited, and liable to express myself more violently than usual.

If the impossible were possible, if he were with me now, and working with me every morning, would it continue, the exultant, exhausting exercise of mind, continually straining against, continually quickened by, the pull of Ben's presence? Or would it be too much for more than a few weeks? The sinews of work and love distorted by too great a strain, energy wasted and balance lost? He would believe – for to be here still, after more than seven years, he must be assumed subject to the reciprocal force – being young, he would believe that the high intensity could continue without remission. But is it not more likely to have slackened, either by small gradations to every-day industriousness, or with suddenness, and even quarrelling, broken with the quick, ill-directed responses of fatigue, and then a new effort needed to find each a separate concentration? And how far would the same be true of all we did and felt together?

I do not know, and dare not really consider. The dangers, both of hubris and of despair, are too great.

CHAPTER 22

At the end of January, James drove Ben up to Cambridge. I walked over early to wish him luck before they left; it was a cold morning with a dark red sun.

Two days later, I had to be in London for a rehearsal, and Ben, on his way home, came to lunch with me at the BBC. He thought the interviews had gone fairly well. The extra economic history had been useful; one of the dons had interviewed him brusquely, but he had kept his head and substantiated his arguments. He had been given a room high up over the Backs. He had had to sleep in his overcoat, but the view had been worth it.

'You can't imagine. Looking down along the bridges, in the frost, and the trees bare.'

'You're converted to Cambridge after all.'

'Oh, all right!'

One of my co-producers, Paul, came over to suggest that Ben should watch the rehearsal. I introduced them, and he took us round some of the other studios before showing Ben where he could sit.

'Nice boy,' he said, as we waited for the cast and the other producer. 'You known him long?'

'I suppose I have. He's the son of an old friend.'

'Well... any time,' said Paul, smiling.

I could hardly answer him. My throat was stiff with caution and half-acknowledged, only half-justified, resentment.

Ben came into the kitchen six days later, as I was washing up the lunch. I dried my hands and took the telegram he had put down beside me. It offered him a vacancy at a Cambridge college for the next Michaelmas term.

I shouted with triumph, and he thanked me, and grew red. He was shivering; his clothes were very wet.

'Is it still raining hard? Did you come by car?'

'By bike.'

'That's worse than walking. Here, give me your jacket. Do you want to borrow a pair of trousers?'

'No, it's all right. I'll come by the Aga and steam.'

I gave him coffee and rejoiced again, and he thanked me for what I had done for him – generosity rather than knowledge making his thanks commensurate with my effort.

I dined with his family that night. We drank Ben's health, and he replied with a token sip of James's burgundy. Later, we were left talking together.

'What are you going to do from now till then? Eight months of liberty. Or does it seem too long? If you can't wait to go up – '

'Oh, I can wait.'

'Ben, what's the matter?'

He looked drawn and uncertain. After a moment he said, 'I think I'm just scared.'

'Of going up?'

'I suppose so.'

'I don't think you need be, you know; not seriously, or at long range. You can cope with the work, or they wouldn't have taken you.'

'It's not that.'

'Is it leaving home?'

'Not really.'

'There'll be lots of other people on their own for the first time. Do you know anyone going up? Anyone from school?'

'One or two.'

'That'll be a help. And I know some of the English faculty. I'll tell them to look out for you. But you can hardly avoid making friends anyway, living in college, – '

'I suppose not.'

'– if that's what's daunting you.'

'Oh, it doesn't *matter*,' he said suddenly.

'All right.'

We were silent. I felt in my inside pocket.

'Hadn't I better give you back your driving licence, by the way?'

I held it out. He did not take it, but said, 'If you think so.'

'Well, what do you think?'

'I was leaving it to you.'

'And if I'd forgotten?'

'I don't know.'

I smiled and threw the licence into his lap.

He smiled back for a moment, put it in his pocket, and then didn't know what to do next, and got up and went to the window.

The pane was black and wet, and I could see his hair and face pale in it.

When Ruth and James and Bridget had finished clearing up – Ben and I, as hero and guest, respectively, of the evening, were not allowed to help – and had sent Mark to bed, they brought in coffee and brandy. When I had said, some time after that, that I must be going, Ben suggested that he should drive me home. It would have been convenient as well as appropriate: the night was still very wet. But the car turned out to have a flat tyre.

'I'll walk.'

'But you'll get wet.'

'I can always get dry again. Really, Ben, don't bother. I'd like the walk. Change it tomorrow. Go in now. It's cold for standing about. Thank your parents again for such a good evening.'

He turned to go, and I said, 'Sleep well. And I am so pleased about Cambridge.' Then, as he reached the house, and called 'Good night,' I called back,

'I'm away tomorrow. But the day after – drive over and have tea, or coffee, or something.'

CHAPTER 23

I went to the New University next day for a seminar, and before coming home I had an hour in their bookshop. A rich, untidy, second-hand department had just opened, and I found a book I thought Ben would like to have, to mark his success. I missed the bus home and had to wait a long time for the next one.

I intended to get up in good time next day and make some scones before starting work.

But I woke aching with fatigue, and let time pass uselessly, without the will to prevent it. The sun hurt my eyes as I made breakfast, and afterwards even when my back was to the window. I could not eat or finish my coffee, and eventually I went back to my room, and lay down again.

I woke about eleven, worried that Ben would arrive. There was nothing to offer him, and the kitchen was untidy. I got up, but by the time I reached the bathroom, I felt too ill to go downstairs. I realised that I had 'flu, or something of the kind, and went back and slept again.

In the early afternoon, my sleep became confused and patchy, and gave way to uncomfortable thirst. I lay in the heat of the blankets, and thought about getting some water. In the end, I pushed the blankets down and began to cross the room. My stomach rose against the pain in my head, and I stopped and lay down, halfway to the door.

When I realised what had happened, I could not get up. I stayed on the floor, sweating and shivering. Twice, a car went past the end of the lane, and I wondered each time what could be done if the engine-noise turned and came up to the house; and what could be done if it didn't – if nothing came. Then, through sleep, or further unconsciousness, I heard another car grow loud, and stop. I woke fully as the front door opened.

I called, 'Ben? Hello? Ben?' and heard an indoor latch, and feet in the living room.

Ben's voice said, quite quietly, below me, 'Alan? Are you there?' and then, 'Oh, well!'

I said, 'Here. Upstairs,' without being able to make much noise; the front door opened again, and I brought my voice to a half-shout, and banged my hand against the floor.

Ben came up the stairs and into the room.

'Alan.'

Sick and exhausted, I said, 'Oh, good.'

He came down beside me, looking startled. I took the cuff of his coat and said, 'All right. It's 'flu. That's all.'

'God!' said Ben, 'How long have you been there?'

'Some time. I don't know.'

'You'll get cold, that's the worst thing. Here.'

He took a blanket and put it over me, then fetched a glass of water from the bathroom and held it for me to drink. After a little longer, he said, 'That's the bed done now. Can you get that far?'

I tried to raise my shoulders, and said 'No,' and unemotional tears ran back into the edge of my hair.

'It's all right. Have another drink.'

Then he put one arm round behind me and under my arm-pit, got me to rise, and took me across the floor, making little meaningless remarks as we went, as a man makes to a horse. 'That's it. Well done. Come on.'

When I was in bed, he brought the extra blanket from the floor, and then went away.

'Don't go,' I wanted to say, but turned instead to lie on my side.

Some time passed, and Ben came back.

'You ought to have a telephone by your bed, you know. He says it's going round. Aspirins and plenty of liquid, and I'm to ring tomorrow if you're worse.'

'I might as well ring myself, if I'm ringing you.'

'No, because I'm staying the night.'

I did not argue much. He had nothing else to do (he said), and his mother was busy, with Mark also in bed. I had never been

89

overborne by Ben before. I did not mind, though I was partly ashamed to let him stay. I was also partly delighted, though I could not attend to the delight as I might have done.

He brought me aspirins and a jug of water, and carried the paraffin stove up from the shed, filling it and lighting it with my advice.

The room grew unfamiliarly warm, and I heard him playing Haydn on the gramophone below me. I slept deeply, but woke remembering shallower patches, with the stirring of the door-latch and Ben's momentary nearness. He came again, and seeing that I was no longer asleep, found a thermometer and sat on the bed for two minutes while I took my temperature. He read it for me: it was at 102.5. I said that he should wait until next morning before ringing the doctor again.

He straightened my bed, and then I heard him in the spare room, making the bed and getting undressed. There was no stove there, and he was used to electric heating. I knocked on the wall, to tell him to take my stove, but he did not hear, and I fell asleep.

Next morning, my temperature was lower, though I was still weak. Ben helped me along the passage to the bathroom. In principle, I resented this debility. But principle – particularly irrational principle – did not have much effect on my spirits. I no longer felt ill. Water tasted like water again, the room was warm, and my weakness had blamelessly and involuntarily secured me Ben's care and frequent company.

He stayed for four days, I suppose – certainly for less than a week. But the tranquil, accepted irresponsibility of those days overflowed their period, and spread into the succeeding weeks, so that Ben went home, and I resumed my work, but our familiarity did not recede to its former bounds and level. Friendship, carried over and beyond the practical limits of acquaintance, did not immediately subside and shrink again. Buoyant above the earlier flood-marks of our intimacy, we left now well out of reach our footing in social pretext, in inequality of age and status, or in necessary and half-necessary occasion.

We played chess in the evenings while I was ill, and Ben read aloud to me, and I to him. He would have resisted his part,

I think, unconfident of his ability before my judgement, but I asked him first only for a review in *The Times*, while my eyes still could not stand the light, and then for a passage in *Twelfth Night* to which it referred (inaccurately). He read aloud well, with a limpid, self-forgetful attentiveness to the author's purpose (though with proportionate embarrassment when a mistake or stumbling recalled self-consciousness).

Now good Cesario, but that piece of song,
That old and antic song we heard last night.
Methought it did relieve my passion much,
More than light airs and recollected terms
Of these most brisk and giddy-paced times.
Come, but one verse.

I quoted some more of the scene, and between us we finished it, the light turned away from the head of my bed and onto the page between his hands.

Next day, I was able to read for a short time. He brought the books I wanted, and when he asked me about one of them, after supper, I began to read – Drayton's sonnets, I think – and handed him the book when I grew tired. He took over with only a little hesitation, and we read Wyatt and Sydney then, and later some Spenser and Ben Jonson, and at another time, at his request, the first book of *The Prelude*.

He wanted to know about my current work, and I read him some passages from the Cycle. He liked it, which gave me pleasure, but he would not read it aloud himself. I pressed him – a little hard – but after one or two attempts, he put the typescript down.

'I know I'm massacring it. Don't make me. I can't get the metre.'

'All right. But I can't do any more at the moment. Read me something else.'

'What?'

'You choose.'

So he found an anthology and read Vaughan and Blake and Hopkins (to my interest and delight); and Dylan Thomas (with my judicious silence); and Day Lewis.

'Read me some more of your Cycle some time?' he asked, when he was taking the tray away.

'If you like,' I said, very much pleased. 'But there won't be time for much of it.'

'I *might* come and see you, even when you're all right.'

'Right. We'll have penny readings. But you must bring something, too.'

He did. I got up the next day, and he went home the following morning. There was no justification for asking him to stay longer. But he was back within a couple of days, bringing Ruth's offer to do my shopping and laundry, anxious that I might be doing too much. We made tea – I recognised his careful unofficiousness in my kitchen – and afterwards he read some Corneille that he had brought – extremely well, as far as I could judge.

He made me take a part, and laughed at my failure to prevent the Alexandrines from degenerating into an anapaestic gallop. It was a gentle revenge, perhaps, for his difficulty with the Cycle. I read him the play of Abraham and Isaac before he went home, and, through the weeks that followed, several other plays from the Cycle, and much else besides.

I was extraordinarily happy. During the day I would mark with a scrap of paper something that occurred to me to read in the evening. I usually made enough supper for two, and whatever I made seemed to turn out well. Ben came in more evenings than not. We read Shakespeare, too, taking the different parts. Ben suggested the Sonnets, and even then, I felt only their glory and our continuing, companionable happiness, which seemed sometimes to lack no completeness, to have no reason to change, except in degree.

I was concerned only that he should make full use of his unrepeatable liberty between school and college. He evaded this subject at first, when I brought it up, then he told me that he had not been well. A few weeks after his return from Cambridge, at his mother's insistence, he had gone to the doctor. He was told that he was run down – the doctor suspected glandular fever – and he must rest for a couple of months. He had not told me before because he did not want to worry me with it when I had just been ill, and also, I think, because he imagined me more stoical than I am about my own health. I was touched by his reticence and upset at my own lack of perception.

He would go abroad in April, if the doctor was satisfied; and he fretted that he could not get a job before that to pay for his travels. He did not want to borrow the money from his father. On condition that his parents and his doctor agreed, I offered him a job correcting the proofs of the paperback, which were soon to arrive from the Press. We agreed on four hours a day, at a rate which was lower than he could have earned, in full health, working at Bracknell's, though rather more, in fact, than I could afford. I limited his time carefully – bringing him a glass of milk as the clock struck, like Leonard Woolf. And though he did not altogether admit it, I realised that he could not have done very much more. The need for real accuracy is very trying, to start with, especially to anyone unfamiliar with Middle English orthography.

To be working at the same thing, though on different parts of it, was a considerable happiness. And though, spending so much of the day with me at the cottage, he spent more evenings with his family, he usually stayed to lunch, and we would sometimes take the afternoon gardening or walking, or, if it was wet, listening to music.

There was a swivelling of focus, a change in the angle of our reciprocal regard. With our sights directed no longer diametrically, each towards the other, but in parallel, or even converging, towards a common object, we were less conscious of each other, or of the reflection of each in the other, but, for this time at least, I felt, nearer than before.

CHAPTER 24

By Easter, the BBC series was finished. They did the plays adequately in the end, I thought. Ben thought they were very good. The paperback was published, with some nice illustrations from roughly (in some cases, very roughly) contemporary manuscripts, and a band round the cover printed with some rhetorical and misleading reference to the broadcast. The sales were good.

Ben left for France immediately after the public holiday. The doctor was pleased with his health, and he hoped to go on to Italy, and perhaps even to Greece. He bought a sleeping bag and a framed rucksack with money left over from his fare, and showed me the various pockets and contrivances with childish precision. He had no address beyond the *Poste Restante* at Dijon; I wrote to him there, and contented myself with knowing that I could expect no reply for ten days or a fortnight.

He wrote sooner than I expected, at length and warmly. He had not stayed long with his French 'exchange' family of the two previous years, but had travelled on southwards through Burgundy, and then into the Alps. He would cross to Italy next day, and spend a night or two in Turin before looking for a lift to take him east across the plain. I sent a prompt postcard to Padua, to tell him not to miss the Scrovegni Chapel. My thoughts followed his journey in more detail – his seeing of Italy for the first time.

I had a postcard from Padua, and another from Venice. By the middle of May, he hoped to see Ravenna and go on to Florence, where he was planning to stay, or at least to be based, for some weeks.

Before the end of June, if I worked hard, I might be able to finish work on the Old Testament part of the Cycle. Douglas would revise my last few plays in his summer vacation; I had already revised most of what he had sent to me. The New Testament plays were longer and more numerous. Still, it would be a milestone, and I began to consider whether I should celebrate it with a holiday. I could find reasons to go to Rome. Should I suggest meeting Ben there? And afterwards, perhaps, we might travel to Brindisi, and take a ship for the Piraeus.

I wrote to Ravenna, mentioning my holiday in general terms, and had a postcard, in answer, from Florence. He was having difficulty in finding anywhere to stay; it was already very hot, and the Uffizi was full of shouting German guides; he would write properly soon. I started to work as fast as I could, straight through each day until supper. There were nearly five weeks before I must determine my plans.

Two or three days later, Douglas rang up. He had been granted leave for a couple of weeks' lecturing in Austria before the vacation began, and he asked if he could spend a long weekend with me on the way. I warned him that I was working hard, but I was glad at the prospect of seeing him. He looked over his lectures, or walked with his dog, while I worked in the mornings, and in the afternoons he drove us to places beyond the compass of my own explorations. The sides of the lanes were rich and white with cow-parsley, and the trees full and damp in their own shade. The dog came with us, waiting discreetly in church porches and stable yards. We worked together in the evening, and disentangled several knots in the text, left till now as indissoluble.

When Douglas packed his case, the night before leaving, the dog became very much distressed, following him into each room or lying still with his chin on the case. He was to be left, Douglas said, at a kennels near the coast. I thought that Douglas was almost as much distressed himself, and I offered to keep Sam with me instead. Douglas could fetch him on his way back three weeks later, and he could pick up most, if not all, of the remaining Old Testament plays at the same time. I insisted, with as much gravity and vagueness as I could combine, that I must be free to leave in four weeks, at the latest.

The dog was well-intentioned and tiresome, like most dogs. After one or two long walks at unorthodox times, he became fairly well reconciled to Douglas's absence, and I thought he would be all right as long as he had a walk every afternoon. It would not shorten my working hours significantly, and it would provide a kind of company. Exams had started at the university, and classes were over; I was working very hard, and had almost no other distractions.

Shopping on Thursday took longer than usual. I did not trust Sam in traffic, and had therefore to lead him and push the bicycle the last mile-and-a-half of the way. His burly, eager, shoving body complicated my passage along the pavement between gregarious shoppers, and I could not find anything to tie him to outside the grocer's, which did not admit dogs.

Mark was at the counter. He put down two baskets and came out to me.

'If you can hang on till I've paid, I can hold him for you.'

When I brought him his baskets and took the lead, thanking him again, he said, 'I didn't know you had a dog.'

I explained Sam's visit, and asked if they had heard from Ben recently.

'Not a letter, but he rang up from Florence.'

'He's still in Florence?'

'Well, he was there on Tuesday. But he's coming home. He got ill. Mum's gone out to him.'

'I see.' I put down my bag of groceries. 'What's wrong, do you know? I'm so sorry.'

'I don't know, really. They think it's probably what he had before. Anyway, Mum's gone out to him. Dad couldn't leave the soft fruit.'

'Are you... managing all right? Is there something I can do to help?'

'It's OK. Thank you very much. I've got half-term, so I can shop. And Bridgie cooks sometimes; and it's mostly cold meat and salad anyway.'

'Well. You've got my number. Do – if there is anything –'

There seemed to be nothing else to suggest, or ask, or any other way to prolong the conversation.

'I must get some stamps. Well... Come on then, Sam.'

Mark patted his side.

'Let me know how Ben is, when he gets back. Or when you hear.'

I forgot the stamps. Worry welled up in me in a sickening tide, receding only before immediate, practical problems, but returning as soon as I realised that it had receded. It was like the beginning of flu – heaving beneath my sense of balance, and making the skin across my shoulders creep and shiver – but without the shrinking concern or the recurrent oblivion.

When I had had tea, I realised that I must work. What I did was not very good, but it was incompatible with anxiety. I thought about Ben only when I stopped. I went on till after midnight, and had a glass of whisky, and slept.

Sam came into my room in the morning while I was still sleeping. It was quite late, and I went downstairs in my pyjamas to let him into the garden. The morning was fresh and warm, and it occurred to me that Ben might not be more seriously ill than he had been in February.

Over breakfast, I began to feel that this was a dangerous idea: a more fearful assumption would be safer. It was a rationally untenable piece of superstition, but it paralysed me between the more and the less immediate dread, and could not be exorcised until I had called Sam in, and given him his breakfast, and started work.

Douglas had sent a card from Salzburg, describing his travels and his welcome at the university, and suggesting that he should take the full four weeks away. I could not see any sensible reason not to agree. I decided to finish the Old Testament plays, and get at least one New Testament play done, as well, before his return. I worked all day, with one short break for Sam, and did as much as I had hoped, though it was more tiring than usual, as though I was driving against the brake. By the evening, I saw index numbers whenever I closed my eyes.

My fear about Ben, banked down by work, broke out again as terror at night. But next morning I looked at a recurrent, unknown word which had baffled both Douglas and me from the beginning, and knew immediately what its origin must be. I spent most of the morning with the etymological dictionaries of various early Germanic languages, and proved my derivation almost beyond dispute: it was a very rare local variant of a Norse borrowing – a technical term for a particular carpenter's tool. I even found a parallel in a much earlier text. I nearly sent Douglas a telegram, but restrained my triumph to a postcard, adding that Sam was well and would be welcome to stay with me until the end of the fourth week or even longer, and that I thought the Old Testament plays would be ready to collect at the same time.

I worked straight through Sunday, and on into the following week. My conscious mind had only a small space for Ben, but the full width of half-conscious thought was occupied with a perpetually repeated calculation: how soon might Mark ring? And if he didn't, how soon might I, without appearing unsuitably anxious, without increasing their various burdens, their strain and anxiety?

My wariness seems strange to me now. To ring up and enquire for Ben, as soon as I heard of his illness, would have been the most natural thing for any friend of the family to do. But some decisions – particularly decisions of timing or proportion – can properly be made only by instinct. And if, for any reason, one dare not trust one's instinct, one is left without any serviceable criterion.

I began to feel very tired. I would jump rigidly awake in the night, and lie for a long time, unable to unclench my muscles or my thoughts. In the day, I was subject to trivial obsessions. I had to set the kettle in the middle of the hot-plate, to open letters without tearing the envelopes, to count the number of times the telephone rang before I reached it – an irrational discipline, to propitiate a fate I did not believe in, but dared not offend.

I would ring, if I had not heard, on Thursday. On Thursday morning, I woke with a steady, cool, empty sense of terror and relief. Nine o'clock was probably the earliest I could decently telephone. By nine o'clock I could not do it. I did not know how to begin the conversation, or to explain why I was ringing now, rather than at any other time, or indeed why I had not enquired for Ben before. The afternoon was a better time – less urgent, less deliberate – and I could think, meanwhile, what to say.

I knew that there were answers to all this, but I continued to do nothing, sitting by the telephone, feeling light-headed and sick. When it rang under my hand, I jumped and shuddered.

'Hello?'

'Alan?'

'Yes?'

'It's Ruth.'

'Ruth.'

'Alan... Are you all right?'

'Yes. Yes, I'm well. How are you?'

'I'm all right. But – '

'Yes... Ben...'

'He hasn't been well.'

'I know. Ruth, I wanted to ring, but – '

'I know.'

'I wasn't sure when you'd be back. I didn't want to keep bothering them before there was any news.'

'I thought so.'

'It's good of you to ring me now.'

'I thought you'd want to know...'

'Yes. Yes, I do.'

'Well, he's basically all right, Alan.'

I put my elbow down on the table, and the other hand on Sam, who had come in.

'We got back on Tuesday night, and he saw Dr Franks yesterday, and there's nothing really serious, thank God.'

'Thank God.'

I realised that she had not spoken in reply, and asked, after another moment, 'What... do they know? What was it then?'

'Well, partly the glandular fever coming back, but they don't seem to be too worried about that; they think he can get over that, as long as he rests. A lot of it was the heat, I think, and trying to cope on his own when he first felt bad; and then there was some problem about finding a doctor.'

'Poor boy.'

'I know. It was horrid when he telephoned, sounding so wretched, and being so far away – '

She broke off and I felt what she had felt, and wondered that I had not considered it more, before.

I asked about the journey. She had gone up to London that night, and caught the first flight next morning. He had had a miserable three or four days by the time she arrived, but once the landlady understood what was wrong, she was eager to help – sent her husband for the doctor, and made Ruth up a bed on the parlour floor.

'How is he now?'

'Enormously relieved to be home.'

'I can imagine.'

'And quite a lot better, already. But he's going to have to take it slowly, and I think the boredom will set in as the relief wears off. Boredom and disappointment.'

'Poor Ben.'

'He'd love to see you, Alan.'

CHAPTER 25

I went that afternoon. He was in the house, in their spare room, and I sat on the end of the neat, quilted bed, and heard about the Scrovegni Chapel, and the Carpaccios in the Church of the Schiavoni, and Torcello, and Chioggia, and leaving his passport in the vaporetto. I kept to a careful half hour, and went home before he got as far as Florence.

By the end of the next week he was well enough to move back into his own room in the yard; going to see him became more ordinary, and less like sick-visiting. He looked white, still, and had to rest for some part of the day, but he was accepting his limitations with admirable good sense and purpose. He read in the morning – he had started Trevelyan's *Garibaldi* – rested after lunch for a couple of hours, and was free then to walk in the garden, or make a cup of tea.

He told me more of his travels – determinedly avoiding all repining, except once when he said, interrogatively, 'I could have stayed on. I wouldn't have died of it.' And I answered, 'It wasn't really a case for trial and error.'

He showed me his photographs, and some absurd Italian posters (acquired by some extraordinary combination of luck and honest cunning) which I helped him put up on the walls of his room.

The ample relief of his safety, and safe return, gave me an unwarranted feeling of holiday. I could not celebrate it appropriately with Ben himself, without betraying how great my past anxiety had been. On my own, I walked in the garden when I should have been at work, drank beer with my supper, ordered a book I couldn't afford, and put a bunch of white pinks in a jug on the mantelpiece.

The end of the Old Testament plays did not seem to get very much nearer. Because I had said that they would be ready for

Douglas on his return, which was now to be at the end of the month, and because over-running a deadline, even a self-imposed one, would have been a mistake, I started to work through the afternoons again. I walked over to see Ben after supper several times; having slept earlier, he would be up until ten-thirty or eleven. But sometimes I stayed at the cottage, reading or listening to music. I did not want to tire him with too much company, and his presence – his existence – at no greater distance seemed as much as I needed to ask.

Sam got less exercise than he felt was due to him, but he came with me to visit Ben, and we walked for an hour or two on Sunday. The university had gone down; friends there and elsewhere had begun their vacations; and all my other company in those ten days were the Sunday fishermen I spoke to and some children in the lane near a village.

Four days before Douglas was due to return, I reached the point I had set myself. Late on Monday afternoon the Old Testament plays were done, and the first (and shortest) from the New Testament as well. Some references remained to be checked, but that would be only a few hours' work. I was as good as free.

The heat, precariously built up throughout the week, broke next day in a series of storms. The roof leaked in several places, and the little apples were scattered on the lawn.

The next morning was fresh and fair. I cut some bread and ham, took the one-inch map, with footpaths, and set out, irresponsible enjoyment augmented by Sam's obstreperous good spirits.

We walked a good way, in a part of the country I did not know well, over towards Harchester. By noon the sun was hot, but the long grass was still wet below the top, against our legs, and so were the inner leaves of the hedges, when we brushed by them. There were puddles in the cart-tracks big enough for Sam to stand in and drink. From the smaller, sunken roads, the pale green wheat was above my head; it looked glossy and thick, a blueish layer floating between the stout ears and the stalks.

Sam quested on his own, returning now and then to me, as the moving centre of his successive arcs of exploration. Where we stopped for lunch, there were white dog-roses in the hedge above us. There was an Elizabethan splendour about the day, and when we went on I found myself repeating some of the Sonnets.

We bathed in a stream – startlingly cold – just before we were to turn back. And then, refreshed against the afternoon heat, went on a little further after all, to find a small Saxon church standing in an oatfield, unroofed, with a dragon on one of its capitals.

It was a long way back. My thirst was growing and my feet were sore when we were still an hour or more from home. To cut off a loop of the road, I turned into the side of a broad wood. Sam ran ahead of me into the shade, and when I could see down the track, in the dun light, he wasn't there.

CHAPTER 26

It is not really possible, I think, to understand love in the Middle Ages until one realises how new it was.

> Lenten ys come with loue to toune,
> With blosmen and with briddes roune,
> That al this blisse bryngeth

Love's paradoxes of pain and delight, 'maistrye' and 'servyse', humility and disdain, mutability and permanence; its panoply of images – rose and lily and leaf, birdsong and thorn and sunlight, 'middel smal' and 'colours white and redde' – now the smudged devices on the small change of any routine transaction or account of love, were all newly to hand then, the originals freshly discovered, clear and hard and bright, treasured and subversive.

I was twenty-eight when I first met Ben, and thirty-seven when I acknowledged to myself that I was in love with him. And such love – unhandled and unhackneyed, private and true and precarious, standing in the danger of authority – seemed, like any 'amorous worldlie love' of the Middle Ages, 'fressher than the May with floures newe'. A sole, small gain to set against the great losses of any love that is not orthodox.

But that night as I went to bed, it seemed all gain. I woke early, with a serene sense of achievement, and lay for more than an hour before getting up, contemplating my happiness, and its object, while the light broadened.

Time seemed to expand before my accepted love: since I knew, now, where I was going, since I need not wait on chance, or let divergent aims delay me, I no longer had any anxiety about when I should arrive. I almost felt that Ben, as the acknowledged centre of my love, was bound to bring me to him, in the end, as I wanted to be brought.

The recognition of him, now, as the focus of my vision, drew all my passions and affections into a lucid order: my delight in his company; my longing for his body; my desire to protect him and to leave him free; the sharpness of anxiety for his wellbeing and well-doing, even the occasional counter-sharpness against a threat to either – each fell into a place, accepted and essential, in the centripetal pattern of my mind.

The particular truth of the situation answered and dispersed the general anxieties I had been parrying for so long. Were my feelings to be considered normal or abnormal? Permissible or impermissible? Fundamental to my nature, or a single aberration? It did not matter – I was in love with Ben.

CHAPTER 27

There were no problems that could not be solved next day. The text was ready for Douglas by the end of the afternoon. I put all the pages together and squared them, dropping them edge-down, through my hands, against the desk. I looked round, stretching, and saw Ben standing in the doorway with the sun in his hair. I did not say anything.

'I'm not disturbing you?'

'No. Not in the least.'

I had been concerned, the night before, that my joy when we next met would show openly and dangerously in my face. Coming so suddenly, forestalling my expectation though he answered my hope, he had prevented the greater risk that anxious anticipation would culminate visibly in embarrassment. My happiness in seeing him seemed simple and clear, without confusion or the need for concealment.

'It's a long time since you've walked as far as this. Come in and sit down.'

He came into the room, and I got up from the desk and turned an easy chair towards him. He sat down immediately, his shoulder grazing past my hand.

'I wanted to see you,' he said. 'It's more than a week.'

'I know. I've been busy.'

'*Sure* I'm not disturbing you now?'

'Entirely sure. Look. I've been working on this section for two years, and I finished it this afternoon.'

'Honestly?'

'Honestly. References and all.'

'That's fantastic.'

I had picked up the pile of stacked papers to show him. He took it from me, onto his knee, and looked through it, keeping the order of the pages, respectfully.

'I'll put the kettle on. No, stay there. I shan't be more than a moment.'

I was several minutes more, and Ben eventually came into the kitchen.

'Sorry to be so long. The Aga was low.'

'Don't hurry. Alan, what's the matter with Sam?'

'Is something the matter?'

'He keeps wandering about, smelling the edges of doors.'

'I know. He is restless. I think he's looking for Douglas.'

'His master?'

'Yes. He'll be coming to fetch him at the weekend.'

'How can he tell?'

'God knows. I haven't started getting anything ready yet. But I think he does know.'

'Will you miss him?'

'Yes. Much more than I should have expected; or than is reasonable.'

Ben leaned against the Aga, holding Sam's throat against his knee, and rubbing the fur on the top of his head.

'I wouldn't have thought reason came into it, really. Some kinds of company you'd always miss; specially a kind which can count as solitude as well.'

The prospect of Sam's absence, being so well understood and defined, was immediately less bleak; it began, too, to be the source of another happiness.

The kettle boiled. Ben brought the pot to be warmed, turned it and tilted it between his hands, and emptied it at the sink. Bringing it back, he asked, 'Have you seen *The Merchant* at Harchester?'

'*The Merchant?*'

'The Rep. are doing it; we thought we might go next week. Would you like to come with us? They've been good recently.'

I felt warmed by his asking, and especially by what I took to be his reason for asking now.

'I'd like to very much.'

'Good.'

We agreed on a day for the theatre, as we took the tea into the sitting room; there was nothing to eat with it but bread and cream-cheese, but it did not matter. We drank a good many cups, discussing Shylock, then Sam and I walked most of the way home with Ben, turning back only within sight of their house.

I did not want to go in; his supper would be on the table. We left him at the field-gate and stopped when we had gone a short way apart, then watched him going along the road and turning between the hedges in the luminous June air.

CHAPTER 28

I suppose that I should try to describe what Ben looks like. I want this account to be complete, but I don't know how far I am able to be objective and accurate even about the separate, visible facts, let alone in conveying their sum and wholeness.

He is quite tall now – about my height; his hair is a brownish fair, and does not stay in place above his forehead. The angle of his cheek-bone is square; his eyes are an uncertain colour, between blue and grey, and are very wide open when he is startled or concerned. His ears are set far back on his head, like a hare's, and when I first knew him his hair was too short to push behind them when he wanted it out of the way, though he often tried.

His hands are large and long, and lie absolutely loose in his lap when he is listening, but hold his knees, or the arm of his chair, and occasionally lift outwards, when he talks. He moves with a certain tentative untidiness which becomes more pronounced when he is unsure; his voice, after it had broken, kept some of its roughness; and the pace of his speech changes with deliberation or eagerness. He smiles either quite privately and involuntarily, or openly – sharing the cause – with no reserve at all; never just from courtesy, though he will give his whole consideration and gentleness when courtesy is needed. His clothes are unremarkable, except when his good suit makes him look tidy and vulnerable. He used sometimes to wear jerseys and trousers passed on by James, which were too short. His skin is fair.

None of this is, strictly speaking, essential to him or, therefore, to my love. Just as I can love him if he has forgotten to shave, or if a cold has made his eyes and nose red, so I should if his hair were darker, or his frame narrower or broader, or even if the movements of his shoulders in walking, or of his eyes in speech, were to change. And yet the fact of seeing him was always important. His appearance, breaking each time through the mould that memory and expectation had prepared, was a touchstone for all my sense of him.

Walking home alone that evening, my awareness of his physical presence beside me not yet entirely shifted from fact to memory, I could consider my own feelings, and what I knew of his, and what should or should not be done, with an unhurried, stable consideration, proved continually against my continuing sense of his reality:

> Whilst thus to ballast love, I thought,
> And so more steddily to have gone.

There was no need to hurry. There was also some need not to. I did not know whether Ben was so constituted that he could return my love. Beyond his undisguised and affectionate friendliness, I had no evidence either way. But in any case, to demand it of him too quickly would be both unwise and unprincipled: unwise to startle any love, and *a fortiori* a love which might seem alien, before it could settle and grow familiar; unprincipled, because he was still very young. He was my pupil – officially once, and still in his respect for my knowledge and advice, the importance which he attached to my approval and disapproval. Offered my love now, and asked for his in return, he might feel either honoured or appalled; he could not give a true reply. He could not reject or accept, withhold or give – could not indeed (if it came to that) decide whether or not to break the law – with the liberty of true love:

> Whan maistrie comth, the God of Love anon
> Beteth his winges, and farewel, he is gon!

I must wait. My dominance must diminish, and his assurance increase, until he could consider love from something like equality.

It did not seem, that evening, a very difficult thing to do. I had all the time in the world. To love him, consciously and unreservedly, was happiness enough at the moment.

Last night, waiting to sleep, I had thought over the eight or nine years of our acquaintance. One or two more was not so long to wait for its fruition.

I was comforted, a day or two later, to find that I had Plato's approval: that, in his view, a good man will not take advantage of a boy who is too young to judge for himself.

But my decision was only partly Platonic virtue, or even tactical wisdom, I think. Some of it was an instinctive and unacknowledged caution, a determination to shelter my happiness for some time more, to hold it hidden between my hands like a match-flame, and draw it up, stronger, before risking it in any wind.

CHAPTER 29

Douglas affected to be unsurprised at the amount of work I had done.

'I knew it,' he said, while he manoeuvred his case from the car round Sam's uproarious helpfulness.

'What do you mean, you knew it?'

'No, Alan, it's great. It was just when I saw you standing with Sam at the gate – the way you stood. He's finished the Old Testament plays, I thought. Either that, or he's fallen in love.'

I laughed, with warmth at his quick apprehension, and with the confidence of my own unassailable secrecy. I was very glad to see him again, and we talked late that evening, and the next, about Salzburg and Mozart and Austrian universities, as well as about the Cycle. Sam redistributed his loyalties, lying close to Douglas's chair, but rising when I rose and staying with me, pushing his head up against my hand, until I sat down again.

They left together, quite early on Monday morning, and when I had seen them go, Sam standing broadside to their direction, waving his tail against the roof of the car, I allowed myself the day off, to catch up on letters, before I should start on the main body of the New Testament plays. Then I re-read *The Merchant* in the evening.

I walked over the fields without Sam to the Graysons next day. But there was plenty of hilarity at the family high tea, and then there was hardly room for us all in the car. Mark was crouched behind the back seat, and I sat with my arms along its back to make room for Ben's and Bridget's shoulders on either side. Expectancy about the play, Ben's closeness, and the burnished, cool air over the fields suspended me in unfathomed content.

As Ben had predicted, the production was unusually good for provincial repertory. They played it straight, not sparing the danger or the cruelty on either side. When Salario and Salarino began to taunt Shylock with Jessica's defection, moving in steadily from either side, keeping between him and the exits, I heard Bridget, next to me, say under her breath, 'Oh, *no!*'

Earlier, in the second act, I had looked along the row and seen Ben leaning forward in anxious concentration, and tried to read the shadowed line of his face as Salarino described Antonio's first farewell to Bassanio.

Over coffee afterwards in the little theatre buffet, James wanted to know whether it always seemed so close to tragedy.

'I think it's all there in the play,' I said. 'It's not always emphasised so much, of course; a lot of producers would make it more light-hearted.'

'You think they overdid it, then? The gloomy side, this time?'

'Well... I don't think they cheated, no. They gave a good deal of weight to the tragic side, but I'd say they kept the balance. Some of the pure comedy was really very funny.'

'Very funny,' said Bridget. 'Especially Gobbo.'

'You were crying,' said Mark, withdrawing half his attention from the actors at the next table.

'Not over Gobbo.'

'Over Shylock.'

'Only in one bit.'

I asked, 'Which bit was that?'

'"Hath not a Jew eyes? Hath not a Jew hands? ...fed with the same food..." What is it?'

'"...hurt with the same weapons, subject to the same diseases, healed by the same means, warmed and cooled by the same winter and summer as a Christian is?"'

'Yes. That's magnificent.'

She and I smiled in a short, entire encounter of feeling.

'I don't think that's the most moving bit of all, though,' said Ben.

'What is, then?' she asked.

'In the trial, when Antonio's saying goodbye to Bassanio.'

'I hate Antonio.'

'I know. I know... but... It is very sad...' He broke off and began to drink his coffee.

CHAPTER 30

Ruth and James took their family to the Lake District for three
weeks in August. They told me on the night of *The Merchant*
that they were looking for a farmhouse to stay in, and I started
to plan the work I would do while they were away. I felt it as a
kind of test: something which I should – and fairly certainly
could – achieve, in order to know that I should be able to cope
thereafter: to live separated from Ben, after I had acknowledged
his importance to me; to work, and not to repine, until he came
back. Ten days later, they asked if I should like to join them.

The farmhouse was at the head of a valley, at the far end of
Wast Water, where the road stopped. Small fields, very green, went
sharply up behind the outhouses, the grass littered with the grey
stones still left after all the walls were built. A track went, fading,
through three or four fields, among sheep and younger lambs, to
the open hillside.

We walked most days that it was fine, carrying our lunch, and
returning only in time for vast plates of supper in the kitchen.
There were other walkers on the well-known tracks, but otherwise
the hills were empty. The hard slope towards the heights in the
morning, and the sheep-scattered emptiness of green and grey, all
round us for so large a part of the day, brought us together in an
unenclosed privacy. Physical help and need, practical difficulties
with maps and shoelaces and tin-openers, opened a way for me
into direct, companionable communication within the family.

The lie of the ground, our varying strength and wind, often
broke us into groups of two or three, but my wary eye and
cautious exploitation of chances to climb alone with Ben were
relaxed before the end of the first day: his company was as
frequent, and as natural, as that of any of the family – a little
more, perhaps, as we were two of the faster walkers. To find him
with me, pulling ahead of the others, or waiting for them at the

shoulder of a hill, was to feel the day expand with happiness, the curves of the landscape surround us in celebration; but this was not destroyed when the others came up with us – only contracted to something less comprehensive and more various, in an alternation of major and minor joy which I could accept with contentment, though I could not predict it.

One morning in the second week, Ben had a letter at breakfast; he opened it before he sat down, and then put it, under the envelope, beside his plate, and began to discuss the day's walk with James.

'Is that from Italy?' Mark asked later, taking Ben's empty porridge plate.

'Yes.'

'How does anyone in Italy know you're here?'

'How do you think? I gave them the address.'

'Who's it from?'

'It's from a school in Verona,' said Ben, 'offering me a job.'

'Why do they want you to do a job now, in the holidays?'

'They don't. They want me at the end of September.'

Ruth looked towards James, unhurriedly, and said to Ben, 'I think the sausages are in the oven.'

Ben got up to fetch them, and helped us all, bringing mine last as he sat down.

That morning, Mark and Ben walked together, developing some interminable joke about the sheep, while the rest of us combined and recombined in various pairs. I walked with Bridget, high up on a grassy ridge towards the top. She was reading *Wuthering Heights*, I remember, and talked about it with quick intelligence and no pretension, and we discussed the North Country and its differences from the South. She had a good ear: recalling a conversation she had heard at the farm, she fell naturally and accurately into a Cumberland voice. The movements of her head and eyes, looking towards me and back again at the path, were like Ben's.

We stopped where the last stony shoulder rose suddenly up to the bare top. There was a distribution of chocolate, and when we began to climb, I was beside Ben, and soon we were both beyond the others. The steepness increased, and there was neither breath nor opportunity to discuss anything except the way. We seemed to climb very fast, and yet to take a long time to reach the summit. At last, we almost ran up a few yards of pebbly, lesser steepness, the sky came up round us on all sides, and we let out breath in sharp gusts and dropped onto the slab of rock at the top.

For some time we sat still, getting our breath and looking out at the great distance. Then we began to move, taking off our knapsacks and stretching, and putting the hair out of our eyes. I loosened my boots, and Ben turned his shoulders to look north-west.

'I think that's Scotland. Have you got the glasses?'

I took off the binoculars and gave them to him with one hand, putting the strap over his head with the other.

'It is, you know. And that must be the Isle of Man.'

For some minutes he looked all round, and then let the glasses fall onto his chest, his back still half-turned to me.

'Glorious. I could stay here for ever.'

'And your job in Verona?'

He moved a little, saying nothing, and then said, 'Alan –'

Mark's voice came up, against the rocks, from some way below.

'Alan! Ben! Ben! Hoy!'

Ben got up immediately, and went to the edge of the steepest part.

'Hoy! Marky! We're here. What's the matter?'

I did up my boots, and joined him, and saw Mark, a short way up the rocky shoulder below us, standing on a boulder and tilting his head back to see Ben and shout to him.

'What is it?' I asked Ben.

'Bridgie's feeling bad. She can't go on.'

'Oh, poor girl. She hurt herself?'

'No. Just stomach-ache. Mum's taking her down to the valley where the road goes, there. And Dad'll go back the way we came, and bring the car round.'

He called down again, 'You coming with us, Marky?'

'No, I'm going with Dad.'

'Come on. We could do the next peak. We might see Ireland.'

'I want to see the milking: we're always too late.'

'OK. Would Mum like some help?'

'Don't think so. They've started.'

'I'll catch them up.'

He turned to start down over the edge. I put out my hand to his arm.

'I don't think you will. And you're forgetting your rucksack.'

'Well... But they'll be slow.'

'Not as slow as that. They haven't got the climb down, to start with.'

He hesitated, looking at the ground.

'I thought you wanted to do the next peak.'

'Oh, all right,' he said without pleasure.

We shouted goodbye to Mark, and good wishes for Bridget, and went back to our knapsacks.

'It's after twelve,' I said. 'Shall we have lunch here?'

'Oh, let's get on with it, if we're going to do the next peak.'

We set off. 'It's not appendicitis or anything?' I asked after a time.

'I don't think so. Just something she gets – you know – now and then.'

I could find no further answer, and our awkwardness was increased.

There was a steep gully to cross, dividing the two peaks; scrambling down to a jumping point, finding footholds, and handing knapsacks across the gap, we spoke necessarily of tactics, then paused at the further edge, finding that the sun had gone in, and got out sweaters. We settled one another's rucksacks again, and smiled, but the long, steep walk towards the top provided nothing more to say. I was beginning to feel hungry, and wondered how soon we should get there. I did not feel inclined to suggest eating before Ben did. We followed a sheep track round two sides of the hill and walked into mist.

'It's not thick,' said Ben. 'The sun's still out on the far side.'

We went on, following the track, at first easily, and then by the cairns beside it. When we could no longer see from one cairn to the next, I said that we had better go back.

'I really think we'll be out of this in a minute,' said Ben.

'But meanwhile, there's not much to stop us going over a precipice.'

'Except that there aren't any precipices.'

'How sure are you about that?'

'Almost certain.'

'Let's look at the map.'

He looked in the outer pocket of my knapsack, and I did the same for him. Then we unloaded, and each looked right through his own. Neither of us had the map: it was still with James.

'I think we can manage without. It's not very far.'

'Still far enough to be a risk.'

'If we went *very* carefully – '

'No, Ben, I'm sorry. Absolutely not.'

Our sweaters already had drops of water lying on the outermost hairs of the wool. We brushed them with our hands, and put waterproofs on over them.

'The way back should be all right,' I said. 'We know how the track goes, and there's nothing till we get to the gully.'

'And if we get back into the sun before that,' said Ben, 'we can get up to the top from that side.'

We turned and started back. I let Ben take the lead. The mist seemed evenly thick at a little distance round us, but near at hand it was patchy. Sometimes we could see our sheep track for some yards; sometimes we had to cast about for the next step. When the track began to run straight down the slope, almost too steeply for steady walking, I knew that the mist had spread back, well beyond the turn where we had first walked into it.

'We'll have to give up the top, this time,' I called to Ben. 'We're nearly back at the gully.'

He turned. 'It's getting thinner. I'm sure it's – '

His voice stopped, and the mist came in more thickly where he had been. I ran until I could see where the path broke off, then crouched my way to the edge of the gully, and looked over. Ben was sitting a couple of yards down, just visible between two rocks.

'I'm all right. Sorry.'

'I should think you bloody well are sorry. A thick mist, and no map, and that's not enough. You can't even look where you're going.'

I clambered down to him, and helped to disentangle his knapsack from the rocks. A patch of it was very wet, where the cap had come off his water bottle.

'My God, you did give me a fright.'

'I know. I really am sorry. It was bloody stupid.'

'Well, anyway – it's thicker over there. I don't think we can get across. What are we going to do?'

'We could always have lunch.'

We found a shelf of ground above the track – flat though very narrow, with a firm rock below it – and got out our sandwiches. Ben winced when he put weight on his right foot.

'I thought you said you were all right.'

'Well... I'm not *dead*.'

We laughed.

'You won't be much lighter to carry, alive, if you can't walk on that foot.'

'It'll be all right. I think I've just sprained the side of it a bit.'

'Put it up.' I pushed my knapsack under it, and we unwrapped our sandwiches and began to eat them, damp in the moist air. Ben did not look as if he was in pain.

'Ben – .'

'I know. Verona.'

I waited.

'Alan, I've been trying to talk to you about it.'

'You seemed to me to be trying to do almost anything else.'

'I know. I know. When it actually came to it, today, I just couldn't. I couldn't *bear*...'

'Can you now?'

'It's more that I've no alternative.'

He put his sandwiches down between us.

'Alan, I don't want to go to Cambridge. And I know it seems crazy, and I know you'll disapprove, and I'm very sorry about it. But I don't want to go, and I'm going to go and teach English in Italy. In Verona.'

He waited for my reply, and I tried to think how I should begin.

'How long have you felt like this?'

'I've never felt really certain about going – not after the first moment, when I was pleased. And then when I was ill, I thought perhaps it was just the illness. But it went on when I was better, more and more; and in the end I knew it was no good – I just couldn't go.'

'How long have you been meaning to tell me about it?' I asked, unjustifiably.

'I've wanted to – well, partly wanted to – ever since I wrote to the school. That was the week before we came up here. And every day I've meant to tell you. But every time – it's all such fun – I just couldn't – '

He broke off. I said nothing, and after a moment, he went on in a lower voice, not looking at me, 'I knew you'd be furious. And you'd ask me about it, and try to get me to change my mind. And I feel ungrateful, too: you did such a lot – helped me – '

'What is it you're worried about? Why don't you want to go up?'

'That's just it. I don't know. Or anyway, I can't explain.'

'You can try. I might understand some of it.'

'But I don't *want* to try. Don't you see? There's nothing I can say which will make you think it's reasonable. It's no good talking about it. It'll just make us both miserable. Please, Alan, can we just leave it?'

I sat silent for some time, trying to examine my various feelings: disappointment so strong as to be suspect; desire to help – and persuade – baffled to the point of anger; and irritation at the idea that I might fulfil Ben's expectation and lose my temper.

He began to eat another sandwich.

I said, 'I don't think I can leave it, Ben, I'm sorry. I've no right to ask your reasons, let alone force your decisions. But I don't think I can just let you decide something as important as this – and from my point of view as unwisely as this – without saying anything: just let it go by default. It would be irresponsible. And I think it would be irresponsible of you not to listen.'

'All right. I'll listen.'

'Obviously, I could be quicker and more to the point if I knew your objections.'

He did not answer.

'All right. I'll be as short and factual as I can.'

I made every point I could think of: the intrinsic interest of his subject; the unrepeatable chance to spend as much time on it as he liked for three years; the waste of training, and using, a good mind inadequately; the internal and external advantages of a good job when he went down; the growing tedium of an unqualified teaching job abroad, and the difficulty of moving on to anything better.

He disputed none of it, saying only, 'I know. Yes, I know,' dispiritedly, from time to time.

I talked of the other pleasures of Cambridge: the courts and the river, the Fitzwilliam, choirs and concerts and plays, architecture and argument and company.

'Company? Oh, for God's sake, Alan, it's all so *pointless*.'

'What's pointless?'

'Going to Cambridge. Reading history. Trying to persuade me. And I'm thirsty.'

'Well, I didn't bring any water, so you'll have to stay thirsty. And meanwhile, why do you think going to university will be any more pointless than teaching English to Italian schoolboys?'

'I didn't say university. I said Cambridge.'

'And which did you mean?'

'All right, suppose I meant university. They'll be learning something they can use, and I'll be helping them.'

'And there's nothing you could usefully learn at university?'

'Stop it, Alan; that's not fair. I'm not being conceited. What if I just don't want to spend three years on those particular things?'

'You could always change your subject – after the first tripos anyway; possibly even before. You could read French, or English.'

'I don't *want* to read French or English. No, all right, I do. But I can read them on my own.'

'It's not the same.'

'What's the difference?'

'Time. And seriousness. Scholarship. Learning to use your critical faculty properly.'

'Criticism. Miles and miles of print, all trying to prove what's unprovable anyway.'

'Do you think you should actually read some before you decide it's a complete waste of time?'

'Look, I've said. I'm not being arrogant. I'm just... Oh. God. I'm sorry. I didn't... I only meant for me.'

'And you think that makes it less arrogant?'

'Alan, I *told* you. I said it was no good talking about it. I knew I'd start saying things I didn't mean. And now I've... Oh God!'

'I think we'd better start back.'

I put the sandwich papers in my pocket and did up my knapsack.

'Alan, *please* – '

'I'm going to cross there if I can. You hand over to me.'

I went down, checking my footing with the deliberate care of ostentatiously controlled anger. Without looking round, I jumped into the mist, now thinning a little, on the far side. Ben came down more slowly, managing the two knapsacks with difficulty. He swung them across to me and got ready to jump. He changed his footing two or three times, and then said, 'I don't think I can make it. I'm sorry. It's my foot.'

'Is that true?'

'Yes, it bloody well is true. D'you think I want to sit here for another hour's inquisition?' He sat down. 'And anyway, I'm thirsty.'

'I know you're thirsty. And you know there's nothing we can do about it. So for Christ's sake shut up about it, and stop being so childish.'

I wedged the knapsacks between two rocks and the ground, and sat against them, looking along the gully. The mist grew no thinner. I looked at my watch. It was twenty-five past three. Looking sideways, I could see Ben on the other side, digging trenches in the ground with a stone. There was more I might say to discharge my anger. I gripped the fingers of one hand with the other and tried to think what it was that he was feeling, what there could be in his decision besides perverse misjudgement and short-sightedness. Neither of these was characteristic of Ben.

What could he have heard or seen about life at Cambridge which had alarmed or distressed him? And why was he so reluctant to talk about it, even to tell me what it was? Could it be embarrassment that was holding him back? Fear? Shame? My disapproval would not mitigate his fear. After half an hour he had still said nothing.

'Look, are your parents going to be worried?'

'I don't think so. Not if we're together.'

He moved suddenly, with an anxious, quick look towards me, and then began to laugh. In a moment I laughed, too, as the irony seemed more and more ridiculous. I pulled out the knapsacks, called to him to catch them, and jumped back to his side. We sat down, to laugh more easily, leaning against each other on the precarious slope.

'But seriously,' I said finally, 'if you think they'll worry, I could leave you here and go back and get James to help. Only I'd rather not leave you on your own.'

'I think it's all right, really. We never get back much before supper anyway.'

'All right. Let's stay. As soon as it clears we can look for an easier way across. And I promise not to mention the university before you do.'

Clambering back, up and along the slope, we found a slab of level rock wide enough to sprawl on. Ben took off his boot at my suggestion (a suggestion I should have made earlier): the side of his foot was swollen and reddish-black, tender to the touch. I was doubtful whether he could get home, but there was no point in saying this until the mist cleared.

We talked about the way, and then he taught me a paper-game. Looking for a second pencil, I found some mint-cake at the bottom of a pocket, and offered him a piece, but he shook his head. I thought his foot was beginning to hurt again. When we were tired of guessing each other's words, we lay back with our heads on our knapsacks and looked into the mist. I turned my head to say something to Ben, and found that he was asleep.

I turned on my elbow and watched him sleeping. When he stirred, I moved my head back, out of the line of his vision. He breathed rather quickly, and his tongue ran, now and then, along one or other of his lips. The edge of his hair was wet against his skin, with the mist. I began to look down into the gully. The summer had not been unusually dry; a cleft as deep as this must have water at the bottom. I edged the strap through the buckle, and took his water bottle and its lid out of the top of his knapsack, without waking him. Then I wrote 'Back soon' on a piece of paper, weighted it with a stone, and started down the gully.

I went slowly, as it was important that one of us should not be lame, and it took me rather longer than I had expected. The mist was thicker further down; there were one or two tricky places; it was all steep; and several rocks were loose. Once, I nearly fell. But then I began to hear water running, and found a way down over the steep, final drop, and into the thick strand of white mist at the bottom. There I could kneel on a flat stone in the brown, secret, weaving water. I drank as much as I needed, refilled the bottle, screwed the cap on tightly and stood up. Then I knelt again, and soaked my handkerchief, and wrapped it in the sandwich-paper.

The mist seemed thinner as I climbed back, and when I sent a stone down from under my foot, I heard Ben call, 'Alan! Alan, I'm here: this way. And the sun's coming out.'

He gave me a hand, to pull me up onto the slab. A blade of sunlight was thinning the mist at the grass edge above us, and the air was warmer. I handed him the water and undid my coat.

'Have some yourself.'

'I've had plenty. There's a stream at the bottom.'

He began to drink, shutting his eyes. Some of the water ran down over his chin.

'Take your time.'

He drank more slowly, until he had half-emptied the bottle, then gave it back, thanking me. I rinsed my mouth and put the bottle away. Then Ben sat down, and I bound his foot with my wet handkerchief.

'Do you think you can walk on it?'

124

'Well – . Enough, I should think. It's much better like this – lovely and cold.'

We ate some mint-cake; and moved along the edge of the gully, as the sun shredded the mist, to a narrower crossing-place I had seen from below. Ben managed it, taking most of the weight with his hands, and scrambling up the far side on all fours.

At the next rise we found the sky almost clear, though the sun was going down. We could skirt the base of the shoulder we had climbed that morning, and take the shortest way to the road, as Ruth and Bridget had done. We should be able to get a lift, or find a telephone, before dark. The going was not difficult, but it would have been nearly an hour's walk at our ordinary speed.

After a few yards across the grass, Ben was limping heavily, and we had no stick. Eventually, I took his arm across my shoulders, and then we went on together at a fair pace, stopping when the handkerchief worked loose, damping it again and tying it up. The foot began to hurt quite a lot, and Ben's breath came roughly, leaving him little to spare for talking.

Venus was out before we reached the valley, and I quoted *Lycidas*:

Oft till the star that rose at evening bright
Toward heaven's descent had sloped his westering wheel.

I went on for a few lines, and then started again from the beginning, to see how much I could remember: it set a rhythm for our walking, and encouraged Ben in a way that needed no reply.

It seemed to me that his pain and fatigue did not really taint the evening's happiness. The lake of dark air as we went down into the levelling fields; the retrospect of dismay surmounted; the prospect of rest; the close agreement of our pace and the affection of our truce: none of these were damaged for him, I felt, nor, therefore, for me.

CHAPTER 31

We had said that we would sleep late next morning. James had had a long drive to find us after we had telephoned from a farmhouse, and by the time we had got home, and eaten, and seen to Ben's foot, it was well after midnight. Rain was forecast for the whole day, and we agreed that it should be a *dies non*.

I slept heavily and woke very warm, hearing Mark talking in the passage, and smelling bacon frying. Then I must have slept again. I had no notion what time had passed when I heard the latch of my door fall.

'Hello?'

'Alan, may I come in?'

'Ben? Yes. Come in.'

I started to sit up. 'Lord!'

'What's the matter?'

'I'm stiff.' I turned on my side and pushed up onto an elbow. 'Aren't you?'

He considered. 'Perhaps a bit.'

'How's your foot?'

'All right.'

'It didn't keep you awake?'

'Not much. A bit.'

He went round the small room. My clothes were lying on the only chair. He put my handkerchief, folded square, on the corner of the washstand, and sat down on the low windowsill, blocking some of the rainy light.

'Look, Alan...'

'Yes?'

'I'm sorry about what I said yesterday. About criticism. I *really* didn't mean it. I have read some criticism – not enough, but some – and I don't think it's at all a waste of time. Some of it was great. I was just cross with you, and said what I didn't mean. Didn't mean anyway, let alone meaning to hurt your feelings.'

'I know. I knew it quite soon, really. I just felt entitled to take umbrage. And with less excuse than you.'

I looked towards him, but he kept his head down and put one hand on the window-catch beside him.

'And the other thing is – I think you're right. I should go to Cambridge. So I'm going to write to Verona today and turn the job down. Only – only I am scared.'

'Would it be any good telling me what you're scared of?'

'I'm not sure, really. And anyway... But thank you.'

The wet, grey light ran along the back of his bent neck. Bound by my stiffness, I could only try to will encouragement and affection towards him, where he sat. He looked up and seemed to receive some of it, but his face was long and irregular with tiredness.

'I'm sure you're right, anyway. And I'm very glad. Come and talk more about it any time you want to. But what you want most at the moment, I think, is more sleep.'

He slept till nearly midday. I had breakfast with Bridget and James, and then worked peacefully, looking out on the farmyard.

When Ben had made the decision I wanted him to make, and slept after it, he seemed contented and refreshed. But if he had shifted the responsibility to me, I did not feel it unduly. For the rest of the holiday we were both blessedly free of the necessity either to decide, or to defend the decision. We sat with the others by the sitting-room fire, reading, or writing letters, or doing a little peripheral work. We played Racing Demon, six-handed and very noisily, in the evening. When the rain stopped, late in the afternoon next day, Mark and Bridget and I walked to the village at the far end of the lake, and bought chocolate and postcards, and stopped at the pub for a drink. Mark drank lemonade, but Bridget was halfway through her cider before I realised that she should not be drinking it there at all, as she was not yet eighteen. I did nothing about it – there was not much I could do – but she and Mark both laughed, on the way back, at my consternation on finding myself in breach of the law.

Ben's foot recovered steadily, but not fast enough for him to walk all day as soon as the weather cleared. The family were reluctant to leave him solitary at the farm, but he did not want to curtail their expedition. We discussed it over breakfast, and in the end I persuaded them that I had wanted for some time to see Dove Cottage and the Wordsworth Museum.

We dropped the others at the top of the pass, and drove on to Grasmere. The sun was warm, and all the leaves were wet. Ben took an accommodating interest, I thought, in the various memorabilia. Then he told me, as we walked up to the church, that he had read the whole of *The Prelude*. He had found it heavy going in some places, but often glorious, and understood now why it mattered so much. I told him about Dorothy's journal, and he bought a copy at the museum shop, and borrowed my pen to write the date and place on the flyleaf.

His foot was sound again by the beginning of our last week, and we could all walk together again, all day, in the strong sun and wind, coming home, hungry and late and complacent, as it got dark, singing absurd choruses to help us along the last stretches of the road.

They took me to Carlisle on the last day, and dropped me there at the station before turning south. I said goodbye to them all, and to Ben, for twelve days, and caught a train north to visit Douglas.

CHAPTER 32

Edinburgh was handsome and invigorating, and Douglas very welcoming. We did some useful work together, dined with several of his colleagues, and went to the opera. And I found that I could keep my sense of separation from Ben fairly well within bounds. Congenial company and talk prevented my continual thoughts of him from accumulating unmanageably, except sometimes at the beginning of the night. One part of my mind did seem to be persistently occupied with fruitless little calculations of the fractions of time until our next meeting. But it was a small part, and, unless I was alone, an unobtrusive one, and I judged it to be harmless.

In the train going south, I took stock of the weeks that remained before Ben went up to Cambridge, and of how much time I could spend with him then and afterwards. The most sensible thing would be to take only the opportunities that arose naturally. I did not feel our friendship to be so equal and unquestionable that I could simply make, or suggest, a regular plan for meeting. But I could not bear to wait wholly on chance either, or even on chance modified by Ben's friendliness. That modification should at least be mutual. I could not be as careless as a young man of his own age – or even a young woman – might be in asking for his company, but I must not let him think that his affection was not returned.

He had four more weeks at home, when I should be able to find several occasions for visiting him or for asking him to visit me. And then, at Cambridge, the term was eight weeks long. Could I allow myself one visit a term? There were books to consult in the Library, and to buy, or consider buying, in the bookshops, and friends whose advice I might value on problems in the Cycle. One of them would probably put me up for the night. The vacations were long. He would travel, of course; he should.

And he would have to read, and probably to earn some money. But these parts of his plans could not yet be decided, and until then calculation was profitless.

On my return, I found that Ben had taken a job in Bramston for four weeks. I saw him when I went in to shop, each Thursday, and on two other days, when I allowed myself to think that I should concentrate better next morning if I could spend the afternoon in the town. Otherwise, I worked very hard, on the Old Testament appendices that Douglas and I had planned in Edinburgh, and then on the next New Testament play. In the afternoons, I dug peat and hop manure into the garden for the autumn.

I spent a Sunday with the Graysons, and Ben showed me the books he had bought on the recommendation of his director of studies, and the suitcases his parents had given him, and the clothes he had bought to take to college, with some of the money he had earned. I could not see that these were very different from what he had always worn, but he was so casually proud of them, so anxious that I, too, should approve of them, that I extended my enthusiasm slightly beyond candour.

One early-closing day, he walked back from the town over the fields and came to see me. He had brought me some bulbs in his pocket, and he found flowerpots and planted them for me, and put them in a dark place under the stairs.

'I think they should come up at different times. As long as you remember to water them. You can take them out when there's a good green spike.'

When I asked him what flowers each pot would produce, he laughed and would not tell me.

I did not know how to say goodbye to him. I was hampered again by having no guide except my all-too-biased instinct. His family had already given me more hospitality than I had any right to expect, and I found I had not the spirit to organise a family party at the cottage.

In the end, I went over to see him the evening before he left, with the book I had bought for him several months before in Harchester. His room was dark, and so was the kitchen window.

I went round to the front door, and Bridget let me in. When she told me that everyone else was out, my disappointment almost unnerved me. They would not be back until late; I felt hollow and scattered, and then, for the first time, afraid that my feelings had not been properly concealed. We had a glass of sherry, and I talked as irrelevantly as I could, then wrote a note to leave with the book.

Dear Ben,

I'm sorry not to find you in. I thought you might like to have this – an early, though not I think a first, edition – among your books at Cambridge. It seems to me to belong both to your subject and to mine, and it brings all my good wishes.

Alan   *4.x.1962*

He replied from Cambridge. The letter came early the next week.

Mon. 9th Oct.

Dear Alan,

I wanted to come over and say goodbye, or at least telephone, but the last few days at home seemed to have no gaps in them at all, until we got back from our cousins on Tuesday night, and then I was afraid you'd be asleep. But perhaps it's better to write, after all, as now I've got time to thank you properly for the book of Characters as well.

I am <u>really</u> pleased to have it, and I'm very touched that you should have taken so much trouble to find me something so appropriate. As you say, it combines literature and history – and some [appropriate – deleted] pertinent comments on university life as well. I hope I shall not become like the 'Young Gentleman of the Vniuersitie' whose 'Study ha's commonly handsome Shelves, his Bookes neate silke strings, which he... is loth to unty or take downe for feare of misplacing.'! This book, anyway, being as interesting inside as it is handsome outside, will be on my table as often as on my shelves. Thank you very much. I shall treasure it.

Cambridge is fine so far (i.e. after three days). My room is small, and up rather a lot of stairs, but otherwise great, and if

I lean out of the window I can see one of the pinnacles on King's Chapel. You must come and see it for yourself.

My supervisors both seem good: one <u>very</u> interesting, if a bit formidable; one more easy-going (Roman History) though more straightforward (but that might just be the subject).

Everyone is very friendly, and I am beseiged [sic] by people wanting me to join clubs, teams, churches, political parties, etc. But I haven't much. One or two people from school came up this term, too, and a fellow first-year historian lives on the floor above (he must need oxygen) and plays Brahms at strange hours. It's easy to make friends in hall, too, by deploring the food (actually it's not bad).

How is the Cycle? Are you past John the Baptist yet? The paperback looks very good in Heffers' window.

I had sherry with the Senior Tutor on Friday, and he said he knew you, and sent you his love (or regards or something).

I must stop and write an essay on the Concept of Monarchy.

Thank you again for the book – and for much else besides.

Love, Ben

p.s. Remember to water the bulbs.

I waited for rather more than a week, and then wrote back. Six days of desolate and unmanageable disappointment had paid in advance for some years of correspondence – for a point of expectation in every week, for continuing knowledge of each other's doings, and continually increasing closeness of communication; more than that, for a habit which could, I thought, be renewed without excuse whenever we were far or long apart.

CHAPTER 33

I have kept all Ben's letters (apart from that first, lost one from Norfolk). I should like to quote them all, but while they are at hand, in a drawer of my desk, there seems to be no real justification for it. I can read them as they are, with greater delight, and there is no other reader to consider. (Even if this account were really for Ben's eyes, he would hardly need to re-read his own letters to make it complete.) I will copy only what is necessary to the account, or at least what is most relevant. And I will do the same with the rough copies I have kept of some of the letters I wrote to him.

Tues. 24th Oct.

Dear Alan,

Thank you so much for your letter. Yes, do please come and see me if you are in Cambridge next week. I have lectures all Wednesday morning, but only one on Thursday, which I could cut. Otherwise, I'm absolutely free, apart from things which can be fitted in anywhere (like work); and I'd love to see you and show you my room and give you coffee, or tea, or whatever fits in with your plans.

They are beginning to pile on the work a bit, and Mr Ridley (Renaissance History) expects an alarming amount of reading, but so far I seem to be managing more or less all right –

(pause here to convince a Moral Re-Armer that I'm not a hopeful case for conversion; it took half an hour.)

– and he (Mr R.) said my last essay (on the Italian City States) was very good!

I've been asked to lunch on Sunday by someone called L. R. Forman. Is he a friend of yours? I think that's what his letter says, but it's rather hard to read. Anyway, it's very kind of him (and you?).

All my other news – and yours – when we meet. Let me know when – or just come, and I'll leave a note if I'm out.

In haste, Ben

p.s. There's a concert in the chapel after hall on Thursday. Would you like to come if you've got nothing better to do that evening? It may not be very good, but a friend of mine is singing in it, and it's a nice programme (Mozart, Brahms, Britten). B

Postcard

26.x.1962

Many thanks for your letter. Not sure what time the bus gets in, on Thurs. morning. I'll try to look into your rooms on my way to the Library, but you shd. certainly <u>not</u> cut a lecture for me. If you leave a note, we can meet later. Or you cd. get in touch with me at Christ's, c/o Dr Lawrence Forman. I'd like to hear the concert, but must first discover Lawrence's plans, if any.

Alan

The country bus got in late, as I had supposed it might, but it seemed worth curtailing my morning at the Library by another ten minutes to go round by Ben's college. The time fell awkwardly: he would not be in, unless his lecture was at twelve, but I was not sure that I could concentrate until I knew when and where I should be able to find him.

He was in. I put down my case to draw breath, and saw the crack of light below his door. I stood for a minute, feeling the warmth of his imminent company. Then I knocked, heard his voice, and went in.

He looked very well, his cheek rounded, and an extra alacrity in his movements and his eyes. He made me welcome, and fetched coffee in brightly coloured mugs, and put a packet of chocolate biscuits between us on top of a stack of notes. I had had breakfast early, and I ate a number of biscuits with my coffee. While the kettle was boiling for second cups, we leaned out of the window into the sun to see the fractional view of King's chapel. Then he showed me what he had been reading, and we talked by the fire until I judged it was time to go.

'I'll come with you.'

'Won't it be out of your way? Where's your lecture?'

'I haven't got one.'

'I thought –'

'That was at ten.'

'You shouldn't have cut it for me. If you did.'

'Only partly. It's one I cut now and then anyway, actually.'

'Oh, I see.'

I put my coat on and took up my case. Ben took a jacket and a clutch of books and note-books, and we started down the stairs.

'And then this morning, anyway, someone came down to borrow some notes.'

'Your fellow historian?'

'David, that's right. He wanted some stuff on Machiavelli. And then he was trying to persuade me to audition for the first-year play.'

'What are they doing?'

'*Richard II*. They're short of people for stray lords. I don't know if it would be fun to be one.'

'"One that will do

To swell a progress, start a scene or two...?"'

'That's Eliot?'

'Yes. *Prufrock*:

> Advise the prince; no doubt an easy tool,
> Deferential, glad to be of use,
> Politic, cautious and meticulous,
> Full of high sentence, but a bit obtuse.'

'Perhaps I don't really want to be one!'

I laughed. 'Theatricals do take up a lot of time. Can we get across the Backs this way?'

We had a late lunch together in a coffee shop near the Library, before I returned to the reading room, and Ben to college. I had finished soon after four, but I walked down the Backs in the late, smoky sunlight, past the bridge we had taken in the morning, and had a cup of tea at the Copper Kettle and a profitable browse in Bowes and Bowes.

Dinner was convivial. I sat between Lawrence and an excellently sceptical theologian, and we talked of Milton and then of Darwin; afterwards, in the Combination Room, I met their other English fellow, very young, who had liked my *Chaucer*, and had some curious ideas about allegory in *Troilus and Criseyde*, which I encouraged him to write up for one of the quarterlies.

I enjoyed it all, but could not decently go very soon. It was late when we came out into the court, but Lawrence still had some work to do, and I thought I might manage to hear the last part of the concert. I went quickly through the darkish, chilly streets, past the porter and across the court to the Chapel door. It was heavily shut, and going round to the side I saw that the lights were out. Ben had not been counting on my company: we had left the plan open; but I felt a sort of guilt as well as disappointment, and I wanted to see him.

There were voices in his room, and as he opened the door to me, I saw another young man sitting under the lamp on the far side of the fire, with his elbows on his knees and his head in his hands. Ben accepted my explanations equably, and put the kettle on, and introduced his friend.

We all exchanged a few remarks about the concert while Ben found mugs and coffee; then the young man said suddenly, 'None for me, thanks, Ben. I ought to go.'

'Have a cup first?'

'No, really. I've got some work – an essay for tomorrow. I've hardly started. Thanks, anyway.' He turned to me, stood on one foot, and said, 'Anyway, nice to meet you,' and went away.

'I didn't drive him away?'

'No, no. Careful, it's rather hot. I think he really has got to work. And he's feeling like being on his own.'

I stayed half an hour – long enough to cancel my sense of having renegued on a plan, and long enough to fill up my stocks of his company, the emergency ration of his voice and feature and movement, to take away with me next day.

CHAPTER 34

Wed. 15th Nov.

Dear Alan,

Thank you for your letter. It was great to see you, and I'm glad you approve of my room.

I seem to have got involved in Richard II after all. I do start one scene, and even advise the Prince! But my part (Salisbury) isn't really long enough for being politic, cautious and meticulous – three scenes (one just walking on) and about twenty lines! However, I am understudying a friend who is Aumerle, and it is fun to be in it. We've got an excellent Richard, and I think Bolingbroke may be good when he knows his lines. Rehearsals don't seem to take up too much time, so far, except in finding enough sweaters – the hall where we rehearse is freezing.

Work is still going quite well. Yesterday I kept Mr Ridley going for the whole hour, on Castiglione, to save Jonathan (my partner) from having to read his (non-existent) essay.

So I hope he's prepared to do the same for me some time.

4th Feb.

Dear Alan,

Thank you for your letter. We've got snow here, too. The courts look ravishing, and so does King's.

Yesterday we got so cold rehearsing that the [pro – deleted] director took us all back to his digs (he's a post-graduate) and made Sergeant-Major's tea. Have you ever had it? Dry tea, sugar, water, condensed milk, and rum, all boiled up together. It tastes quite extraordinary, but it's certainly warming. The performance is now theoretically fixed for the fifth week. Do come and see it if you'd like to, though I honestly don't know if it will be worth *seeing – or even if it will happen at all. There seem to be so many problems and disagreements at the moment.*

It looks as if I may have to be Aumerle, which I don't much want to be. Still, Shakespeare's always Shakespeare, and if you would really find it interesting, or even useful to your ideas on drama, do come. I do think it's interesting as a Tudor view of a Mediaeval view of a king's view of kingship...

12th Feb.

Ticket for Thursday night enclosed. Cross your fingers for us. See you afterwards.

Ben

CHAPTER 35

After the play, I waited fifteen minutes for Ben at the entrance, and then went out into the sleety dark, and round to the stage door. The close, shrill, moving crowd of people in the hot room did not seem to contain him, and a little way in from the door it was even harder to see if he was there. A young man with a grey beard was sitting on the floor by my feet, while another young man pulled off his boots. I asked him if he knew whether Ben Grayson was there.

'Ben? Should be. Hold on.'

He got to his feet, and shouted over several heads, 'Charles, know where Ben is?'

'Don't you?'

'Joanna will know,' said his friend from the floor. 'I can't get them off if you stand up.'

'Joanna's gone on,' someone said from behind me.

'Already? Ben probably has too, then.'

'He's gone?' I asked.

'To Julian's. The cast party.' He sat down again. 'If you like to hang on a minute, we'll all be going.'

But I asked the address and went out alone, buttoning the neck of my coat. Recent expectation and present uneasiness of various kinds propelled me without decision or resistance towards the party. A party which Ben had not mentioned, and to which I had not been invited. The house was some distance down the Trumpington Road, and I was cold when I reached it. But he was not at the party either.

Half a dozen undergraduates offered me mulled wine, tried to take my coat, suggested and discussed where Ben might be found. If he wasn't in the dressing-room, then he must be on his way. Lots more people would be coming in a minute; they were still changing, or they were on the way. Joanna must be on the way, and Nick.

'I don't think so,' said the host, coming in with another tray of glasses. 'Most of that lot left before I did. They can't be coming.'

'Nick always has trouble with his boots.'

'All right – Nick. But the others.'

'But why not? Everyone was coming.'

'I don't know why not.'

'And Ben was great. After less than a week.'

'Yes, he was. Ben was great. But I think he's gone off somewhere. Him and one or two of the others.'

I drank half a glass of the wine, said that I had enjoyed the play, and walked back down the Trumpington Road in increasing vexation. I stopped under a lamp-post to re-read Ben's note. He had expected me on Thursday, and he had said that he would see me after the play. And now he had gone with his friends to spend the evening somewhere else. There seemed no very profitable way for me to spend the rest of the evening: the Library would be shut; it was too late to visit friends; and besides, it was cold and very wet. I was to stay in the guest-room of Ben's college, if he had not forgotten to book it. I might get some work ready for tomorrow.

But by the time I had found the room, I was too cold and tired, and too dejected, to want to do more than go to bed. I took out my papers and my things for the night, and started to undress. Standing by the window, unbuttoning my shirt, I began to work out which Ben's window must be in the tall building across the court. His was the corner staircase, and the second highest floor, so... But the light was on in that window. I might be wrong about the staircase. I worked it out again, and made sure that I was right.

While I had been walking about Cambridge in the sleet, had he simply gone back to college? Perhaps he had expected me to meet him there? No. He would certainly have explained, and I should have remembered, if we had had to make our way back separately after the play. He had gone without remembering, or bothering, to look for me before he went.

My irritation rose level with my desire to see him. I did not feel inclined to claim, or even to accept, the hospitality he had forgotten. But I owed him seven and sixpence for the ticket. I could pay my debt now, and see him, and save a stamp.

I put a coat on over my shirt, took a ten-shilling note from the dressing-table, and went quickly across the court and up the stairs to his room. Ben came out onto the landing as soon as I knocked.

'Alan. Thank God!'

'Were you expecting me to meet you here?'

'Didn't you get my message?'

'No, I didn't. I just came to give you this, for the ticket.'

'But Joanna said she'd tell you. Didn't you see her?'

'How do you suppose I should have known her?'

'Joanna Brooke. Duchess of York. She said she'd look for you.'

I said nothing.

'Oh, hell. Come in. Oh, please, Alan. I really need your help.'

'You could have had it about an hour and a half ago if I'd known where you were.' But I went in. There was no-one else in the room.

'God, I'm sorry. Come by the fire. Your shoes look wet. How did you get back?'

'Via the party in the Trumpington Road.'

'Oh, no! Damn Joanna. What the hell was she thinking of?'

'Perhaps she thought that looking after your guest was your responsibility.'

Ben looked at me, not altogether apologetically. There were lines of brownish make-up at the edge of his hair, and down the sides of his neck.

'All right, I know. It was. And I'm very sorry, specially on such a foul night. But I don't think I could have done anything else.'

I hesitated to reply, and put the ten-shilling note on the mantelpiece.

'Sit down, and then I can tell you about it,' said Ben.

We both sat down, and I stretched my wet feet to the fire.

'It's David. I had to come back with him. He's in a terrible state.'

141

'He lives upstairs?'

'Yes. He's quite a friend. I've got to know him pretty well over the play.'

'He was acting?'

'He was Salisbury. David Williams. But to start with, he was Aumerle and I was Salisbury; I think I told you. We had one scene together, and I was supposed to be understudying him, too, though the understudies never actually rehearsed or anything. We used to hear each other's parts.'

'And he fell out?'

'I never really knew what happened. There was some row. Julian was very angry. David said he wouldn't act. I wasn't rehearsing that day. The first I knew about it was taking on Aumerle about a week before the opening.'

'You did very well.'

'Oh. Oh, did I? Good. Great. Obviously, I was worried about taking David's part. I asked him, and he said, go ahead: he was thankful to be out of it. There didn't seem to be much else I could do, anyway, but still, I wasn't sure. And then he began to get so low, being out of it. He looked so sad, and he was always coming in after I got back from rehearsals and asking me how it was going. In the end, I talked to Joanna, and she talked to Julian, and they offered him Salisbury, which they'd been going to cut. I wouldn't have minded changing back, but Julian said I couldn't.'

'Yes, I see.'

'So that seemed all right for a bit, and then something went wrong at the dress-rehearsal.'

'That's not unusual.'

'I don't mean that sort of thing. Somebody told David that Julian thought he was no good, or liked my Aumerle better than his, or something. And only let him have Salisbury because I'd said I'd throw up Aumerle if he didn't.'

'Was that true?'

'No, of course it wasn't. I'd just said David seemed low, and was there any chance of a part. But David thought it was true – or might be – he was in a funny state – and got terribly worked up.

He went through with the part – it was too late to back out – but he's been looking more and more strung up and miserable at every performance. And then tonight he missed a cue; and made a mess of his only long speech. He has to stay on for about a hundred and fifty lines after that, saying nothing. I was on stage with him, and I could see he was almost out of control.'

'On the Welsh Coast? Where you try to comfort Richard, after he hears he's been deserted?'

'Yes, that scene. I keep having lines like "Comfort my liege! Why looks your Grace so pale?" – and all the time I was trying to will the comfort at David instead of the king.'

'I can imagine.'

'I went after him as soon as we got off stage. He was almost hysterical, saying he wouldn't go on again. I got him some whisky – there were a few minutes while they put up Flint Castle – and then got him to walk on beside me. He didn't have any more lines, thank goodness: just standing about on the walls.'

'That was well done.'

'It calmed him down a bit, and I persuaded him he should stay till the final curtain. Barbara went and talked to him while I was on.'

'You still had all your big scenes to come.'

'That was the problem – one of the problems.'

'You were very professional about it. I don't think I'd have known. Your last scenes were the best.'

'Desperation or something. Still, I'm glad you thought so. Anyway, David went rushing off as soon as it was over – just like that – costume, make-up. I couldn't catch him. I had to find Joanna and leave you a message; but I thought he'd probably come back here to his room, so I came straight back, too.'

'Also without changing?'

'I put a coat on. I'll have to go back for my jeans and stuff tomorrow.'

'And was he here?'

'Yes. He's upstairs now, in his room. But, Alan, I'm terribly worried about him.'

'Have you talked to him?'

'I've tried to. I went in and he was lying there on his bed, still in his costume. He just told me to go away.'

'And you did?'

'No, I didn't. I sat down and tried to talk to him: said he'd been very good; nobody had noticed where he'd gone wrong, he'd covered up splendidly; people often forgot things – Gielgud, Olivier, everybody – and as long as they kept going, covered up and kept going, it didn't matter a bit; it was fine. And I said, why didn't he get some other clothes on and come to the cast-party? But it was no good. He wouldn't really answer – just kept saying there was nothing I could do, nothing anyone could do; saying I couldn't help, would I please leave him alone. Stupidly, I suppose, I said there'd be lots of other plays, other chances. And that was what was really sad: he said what was the point? Whatever he tried to do, whatever he most looked forward to – Aumerle, Salisbury, the concert – always went wrong. It would be better not to try, not to look forward to anything. I just didn't know what to say, but I was pretty worried about him by that time, so I stayed there – '

'What were you worried about?'

'Well, what he might do; that he might – anything, really.'

'Do you mean that he might try to take his own life?'

'Well – . Oh God – *yes!*'

I jumped up.

'His door's locked,' said Ben.

'But anyway – '

'I think this is the best place to be. I can hear if he walks about – better than outside his door. He hasn't moved since I came down here. I listened hard, even when I was changing. He must be still lying on his bed. I hope he's gone to sleep.'

'No pills or anything – nothing he could use – near the bed?'

'No, I don't think so. I've been working it out while I've been waiting here. He has got some codeine or something, but he keeps it in a drawer, the far side of the room. I know he hasn't got a gun. The window's very small, and set back – it's not a clear drop, and anyway it's flowerbeds underneath. And I can't think of anything else that wouldn't take ages, and lots of moving about.'

'And if you did hear him moving about?'

'I reckoned there'd be time to go and wake Jim, across the passage, and between us we could get the door open. Unless you'd come by then.'

'I see. I see.' I sat down again. Then I said, 'He locked you out?'

'I was going to get him some water – he asked me to – and the minute I was outside, he slammed the door and locked it, and wouldn't let me in again. I suppose I should have thought... But he did go straight back to the bed. I could hear him lying down again while I was trying the door and asking him to let me in. He hadn't time to get across the room. And then he was lying there, crying: crying and not answering; and then quiet. Eventually I came down here.'

I was silent. Ben said suddenly, 'Alan, I've been so scared.'

'Of course you have. But I think it should be all right now; now there are two of us. I wish you hadn't had to wait so long before I came. What do you think we'd better do now?'

'I'm not sure.'

'What about his tutor?'

'I don't know. If we have to, obviously. But I don't want to bring a whole lot of people down on top of him. He's told me quite a lot about it – about the whole thing. If he thought he couldn't go on talking to me – I was telling the whole college – telling anyone – '

'You've told me.'

'Well, I had to. And I knew I could, that you'd understand. Anyway, you're sort of outside the whole thing.'

'I imagine there's rather more to it, isn't there, than forgetting some of his lines?'

'Well...' Ben leaned forward to turn up the fire, and footsteps went diagonally across the floor above. We kept still. They stopped above where we were sitting, and there was a little scraping and creaking of furniture, and then nothing more.

'The armchair,' said Ben, letting out his breath. 'Not the drawer.' He sat up again and rubbed one hand over his face and up into his hair. I put my hand on his other arm, touching his wrist where the cuff of his sweater stopped.

'All right so far, then,' I said, and sat back. 'But I don't think we – you – can go on waiting like this indefinitely. Is there no way we can get into his room? Would the porter have a key?'

'He does have them. But David lost his at the dress-rehearsal; he's probably got the spare one already.'

'Hmm. What about the window?'

'I don't know. We might try from the roof.'

'Is there a way onto the roof?'

'I don't think there's an official one, but some people were up there last week. Rugby players: we'd won a match or something.'

'Can you find it?'

'Jim would know; he's in the college fifteen. Or we might be able to find it and not wake him up. I think they went up our staircase.'

'If you go and look, I can wait here.'

Ben went out quietly, and I sat and listened to the singing of the gas fire. He came back in rather less than five minutes.

'I think we may be able to do it.'

I followed him up two flights of stairs and down a long passage, into a pantry with a sink and a gas-ring, under a sloping roof. The window was open, and it was very cold. I shut the door. Ben climbed onto the draining board and stooped through the window. I followed, with less than his agility.

We found ourselves in a gully between the steeply sloping roofs of the two gables which looked out onto the first court. The gully was blocked at each end by a sheer wall. There was no way through which would allow us to reach – or even to see – David's window in the facade of the western gable.

Ben scrambled a little way up the slope of that roof, and looked over the edge.

'Do be careful.'

'It's all right. His room's further along.'

'I know.'

'Oh. Yes. I'm being careful. I can see his window. But I'm not sure how we're going to get to it.'

He hung over the wall, calculating the drop to David's windowsill. I joined him.

'It wouldn't be safe,' I said.

'I think it's safe enough.' He pulled himself further up the slope.

'Ben. *Wait.*'

'We can't wait, Alan. We've been out here ten minutes already – more – while he's on his own.'

'But there's a skylight or something.'

A little below the roof ridge, on the far side, a glazed trapdoor projected from the slates like the top edge of a box. Ben tipped himself across the ridge, head down, and pulled at one corner of the frame. It would not open. I took the other corner; we tugged together and managed to lift it. Then Ben straddled the roof-ridge, and turned, and let himself down through the dark hole of the skylight. I followed him. It was not far to the floor.

We were in an attic, which seemed very warm after the roof. Two or three narrow lines of light cut across one end of the floor. We stood still until we could hear that there was no movement from below. Then we groped our way past blunt, wrapped shapes, sticky with dust, to the place where the planked floor stopped and the plaster of the ceiling below had shrunk away here and there from the big old beams.

Ben lowered himself and lay flat on the planking, one line of light from below yellowing his skin like a streak of pollen. After some minutes, he beckoned and I lay down beside him, but, looking through the next crack, I could see only a piece of painted wall. I shook my head, and Ben put his mouth close to my ear.

'Still sitting by the fire.'

'No pills? Drawer open or anything?'

'Not that I can see.'

We lay quiet for some time more. Now that action was no longer necessary, and anxiety at least a little delayed, happiness started to move through me, lying next to Ben on the dusty, private floor.

There was a stir below. Ben stiffened, and I waited.

'Putting the kettle on.'

'Good sign?'

'Could be.' I felt him laughing.

'What's funny?'

'Water there all the time, in his kettle.'

'Ssh!'

'I don't think he can hear us, whispering like this. He's making tea.'

'Doesn't look like despair.'

'Unless it's to take the pills with?'

'At least he can't have taken them already. Tea's a stimulant: no point in drinking it later.'

A smell of tea and hot metal came up to us.

'God, I'm hungry,' said Ben.

'Still no pills?'

'Not so far.'

'When did you last eat?'

'I dunno. Lunch or something.'

I felt in my pockets. 'Cough-lozenge any good?'

'Yes, please.'

I transferred the little, rustling packet into his hand.

'You?'

'No thanks.'

He took two, and sucked: his breath became fruity and antiseptic. A head with dark hair came into my view, and then shoulders in a loose, white shirt.

Ben asked, 'What's he doing?'

I shifted a little, and saw further down the wall.

'Writing? Working? At his desk, anyway. A loose-leaf book, and I think an Oxford standard text. And a cup of tea. Must be work.'

'Must be. He's got a supervision tomorrow. Look,' Ben went on then, 'he can't be too bad. Do you want to go back and get some sleep?'

'What about you?'

'Well, I would, too – and something to eat – only...'

'It's later that's worrying,' I said.

'Yes.'

'Perhaps we'd better both stay?'

'Well...'

'I think I'd rather. We needn't both stay awake.'

We lay silent for a long time. Once David crossed his room out of my field of vision, and back again, getting another cup of tea. I began to feel tired, and realised that we hadn't agreed who should sleep first. I listened for Ben's breathing: it was slow and even.

David pushed his cup further from him, laid his arms on the desk, and put his head down on them. As I watched, he turned his head sideways, and I could see that he was sleeping, or falling asleep. He looked young, with a round, vulnerable cheek, and thick, dark hair lying across the stage make-up on his forehead.

'Alan?'

'Ben. You awake?'

'Now I am.'

We were silent for a time further.

'It doesn't feel as if this is really happening,' said Ben.

'What?'

'Us lying here; and David – I can't really believe it. Or at least I can't imagine it – feeling like that, *that* much.'

'You've never felt anything like that yourself? Even enough to imagine it, I mean: to be within reach of what he's felt?'

'No. No, not really. Unhappy, obviously, or disappointed, or left out. I mean, everyone has. But not like that.'

'When did you feel left out?'

'Well – oh – in France. Once. A bit. Have you, ever?'

'Felt left out?'

'Felt like David.'

'Not, I think, like that. Unhappy – as you say – of course, from time to time. And more than that – once or twice – desolation: the being without any conceivable consolation, even, for a time. Or thinking I was. But never despair: I always assumed my life had to go on. And never in such a *hurry* either.'

'You think he needn't have got in such a state, so soon?'

'Oh, need. How can one know, for someone else? It can be very painful – exclusion, broken affection, jealousy.'

Ben turned his head.

'But this I do think,' I went on. 'When someone else is in despair, you can see that it won't last forever, that one can survive.

And I think one should decide in good time to remember that, if one's ever in the same state. Remember it, or at least act on it.'

'But how could you act?'

'Hold on; refuse to despair finally, I suppose; endure while you have to.'

'I don't think everyone could manage that – not alone, anyway.'

'You think one should get help?'

'I think you'd have to: you'd have to go to a friend, or someone.'

'It could be. For some people, that could be the best way: to make your friend your resolution; to say, "I know this can't go on for ever – this despair, this agony – but I feel as if it will. Hold on for me until I come through."'

'It would be the only way, I think. But then if...'

'If?'

'Well, if your friend – the only friend close enough – was part of it already, part of the trouble, or the despair – .'

'Was that part of David's difficulty?'

'In a way. Sort of.'

His voice had an ambivalent reluctance, as if he was trying to keep, but wanting to unload, a burdensome confidence.

'It's getting very cold in here,' I said after a moment.

'It is a bit. Better than the roof, though. When did you feel so desolate, Alan?'

'When my mother died, principally.'

'I'm sorry. I shouldn't have asked.'

'No, it's all right. I didn't mean to sound stiff. It was a long time ago, and I haven't talked to anyone about it for some time – or at all, perhaps, really.'

'How old were you?'

'I was thirteen. My father had died when I was very young – four or five, I think.'

'So then you were on your own?'

'In a sense, yes.'

'What did you do?'

'I had some cousins on my father's side. I went to live with them.'

'Was it all right, with them?'

'They were kind and, I think, sensible. But I had felt very close to my mother.'

'What was she like?'

'She was – humorous,' I said slowly. 'Humorous, and easily delighted. Quick to feel other people's feelings – even to the point of distress. Not, I think, patient by nature, or practical, but both, very adequately, because she thought it necessary. Argumentative, but generous in argument, and honest: honest in everything – except perhaps where she let affection modify the truth a little. Easily alarmed, I suspect, though she gave me freedom and didn't try to keep me too safe. Inventive: she could tell stories and make up games; she used to write verses for me, for special occasions.'

'What sort of occasions?'

'Oh, birthdays, starting a new school, scholarships – that kind of thing. One I remember when I first learnt to swim.'

'Did you write poems for her?'

'Not very much. I used to draw maps for her – imaginary maps, usually, with a great many coloured pencils.'

'Is it really better, do you think?' Ben said, after a moment. 'Better to have loved and lost – you know?'

'I think it is. Yes, I'm sure it is; much better, though not necessarily less painful. Especially if you mean all kinds of love: parents and children, friends – '

'Have you ever been in love?'

'Have you?'

'Well, no, not really. Do you think I should have? I mean, by my age?'

'I don't think there's any "should" about it. What are you? Nineteen?'

'Yes.'

'Some people who have loved better than most have started a great deal later than that.'

151

'Sometimes – everybody seems paired off. Well, not everybody, but such a lot of people. Or at least wishing they were – I mean, wishing it about a particular person.'

'But you've found friends?'

'Oh, friends, yes. David's a great friend, and Nick, and Joanna, and Jonathan.'

'Joanna was the Duchess of York?'

'That's right. She's a great girl.'

'But no more than that?'

'No more than that. Less, when it comes to giving messages.'

We laughed, and Ben rolled onto his side, which brought him close to my ribs. The floor creaked.

'Sshh!'

'OK. I'll keep still. What's the time?'

'Nearly three. Go to sleep. I'll watch.'

'OK. Wake me up when you want to.'

'Sleep well.'

He put his head down on the crook of his arm, and I lay and watched him, and looked down from time to time on David, also asleep. After some time, Ben shivered in his sleep. Without waking him, I put my hand on his, and found that it was very cold. I sat up and took off my coat, and lying down again, closer to Ben, I spread it over us both.

At about half-past four, David raised his head, shivered, and stretched. He stood up shakily and moved away from the desk, and out of sight. I was edging towards another crack, when the light went out and I heard the scramble and creak, and the double thud of shoes, as he got into bed.

There was not much that he could attempt without switching on the light. I felt very tired. I pulled my share of the coat round my shoulders, and went to sleep.

'Christ! What's the time?'

'It's between five and ten to nine.'

I saw Ben in the pale, grubby light, sitting up and rubbing his hands in his hair.

'You didn't wake me for my turn.'

'It was all right,' I said. 'I got some sleep, too. He put the light out and went to bed. Nothing he could do, really, without putting it on again and waking us up.'

'No, of course.' Ben looked down. 'And he's still there, thank God.'

'Could we go back now? What do you think? Go and make some coffee? If we hear him stirring, we can see if he'll let us in. He'll have had some sleep; he may be feeling more rational.'

'Right. Yes, I'm sure we could. The only trouble is, I've got a supervision.'

'When?'

'Nine-thirty.'

'Can you get out of it?'

'I don't think so. *And* I'm supposed to have done an essay.'

'What are you going to do about that?'

'I'll have to borrow one from Jonathan: his girlfriend's in the second year. Yes, I know, but what else can I do, without giving David away?'

'All right.'

I made the coffee while Ben ran across the court to Jonathan's room, and then came back to change his shirt and shave. His trousers were grimy, and torn at the knee, where he had pulled himself back through the skylight, but his other pair were still in the green room.

153

CHAPTER 36

Two hyacinths were coming out in the pot on the kitchen table when I came home. I had gone to sleep in front of the fire while Ben was at his supervision, and again on the bus, but I still slept long and heavily that night.

The essay had been safely accepted. 'He said my style wasn't as good as usual,' Ben reported, with mock - complacency, and an eye on my reaction.

A little before twelve, we had heard David beginning to move about, and Ben met him on the stairs, coming down to borrow sugar. We persuaded him to stay while we made more coffee and toast, and when the talk turned to his interest in the early Renaissance, I offered to show him my Jacobean translation of Boccaccio.

'Ben can bring you over,' I said, 'any time you're visiting him.'

'I was going to ask you,' said Ben. 'What about Easter?'

David was looking white, and the skin round his eyes was thick, but he seemed tranquil, and now he smiled at Ben with real pleasure.

'I'd love to. I suppose I'd have to bring some work.'

Ben thanked me for the suggestion, when we were alone, and I apologized for making free with his hospitality.

'No, it was a great idea. I don't know why I hadn't thought of it. He seemed fairly all right, didn't you think?'

I woke next morning with the sense of a pool of hope and contentment lying below the surface of my mind. As I made the breakfast and sorted out my papers, a spring broke through into the daylight of conscious expectancy: I thought that Ben might be capable of falling in love with a man.

The evidence was not substantial. If he had told the truth, (and I thought he had), he had not yet fallen in love with a young woman. There was still time, as I had said. (I had been honest, too, and really evasive only once.) But at least the way was still clear; and I thought that any homosexual inclination was likely to lie unacknowledged, or even suppressed, for longer than a heterosexual one. He seemed to have felt some sense of isolation already. (Could I really rejoice in that? How could I not? I could perhaps wish for a change in the whole of society, to avoid wishing for one in Ben.) Even at College, he was aware of the pairing off – 'or at least wishing they were' – in which he was not included, though I did not think he was deeply or continuously concerned about it.

In France he had been really unhappy. I had known that already, and now he had given me the basis of an explanation, though I must not build too high on it. He had felt 'left out... Once. A bit.' More than a bit, and I could not believe (even allowing for subjectivity in my judgement) that Ben, at eighteen or so – and speaking good French – would be left out so blatantly from personal antipathy or national prejudice.

I remembered my mother telling me once about a dance she had gone to as a girl. Most of the other guests had known one another much better than they knew her; the young men in her party soon found other friends; and when the dancing began, she was the only person without a partner. Somebody's uncle danced with her once, and a glum young man asked her for one or two dances, and then wandered away and left her, tall and shy, to stand against the wall. There was nobody to take her in to supper. She went upstairs as if to do her hair, looked at the shawls and furs lying on the bed in the spare room, and longed to crawl under them and go to sleep until it was time to go home. She had cried most of the way home, in the borrowed car, when her father asked if she had enjoyed herself. And he had stopped the car, lent her his handkerchief, and told her that the young men at the party weren't worth a second thought, let alone a tear. 'Those lounge-lizards? It's their loss, my dear.'

'I was comforted,' my mother had said. 'He knew how to make me feel better. But I can still remember how I felt that evening – how utterly left out I felt.'

Was that what Ben had suffered in France, but for three or four weeks? I could imagine a group of young men and girls, well-acquainted, amorous, on holiday, falling in and out of all the various stages of love and dalliance, 'so priketh hem nature in hir corages'. And Ben among them, isolated, not by the pangs of despised love, nor, like my mother, simply by being unsophisticated and unintroduced, but perhaps (it was just possible) by being unable to share in the emotions of those around him.

At Cambridge, I thought, some of the emotions around him were different. It seemed fairly clear that David's distress was based on something more than a moment's theatrical inefficiency. And whatever the emotional complications back-stage, they apparently involved Ben himself – as David's friend, and also, perhaps, as his rival. It was not a willing rivalry. Ben's only emotion in the whole affair seemed to be his kindly and (I was fairly sure) non-romantic concern for David. Nevertheless, it seemed to be an encounter – quite probably his first – with erotic feelings between young men. And as both the confidant and the object of such feelings, he had shown sympathy rather than disapproval or disgust.

There were other sources for my happiness: an irrational pleasure that someone else had appreciated even a little of Ben's worth; and an even more absurd complacency that he had come to this appreciation later than I had. A much deeper satisfaction, a warm current, now, running below all my thoughts, was the fact that Ben had wanted my help, and had asked for it. In spite of my hasty and self-important assumption of his neglect (which might fairly have cost me the whole night's company), he had welcomed me with open affection and relief, and had been anxious to confide in me as far as he could without betraying David's confidence – further, I thought, if I had pressed him a little, exploiting his anxiety and yielding to my own.

In other ways he had been more determined and less biddable than before, disregarding my advice, and even my reproof, with an *insouciance* in which, eventually, I rejoiced. The equality and independence of judgement, for which I had undertaken to wait, were developing fast, now; and there was something which delighted me, too, about the form they took – the movements and gestures of his incipient defiance.

Spending the whole night together, depending on each other, in the uncomplicated intimacy of danger, we had come unusually close. But even that closeness, and the corresponding physical proximity, Ben's back lying against my ribs, I would have forgone, or at least deferred, rather than lose one of his reasons for entrusting his anxieties to me:

'Well, I had to. And I knew I could – you'd understand.'

The Cambridge term would be over in three weeks. The Christmas vacation had been cluttered with visiting cousins for the Graysons, and shortened for me by a conference on Mediaeval studies. I had hardly seen Ben by himself for more than a few minutes. At Easter, there would be time for him to visit me. If David was staying with him, I could ask them both to supper, or to spend a day, to see my books. And I could stop at the Graysons' sometimes, in the course of a walk.

Near the end of March was Ben's birthday. I might find him a book of Mediaeval Lyrics: I did not think he would find the Middle English too difficult, and I should like to think of him reading them, to feel that they were, in some way, addressed to him. I wanted to give him Shakespeare's Sonnets above all else, but I thought that it was not yet the time. I would give him the Sonnets when he was twenty-one, if I could find a nice edition. By then, he would be fit subject for such a declaration – and fit to understand it, if he wanted to. I began to think of March next year as a threshold. Meanwhile, it was too long since I had visited Ruth and James. I might see if they were in tomorrow, and give them Ben's news, or some of it.

I worked hard in the next three weeks. Time in the autumn term, once it began to be marked out dependably by Ben's letters, had moved at a tolerable jog-trot. And leisure had gone briskly as well as work, except sometimes, when I was listening to music. But now increase of hope, or twelve hours of Ben's close company, or the two together, made me ache and strain for him like a dog whining and straining against a door. Mental calculation of the days and hours left until he might return, or even write (though he would hardly have time, before the end of term, to answer my letter of thanks), did nothing to alleviate the prickling, bodily longing for his immediate presence. After a long session of neglected work and profitless multiplication and subtraction, I would look at my watch again, to improve the result by half an hour, and find that it had moved only seven or eight minutes. It was an intrusive, dominating hunger which I must discover how to shake off, or at least to endure. He might be gone for much longer than this another time – abroad in the summer, for instance. But all my resources of self-control were not enough to restore common sense and concentration. I scribbled in the margins of my notes, writing Ben's name again and again, and then wasted more time tearing off the strips of paper and burning them over the hearth. I forgot to fill the Aga at night, and spent half the next day trying to light it again. I went up- and down-stairs to the bathroom half-a-dozen times in a morning.

In the end, I set myself a great deal of work to get through in the remaining weeks, and simply worked every day until I had finished the allotted number of lines. I had supper at nine, or ten, or whenever I had done. I vowed I would not visit Ben, whenever he came home, until I had finished. By the middle of the second week I was tired, but I slept well, and my mind began to keep to a channel of work and the routines of housekeeping.

At the end of the third week, with rather more than a day's work to go, I had a letter from the Press, asking me to be on the Committee for the new Dictionary of Middle English. The work would begin in October, and was expected (rightly) to take several years. The Committee would meet in Cambridge twice a term. Philological, professional, and personal delight did delay me that morning.

I still had over half a day's work to do, at nine in the evening, when Ben rang and asked me to walk over next day to see him and David.

'We got back today. Come and have coffee after lunch. We might go for a walk or something.'

If I asked them to walk over to the cottage instead, I should not be visiting Ben. But that was prevarication.

'I'd love to see you both, but I've got some work to finish first. May I ring you tomorrow, when I know how far I've got?'

After midnight, my eyes stung and began to drop shut involuntarily. I set my alarm early, and finished, with continual cups of coffee, in time to ring Ben at a late breakfast. Ruth answered, and told me that he and David had gone out already. She could ask them to ring me back when they came in.

I put the telephone down and cursed my pedantic obedience to private deadlines. I did not even know how long Ben would be staying at home. I might have missed him altogether. It was sheer priggishness, self-congratulating delight in the exercise of will, an illiberal spiritual pride I should have grown out of. And now what was I to do with the rest of the day? I went out into the garden to calm my irrational, *post-hoc* rage of recantation, and Ben and David walked through the hedge, where they had leant their bicycles.

'Good, we're not too late,' Ben said. 'We thought we'd come before you started work, only my chain came off. I thought we could make a plan, and then go away and leave you to work.'

'It's all right. I've given myself a holiday. You needn't go away.'

I made them coffee, in a state of excitement I could not altogether control. All the counter-tensions of the past weeks were released now, but so abruptly, and all together, that I was left quivering with the residual vibration. I moved so quickly that I burned my hand on the kettle. It did not seem to hurt very much, but Ben spread butter on it with a direct concern which made me light-headed.

He took the cups from me, and carried them to the windowsill in the living-room, and there, sitting in the strong, early sun, listening to him and David make plans and jokes and include me in both, I began to calm down, to forgive my scrupulousness, and to let my coffee grow cold in the cup on my knee.

There were places in the neighbourhood that Ben wanted David to see. As they talked, it occurred to me how many reasons there were that I should have a car. The Cambridge bus was intolerably slow and unreliable, and I should soon be going there twice a term. Driving myself would save well over an hour each way: nearly three hours more for work at home; or for Cambridge. How much would I have to pay for a small car, second-hand? I thought James would know.

The boys knew, too, and offered me complicated and sometimes contradictory advice as we walked over the fields to a pub. Ben caught my eye interrogatively while David was climbing a stile, and I nodded back: he was cheerful without strain, though his face fell into sad lines in repose.

We drank beer and ate bread and cheese in the pub, and talked about Cambridge. David was thinking about staying on after his first degree, to do research. He seemed uncertain, and I guessed that his doubts were not only academic, but we talked about the more objective grounds of decision: his chance of a good degree; his choice of a subject; what it was like to do research; and the difference from undergraduate work: the greater freedom and excitement, and the correspondingly greater need to be systematic.

'Are you sure it's your sort of thing?' Ben asked David. 'Up at the same time every morning; two hours' work before breakfast? I can't see it.'

David had heard me with intelligent attention. Now he moved Ben's glass and held it out of reach.

'Why not? As long as you're strong-minded. Maybe Ben should go into the army?'

I laughed. 'I think you'd do very well, David. Ben, you're drinking my beer.'

'Oh, sorry. I thought it was David's. Give it *back*, blast you.'

'Admit you get up quite as late as me.'

'If you don't both sit down, you'll spill all our glasses.'

'Only now and then,' said Ben.

'Always. Always, unless I've been having a rehearsal,' said David. He looked suddenly white. Ben sat down, and David pushed his glass towards him over the wet-ringed table.

'I'd like another pint,' I said. 'You can get it for me, Ben – you had half the last one. And for yourself. David?'

'No, thank you.'

'I know what you mean about rehearsals,' I said. 'They seem to displace everything while they're going on – sleep, time, sense of proportion.'

'Yes. That's quite true.'

Ben brought back three pints after all, and David accepted his with a brief look towards me of surprise and gratitude.

The two boys were working for their preliminary exams, and they spent each morning reading – all of it in principle, and at least some of it in fact. There were books of mediaeval history on their reading-list, however, which they had not been able to find in the College library, and passages of Latin which were beyond their limited powers of translation; and these quite often provided a reason to visit the cottage as part of a morning's work. They would ring up (until I told them not to bother) and arrive, with a good appetite for coffee and biscuits, in the middle of the morning.

We spent one wet afternoon looking at my books. I showed David my *Boccaccio*, and found several other things I thought might interest them. Many of these Ben had not seen before, either, and he was more impressed and excited than I had expected. He particularly liked a little nineteenth-century *Gawain* – one of the first printed transcriptions, with oddly appropriate pre-Raphaelite wood-cuts – and I considered whether I should give him that, instead, for his approaching birthday.

They often stayed to lunch, after a morning visit, or took me home with them. And then, if the afternoon was fine, we walked or bicycled to further villages, to show David a church or a tithe-barn or a pretty green. Mark came with us, when his holidays had begun, and Bridget once or twice, when she was not too busy with work for her A-Levels in June.

It was a halcyon time. Happiness continued, and hope; but hope was not disturbing, because nothing could change before next March. That was the accepted point, now, before which I would make no open attempt to secure, or even to discover, Ben's affections. I did wonder, now and then, what I should do if he approached me before that time. He was certainly seeking my company a good deal, and though it was always with David, there were moments when he met my eye in a joke, or my mind in the nuance of a phrase, which made me imagine that he must also share feelings of a different order of magnitude. But I did not decide what I ought to do in such a case: I thought that it was not really very likely to happen – it was impossible to decide in advance how I should respond – a decision made on the spur of the moment is often the best (particularly since it often corresponds with what the decider really wants). I could wait and enjoy his young company, and David's, and add to my hope.

It was when David had gone home for the last part of the vacation that the cheerful serenity of the time began to gather into something fuller, more distended with possibility. I had sent the Victorian *Gawain* to be rebound, and it had come back not, as I had hoped, in time for Ben's birthday, but two or three weeks later, in the middle of April. We had celebrated the birthday all together, with a family dinner, and the festivity had seemed not much diminished by the lack of one present. Now I wrote his name in the book, and a couple of lines from the third fitt (Gawain's speech to the Lord of the Castle, when they keep their first bargain), and put it by his plate when he was coming to tea. He was very pleased, and read the inscription aloud, pronouncing all the thorns as 'p's, and put an arm on my shoulder to thank me. After tea, we sat by the fire and talked, and he thanked me then for what I had done to help David.

'I meant to write after that night. I'm sorry I didn't. I wanted to wait till I could write properly – really thank you properly – not just a scrappy letter. And then the end of term – you know what it's like...'

'I know. I was busy, too. How do you think he is?'

'I think he's pretty good. He got a bit low, now and then, towards the end of term, but never so bad, anything like. And while he was here, it was great; he seemed absolutely happy – even talking late at night. It *was* a good idea, asking him. You've done such a lot for him.'

'No great effort being hospitable at your expense. And Ruth's.'

'No, but when he was here. You were so kind – having him round, and talking to him and everything.'

I could find no immediate, honest answer.

'He thought it was terrific.'

Remembering our conversation later, I glowed at Ben's gratitude, and at a stronger warmth which had reached me occasionally; but I felt a dissatisfaction, too, like a clinker somewhere within the glow of the embers.

CHAPTER 37

I thought of taking a holiday early that year. Three weeks in Italy over the turn of May and June would bring me home before the universities came down. But some disappointment lingering from the year before made Italy on my own look bleak – not inviting enough to overcome inertia about breaking off work and deciding on dates and tickets and hotels. And I did not want to mortgage the rest of the summer: I certainly could not afford two holidays.

I spent one weekend in Cambridge, just before May Week. I had a useful preliminary talk with one or two other members of the Dictionary Committee, and Ben took me on the river with David and Joanna. She seemed a sensible, humorous girl, quite good-looking, and more adult than the two young men. It was fine, hot weather, and Ben and David vied with each other in the speed and dexterity of their punting, teasing each other, and splashing us all with river-water. Ben lost the bottom for a moment, where the river was deeper, and David took up the paddle with a provoking show of helpfulness. Ben tapped it out of his hands, and as it floated away David stood up and dived with some elegance over the bows.

'I hope you knew how deep it was,' I said, when he had surfaced and retrieved the paddle.

'Oh, pretty deep,' he said, shaking water and hair out of his eyes, and holding the side of the punt. 'And I knew you'd bring Ben to justice if I broke my neck. Hey, Ben, stop it. Let me get in.'

Joanna took the pole while Ben and I helped David back, and then she continued to punt, with more skill than either of them, while they took their wet shirts off and spread them in the stern.

'I shall burn,' said Ben, half-turning his head.

'There's some sun-stuff in my bag,' said Joanna.

I liked her increasingly, and I could see no sign of anything more than equable friendship between her and Ben, though

I thought she looked at David occasionally with something more – a hopefulness for which I judged there was little foundation.

We had supper afterwards in David's room, with cold food and a bottle of wine, and a good deal of hilarity – increased, for Ben and me, by the complicity which seemed (in the way of shared secrets) irresistibly funny, in spite of its gravity. We had to avoid looking at the cracks in the ceiling, and to change the subject quickly if our eyes met.

I came home full of sun and air and high spirits. The hedges seemed very close together after the great, uninterrupted Cambridgeshire skies.

Ben stayed up after the end of term for a May Ball in a party of friends, and from there he went to London to stay with David. I worked on, taking patience from the blessed length of the Long Vacation. The completing of the Cycle was beginning to appear on my horizon – at a great distance still, but a calculable one. If all went well, and Douglas and I could both work steadily, the text should be done in another twelve months. That would leave the glossary and the bibliography, and a long introduction, as well as a final, detailed checking of the text. But it could not be far into the following year before it was ready for the Press. Allowing twice as long as usual after that, for arguments about the extent of the notes, it should be through the Press by early summer – less than two years from now, and a few weeks before Ben's finals. The rest of the money from the Press was due to us on publication. That would be the summer for a real holiday.

Towards the end of June, Ben came home. He had enjoyed London, seen several plays, and spent all his remaining money. He came to see me soon after his return, and brought me David's news and greetings. His own summer plans were still vague. The first necessity was to earn some money, and he was afraid that he had left it late; school would be ending in a few weeks and then there would not be much extra work going until the harvest. In the end, he found a job on a milk-round. He had to get up early, which limited his freedom in the evenings. Visiting friends too often after supper would reduce his night's sleep beyond what was good for him. But his round included the cottage, and I began to wake before half past six, hearing the grind of the reversing van, and then the glassy chink of the bottle on the step. If I was quick – and I became quicker – I would see the top of his head, and his shoulder, stooping by the door, and my love would run, for a rare moment unchecked by the caution of appearances, through the fresh, gilt air of the morning to his easy, brisk, retreating back. Once he pulled a rose towards him, on his way to the gate, and bent his head to smell it.

I slept without the curtains drawn so that the sun helped to wake me, but one morning when it was overcast I did not wake until twenty to seven. I felt an almost superstitious disappointment, as if I had lost the talisman of the day. I was not surprised that it was raining; it was not worth trying to go back to sleep.

I went downstairs to put the kettle on and fetch in the milk, and met Ben setting down the bottle on the doorstep. He had been delayed by mud in the lanes, and hoped I hadn't been waiting for my milk. His shirt was very wet already. I made him a cup of coffee and found him a dry shirt and a waterproof jacket. He changed by the Aga, rubbing himself dry on the dry tail of his own shirt before I could fetch a towel.

'I mustn't be long. I'm late already.'

'Better than being off work with a chill.'

'That's what my mother would say. And, why didn't I take an anorak in the first place?'

'And she'd be right?'

'Of course. God, that was good. Thank you so much.'

'Any time. Even if it's not raining.'

He had not known what time I usually got up. I could change it without any declaration of intent. We drank coffee together early every morning – sitting on the doorstep, if it was fine. My love, in that short space, could no longer be open and unobserved, but I could feel it, not much inhibited, moving towards him as he sat beside me, with the mug between his hands, and the sun on his knees and his rough hair.

Milkmen seemed to be well paid. After six weeks, Ben thought, he would have earned enough to go abroad. A few days before he finished, he arrived with a message: James had heard of a car which he thought might suit me. Would I like to go over for a drink that evening and hear about it? I did some accounts before I started work, and decided what I could afford.

In the evening, as we sat in his garden and drank cold, summer drinks, James told me about the car. An acquaintance of his in Harchester wanted to sell it because he was going abroad. It was in good condition, a reliable make, the right size, and the price was several hundred pounds more than I had reckoned to spend.

I could not immediately dismiss the plans for the autumn already forming. Should I buy it, adding the money set aside for a holiday? I asked James if I might have time to think about it.

'Of course. He doesn't need to know straight away.'

'Very good of you to let me know about it, anyway. What are your plans for the summer?'

'Ruth and I are hoping to get away later on.'

'When the fruit's all picked?'

'That's it. And Mark with us, unless it clashes with a pony-trekking holiday we've promised him. Bridgie's the one with exciting plans,' he added, as Bridget came out, carrying a garden chair.

'What are you doing, Bridget?

She set down the chair, and James gave her a drink. 'I've got a job looking after children in Barcelona.'

'That does sound fun. And strenuous?'

'Well, it might be. I don't know what the children are like. But anyone who's looked after Marky has had plenty of practice.'

'What's Ben doing?'

'Who knows?'

'Least of all Ben,' said James.

'He's not going abroad?'

'I should think he's quite likely to, in the end. But he and his friends seem to think it's unadventurous, or something, to plan more than three days ahead.'

'Ben,' called Bridget, 'they're slandering you.'

He came up the path from the fruit-cages, his hands and shirt blotched with red.

'Have a drink,' said James.

'That's the last load in,' he said, and smiled and nodded to me, stretched, and sat down on the grass.

'That's good of you, Ben,' said his father. 'Specially when you've been working all morning.'

'You finish the milk round on Saturday?' I asked.

'Sunday.'

'And then?'

'Sleep.'

I laughed. 'Any secondary plans?'

'Well, I'm not really sure.'

'Ah!' said James.

'David wants to go to Greece,' Ben went on.

'That would be wonderful.'

'Well, yes, it would. But I don't know. It's a long way. And then Tim and Joanna and some people were thinking about driving through France, if Tim can get a car.'

'Join up with us,' said Bridget. 'Give Rosie and me a lift across France, and we'll help with the petrol.'

"I don't know. I don't know. I really must ring up Tim.'

In the end, I did nothing about the car.

As I waited for Ben to decide where he would travel, I began to make my own plans. If he could be vague, so could I. My holiday must, after all, depend on the state of my work and the state of my bank balance, and no-one else knew enough about both of these to determine with any accuracy what itineraries, or what degrees of certainty or uncertainty, they might warrant.

When Ben had made up his mind, I could make up mine in the same direction. To make it appear a coincidence would come nearer to dishonesty than I liked, or than I had ever come, with Ben, but I did not know what else I could safely do. A car – if I could find a cheap one – would provide a good reason for combining our journeys, but I was now afraid to buy one before I knew where I wanted to go and what the journey would cost. By the time I knew that, I might not have long to look for a car.

My immediate future had not been so uncertain for a long time; it had not often depended so completely on someone else's decision since I was an adult. I preserved some sense of certainty by making general preparations: returning books to the library, cleaning out the larder and the fridge, mending clothes, and putting together some portable and replaceable work.

On the Thursday after Ben finished his job, I met Ruth in the post office. She told me that he was leaving early next week, for Spain.

'Spain! What fun. Whereabouts?'

'I don't think they've really settled. One of them wants to see the Moorish stuff in the South. Ben's rather fascinated by the route to Compostela.'

'That doesn't sound very compatible, unless they have quite a long time. Or a car.'

'That seems a bit uncertain, too. And then of course they ought to see Madrid – the Prado...'

'I've got to be in Madrid myself at some point this summer.' I needed to say it, but I could not find a voice that would convince either of us.

'Has he read George Borrow?' I asked instead. '*The Bible in Spain*? I might bring it over, if I can find it.'

The evening was cool and rustling loudly with the early burning of a stubble field beyond the road. I declined James's offer of whisky, and found Ben in his room, sorting shirts. He put the bulky volume of Borrow beside his knapsack as doubtfully as it deserved.

'I don't suppose you'll have room to take it with you,' I said, 'especially if you're walking. I just thought you might be amused to look into it, if you have time before you go.'

'Well, that might be great,' he said, picking it up again with polite interest and relief, and turning over some of the pages. 'I'm not actually sure how we are going. We may have a car – Tim thinks he can get hold of a car, but he's not sure.'

He put the book down on the shirts, then picked up the whole lot and started to push them into the knapsack. 'If we do have one,' he said, 'I was going to say – I wondered – if you'd like to come? I mean, without a car it might be a bit rough. But it's probably too short notice, anyway. I don't suppose you could get away by then... by next week.'

I said that I was hoping to have a car before the end of next week.

I walked home with the pulse of happiness beating through my thoughts like a kettledrum. The flames over the stubble had gone out, leaving only their tall smoke to hide one track of the sky. My shoulders and arms felt electrical with unexpressed delight, their skin so tender that I thought it would be dented by the mere pressure of the air – the smoky, semi-translucent air that circled my journey home.

Early next morning, I telephoned James's friend and heard that he had sold his car. Then I bicycled into Bramston and asked at the garage if they knew of a car for sale. They rang me at the cottage at lunchtime: one of the mechanics had a cousin who wanted to sell a small estate car; it would probably cost slightly more than the one James had suggested.

I left the table uncleared and rode into the town again to see my bank manager. I showed him my accounts, told him my immediate expectations, and explained my need for a car in the autumn. He agreed, with an unexpected and unsurprised readiness, to allow me an overdraft of six hundred pounds.

I bought the car the same afternoon. The garage declared that it was mechanically sound, and on the whole I trusted them. There was not much I could have done if I hadn't. I collected the log-book, handed over the banker's draft, and drove away. I was reluctant to discuss the price with James, and besides, I thought the car would look more reliable when I had washed it. I drove home, and did not telephone Ben until the insurance was arranged, the car was clean, and my bath was running.

CHAPTER 38

By the beginning of the next week, Tim was still negotiating about borrowing his brother's car, Joanna was undecided, and David was in the country without a telephone. We decided to start making plans without waiting for their final decisions. I spent Monday afternoon telephoning ferry lines, while Ben sorted my maps and spread some of them out open on the floor. The first five car ferries had no places for the next month. The sixth had a cancellation on Wednesday for a crossing to Boulogne, and a reduction if we booked the return at the same time, for a month later.

'Let's take it,' said Ben, as I waited with the receiver in my hand. 'Don't you think? The others can come with us if they're ready. And if they aren't, they can catch us up by train. Plane, if they're feeling rich.'

'And if Tim does get the car?' I said.

'Then there'll be lots of room, even if Joanna's coming, and maybe he can bring Celia and what's-her-name as well. But they'll be lucky to get a ferry place, won't they?'

'Very.'

I shut up the cottage next day, and drove over to spend the night at the Graysons'. I slept in the spare room – tidy and a little alien, with only a trace or two of Ben's invalid occupation. It was strange to sleep for the first time in a house I knew so well, waking, and had thought of so often from a distance as I fell asleep.

We left next morning at six, drinking coffee quietly at the kitchen table, and calling goodbye to the sleepy family round bedroom doors. It was a fine, fair morning, the car ran well in the empty lanes, and the sun was soon high enough to warm us as we went.

We took five days to reach Spain, as that was the time we had before meeting the others just over the border on the north coast.

Stopping places and dates are in my diary, and, I think, in Ben's, but other memories are more immediate, and perhaps more relevant. There are certain places – the ruined Abbey of Jumièges in the early morning, the great blue glow of Chartres, the first sight of the Pyrenees – which have acquired a kind of grace in my memory, a blessedness which, between lovers, might have made them a symbol or a password. But it was the journey itself, for me, which gave the whole enterprise, the whole summer, the luminous clarity of joy.

We slept on the grass, side by side, or, where the level ground was narrow, head to head, in our sleeping-bags, talking more and more slowly, studying the stars. When it looked like rain, in the foothills of the Pyrenees, we slept in the back of the car, with the seats folded down and our shoulders on the tailgate, closer together though we missed the closeness of the wind and the grass. We went to bed not long after it was dark, and had slept enough by early morning.

I usually woke before Ben, and would lie with a book and watch him sleep, lying very loose and heavy on the ground, looking very warm, from the warmth of his cheek between his hair and the edge of his sleeping-bag. If he was still sleeping after seven, I would get up, and light the primus-stove, sometimes quietly enough to let him sleep on. But he would always wake at the smells of bacon and coffee, and stretch, push back the sleeping bag, and begin to fetch knives and mugs. We did not say very much until we had started eating. Then Ben's drowsiness would give way to coffee and holiday expectancy, and he would run his fingers through his hair and take up the conversation from where it had ended last night, or from the way we might go that day, or from what he had been dreaming.

When the kettle had boiled a second time, we finished our coffee and began to get ready to go. Ben usually washed up, still in his pyjamas, kneeling on the ground by the bowl, while I packed the primus and rolled the sleeping bags round the pillows and stowed them all in the car. We would get dressed, then push the bundle of pyjamas among the sleeping bags. Once, getting our clothes from the front seat, Ben threw me his own shirt by mistake. I held it in my hand and wondered whether to put it on, but in a moment I said, 'Wrong shirt!' and threw it back. I was not sure that I could make such inattentiveness credible; and it would be dangerous, too, to let myself start pursuing such contacts at one remove, such secondary totems.

While the sunlight was still cool, I would steer the car over ruts and stones to the road; Ben would walk ahead, guiding me, and go back to see if we had left anything behind. Then he would run up, and jump in beside me, and spread the map on his knees.

We had to stop in a village before midday, sometimes for petrol, always for fresh water. We would try to find one which baked its own bread, and might have cheese or pâté, too, and olives and fruit. If there was a river accessible and deep enough, we would leave our lunch on the bank with our clothes, and swim before we ate. I would have done first, dry and put my clothes on, and start undoing brown paper and breaking bread while I watched Ben duck-dive through the wavering translucency, or lie on the water, arched back, his eyes nearly shut in the sun. He would finish, suddenly, running up the bank in a scatter of water, wrapping a towel round his waist, apologising hungrily. 'Sorry. Are you starving? Why didn't you start?'

He would eat as he was, not waiting to dress, the drops drying as they ran down his arms, his hair lifting as the sleekness and darkness of the water left it. When I had eaten enough, and convinced Ben that the last bread and cheese, the last fig or peach, either were his by right, or would be wasted if he left them, we would lie and doze in the sun, or talk, or read, arguing peaceably now and then about the probability of Ben being sunburnt before he put his shirt on.

When the sting began to go out of the sun, we would roll up the papers and wipe the knives, take up our towels, dry and sweet from the sun, and go back across the fields to the car. We had usually covered a good distance in the morning, and could take time for wandering in the rest of the afternoon, turning off into even smaller roads to find a monastery, or a bridge, or wall paintings in a village church, or walking, once, up the silent perspective of a grass-grown avenue to a little empty manor-house.

Early in the evening we would look for somewhere to have supper. We ate cheaply. Ben took it for granted that all our bills should be equally divided, and I did not want to insist on doing more (though I hoped he might forget about the petrol). But in the little brown dining-room of an inn, or a café-bar clattering with television and table football, we would have home-made soup and good steak – or the casserole we had smelt cooking when we came in, or fish from a river nearby – and take our time, and drink the local wine moderately – or rather less moderately when we were within a walk of that night's camping place. When we had coffee, Ben would dip a big oblong of sugar into his cup, watching the coffee rise through it, almost to his fingers, until he lifted it and ate it, the moment before it crumbled.

We would come out at last into the last light, and the night would be half-dark, with the moon rising, as we got out our sleeping bags – quite dark, when we camped in a wood.

We crossed the border out of France and into Spain quite early on Monday morning – a blue-grey morning, with clouds blowing off the mountains, and letting the sun into the narrow passes. The sleepy officials in the customs shed let us by easily, and then we drove up high out of the pass, and stopped and walked about and ate biscuits in the sweet, snowy air, before we turned west and downwards towards the town and the sea.

We looked for the others at the railway station, as we had agreed, and then at the dock, and eventually at the small airport as well. Waiting in the car, while Ben collected a timetable and read the board of arrivals at the airport, I began to think about travelling with him alone through Spain for the rest of the summer. It was the kind of chance I had not let myself foresee – and even now, I would not hope for Ben's disappointment. I did not know how disappointed he would be. He returned, undistressed but not triumphant. 'No sign. Useless lot. Let's go and look at the Cathedral.'

'I suppose we could ask at the *Poste Restante*, then we'll have to give them up till tomorrow. It's probably on the main square.'

There was a letter for Ben there, from David, as well as one for me. He opened his, standing on the post office steps.

'Late tomorrow.'

'Something delayed them?'

'Hmm.' He handed me the first page.

'That's all tomorrow for the Cathedral, then,' I said. 'Shall we have some coffee?'

We sat at a café table in the square, and I read the first page of David's letter, and Ben read me parts of the other pages. Tim had let his passport run out and could not get it renewed before Monday (that was today). David and Joanna were waiting for him, but they hoped not to delay us too long, as they had found a cheap flight next day. Tim had not managed to get hold of a car, so there was no need to wait for a ferry.

'Do you think we can all fit into Alan's car, with our gear as well?' the first page ended. 'Marvellous if we could, but of course, not if A. thinks it will break the springs. Only he'd – ' I gave the page back to Ben.

'Tim – honestly!' he said, looking through the other pages. 'Wait a second... "We'll only have what we can carry," – well, obviously – "sleeping-bags... buy a tent if it looks like rain... someone could always hitch-hike." Or go on the roof. They are idiots.'

'I think it should be all right,' I said. 'We always knew Joanna might be coming. Any other news?'

'Not really. Do you think they'd have postcards inside? I ought to send one to my mother.'

'I should think so.'

'As long as you don't mind,' he said, coming back with several cards, 'and you really think the springs'll stand it. Can I borrow your pen?'

I took it out of my pocket, and with it my letter.

'And as long as that's not three more people coming without a car,' Ben said.

I opened it. It was from Douglas.

15ᵗʰ August, '63

Dear Alan,

I hope this will find you; I'm sending another to Pau. I'm never sure how far one can rely on Postes Restantes – or indeed on friends to stick to their itineraries.

I had a letter from Jackling at the Press yesterday. They're putting together a report, for the new Secretary to the Delegates, on work in prospect, with a prediction of costs and so forth, for the next five years. He thinks there's a chance we could get them to agree to a really comprehensive edition, if we put our case now, before everything is settled. Later on, he's afraid they may be in for some economies, and if it hasn't all been agreed before, they might want to argue about some of our 'extras' (i.e. the bibliography, and other basic necessities).

Is there any hope you could get back in time for meetings starting on Friday, 24ᵗʰ August? I know this will be a fearful nuisance, and I ask it most reluctantly, but I'm due to start lecturing at Uppsala on Tuesday 21ˢᵗ (Middle English analogues to the Sagas) and I can't see any way to get out of that, or even postpone it. I know you'll feel as strongly as I do that it's a chance we ought not to miss: to have as much space as we want for the notes, let alone saving the bibliography, appendices, etc. from mutilation.

I'm sending copies of everything I've got this end that might be relevant, direct to the Press. I wish I thought that would be enough to get a sensible decision out of them, without one of us being there to thump the table.

I hope your travels have been good so far, and the weather clement. I really am sorry the timing of all this is so unlucky. Next time it will be your turn to interrupt my idyll.

D.M.R.

Ben was still writing postcards. I sat still and reminded myself that tomorrow, in any case, all the others were arriving – Joanna and Tim and David. I began to work out how soon I should leave, how long the meetings were likely to take, and how much money

I should have left. I put Douglas's letter back in my pocket, and Ben looked up and said, 'Sorry. I won't be long.'

'No hurry,' I said, and then, 'I might look round the square while you finish them off.'

He caught me up on the far side, and we wandered down a side street towards the quays and found ourselves at the side door of the Cathedral.

Inside, it was very dark, and sweet and stuffy with incense. Eight or nine old ladies were following a service at a flickering, golden altar. We walked across behind them quietly, and sat down. Then I felt I could not walk any further for the moment, and studied a bright, mawkish Assumption much longer than it merited.

Ben had gone off into a transept; he came back through the arches, and I said I'd seen enough. As we went out through the main door, I said, 'I'm afraid I'm going to have to go back to England.'

Ben stopped. 'You mean, soon?'

'Yes. Tomorrow or Wednesday.'

'Alan!' He looked at me, and then said, 'Nothing's wrong? Nobody's ill? *You're* not ill?'

'No, I'm not ill. There's nothing wrong.' He was frowning, looking at me dubiously. 'Look.' I gave him Douglas's letter and he began to read it, leaning against a pillar.

'I suppose you absolutely must go?'

'Yes.'

'That's what I thought. God, how sickening. Why couldn't it be three weeks later?'

'I'm really sorry, Ben. I wouldn't do it – I don't want to do it – only it's a great many years' work. And it's very important to Douglas, as well as to me.'

'Don't be silly. Of course you must do it. It's just that it's such a shame. France was great. Oh well – it'll be different with all the others, anyway. It's you it's rough on, cutting into your holiday. Well – David'll be disappointed, too.'

'I thought I'd leave you the car.'

'I didn't mean – not just – . But you can't. How would you get back?'

'I can fly. Have you got that timetable? I ought to be back by Thursday, to get home first and sort out my papers.'

'But you could still make it by car, couldn't you? And change the ferry booking?'

'I thought you'd like to have the car, all of you.'

'Well, obviously, it would be – . But look, you don't have to do that. We'll manage. They said they'd only bring what they could carry.'

'And you?'

'Well, I...'

'You'll manage much more easily with a car.'

'Look, Alan, seriously. It's a lot. I don't want it unless you're really happy about it.'

'I think I'm happy about it, if you're driving. What about the others? Have they got licences?'

Ben was blushing. 'I'm not sure. Tim has. I'm not sure about the other two.'

'Well, I'll leave that to you. Anyone who's got a licence can drive, if you think he's safe and sensible.'

'Or she?'

'Or she. But if anyone drives without a licence, I won't be responsible for anything that happens – and I won't come and fish you out of a Spanish gaol, either.'

'No, of course. Of course not. Alan, it really is... I think it's the most generous thing anyone's... even you.'

He folded the letter, and handed it back to me.

'At least, if you're flying, you can stay a couple more days.'

'That depends on the flights.'

We sat down in the porch of the Cathedral, and studied the airport timetable. There were flights to London on Tuesdays, Thursdays and Saturdays, in the afternoon. Thursdays would be too late.

'In that case,' said Ben, 'I'm going to take you out to dinner.'

We found a place to camp a few miles beyond the airport, among rocks and gorse, near the sea. The wind put the primus out until we lit it in the angle of a rock. We boiled a kettle, and shaved, and made cups of tea with the water that was left. Then we put on proper shirts, clean ones, and ties, and laughed at each other's respectability.

Much later on, full of wine and excellent paella and figs and coffee, we found our camping place again in the windy dark, and groped for places clear of gorse and rock to lay our sleeping bags.

Ben put his hand down on top of mine, and laughed and said, 'Sorry,' and then said, 'Alan, it has been great. And I am grateful,' before he moved his hand away.

CHAPTER 39

The meetings at the Press were long and strenuous. I fought hard for full scope for the whole edition, and spent the evenings gathering and arranging material from Douglas's papers and my own, and working out predictions of the space and time we should need.

But after a preliminary talk with Jackling, and the first, brief committee meeting on Friday, I had to wait until Monday to get down to details with the young man recently put in charge of Middle English texts. I stayed in college rooms and worked looking into a sunny quad, full of wallflowers and almost empty of people, except for the tourists of the afternoon.

There was plenty to be done, and young Robson asked me to dinner on Saturday evening (the college kitchens were closed), but I grudged the extra time fiercely. Perhaps I could not have presented our case so well on Monday if I had waited for Saturday's flight: I should have had scanty time to get down to the cottage, sort out the papers, and arrive by Monday morning. And perhaps in Spain, with five of us, my journey with Ben would have ended in awkwardness and disappointment – even, for me, in loneliness (though I did not think Ben would have allowed that to happen); or at least with a more ordinary, multifarious cheerfulness which would blur the clear, single happiness of our journey in France. Perhaps it was as well to have ended that abruptly and privately, keeping our companionship intact and uninvaded, right up till the last few, uneasy minutes at the airport, when it began to be pulled apart again into two solitudes. All that might be so, but a half-hour's talk and one fifty-minute meeting, half of it occupied with courtesies, had cost me four days with Ben.

By the next Friday afternoon, Brian Robson and I had drafted a complete scheme for each section of the edition, with allowances of time and space worked out in detail and almost meeting my demands. I hoped Douglas would think my few compromises justified, and I hoped even more that my predictions of our needs had been accurate, and that the small margins I had managed to insist on here and there would be wide enough.

The full committee met again on the following Monday. At the weekend, I wrote a long letter to Douglas in Uppsala, and a postcard to Ben at the *Poste Restante* in Madrid. I considered spending the rest of the time on ordinary work on the Cycle, but the draft done, and the cost of doing it, had earned me some indulgence, I thought. Late on Saturday afternoon I went swimming in the river bathing-place, but the water seemed cold and muddy. I saw a Bunuel film at the little arts cinema in the evening, and spent much of Sunday at the Ashmolean museum.

On Monday, when we showed the draft to the committee, they took some time to discuss two of the appendices, and much longer to discuss the notes. Adequate notes would certainly make the book impossibly bulky. Our solution was to put them into a separate volume, which could be used side-by-side with the text; theirs was to have inadequate notes. Brian Robson stood by our draft with me, and we argued together, against his seniors, for most of the afternoon. In the end, our persistence was longer than their patience, and the draft was passed with very little alteration.

I took Brian to have a drink at the Bear, and after some general, celebrating talk, he began to produce his own further ideas for the Cycle: a paperbacked edition for students, and a translation for the general public as well – perhaps even a verse translation. He spoke warily, evidently unsure of my attitude to popular editions of this kind.

'I'd have nothing against either of those. As long as the text is *there*, properly annotated, available to anyone, there's no harm in a popular version. I imagine the students' edition would have to be simplified a good deal, too, wouldn't it? Textual and linguistic apparatus reduced to the minimum; everything put into the glossary, as if it were beyond dispute: that sort of thing?'

'That's about it.'

'I don't know how much good I'd be at verse-translation, though, or Douglas. We'd have to keep to the verse-patterns, or we might as well do it in prose...'

'I suppose so.'

'But some of those stanza forms are fiendishly complicated. And then the way the alliteration is interwoven with the metre and the rhyme... We'd have to see.'

'We could always get one of the university poets in on that, if you liked. They'd love it.'

We both drank slightly more than we meant to, and I told him something of my holiday. He was apologetic, and hoped the interruption had been worthwhile for me. I said it had.

'I was going to ask,' he went on, '– another drink? – I was wondering whether you'd feel inclined to stay on tomorrow and come with me to Jackling about these other ideas – the translation and the paperback. But you must be longing to get back to Spain.'

'Not really,' I said. 'I couldn't get a flight before Wednesday or Thursday, and they'll be starting back by the end of the week. I don't really know where they are by now, anyway.'

'Oh, God. I'm sorry.'

'That's all right. I'd like to stay. I can always see Spain another time.'

CHAPTER 40

I came home with just over a week to go before the car was booked to return on the ferry from Boulogne. Work on the Cycle went forward steadily, though I now kept two extra notebooks to hand, for ideas on translation or commentary in both the popular versions. The weather was grey, and the familiarity of the countryside seemed alternately reassuring and uninviting. I left it unvisited, and spent the afternoons on chores in the house – cleaning, mending, tidying – that were long overdue.

On the day after the crossing, I could not settle to work: three times the telephone rang – always for something trivial – and twice a car turned up the lane, and I had gone out before I knew I had taken a decision, and then had to spend more time helping a misdirected stranger to turn, and discussing prices and weather with the firewood man. There was no housework left to do that afternoon, but I did not want to be away from the telephone long enough for a walk.

Eventually I did some desultory weeding, and scratched up some moss on the path. I did complete the day's work before bed, but the night was hot and restless, and I did not fall asleep for a long time.

In a dream in the morning, I was standing on the tiles beside a pool. A young man with a tray of glasses came along the edge, between me and the water. I told him I wanted to swim. 'Not without a driving licence,' he said. 'I'm afraid we have to insist on a licence.' I could not show him my licence because I was not wearing any clothes. 'Just let me swim far enough to find my jacket,' I said, and tried to dodge round him, but he held the tray high over his head with one hand, and with the other he pushed me away from the water's edge. I fell deep into the earth, struggling, smothering. Then, on the other side, further from the pool, I heard splashing strokes, and the continuous, soft roaring of the sea. I called out very loud, 'Ben, are you there?' and woke myself up in the bedroom, with the hot sun coming through the curtains.

It was nearly ten o'clock, and I had slept through the alarm. I was very hot and shaking slightly, and I could still hear the distant sound of the sea. It stopped, and I heard a car door bang. I jumped up and looked into the garden, and saw Ben coming through the gate, my car in the glare of the sun behind him, and two or three others getting out of it. I pulled on shirt, trousers and sandals, flattened my hair with my hands, and reached the front door as the others caught up with Ben on the doorstep.

Joanna put her arms round my shoulders as I opened the door, and we were all involved in a general embrace of welcome and gratitude.

'You've got here – marvellous,' I said, at the same time as they said, 'Come and have a look, Alan. Come on, come and see.'

David took my arm and Joanna my hand, and I was drawn down the path among them to where the car stood at the gate. It was shining with a flat, white gleam in the sun, and, reaching it, I saw that all the familiar scrapes and hollows and rusted flaws had been evened and painted, under the high, unfamiliar shine. The light sprang off the chrome bumpers in white sprays, the tyres were black and glossy, and the windows were invisible.

'My goodness! It's like a new car.'

'We were working on it all yesterday,' said David.

'I'm sure you were – if not longer. That's a tremendous amount of work. Thank you very much indeed – all of you.'

'You'd been so kind to us,' said Joanna. 'We couldn't give it back to you all dusty.'

'And that's not all,' said Tim, opening the bonnet.

I looked into the engine, and said, 'Aha!'

Ben's hand touched my arm for a moment, and he said, behind me, 'We thought you'd be pleased, specially about the battery terminals.

'The battery terminals are magnificent.'

'We checked it all.'

'Cleaned just about everything you can clean.'

'Tim showed us which bits: he knows about the engine.'

'It was David's idea.'

'It took till after dark till we got it all fixed.'

'Tim was an absolute slave-driver.'

'I think it should run a bit better now,' said Tim, leaning over and tightening something.

'It was great before,' said Joanna.

'Oh great, fantastic. But I think we've got rid of the tapping, and the timing should be better.'

'We didn't know what to bring you,' said David.

'You didn't have to bring me anything.'

'Well, but – '

'And this is tremendous. I didn't expect it at all. I can hardly believe it's the same car.'

'Anyway, in the end we thought – '

'Joanna thought olive oil,' said Ben.

'It's what my mother said to bring back for her.'

'It's terribly good and cheap.'

'And then I found – ' Ben started, and opened a door, and knelt backwards on the back seat in a hot smell of petrol and polish, and brought some parcels up from behind the seat. David took them from him and put them all into my arms. The paper round them was coming unwrapped.

'Good heavens – more glories! Shall I unwrap them here, or shall we go in and make some coffee?'

'Coffee would be great.'

'We got up so early; there was still all the polishing to do, or we'd have been here sooner.'

'We were terrified it would rain.'

We went back along the path, and Ben put the kettle on while the rest of us sat at or on the kitchen table, and I took off the tattered paper with Spanish words printed across it. They had brought me five litres of olive oil in an enormous, rectangular can, and a rug, striped in green and bright blue, and a little wooden guitar.

'Ben said your curtains were blue,' said Joanna, 'so I thought it might go. On the floor, or over a chair, or something. And David said you were a good cook.'

'I know you don't really play the guitar,' said Ben, 'but I thought you'd like it, somehow.'

'I do, very much. And all the other things. If any of you would feel like going down to Mrs Harris for some eggs, later on, we could have omelettes and salad for lunch, and try out the olive oil.'

I keep the guitar on the top shelf of the bookcase. It is a very pretty shape, and I have found out enough about it to play the top line of some early music I found in Cambridge, when there is no-one else to hear me.

Ben's friends went home next day, and he spent the last month of the vacation reading. I did not feel I should give him any reason to make that short time shorter still, but he came once or twice in the afternoon, and helped me pick apples. And his parents asked me to lunch one Sunday, and another day to drive with them all to a bird-sanctuary, some miles away on the coast. We ate a picnic lunch beside the estuary, bargaining mildly about turns with the field-glasses, and watching seabirds plane and swoop with the wind, and flap back against it.

Mark challenged Bridget and her friend – just back from Barcelona – to swim. Ben said it was too cold, and lay back and looked up at the sun, creasing his eyes.

'Have you decided when you're going up yet?' I asked.

'Not exactly, but it might have to be a bit early. I've got to find somewhere to live.'

'But, Ben – good heavens – I thought you'd got somewhere. Somewhere with Tim, ages ago,' said Ruth.

'Yes, well, I had, but that fell through.'

'But will there be anywhere left by this time?' asked James.

'Oh, I should think so.'

'Why leave it so late?'

'It's not really all that late. September's a good time, honestly: everyone's moving.'

'Well, I shouldn't leave it too long,' said James. 'What do you think, Alan?'

'No,' I said, 'I shouldn't leave it too late. Have you got any other possibilities?'

'Jonathan said something at the end of last term. He was going to ask his landlady.'

'What about ringing him up?' asked Ruth.

'All right, *all right*.'

'I mean, it would just be another place to try.'

'Yes. I know. I will.'

There was a silence. Eventually James asked, 'And if you don't find anywhere by the beginning of term?'

Ben rolled over to look away from the sun, into the sandy grass.

'It wouldn't be the end of the world: there's someone's floor I can sleep on. But I'm bound to find somewhere, in the end.'

CHAPTER 41

18th October

Dear Alan,

I'm sorry it's taken me so long to answer your letter. The college thought I was living out, and gave it to the messenger, and he couldn't find me (not surprisingly, as I'm actually borrowing Jim's room in college till he comes back next week – but not officially). So I didn't get it for a bit, and then there have been college exams (not too good), and room-hunting (no good at all), and a silly late-night concert with David and people, and a stack of reading they seem to think I should have done in France, or Spain, or on the milk round, or something.

Anyway, I gave in my essay this morning, so it's a good afternoon for letter-writing.

I'll let you know my address as soon as I've got one; till then I suppose it'd better be college. Perhaps the porter will think I'm a devoted College Man who comes in from my digs for breakfast every morning.

I got to Cambridge very early for the first meeting of the Dictionary Committee: the journey by car was quicker even than I had reckoned. I started while the sun was still red, and there was mist in the lanes, and drove into the town and parked the car just as shops were opening and undergraduates on their way to early lectures.

I had written to Ben, at the new address he had sent a few days ago on a postcard, but I was not sure he would have got the letter yet. I had not had much breakfast; I didn't think he would mind even an unexpected visit. I took my case of papers, and a book to return to the library, and crossed Parker's Piece, then walked through the little, shabby streets of the Kite. The house had a railed front garden, about two yards across, and a red front-door, half-open. The curtains of the ground-floor room, which I thought was Ben's, were still drawn, but the light was on. I went into the hall and knocked.

'Come in.'

In the room, a young man in stocking-feet was winding some paper into a typewriter.

'I'm so sorry. I'm looking for Ben Grayson.'

'I'm afraid he's out. Gone to see his supervisor.'

'Oh, I see. Do you know when he'll be back?'

'He said about an hour.'

'Ah. Well, perhaps I could leave him a note. I'm sorry to have bothered you. Is his room at the back?'

'No, that's the kitchen. This is his room.'

'I see.'

'Leave it on my desk if you like.'

'On your desk?'

'This is my room, too. In fact, it's my room altogether. Ben's staying with me.'

'Good heavens, is there room for you both?'

'There's room for a mattress if we move the armchair.'

'Yes, I see. Well, it's very good of you. I suppose he still hasn't found anywhere for himself?'

'I think you are Alan Pearce.'

'I am, yes.'

'Ben was expecting to hear from you – but by letter, I think, or by letter first.'

'I did write. It can't have reached him.'

'Would you like some coffee?'

'Thank you, I should, very much.'

He put his shoes on, drew back the curtains, and started to make coffee in a percolator.

I looked at the playbills on the walls.

'So Ben has an early supervision?'

'Not a real one. It was just about his college exams.'

'Have you been having exams, too?'

'Not any more, thank God. I'm doing research.'

189

'In history?'

'In English.'

'Really? What's your subject?'

'The Scottish Chaucerians – mainly. Milk? At least, so far it's Scottish Chaucerians only. What I really want to do is a comparison with Beckett, but I've got one of these tremendously conformist supervisors: "Can it be a good idea if Leavis hasn't thought of it?" What do you think?'

He looked up as he poured out the coffee, waiting with a little amusement, I thought, to see if I could steer between conventional disapproval and dishonest approbation.

'I don't know Beckett well enough,' I said. 'It's certainly not the first comparison that would occur to me. Thank you.' He handed me my coffee. 'But if you really think it could be illuminating, I shouldn't let Leavis deter you – or lack of Leavis.'

I meant what I said, but he caught my eye with a sort of humorous acknowledgement, conceding me the point.

'Who's your supervisor?'

'Adrian Camm.'

'I should take his views fairly seriously. He's pretty good.'

'But not infallible?'

'No, I should think he's as fallible as most of us.'

'Good God: Alan!'

Ben had stopped in the doorway.

'All right?' the young man asked him.

'Not very,' he said, coming in and folding some papers and putting them down on the corner of the desk.

'Coffee?'

'Please. Alan, when did you get here?'

'Not long ago.'

'I'm sorry: I didn't know, or I'd have – well, if I could have – .'

'That's all right. I don't think you got my letter. Your friend very kindly let me wait, and gave me coffee.'

'Of course. Sorry. This is Julian Foster. Alan Pearce.'

'Yes,' said Julian. 'And in fact we have met once, I think.'

Ben asked, 'Where?', while I waited to discover.

'In Trumpington Road, once.'

'I don't remember,' said Ben.

'You weren't there.'

'But – you never said.'

'You were otherwise engaged.'

'You were involved with *Richard II*?' I put in.

'He directed it,' said Ben.

'A very interesting production. And your Bolingbroke was excellent.'

'It was fun to do,' said Julian. 'I'm glad you liked it. Though it had its problems. But I'd like to know what you think about the Chaucerians. Have I really got to stay in the fifteenth century all the time? Or stay in Scotland, come to that? The other chair's in the kitchen if you want it, Ben.'

Ben sat down on the floor.

'Well.' I considered it. 'I think you ought to be clear whether you're discussing influence – and that's a subject in itself – or simply making a critical evaluation.'

'*A la* Leavis?'

'In a sense. But in another sense, if that's what you want to do, you need call no man master. You can use any material you like – make any comparison.'

'Anything at all?' Ben asked.

'I'll tell Adrian that. And that it was you who said so.'

'Anything, as long as he can justify it critically. But if you're looking at them as a source of influence, or indeed at their own sources, then you've got to be much more rigorous. Rigorous in a different way, perhaps.'

'More scholarly?' Ben asked.

'You can tell me,' said Julian. 'What were Henryson's sources? Besides the obvious ones.'

We talked about them for some time. He was unusually well informed, and quick to see the significance of the parallels I suggested. Ben sat and listened to us, occasionally asking a question, which Julian left unanswered.

Ben made us some more coffee, and then moved about the small room, collecting books and papers. He knelt by the bed, where Julian was sitting, and felt about underneath it.

'Isn't there an analogy there with Boccaccio? The point you made in your *Chaucer* – Ben, what are you doing?'

'Sorry. I'm looking for *Imperial Spain*. And my wallet. I've got a lecture at eleven.'

'It's not quarter-past ten yet.'

'I want to take some books back first.'

'I'll come with you as far as the University Library,' I said. 'My meeting's at eleven.'

Julian got up and filled my cup again.

'If you've got a moment – it's not a quarter of an hour to the English Faculty from here – I'd love to show you my draft plan. If it wouldn't bore you?'

'I'll go on, then,' said Ben, discovering a book on the mantelpiece. 'What about lunch, Alan?'

'Don't rush, Ben,' said Julian. 'You haven't told us what Ridley said about your exams.'

'Oh, not much,' said Ben, looking round the room. 'It might have been worse. I could meet you outside the University Library, Alan, or... Julian. Don't. Give them to me.'

'"Gamma query plus. Delta." *Delta?*' Julian was unfolding the papers Ben had left on the desk. '"Don't make sweeping statements until you know something about the period... Have you read Elliott? Or Mattingly? Or any of the books on the list?" I thought you said it could have been worse?'

I stood up. Ben took the papers from Julian's hand, looked at me, pushed them into his pocket and pulled them out again.

'You didn't tell me,' said Julian.

'I know I didn't. Anyway, you know now – both of you. I've got to get to the library.'

He put the papers down on the arm of my chair, and went out.

'Oh God,' said Julian after a moment. 'Oh God, poor Ben.'

I said nothing.

'Why didn't he tell me what a mess he was in? He's obviously upset about it.'

'Perhaps that's why.'

'He'd have told you?'

'Only if he'd wanted to.'

'Hm.' He looked at me. 'Even if he'd wanted to – . He minds what his friends think of him – especially anyone he looks up to. You must have noticed that?'

I started to speak, and then stopped. Julian offered me another cup of coffee, and, caught with hope and uneasy curiosity, I accepted and sat down, refolding Ben's exam papers blank-side-out again.

We discussed Julian's draft plan for nearly half an hour and, leaving in a hurry, I left behind the book I had brought to return to the Library.

I waited for Ben on the steps of the University Library. I had been late for the meeting, and had also had to make disingenuous excuses for missing lunch with the rest of the Committee. I was afraid I might be missing discussions, and even decisions, too. But I had not had time or presence of mind to suggest another time for meeting Ben, and I could not think how else to get in touch with him, except by leaving a message in Julian's room.

By thirteen minutes past one, I had decided that he was not coming. Then he came along the path from West Road, rather slowly, and I went down the steps to meet him.

'You did come,' he said. 'I wasn't sure. I – oh, Lord!'

'Where shall we go?'

'There's the coffee shop, or a pub. Or the Italian restaurant, but it's a bit expensive.'

We went to the Italian restaurant, and I ordered plates of pasta and some wine. Then I put the exam-papers down beside Ben's plate.

'You left them behind. I didn't know where to put them away.'

'Oh, Lord. Thank you. Did you look at them?'

'No.'

'Thank God. Well, no. Perhaps you'd better.'

'As you like.'

'Yes.'

I took the papers from him and looked through them fairly quickly.

'Yes. He doesn't spare you.'

'I know. And it was worse this morning. He only kept me about twenty minutes – just sent me away after that. I've never, ever felt so small – such a fool. Almost never.'

'I can see he doesn't suffer fools gladly. But had you been a fool?'

'Yes. But I don't think as much as that.'

'What went wrong?'

'I did do some reading in the vacation. I had read Elliott, and half Mattingly – nearly half. And a few other things. Not as much as I should have, but some. I thought I'd get a beta, about; with nice questions, maybe even a beta plus.'

'But they weren't nice?'

'They were awful. And I'd been up late the night before – it just all went wrong.'

'I see.' The wine came, and I filled Ben's glass.

'I think a good many people make a mess of college exams once in their time. I shouldn't let Ridley – or anyone else – make you feel it's irredeemable. You can catch up on your reading. If you really think you should eat humble pie, you could make Ridley a new set of notes on these questions. Or have you got to re-do them anyway?'

'Not so far.'

'Well, it's worth considering. And then I think you should cheer up. It's not absolutely unknown, skimping your reading, particularly in your first long vacation.'

'Did you, ever?'

'I may not have done it myself, but I have been a tutor, after all.'

He drank some wine, and asked, looking into his glass, 'Were you ever as rough on your pupils as that?'

'Pretty nearly, now and then, I suppose. Perhaps not quite.'

'Would you have been, this time?'

'To you? Not unless I'd thought it was absolutely necessary. As, in fact, I suppose it wasn't, was it? Even a tutor can misjudge how much work a pupil's done, or how thick his skin is.'

'I didn't know what you'd think. Or how I was going to tell you – what I was going to tell you. I thought at least I'd have time to think. And then there you were when I got back. And then Julian told you anyway – '

'I didn't think he should have done that.'

'No. Well. Nor did I. But at least it got it over with – pushed me over the edge.'

'That wasn't his business. It was for you to decide.'

'To jump? Yes. But suppose I hadn't decided?'

'You decided some of it for yourself, just now.'

'I suppose I did, yes. Yes. And decided right.'

'Good. Though it doesn't put Julian in the right. But – here's our lasagne. About time. But, Ben, did you mind – did you really – ?'

He looked up. 'What?'

'Well – I don't know.'

Ben put his fork down.

'Alan, are you sure everything's all right?'

'Yes, I think so. Of course it is. Why?'

'Just – if you start saying you don't know – it's worrying.'

'I see.' He was laughing. 'You abominable boy.'

CHAPTER 42

I dined with Maurice Wakeford and Peter Thorsen from the
Dictionary Committee, and stayed in Thorsen's college. Waking
early, I looked out from my window over the Backs, where
shadowy ducks beside the water were still sleeping, one-legged.
The air was chilly, and there was mist among the bridges. Two
young men in thick, loose, bright clothes came running round
the curve of the far bank, jogging quietly, hardly unsettling
the ducks. The one nearest the water pushed back the hood
of his jacket as he ran, and it was Ben, with his hair in his eyes.
The other young man stopped and crouched to tie a shoelace,
and Ben circled round him, without breaking the rhythm of his
run, and then reached down a hand to pull him to his feet again.
His friend let go just too soon, stumbled, fell back against Ben,
and they pushed apart again, laughing. The sun began to come
over the buildings behind us, and the young men skirted round
opposite sides of a puddle and ran on side by side. At the next
bridge, they turned and ran across, and after a moment another
figure came running the other way, along the far bank and past
my window.

Missing my library book when I unpacked the night before,
I had decided to ask Ben, when I next wrote, to take it back for
me. But I could go round after breakfast, I thought now, and pick
it up before I left. There were one or two things in it that should
perhaps be checked again, and it would not delay me much.

Julian let me in. Ben was kneeling on a mattress in front of the
fire, making toast on a knife:

'Have some breakfast?'

'I'm sorry, I thought you'd have finished. I think I left a book
here.'

'Yes.' Julian took it from beside the bed and put it into my
hand. 'Is it any good?'

'We're late because we both went running', said Ben. 'But there's plenty.'

'Sound rather than exciting. No thanks, Ben, unless you've got some coffee to spare. Yes, I saw you running – my room looked out on the Backs. The two of you – '

'We never met up,' said Ben. He had leaned back on his heels, and he looked straight up at me with a still, anxious, deliberate look.

Julian turned from a cupboard and put down a pile of plates.

'I don't know how you do it, Ben.' He stepped over the mattress and took the knife out of Ben's hand; one side of the bread was smoking and black. 'You really raise incompetence to a fine art. Would you like to make your own, Alan?'

'Sorry,' said Ben. 'I'll open the window.'

'No, thank you. I've had breakfast. My fault for distracting you, Ben.'

'Doesn't leave us much,' Julian said to Ben. 'Three slices, and one's the crust.'

'One'll do me. I don't mind crust.'

'Don't be silly. You said you were starving.'

'Any biscuits left?'

'No. It's after nine. Higgins is open.'

'Higgins is miles.'

Julian handed him some silver.

'I've *got* some money,' said Ben. 'Somewhere.'

'Oh, take that for now. You can pay me back for the ones you burn.'

Ben went out.

'So you saw us both on the Backs this morning?' said Julian, pouring me a cup of coffee and starting another piece of toast. 'I'm surprised you knew us at that distance.'

I leaned against the desk and began to drink the coffee. 'Ben had his hood back. I wouldn't have been sure it was you.'

'Wearing a red tracksuit, like this?'

'Yes.'

His red jacket had the hood pushed back now, and the zip undone as far as the waist.

'And on my own, too?'

'On your own? Yes.'

'It must have been me. Did we miss each other by much?'

'Some minutes.'

'How maddening. Still, at least it's stopped him brooding over his exams.'

'He seemed very cheerful. Until he burnt the toast.'

'He *is* the most – I think he must think incompetence is endearing. So it is, up to a point. What do you think?'

'I think I'd distinguish absent-mindedness from incompetence.'

'He seems to have managed both in his exams.'

'Yes, I'm afraid so. But he can make that good. As long as he hasn't lost too much confidence.'

'If only he wasn't so anxious to please; then it wouldn't hit him so hard when he doesn't make it. He cares far too much what other people think of him. It's asking for trouble.'

'I imagine he cares about the work itself, too?'

Julian buttered his toast, stood up, and went over to the cupboard.

'Would you like a biscuit? There seem to be some after all.'

'Really? Not for me, thank you.'

He came back to the table with a pot of marmalade, and began to spread some of it on the toast.

'The work itself? Well, a bit, I suppose. But I don't believe he cares *that* much about sixteenth century foreign policy. As long as he knew you wouldn't disapprove, for example – '

'There was no need for me to know more about it than he cared to tell me.'

'But he was going to have to stop avoiding that issue, wasn't he? In the end? Meet it head on, and find out just how much he did mind – or how little – what anyone thought?'

'You don't think that's a decision he ought to make for himself?'

'He's young. And he's such an idealiser. It gets between him and reality.'

'And three or four more years give you the competence to disabuse him?'

'Five,' said Julian, and smiled suddenly, and sat down.

'No, you're probably right,' he went on. 'I shouldn't have done it. Ben can't take that sort of thing. Not twice in one morning, anyway. Ridley can be savage enough – my God! Do sit down, won't you? It wasn't fair. I should have left it to him. Please, have the armchair.'

I was still shaking with excitement and antagonism. I sat down.

'I'm very fond of Ben,' Julian went on. 'Is it clear now, do you think? I'll shut the window. He's about the most open, genuine person I know. I just wish he'd rely more on his own judgement. It makes me wild, sometimes. He's got a lot of good qualities: he's bright – and quite industrious, usually; he's not a bad actor; he's got a good deal of charm, and a good heart. Why is he always waiting for someone to tell him he's been a good boy?'

There was a pause. Julian took his plate onto his knee and stretched out his very long legs.

'I don't know whether you could say anything?' he asked, finally. 'He'd listen to you.'

'What do you suggest I should say? Do as I tell you: be more independent?'

'Right!' We both laughed.

'All right,' said Julian. 'Fair enough. But seriously, don't you think there's something one could do – or say – or perhaps not say?'

'That I should say, or not say, for example?'

'Well – I don't know who else could do it. Do it so effectively, anyway.'

'I think you over-estimate my influence.'

'I don't think I do, you know. You should have seen him when he had finally shown you his papers, and the skies hadn't fallen. He was like a child coming out of the dentist's.'

I put down my cup, spilling coffee in the saucer.

Julian looked at me, then got up and fetched another saucer from the cupboard, and changed it for mine. He sat down again and waited.

'You saw him afterwards?' I asked, in the end.

'As soon as he got back.'

'And he told you about it?'

'He told me a good deal.'

'Voluntarily?'

'I hardly needed to twist his arm – except perhaps to stop him talking: he was fairly spilling over with relief. And gratitude.'

'Really? Then I imagine he told you that it was his own decision, this time, to show me the papers.'

'That's what he said. And what he thought, I suppose.'

'It was what happened. I put no pressure on him of any kind. I didn't even suggest it.'

'I can believe you. One doesn't always need pressure to have a tooth out, if the ache's bad enough.'

He got up. Ben was standing at the window, and knocked on the glass. Julian went to let him in. I put my face into my hands for a moment.

Ben came in, carrying a loaf of bread, his cheeks bright with cold. I waited for a moment, and spoke to him; then I said that I must go.

CHAPTER 43

Driving home, I left behind the momentary tranquillity of Ben's presence. My mind could settle nowhere without weighing or rubbing on some sore graze. The conversation with Julian seemed to have made abrasions on every surface of it – and even on the surface of my skin, which burned and tingled as I drove. The morning was half gone, the traffic was thick, and what had I gained by my delay? A fine for the library book – ('Don't forget this, after all,' Julian had said, coming into the hall to give it to me); four minutes of Ben's company, with nothing said and some things unresolved; and a last minute-and-a-half, when he came in, with the cold air, pleased to find me still there – and then I was too much beset by anger and confusion to know how to reply or how to stay.

For that, I had suffered Julian's arrogance, his disingenuous interest in my advice, his patronage of Ben. Beckett, indeed! Ben's good qualities! He certainly relied on Ben's good nature. How could he accuse anyone else of dominating Ben, exploiting his friendship? If indeed theirs could be called a friendship. With nowhere to live, Ben had hardly had a choice, and he would naturally be civil to anyone who gave him houseroom. But to take such advantage of his necessity – to ignore him in conversation, send him off to run errands, expose his private failures and distress, humiliate him before his friends for his own good – to domineer over him entirely as far as I could see – and no doubt a good deal further than I could see... . I pulled out round a bulky van which had blocked my view and sullied my air for several miles. A horn blared in my ear, and a car, coming at speed from behind, filled the side window, very close. I swerved back, just cleared the back of the van, and ran my front wheels sideways across the verge. The hooting from the other car went on, growing fainter. My car hit a gatepost, not very hard, and stopped.

I put on the handbrake, got out of gear, and switched off the engine. My hands were shaking; I put them down on my knees but could not stop them. The car and the van had gone on. Since they had suffered no damage, they had not bothered with further protests.

I was wholly to blame. I had not looked in the mirror before pulling out. If there had been an accident – and I had been luckier than I deserved – it would have been entirely my fault. I held my head in my hands, waiting for the shock and alarm and self-reproach to stop spinning through it. As they began to slow down, I sat up and looked at my watch. Then I opened the door and got out to stretch my legs and relieve myself before driving on. But when I came back to the car, I was still trembling, and the seething of my mind still defied control and concentration. I decided with chagrin that I was not yet in a fit state to drive. I moved the car completely off the road, locked it, and walked through the gate and up a field-track as it began to rain.

I don't know where I went; even if I wanted to, I don't think I could find the way again. I kept my head down, as the rain blew in my face, and saw only the close detail of things by my feet: a wet sack in the hedge, a dead rook with his wings spread out over the tussocks of the headland grass.

As I walked, and the front and shoulders of my coat grew wet, my thoughts began to clear a little. I recalled my state of mind when I started to overtake the van, and realised that it was confusion and anger which had dispelled my usual caution. That was not an excuse, legally or morally, but it was the case. And how far had my anger itself been justified, how far proportionate to its object?

I tried to look back steadily to the conversation in Julian's room. By the additional pain it gave me, like a thorn in the finger, as I approached it, I recognised that my strongest motive for anger was the suspicion that in one of the things he had said, Julian might be right. When Ben had finally brought himself to show me his papers, he had been like a child coming out of the dentist's. I might accuse Julian, with reason, of teasing Ben, bullying him, displaying his weaknesses, testing his submissiveness. But how much more powerful and pervasive was the dominance which needed to exert no pressure, which simply made the tooth ache until it was more tolerable to have it out.

I looked up and found that I was under a tree at the side of a field. I had stood still to grapple with the thought. Had I really acquired, and retained, that sort of dominance over Ben? I had thought he was outgrowing my influence so fast; I had even assumed that by March it would no longer be a bias worth considering. But now he had told me himself, all but explicitly, how much he cared about my good opinion.

How had I brought this about? It had surely been unintentional. I had been waiting for more than a year, after all, for him to reach that equal, un-dependent friendship in which he could justly assess my feelings and his own. It was not in my own interest to keep, still less to increase, my power over him. Was I perhaps incapable of relinquishing such power, even in my own interest? I thought uneasily of our argument about his going up to Cambridge. Or was my desire for his independence unreal – a blind for my conscience, while I consolidated my commanding position? I could not believe this.

I concluded sadly, as I left the tree and went on along the line of the hedge, that my efforts and intentions, however unimpeachable, were not very important. If I exerted too much influence on Ben, it was mostly just by being what I was: older than he, better informed, more confident and decided in my opinions, less flexible, perhaps, in some of them. By being what I was, while being his friend. Should I then stop? Which? Each seemed equally impossible. But human influences, relationships, were always partly dependent on human presence. Could I withdraw the influence by withdrawing my presence? Not entirely, but at least a little – limit the time I spent with him, to give him time and freedom to grow away from his anxious deference.

A part of my mind protested that I spent little enough time with him anyway: a day or two in the term, a week here and there in the vacation, a holiday cut short. But I was still shaken by the irresponsible way I had driven, while I was trying to avoid my present conclusions. In a mood of self-punishment, I determined not to see Ben when I went to Cambridge for the next meeting of the Dictionary Committee.

But those opportunities which I had taken up so joyfully – the committee, the car – that whole pattern of each term's anticipation and delight which they were to make possible: how could I bear to leave them unused, to squander them? There were other reasons for their existence. There were contributions to be made to the Dictionary, and I had calculated that the car would save me three hours on the double journey – three hours would account for a good many lines of the Cycle. I got back to the car, very wet, and drove home in a kind of grey, rigorous calm, no longer concerned to defend myself from Julian's remembered insinuations, concentrating mainly on the traffic, and occasionally on Middle English adjectival forms.

The car had no heater. I was so cold by the time I reached home that I had a glass of whisky and a hot bath before lunch. Lying in the hot water, I let my mind revert to Ben, and to Julian. It would have been easier to dismiss Julian's intrusion if he had been a more negligible person. At first meeting he had been likeable, even delightful: humorous, well-read, very intelligent; even his attitude to Ben could be seen at first as no more than a kind of high-handed and not unfriendly teasing. And Ben liked him, too. I could not really pretend that his friendship was only acquiescence in a practical arrangement, exploited by Julian. 'Friends... he looks up to,' Julian had said. And I had to admit that that claim, at least, was not mere arrogance. Ben did look up to him – was grateful, and perhaps proud, that someone so much older, and of so much ability, had made him a friend, offered him a share of his room. I had thought when he introduced us that, in spite of being startled and preoccupied, Ben was pleased and excited that we should meet – that we should get on well, appreciate each other, discuss our subject – his two knowledgeable, articulate friends. And he had accepted without resentment, though not perhaps without disappointment, his exclusion from our conversation, inadequately mitigated by my efforts.

I could not help a sharp and far-reaching jealousy of anyone who spent every morning and evening, every night, in casual friendliness and at close quarters with Ben. And I did not like the idea that Ben might class us together: look up to us with equal admiration and respect (though perhaps it was not as equal as all that?). But I could not deny that Julian's friendship would have its attractions.

The water from the hot tap began to run cool, and I turned it off. Julian was attractive. Not only in manner and appearance – though he was good-looking, I thought – but in a kind of teasing reserve which invited, how intentionally I did not know, a desire to know more of him: what he was thinking, what he wanted. There was some question, too, some intrigue, even, about another friend of Ben's. Why had he been so anxious that Julian should not know about his running companion on the Backs? I imagined it had been David. Their friendship, I had always felt sure, was not erotic. David's feeling for Julian, on the other hand, had been serious and painful. Had Julian been coming to meet Ben, and had Ben, knowing or suspecting this, steered David over a bridge to avoid him? It would be characteristic of Ben's kindly concern to spare David an encounter which might distress him, or might even revive feelings better left to fade, – especially if Julian was likely to use the encounter (and I would not put it past him) to demonstrate the greater warmth of his feeling for Ben.

I got out of the bath and started drying. That was the centre of the matter, of course: why had I been avoiding it so long? For all he exploited it so arrogantly, Julian was obviously out to secure Ben's friendship. (And his high-handedness might even be part of his strategy. I did not think he did many things by accident.) What were the terms of that friendship to be, in the end? By allowing Ben to sleep on his floor, was he hoping at last to get him into his bed?

I put on dry clothes, and went down to the kitchen and heated some soup. Before I had cleared away my lunch, I had revoked my decision to go to Cambridge without visiting Ben. My friendship might have its dangers for him, but I did not know of any other means to counter-balance a friendship which seemed to me far less predictable and more dangerous. And I should, after all, be on my guard now. I would take particular care to stand clear of Ben's decisions, give no advice, imply no obligations.

CHAPTER 44

12th Nov.

Dear Alan,

    Good. I'll expect you a bit before nine, for breakfast. Bacon and eggs, and porridge if I can manage it. If you have to leave home before half-past seven you'll be ravening, I should think.

    Please note my new address. I'm afraid the parking's pretty bad, but otherwise it's great: two rooms (well, the bedroom's a sort of cupboard, but it is separate), and only one other person using the kitchen, and a nice, odd landlord with four cats; and a view over Christ's Pieces, where yellow leaves, or none, or few do hang at the moment, but it should be lovely in the spring – well, it's lovely now.

    Other good news: David's been advised to go in for a choral scholarship. If he gets it, he'll be richer (a bit), and busier (probably good), and he'll have really succeeded at something. So cross your fingers for him (unless you eschew such superstition?). And Ridley said my last essay was very good, and the one before that 'showed evidence of hard work and hard thinking'. (It took four days reading and two days writing, absolutely solid – apart from lectures – from breakfast to bed, so I'm glad he noticed it!) So I think I really am making up for lost time, now I'm settled in and on my own.

    Julian says to ask you if there is a <u>reliable</u> commentary on the <u>King's Quair</u> (<u>Quare</u>? <u>Quere</u>?). He thinks he's converted his supervisor to his Beckett idea, but now his supervisor has to convert the Board. Meanwhile, he's busy casting <u>Chips with Everything</u> he thinks I ought to audition for it, but I'm not sure; Part I will be looming a bit by next term. Also – did I tell you? – Tim's talked David and me into running for the college (they're short of people). It's a bore in a way, but we aren't taking it very seriously, and it was good while the weather was so lovely.

I'm glad the Cycle is going so well, and work for the Dictionary is fun, and worth all that driving.

Could I give your name as a reference for getting a job in the Post Office before Christmas?

He had the table laid by the fire when I arrived, and there was porridge in a saucepan in the hearth, watched intently and non-committally by a tall, ginger cat. His windows looked across a little, wedge-shaped yard to the cold, stirring branches of the big trees on Christ's Pieces. He fried bacon and eggs in a kitchen down the passage while I had a second bowl of porridge, and when we had finished, we sat on by the fire, talking.

He told me that David had won his choral scholarship, and was, as he had hoped, busy and more self-confident.

'He said he'd love to see you, actually,' Ben said, giving the cat a saucer of milk. 'But I don't know if you'll have time. I said to come in for a drink this evening, on the off-chance. I didn't think you'd want company at breakfast.'

He asked about the plans for the Dictionary, and I showed him some of the first entries I had been working on. I had brought a fair draft of one of the Cycle plays for him to see, too, with a mediaeval view of the Roman army which I thought would amuse him: jousting in tournaments, and sacrificing to Mohammed. He told me that he had decided not to audition for the play Julian was directing.

'Though it is a terrific play.'

'What did you say it was called?'

'*Chips with Everything*. Wesker.'

'Wesker. What else has he written?'

'Oh, *Roots, Chicken Soup with Barley* – and he's started Centre 42, and all that. You know.'

'I don't know more than his name, I'm afraid, and that only in reviews.'

'He's not all that well-known, then?'

'I think he probably is, but I'm shamefully badly read in recent plays.'

'"I could show you ignorance," said the Red Queen. But it's great, Alan. You really ought to read him.'

He stood up and took two thin Penguin books down from a shelf, and gave them to me.

'May I borrow these?'

'Of course.'

'Do you want to put your name in them?'

'Will you forget they're mine?'

'Probably not, but it's a good habit.'

'I think it's in already, actually.'

The first book had an inscription on the flyleaf:

'Ben. "Words do mean a number of things." I.viii.'

'That's the one I didn't audition for.'

'What made you decide against it?'

'Well, a number of things, I suppose. Time mostly. I've still got an awful lot of reading to do. And I'm not sure it's really my sort of thing, anyway.'

'The play?'

'No, the play's terrific. But everything gets so frantic – I just didn't feel I wanted to be in it all again.'

'Is David in it?'

'Too busy singing. And that's probably good, too.'

I put my cup down in the hearth. Ben picked it up, and held it out of reach of the cat, who had begun to stretch enquiringly towards it. I nodded, and while he refilled the cup, I said,

'Ben... your decision not to act: it wasn't anything to do with me, was it?'

He looked at the fire for a minute or two. 'No, I don't think so.'

After another pause, he asked, 'Why? Do you think I was wrong?'

'No, I don't. I'm glad you're working so seriously. Well, obviously, I can't help being prejudiced in that direction. Besides, when you've got a good mind, and an unrepeatable opportunity, it would – . Well, anyway. But I don't want to run your life for you. You must run it for yourself.'

'You don't.'

With an effort, I asked, 'Even indirectly? It is a danger, sometimes, if one's older – . Not on purpose, necessarily, or even

208

consciously. Just by expecting things, or approving, or not approving. Particularly if one does mind – with anyone one's – whose welfare one cares about.'

Ben smiled. 'I shouldn't worry, really, Alan. Nobody could know you for ten years without beginning to get the idea that people ought to think for themselves.'

The cat jumped up heavily and settled on my knee. I stroked her, and she purred delightedly. I was extraordinarily pleased. I had never before known so clearly – perhaps I had never known at all – that greatest and most proper satisfaction of a teacher: to see a hopeful pupil finally fledged, taking off. That he should acknowledge my part in his fledging, even as he left it behind, was a bonus beyond reasonable expectation.

'Did you ever get as far as Plato?' I asked eventually.

'Well – Plato-told-to-the-children: little bits, with a vocabulary at the back; bowdlerised, probably.'

'Do you remember where Socrates says that his followers never learned anything from him? That wisdom is the child of each man's own soul? "Τῆς μεντοι μαιεαις ὁ Θεός τε καὶ ἐγω..." I can't quote it exactly.'

'No – well – that's why I can't understand it exactly, of course!'

I laughed. 'All right. It means that he was only a midwife, helping individual souls with the birth of their own wisdom: "But the god and I are responsible for their delivery."'

'Only the midwife. And yet he spent his whole life teaching them.'

'And lost it.'

'Yes. Still, it's not so little – it's more than most people manage – to deliver wisdom.'

'Yes. It ought to be enough – more than enough.'

'And is it?'

'Is it? Would it be? I don't know. I hope so.'

We were silent. The cat twitched her ears and turned to watch the door.

'Graham's coming up,' said Ben. 'She always knows.'

She extended her forelegs and then her chest over my knee and down towards the floor, hesitated, and then contracted again as her back legs followed.

'She's going to need a midwife soon,' said Ben, as she walked to the door, and I saw that her stomach was rounded.

'She should have handsome kittens,' I said.

She moved to one side as someone knocked. Ben called, 'Come in', and the door opened, just clearing the cat where she stood.

'Ben. Am I intruding?'

'Not at all. Come and meet Alan.'

His landlord came in and stooped to pick up the cat as she shoved against his legs and purred. He transferred her to the other arm and shook hands with me. 'Graham Roskoff.'

'Alan Pearce,' I said.

'Yes. I know your work. And I've heard a good deal about you from Ben. Ben, do you think you could open your window? It's the quickest way down for Jocasta.'

'She's Jocasta, is she?'

'They've all got Greek names,' said Ben, straining to open a little window above his head. 'Orestes, Antigone. There.'

'All from Sophocles?'

'All from Sophocles'; the landlord was letting the cat climb to his shoulder. 'The fourth is Tiresias.'

'He's blind?'

'Blind, but cleverer than all of them – than all of us. "So were I equalled with him in renown..." Well. So you're Ben's greatest friend. Don't worry, Ben. You can shut it now; she'll go down the other way. There is something Sophoclean about cats.'

'I still think it was a bit rash to call her Jocasta,' said Ben. 'Bound to put ideas into her head.'

'I don't think there was much danger of that. The ideas were certainly there already. I must ask you, Ben, may the plumber come to repair the hot water pipe in here this afternoon? Will he be disturbing you?'

It was time for me to go. I finished my cup of coffee as I stood, shook hands again with Roskoff, and found then that I had taken

Ben's hand, contrary to our usual custom, to say goodbye. I thanked him for breakfast, and he brought his two hands together, keeping mine between them.

'Come for a drink this evening if you can. But come soon again, anyway.'

CHAPTER 45

1ˢᵗ Dec.

...David can get tickets, and if you would like to come, do you think you'd be able to give Marky a lift? He's been longing to hear it for ages. But only if you'd like to come anyway. It wouldn't kill him to take a bus...

I had thought it impossible to be a great deal happier than I was on my second drive back from Cambridge. The decision to revoke my self-denying ordinance, and visit Ben after all, had been justified several times over by the event (if events can justify decisions). Our old, companionable ease had returned, undoing the uneasiness and irritation of the earlier visit. He had denied, strongly and thoughtfully enough to convince me, that I had too much influence over his decisions, and denied it with such cheerful and affectionate certainty that I carried the words with me to touch and turn over in my mind like a talisman. He had taken my hand between both of his when we said goodbye, and though this could have been from kindly familiarity or hospitable impulse, Roskoff had suggested, vaguely and believably, that it could have been from something more. He knew me as Ben's greatest friend, and I did not know who could have given him that impression, except Ben.

There had hardly been time to go back that evening for a drink. The committee had ended late, and besides, I think I wanted to rejoice alone, to garner up such happiness entire, before it should be attenuated with sociable pleasure – to harvest present bounty with undivided attention, though without, as far as I can remember, any conscious provision for a bleaker season.

Now all this happiness was set humming and stirring by expectancy, and was drawing into itself the minor joys of the sharp, winter-evening mist, the moving circle of yellow, winter grass in the headlights, and Mark – young and excited, half awkward and half boldly affable – in the front seat beside me. His voice was breaking, his youth just beginning to show through his childhood, and I could feel the first, irregular tugging, now and then, of the attractive force he would have in three or four years' time, as a young man. I could recognise this now, privately but clearly, and even accept it as an ingredient in my present happiness, without trying to misunderstand it for the sake of my *amour propre,* or indeed of my loyalty to Ben. There is a long and evident distance, for me, between mild sexual attraction and the inclination of the emotions, and still longer one between such attraction and its verbal or physical expression. For those for whom these states are closer together, or even indivisible – a large number and, in conventional notion, a majority of men – I can feel concern, or occasionally envy, but no real, direct sympathy, and consequently, perhaps, less right to make judgements.

We found somewhere to park in Grange Road – Mark calling enthusiastically, and signalling with a torch, to guide me into the short space – and walked to David's lodgings where we were to meet and collect our tickets. Ben was not there, but David welcomed us warmly, jumping up to take our coats, and offering us sherry and madeira and salted nuts.

Our tickets were on a table by the fire, in an envelope labelled *'Carol Concert: Ben, Alan Pearce, Mark G.'*

I thanked him and took it to put in my wallet.

'How much do I owe you?'

'Nothing.'

'Are you sure?' I moved a ticket half out of the envelope. '10/-' was printed at the bottom.

'Choral scholar's perks. Which reminds me, Marky: do you want to come and sit in the organ-loft? There's room for a couple of people up there besides the semi-chorus.'

'Will they let me?'

'There's no-one much to stop you, once you're inside. And at the door – who's to know you're not one of the tenors? We could find you a surplice ...'

Mark drank some sherry, looking down into his glass, pleased. David glanced at me as he picked up the bowl of nuts, and we smiled separately.

'As long as I don't have to join in,' said Mark. 'I mean, really be one of the tenors. My voice is a bit dicey at the moment, and anyway – . I could just open and shut my mouth?'

David laughed. 'Don't worry: you won't really be with us. The seats are to one side. But you do get a fantastic view over the chapel – the lights and everything. There's quite a lot for everyone to sing, anyway: you can – . Ben? Come in.'

He came through the door in his overcoat, breathing quickly from the cold.

'Sherry or madeira?'

'Lovely. Alan, how are you? Hello, Marky.'

'Yes, but which?'

'Which? Oh, yes. Well – .'

'Bridgie said to give you this,' Mark said.

'Bridgie? Is it – ?'

'Read it.'

Ben pulled off a glove and slit the top of the envelope raggedly with his finger. He read seriously, and we waited, Mark expectantly.

'God, that's marvellous! Good for her! Terrific!' He said to me, 'Bridgie's got an exhibition to Oxford.'

'Really? That's magnificent.'

'When did you hear at home?'

'Only this morning. The telegram came at breakfast.'

'Wow! Mum and Dad very pleased?'

'Bursting with it. But Bridgie said not to tell anyone else till she'd told you.'

Ben smiled at the letter.

'You'd make a good poker player,' I said to Mark. 'I'd never have guessed.'

'We ought to drink to her health,' said David. 'And I'll mix it half-and-half, Ben, if you don't tell me which you want.'

We drank to Bridget's award, and I looked at Ben as he set down his glass and unbuttoned his coat. His pleasure was real and generous, and not less admirable, I thought, for a strand of pain at being so far outdone in his own achievement (though perhaps the pain was partly my own).

I asked, 'To read French and German?'

'French and Spanish,' said Mark.

'Ah. Not quite so common.'

Ben looked across at me, and David refilled our glasses.

'Drink up, Ben. You've only got ten minutes to catch us up.'

Following Mark out, soon afterwards, into the cold little hall, putting on my coat, I looked back to see Ben waiting while David turned out the fire, and then, as he stood up, handing him a note.

It was very cold going up Burrell's walk, and colder crossing the Backs in the icy damp of the wind. The path was not wide enough for four: David walked ahead with Mark, teaching him the tenor line of one of the carols; Ben and I followed, and I tried to repay him for my ticket, but he said he had paid David only for himself and Mark. We caught up the other two as we came within sight of the college.

'There,' said Ben, 'I knew we'd be early.'

A thick, stationary line of people reached along the pavement in front of us, all the way to the college lodge, and, presumably, beyond it into the chapel court. The porter was turning away people without tickets.

'Sorry, sir: not a chance. All sold out since Tuesday. Not a chance, I'm sorry, miss.'

'Good heavens, David,' I said. 'Are you eclipsing King's?'

He laughed, disclaimingly and with pleasure. 'Not yet.'

'In a few years' time, though,' said Ben.

'Well, as long as Howard's still here.'

'He's your director of music?'

'And conductor,' said David. 'He's fantastic. It's all him, really – all his doing.'

'I didn't know you were coming to this, Alan.' Julian Foster had stopped beside us on his way along the road to the back of the queue. His coat-collar was turned up, and his hands were in his pockets. 'Ben. David. Hello.'

'This is my brother, Marky,' said Ben.

'Mark,' said Mark, *sotto voce*.

215

'Mark,' said Julian, and smiled. 'Have you been before, Alan?'

'No. I gather it's going to be extremely good.'

'David should know. I've only heard the first part.'

'The Mediaeval things? Did you?' asked David.

'In rehearsal once.'

'I didn't see you.'

'Probably not. I was at the back. Howard wanted some advice on the words.'

David looked amused. 'Did he take it?'

'Of course not. But a musician who notices that there are words at all deserves encouragement. Do you sing too, Mark?'

'He's singing tonight, anyway,' said David. 'In fact, if we're to get up to the organ-loft, Mark, I think we ought to be pushing on. OK, Ben? See you both afterwards – by the side-gate's best, probably.'

Sitting with Ben in the warmth and half-darkness of the chapel, I could make out the semi-chorus, or some of them, standing along the front of the gallery, against the small light of the organ. After some time, more light began to grow from the door, then concentrated just beyond the screen, and came through it, under the arch, in numerous candle-flames. The main choir went up the aisle to the chancel, carrying their candles, as an unaccompanied voice from the gallery began the first carol.

The words were the first shepherd's greeting from the Townley Plays:

> 'Hail, comly and clene,
> Hail, yong child!'

It was the best version (England and Pollard) and set to music which I judged to be more or less contemporary with the words.

A second singer began the next shepherd's words, and Ben looked up, glanced at me, and nodded: it was David's voice.

> 'Hail, suffern Savioure
> For thou hast us soght!
> Hail, frely foyde and floure,
> That all thing has wroght!'

He sang very well indeed: the proper mediaeval restraint and impersonality, clear as glass, over the present gentleness and the suffering foreseen.

At the end of the third shepherd's greeting, when the main choir were in their places and light spread round the chapel, all the other voices from both parts of the choir came in, in a final canon:

> 'Lo! he merys,
> Lo! he laghes, my sweting.
> A wel fare meting!'

We knelt for the Bidding Prayer, and I looked at Ben's head, to the right, by my arm: his forehead weighing on the back of his hand, his neck bent, unmoving. Was he, like me, kneeling for decency only, for a conforming courtesy to the traditions from which, at the moment, we were profiting? Or could he be feeling more than that? Could there be anything in his state of mind which corresponded more closely with the stillness, the abandonment of private intention, the fealty of his body?

I hardly imagined that he was praying with entire conviction for Philip, Duke of Edinburgh and all the royal family. Even conventional, practising Christians might surely find that difficult, and I knew that he was not a practising Christian. But was he, all the same, directing his thoughts along some line which converged, however distantly, with the line of traditional belief – the belief which ran back from this service to the *Luda Pastorum*, and back again as far as the Bethlehem legend? He, too, had been moved by David's singing, I had seen. Was he now inclining, or trying, to locate that vulnerable love, that heroic acceptance and transmutation of suffering, in a separate, objective, originating existence? And to give that existence his allegiance?

I thought of it with some incredulity, but also with curiosity, with a kind of envy, and then to my surprise with an almost intolerable access of love. As we rose and stood for the next carol, I did not know how to look at him, for fear my feeling must blaze unconcealably in my face. But he turned to me with such a direct sympathy of delight that I could safely reciprocate his look, the precise nature of my emotion, as perhaps of some part of his, obscured by the other causes of delight around us.

And indeed, by the end of the service the two layers were no longer altogether distinct: the lesser, external joys afforded, besides their own considerable worth, something more than a cover for the brilliant, dangerous, inward glory – more even than the embroidery, on that cover, of the ancient decorations of Christmas. Each layer seemed to have penetrated the other, so that Isaiah and St. John, candle-flames and Tierce de Picardie, the dew in April and the herald angels were informed by my love, and became its outward shape, while that love seemed to concentrate all the wide splendours of the Divine Charity, imagined or apprehended, which we were celebrating, and, like a magnifying glass, to bring the distant and unattainable light into one immediate, burning point.

Coming out of the chapel with Ben, meeting Mark and David at the college side-gate, making our way through the emerging, indecisive crowd, I felt dazed and disinclined to speak, and then very cold. We turned together into the sleety, stinging rain. Mark was excited and voluble, carrying his surplice over his shoulder like a trophy. David was walking behind, and I dropped back to join him and to tell him how much I had enjoyed the service, and his singing especially. He received my inexpert praise with a pleasure which touched and surprised me, and made it difficult to know what to say next.

Ben and Mark were waiting for us, stamping their feet, at the turn into Grange Road.

'Someone's left his lights on,' said Mark, with censorious concern.

'Only sidelights,' said David, as we came nearer.

'It's not you, is it, Alan?' asked Ben.

'I hope not.'

'It is. It's us,' Mark called back triumphantly from where he had run ahead. 'If it won't start, we'll have to stay the night.'

'And where do you think you're going to stay?' asked Ben.

'I don't think we need despair of starting.'

'On your sofa. Couldn't I? I haven't seen your room yet.'

'On my floor, you mean, if there are three of us.'

'I'd have room for one of you,' said David.

'It's only been a couple of hours,' I said. 'It may be all right.'

But surely I might hope for a mistake so genuine to turn out luckily?

Sitting in the cold driver's seat, I switched off the sidelights and turned the ignition key. The engine rattled and died. I pulled the choke out and tried again: this time the rattle was weaker. David stooped to the window, and I wound it down.

'No good?'

'Not so far. Should I try without revving up at all, do you think?'

'It might work. But it's probably the cold as well.'

I took my foot off the accelerator, and turned the key once more, producing only a momentary rasp and scrape. David shook his head.

After a moment, I asked, 'There's nowhere open, I suppose, at this time of night – nowhere I could get it recharged?'

'Not that I can think of.'

He stood up and turned to Ben with the question.

'Then we'll *have* to stay,' I heard Mark say.

Ben looked in through the window. 'How urgent is it for you to get back?'

'Not very. Not at all, really, for me. I am sorry to have been so stupid. But what about Mark?'

'He's dying to stay.'

I smiled. 'Well – . We'd have to let your parents know.'

'Of course. Sure. And you could get it fixed first thing tomorrow morning. David thinks there are lots of places open by eight. What?' He turned half-away. 'Well, it is nearer. Yes, I know you do, Marky. I think it's for him to say.'

He turned back to me. 'David can put one of you up, and I've got room for the other. I don't know which would be easier for you?'

I took out the key and sat quite still for a moment. Then I got out of the car and looked at the three of them standing in the cold. The rain had stopped. Mark said, 'It's –,' glanced at Ben, and stopped.

'Well, Ben,' I decided to say, 'which way round is it to be?'
I looked towards him, and then past him. David's face was just
beyond his shoulder, raw with cold and with something else
as well. In the moment before he looked down, I thought it was a
kind of expectancy – an anxious, undefended hope – and I thought
it was directed at me. Was there something that my decision could
provide? Some advice or help? A chance to talk alone?

I found that I was leaning against the bonnet of the car.

'I imagine there would be a garage nearer you, David,
wouldn't there?'

'Yes. Yes, there would.'

'And it wouldn't be a nuisance? You've really got room?'

'Masses of room. I've even got clean sheets.' He spoke with a
kind of hilarity, and we all laughed.

'The sofa's pretty short,' Ben said to him. 'Where'll you go?'

'Oh, Mrs Slater'll have a mattress; she may even have a camp-
bed. Anyway, I don't mind the floor.'

'That's more than Ben would say,' said Julian. He came across
the road to join us, from the dark of the pavement opposite.

'More than I'd say?' asked Ben, turning.

'You're not often over this side,' said David.

'I never minded a mattress on the floor,' Ben said.

'You weren't too keen on the floor without the mattress,
I remember,' said Julian.

'Well – '

'Anyway, I've still got the mattress, if it would be useful.'

'But the car won't go,' said Mark. 'The battery's flat.'

'So I gather. But the mattress is quite portable.'

'I'll be all right,' said David. 'Honestly. Thanks all the same.
It'd be a long way to bring it at this time of night.'

Julian did not reply.

'I didn't know you ever came this far out – out in the wilds,'
David said.

'They have lectures here now and then – English, History –
they might interest you.'

'Come on,' said Ben. 'He goes to far more lectures than me.'

'I can believe it.'

220

'I'm cold,' said Mark.

'So am I,' said Julian. 'Why don't you all come back and have some rum? I've just been given a bottle. That'll keep the cold out. Then we can think about moving the mattress. If it's too much for David, I might be able to run you back in Piers's car.'

'It's really quite late,' said David, 'and it's raining.'

'It stopped ten minutes ago.'

'Great,' said Mark.

'You like rum, do you?' asked Julian.

'Well, I'm not sure I've...'

'So it has; it's stopped,' said David. 'Now there are so many of us, I wonder if we could try pushing.'

'Alan left the lights on,' Mark said to Julian.

'And you didn't notice them either,' said David.

I turned to open the door again. The original honesty of my intentions about the car – grown weaker with my recent, stronger hope – was beginning to fluctuate disconcertingly.

'You're the lightest, Marky,' said Ben, behind me. 'Hop in and steer.'

I stood aside to let him in, and saw a glance of enquiry go from Ben to David, answered by one which despaired of explanation, or at least postponed it. I opened the window by the driver's seat and Mark, at my suggestion, put the clutch down, got into gear, and let off the handbrake.

David opened the other front window and called, 'Are you ready? Push!' Mark switched on, and the car began to move very slowly down the road.

'Clutch up – slowly,' said David.

'Left-hand pedal up,' I added.

'Yes, I know, but – ' He looked down for it, and the car swung out towards me. I put my hand through the window and turned the wheel the other way: the car touched the kerb and stopped.

'Damn,' said David.

'Sorry,' said Mark and I together.

'It's OK. You're doing fine. Check you know which the clutch is, Mark, and we'll try again.'

David and I put our shoulders against the inside of the window-frames; Julian and Ben bent again to push from behind; and I turned the wheel outwards.

'All ready?' asked David. 'One, two, three: push! And again: *Push*! Come on, Julian; are you pushing or pulling? One, two, three: push!'

The car moved, straightened, and moved faster. Mark let up the clutch, and the engine fired fitfully, then roared more steadily. We were almost having to run. Mark got out of gear, following David's instructions, and began to brake.

'All right?' I called to David across the roof, as we slowed to a halt.

'Right.'

The engine was roaring securely. I looked through the window. 'Keep your foot on the accelerator, Mark, and move over all you can.'

He shifted and leaned to the left. I opened the door and scrambled in, sitting almost on top of him, reaching to take over the pedal and the steering-wheel. As I got into gear, Ben came to the window.

'Keep the engine going,' shouted David. 'Don't let it – Hey! Let go or he'll drag you.'

We checked, then went on, gathering speed. I looked in the mirror but could see only streetlights, and two or three long shadows against them.

CHAPTER 46

The week leading up to Christmas was punctuated by the post. The cottage was on Ben's postman's round. He could not often stay long, but I would have the coffee hot, before I went out of the door to take the little handful of envelopes from his hand. Once or twice he stopped for a mugful, drunk in the hall, and once he stayed a few minutes longer, looking for the receipt-form for a registered parcel of notes from Douglas.

He brought me an invitation from his family for Christmas Day, and we agreed to drive over together when he had finished his round. He would make the cottage his last stop. I usually forgot the post on Christmas morning.

He came earlier than I had liked to hope, when his family, he said, would scarcely be out of church. I gave him a glass of Marsala and, after some hesitation, my present for him, to open now, between us, rather than in the general exchange of goodwill and exclamation in the afternoon.

Standing with the parcel in his hand, he said, 'Actually I've got yours, too, somewhere,' and went out to the van; and I knew that he had followed the same line of indecision as myself.

I had found him an early translation of *Don Quixote* (Lockhart's edition of *Motteux*), and I dallied with the string and sticky tape on my parcel until he had opened his, thriftily keeping separate two occasions of delight. His present to me was a little hand-coloured engraving (early nineteenth century, I think, though Douglas thinks it may be a copy) of the Abbey at Jumièges in the early morning. Two small figures in trousers and blue, swallow-tail coats are crossing the foreground, preceded by their long shadows.

When I thanked him, and wondered how he had managed to buy it without my knowledge, he laughed and reminded me of my impatience (well concealed, I had supposed) at the time he took to buy lunch at Caudebec.

'The shop didn't open till half-past nine. I thought I'd never play out time without you suspecting something. But I knew I ought to get it for you, with the right time of day and everything. And us there in front.'

I turned it, and saw that he had written on the back, 'Alan. Remembering our time in France, and one morning especially. (And a Happy Christmas, too.) Much love, Ben.'

He was pleased with the Cervantes: he had thought of Don Quixote, he said, as they drove in the empty, red plains in the middle of Spain – thought of him, and wished he knew more of him, and often wondered how much, besides the landscape, their travels had in common.

30.i.1964

My dear Ben,

Thank you for your postcard. Of course you mustn't take time writing letters when you need it for work. Having a deadline so much less exact and more distant than yours – (the Cycle is going well, thank you: we seem likely to finish the text by the beginning of the summer, which is oddly difficult to imagine) – I can probably find time to write about as often as before. But I don't want to do this if it makes you feel obliged to write back – particularly to write back at equal length. I found recently a civil-war historian asking a friend to send him a few lines, 'to tell me that you are alive, and that in this dismall time of mutation you are soe farr from change that you continue ever the same to me'. A postcard of that kind is very welcome, particularly any as handsome as this view of your Old Court. But whenever it begins to be a burden, (and even the smallest grasshopper very easily becomes a burden before exams), you mustn't hesitate to drop that, too.

My next Committee meeting is to be tomorrow week (Thursday). I'd like to have breakfast with you again, as you suggest, but I may not be able to leave home in time, unless the electricians arrive very promptly. (I'm not having anything else radical done to the cottage: only a certain amount of 'making good' after the wiring; and some repairs to the little shed at the back.) May I leave it that I'll come if I can, and that you won't make any special preparations? Would you, in any case, be free for dinner that evening? If I don't hear from you, perhaps I might look in a little before 7? But don't change any plans: just leave me a note if you're busy elsewhere...

9th Feb.

Dear Alan,

I've got both essays done ahead of time (extraordinary feeling!) and I definitely need an hour or two off before I start making notes on Pitt's foreign policy. So there's no reason I shouldn't write a proper letter, for once – and, of course, an extra reason why I should. Thank you for the delicious dinner last Thursday. I haven't really been living on sardines eaten out of the tin, but college food does get fairly dreary, and there aren't many alternatives that are quick and easy (on one gas-ring, anyway). All that super food and wine (and food in wine – at last I know what a daube is) really made me feel 'Fate cannot harm me: I have dined this term.'

It was lovely to see you and have time to talk properly. I must say the waiters were very patient and polite – elsewhere, they start meaningly stacking chairs on tables all round you. But there were still things I wanted to go on talking about when we had to go (I hope you didn't have to climb into College?). For instance – but I think I'll have to wait till we meet, if I'm to get Pitt even started this evening. It is great, though, that the Press are being so encouraging (– and so open-handed! But didn't dinner make an enormous hole in your windfall? My turn to stand you a meal next time).

It looks as if I shall be here when you come in March, but only just. There's a reading party at Ridley's house (or barn or something) in Wales, and David and I thought it might be a good way to get some work done. It's straight after the end of term, till Easter, so I won't want a lift home after all, though thank you for thinking of it. If you did by any chance have room for a suitcase

225

and/or a few books in the back of your car, it would be marvellous, but not if it would be a bore.

And the Saturday after I get back is my twenty-first party. You will come, won't you? There will be lots of friends – Cambridge and local – and a buffet supper (my mother says she's started being extra nice to anyone she knows with a freezer!), and we're going to dance in the big packing shed. David thinks a friend of his may be able to bring a steel-band, or if not, there'll be records. Dad and Marky are fixing up lights. Actually, I can't remember if you like dancing, but it doesn't really matter. Please come anyway, or how will you ever know I've really come of age at all? – let alone reached years of discretion! 8 o'clock. Black tie (if you like). R.S.V.P.

Much love, Ben

The drive back from Cambridge at the end of term was happy, all the same. The hawthorn was coming out in the hedges, and part of Ben's work and many of his things were in the back of the car.

Having avoided it a little awkwardly on my last visit, I had had to dine with Maurice Wakeford after the Committee meeting. But in the morning, I had driven round to collect Ben's things before eight o'clock, and a fellow lodger, taking in milk bottles, let me through the front door. I found Ben asleep, or rather he came to open his door to me some moments after I had knocked, not dressed, his hair disordered, and his eyes blinking against the morning light.

'Sorry. Sorry. I meant to wake up half an hour ago.'

I could see, through the other door across the room, the top sheet and blankets pushed back in haste to the foot of the bed.

'I'm a little early. I'm sorry I woke you. There's no great hurry.'

'Are you sure? Is the car OK? I don't think anyone will come round this early.'

His pyjamas, still warm with the undispersed warmth of his sleep, were open most of the way to his waist, and below. He looked down and laughed, and pulled them together, tucking the jacket into the trousers, as most of the buttons were missing.

'Sorry.'

I shook my head.

'Have some coffee and I'll get dressed. I won't be five minutes. Then we can load.'

'Won't you need some breakfast?'

'I can have it later.'

'No, no. There's time enough for that. I'll put the kettle on.'

In the kitchen at the far end of the passage, I found mugs and knives in the sink, and washed them. I made two mugs of coffee when the kettle boiled, and found bread and butter, and went back to Ben's room. He was in shirt and trousers and bare feet, lighting the fire with one hand while he brushed his hair. Sun came into the room from Christ's Pieces. I cut two slices of bread and started to toast them. Ben took one of the knives from my hand and crouched on his heels beside me.

'I hope you're better at this than me,' he said.

'Last time, I was to blame, I think.'

He turned, and understanding of something, at least, more than we had said, travelled along his look to mine, and back again. I put my hand over his and moved it away from the fire as one edge of his slice began to smoke. He laughed and exclaimed, then reached his far hand across to me as my slice flared suddenly, lost his balance and fell against my side, his head on my shoulder. I kept still, and felt his laughter shaking through me. I was laughing too, quite enough to account for my immobility.

Then I took my hand from his, put my arm along his shoulders, and righted him.

'I'm sorry,' I said. 'Perhaps we'd better have bread.'

He shook his head, still laughing. 'I started it. And you saved my bit anyway. Why don't you do them both on your own? We're obviously past praying for together. I'll lay the table. Oh God, you didn't do the washing up, did you?'

The sense of physical closeness remained with us while we had breakfast: the feeling of boundaries no longer defended, of dignity and privacy both caught off their guard – outflanked by intimacy and absurdity. Going up and down, loading the car with Ben's possessions, we felt no need to avoid each other in the doorways or on the narrow stairs. We brushed sides and shoulders, and laughed, and straightened each other's toppling piles of books.

'Are you sure you'll be able to see out?' he asked at last, shutting the tail-gate.

'Are you sure you'll have anything left to read in Wales? Or to wear?'

'I must say, I can't quite think what.'

'You'll have to send me a postcard when you need a clean shirt.'

'If you could ever find it in all this. I thought – I really did think – there was only going to be a suitcase and a few books.'

'I didn't,' I said, and we started to laugh again. Then I moved to put my hands on Ben's arms, just as he moved to do the same to me.

'Well,' I said, 'have a good time in Wales. Good reading and good walking. Thank you for breakfast.'

'Thank you for making it. And for taking my stuff, even more. See you when I get back. And don't bother to take it round specially. Leave it till you're going anyway.'

'Enjoy yourself.'

I opened my hands, but Ben tightened his and lowered his head, as if to rub it against my shoulder. Then he pushed himself back and upright, letting go.

'I'll see you then. Safe home.'

'Goodbye.'

CHAPTER 47

Driving in and out of the shadows of clouds and hedges, feeling warm beyond the capacity of the March sun, I thought about Ben's birthday. It was in ten days' time, at the end of the coming week. Full, public celebration was deferred until after his return from Wales; but that day, Friday, the true anniversary, had been for so long the point I was making for – the head of the pass in the almost interminable climb, the height from which I should be able to see the lie of the landscape I desired, and to know whether I could ever reach it – that I felt I could not bear to ignore it as I went by, leave it wholly unmarked and uncelebrated.

Should I then use it as I had always planned? I could write Ben a letter to reach him on his birthday, wishing him many happy returns, and declaring my love for him. Thinking of it, beginning to find words for such a letter, made me short of breath. I tried to ignore my terror and excitement and consider whether this would be the wisest thing to do. What if the letter arrived early, or late? That was a ludicrous objection – rigidity carried beyond pedantry to the point of superstition.

I tried to imagine Ben reading the letter, at breakfast, perhaps, among his friends; or, when he had read some way, would he put it back into its envelope, and then into his pocket, to read later, away from talk and enquiry and Nicholas Ridley's noticing eye at the end of the table? In the garden? (Did Ridley have a garden?) In the bathroom, for privacy? On the side of a mountain? Then I thought of his face.

Mild expectancy and friendly interest would give way to surprise, perhaps to perplexity, as he began to understand my drift. And would his perplexity grow to confusion? To embarrassment, or even horror? I should not be there to read the warning signs in his face, and change course accordingly – if necessary, towards the harmless, predictable channels of good wishes, and affectionate interest in his doings, and small news of my own. The original course would have been charted, unalterably and unmistakably, right to the purposed end. And I should not even know how dangerous it had been, until it was too late: until everything – even the accustomed wealth of friendship, so long counted secure, even the chance to help him salvage some confidence in human honesty and disinterested affection – was lost in the general shipwreck.

But he might read on with sympathy, with hardly-dared anticipation, and, in the end, with reciprocating joy. He might. And I should not be there to see it. What could be worth the forgoing of those minutes? Scrupulous adherence to my original timetable?

There was still the objection that he ought to have time to consider such a revelation on his own – that my presence might make it difficult for him to find, let alone to give, his true answer. But I should be on my guard against such a danger, as against any danger to my own hopes. I should not press, or even ask, for an immediate answer. At his least hesitation or embarrassment, I should insist on a deferred one. I could trust myself so far.

I would send him a card, to mark the day, and keep everything else for his return.

I went into Bramston two days later, and spent some time looking for birthday cards. I had not realised how many there would be, nor how few that were tolerable, let alone appropriate. I looked through racks of sentimentally photographed flowers and animals, and garishly coloured cards in the shapes of numbers. When I had reached the back of the shop, the proprietor came to offer advice. He explained that the cards were arranged in sections for different occasions. (I was now looking at Easter cards.)

'Looking for anything in particular, were you?'

I asked if there were any cards for a twenty-first birthday.

'Just over here.' He indicated another rack, glanced at me, and added, 'Not a very big selection, I'm afraid. I don't know whether there's anything you'll like.'

There were one or two jokes, of an Edwardian vulgarity; the rest were silver pasteboard keys. He smiled, and realising how much my face must have fallen, I smiled too.

'I'm sorry to be so difficult.'

'No, that's all right. Has to be right, after all.'

'It's not really very important.'

'Still, it seems like it to them, doesn't it? If they only knew.'

'If they knew?'

'Be good enough for some of us, wouldn't it, being twenty-one again? Settle for that, never mind the cards.'

'I see what you mean. Are there any other cards you can suggest?'

'Hmm. Not unless any of the relationship cards would do? That's this side, if you'd like to have a look. Grandma, Grandpa – that's no good; those ones are for the children; but what about these for the young people? Son – daughter – niece – nephew – boyfriend – girlfriend–?'

I shook my head, and he scanned the cards again and said, without looking up, 'I tell you what I'd do. I'd go to the Cornmarket Gallery. You want an art card, really, not one of these. They have them at the desk.'

'Do they? That's a good idea.'

'Beautiful, some of them. That's what you want to do. What I'd do myself, for a special occasion.'

I thanked him for his trouble and advice, and bought a block of paper of the wrong size. There were reproductions from Constable's sketchbooks among the postcards at the Gallery. I bought one of a bend in the Stour, with figures in the distance, bathing from the river bank. Then I drove home by way of the Graysons, to deliver Ben's things.

Following his suggestion, and my own inclination, I had not hurried to do this. Ruth came out to help me unload the car and carry everything across the yard into Ben's room. We stacked it up as neatly as we could, and then she gave me a cup of tea. I gave her a good account of Ben – of his health, and serenity, and purposeful working – and she told me about their preparations for the party. There was a great deal to be done, cooking and moving furniture and clearing out the packing shed. I offered my help, but she declined it for the moment.

'I know how busy you are. And Bridgie's at home to give me a hand, and Ben will be back nearly a week before.'

'Mark must be on holiday, too?'

'Not till next week, officially, though he could hardly spend more time than he does already, tinkering with the lights. Nearer the time, though, it might be marvellous. If any of the children's friends need picking up, or meeting at the station, could I give you a ring?'

There remained only my own preparations. I took my dinner jacket to be cleaned and mended, and, after some consideration, bought some new evening shoes; the pair I possessed were worn across in creases which would soon be cracks. Then, when I had reached a good stopping-place in the Cycle, at the end of a play, and sorted out my notes from the last Dictionary Committee and the work arising from them, I took a whole day off, and went up to the New University, and then on into Harchester, to look in the bookshops. I found nothing all morning – nothing, that is, to my main purpose. I had collected a considerable load, by midday, of books of subsidiary interest, historical, literary or philological, including a complete edition of Olsen's *Etymological Hand-book of Viking Loanwords,* which Douglas and I had almost despaired of finding.

Piling the books in the back of the car, feeling despondent and thirsty, my shoulders aching, I thought of a conversation between Ruth and Bridget, some years before. 'You won't find anything when you're tired and thirsty,' Ruth had said. (Bridget had been going to buy clothes on her own, I think, for the first time.) 'Or if you do, you'll find it's wrong when you get it home. So, here,' taking some money out of her purse, 'have some coffee on the housekeeping – and a bun.'

I locked the car and went to the Swan for steak-and-kidney pie and a baked apple. After half a pint of lager, I realised that there was nothing to stop me taking a day in Cambridge later in the week; after another half-pint, and coffee, the remaining bookshops in Harchester did not seem so unhopeful.

I paid my bill and went down through the small streets to the river, as the sun began to find gaps between the clouds, so that

I could work my way back methodically to where the car was parked, leaving no possible shop unsearched. A little way from the High Street, I saw an evening shirt for sale, at a reduced price, in a shop window. Remembering the two yellowish shirts in the bottom of the drawer at home, I went in, asked the size, and bought it. After I had paid, I saw that it had a small, raised pattern embroidered on the front in white thread. I should probably not have bought it, if I had noticed this earlier, but I decided that I did not mind. I recollected that Lawrence Forman's young colleague had worn something of the kind, and I carried the package out of the shop with a pleasant sense of mild recklessness.

Some way further on, an unfamiliar signboard at the mouth of a side street directed me to a binder's and second-hand book dealer's, recently opened in a narrow house. I went upstairs to the poetry and plays on the third floor, and across the room to the two shelves of Shakespeare. There was a 1760 edition of the Sonnets on the second shelf, an almost perfect copy.

It was a shop for serious collectors: the owner was knowledgeable and, I think, shrewd. He told me a price, and I paid it without demurring, with the elation both of abandon and of capture. Then I walked down again to the river, sat on a bench, and looked at the binding and the titlepage and the fount, and read the Sonnets, until the sun had gone in, and it was time to drive home.

Having a bath before supper that evening, I began to invent a parody of one of the Sonnets. I could recall most of it now, I think, if I tried. It began, 'Devouring Time, don't blunt the Lion's paws', and went on, by way of cats in Cambridge, and dragons in Wales, to urge Time to hurry on the celebration of Ben's coming of age.

After supper I wrote it down, then changed the last couplet (which had at first differed little from the original) for some more standard form of congratulation. I copied it all onto the back of the Constable postcard, and addressed and stamped an envelope for it. Reading it through with greater caution next morning, while waiting for the kettle to boil, I had doubts about the gravity of such a tribute – of such a reference, however indirect. But it seemed, in the end, adequately offset by the absurdity of the verse, and the informality of a postcard – and, perhaps, by the limits of undergraduate knowledge of the Sonnets. It need seem no more than a literary *jeu d'esprit*, or, later, a light-hearted earnest of my present – no more, or only as much more as Ben was prepared to understand.

CHAPTER 48

The morning of the dance was wet. I had been working fast since my day in Harchester, impelled by a kind of urgent, confident energy to get well ahead in the Cycle, besides preparing several of the more complicated entries for the Dictionary. Ben had answered my postcard with a picture of Glyn Ceirog, and a limerick on the back of it:

There once was a student of Chirk
Who meant to do plenty of work,
But he sat in the sun,
And he struck twenty-one,
– And he found it much simpler to shirk!

Many thanks for superb sonnet: sorry this is the best I can do in return – in a daze of wind & sun (quite a lot), and celebratory wine last night (ditto) – and some *history! See you after Easter. Much love, Ben.*

[Written sideways in the margin:] *David sends love.*

He had returned on Easter Monday, spending a night with David in London on the way, and I had seen him once since then, not for very long. He was very well, burned brownish-pink by the wind, and looking somehow larger, as if he had broadened beyond the confines of his clothes (and not only, I think, because there was a split across one shoulder of his shirt). But there was some uneasiness in our meeting. I was afraid that the sonnet might, after all, have conveyed too much (although his reply had been so reassuringly frivolous). I hoped that it was only my own eagerness, so nearly released and until then so tightly restrained, which was overcharging the lines of communication between us. I had stopped at the house in the course of a walk, partly to ask what driving I could do for them. We had spoken for only a few minutes when

235

Ruth came in, and the conversation turned to addresses and the times of trains, until I had to leave.

Now I worked restlessly in the morning, looking out of the window, whenever I found an excuse to get up, to see what weather was prefigured by the western sky. After lunch I wrapped the Sonnets in white paper, and wrote 'Ben with love from Alan' on it – very lightly, so that I should not mark the binding. I might inscribe the book itself later on. I reminded myself that there might well be no opportunity to talk to Ben privately and at length that evening. He would have other presents to receive, other friends to welcome, food and drink and company and music to supply and vary. I would give him the Sonnets, and let the rest of my declaration follow when the time seemed right.

The rain had stopped. I did some weeding, and cleared up the debris left by the builders at the back of the house. Then I had a bath, shaved, and made a cup of tea before getting dressed. There was still an hour before I could start. I took my own copy of the Sonnets from the shelf and started to read them from the beginning, my fitful attention soon steadied and settled, the wearying lurch of nervousness rested, in the strenuously directed energy, the active composure of the lines.

I left the house just before half-past six.

It took less long than I had calculated to fetch Bridget's two friends from the far side of Bramston, and we had to wait to meet the London train on the way back. When we arrived, Ben was standing in the doorway, against the light from the hall, welcoming the first guests. His dinner jacket looked very black; I thought it was new. There was a flurry of greeting and laughing, and parcels wrapped in bright paper. The girl from London kissed Ben's cheek, and he kissed hers in return, shifting his presents precariously into the crook of one arm. More guests came up behind us, and people began to move past Ben into the hall. I stretched to take his hand – the hand that was free – and he nodded at me, without saying anything, smiling, as if to confirm some mutual understanding. There seemed to me to be an instant – a very short instant – of silence, and in it I touched his shoulder with the palm of my hand and went on into the hall. I left the Sonnets with my coat.

I spent the first half hour or so of the party helping James and Ruth to distribute the wine – carrying trays of full glasses, and then bottles from which to refill them, between the two rooms of guests, stopping to be introduced to cousins, or to talk to acquaintances among the neighbours. The middle-aged people making patient, jovial conversation across the spaces of the rooms were gradually joined by the young. They came in from outside, in haste, explaining why they had had to start so late, how they had missed the turn; or they came down at leisure from upstairs, from re-arranging their clothes and their hair.

The two rooms became more and more closely filled. Mark came in from directing the cars outside and asked me if I could see either of his parents: the steel-band had arrived, and wanted to know where to put their instruments. He was wearing a suit, and looked taller and self-possessed. I saw him consult with his mother, and look down suddenly at his shoes, which were very muddy.

I filled some more glasses, and my own, and realised then that it was my third. I went to look for something to eat. Ben came in from the kitchen with a plate of hot sausage rolls.

'Can I take those round for you?'

'Have some yourself first. They're really good: home-made.'

I took two, then held the plate for him to do the same.

'This is all magnificent, Ben. You must all have been working very hard.'

There was still the same sense of complicity – of conspiracy, almost – without any need to talk about it, or about anything, indeed, beyond the most commonplace.

'The others did most of it, really. It was pretty well organised by the time I got home.'

'Hello.'

Ben turned. 'David. You've got here.'

'Finally. I'm sorry. Hello.'

'Hello. How are you?'

237

'Piers's car break down?'

'No, for a miracle. But it's got no windscreen wipers, no petrol gauge, and no maps.'

'You'd have done better by train with Louisa and Geoffrey.'

'Much.'

'Don't worry: the band's only just got here.'

'Have some of these,' I said.

'And you need a drink; we all do. Alan, should we open some more bottles, do you know?'

The noise diminished, and the air cooled and moved more freely. The back door had been opened, and people were making their way across the yard to the dance floor which had been laid down in the packing shed. Ben went after a few minutes, encouraging others to go with him, but his parents' contemporaries stayed to talk, drawing up chairs and refilling glasses with a grateful sense of celebrations well launched, and obligations temporarily suspended.

James drew back the curtains and opened a window. It was a fine night now, half clouds, half stars, and I could see a double track of candles in jam-jars, marking a path across the yard, towards the shed.

It was nearly an hour before someone suggested going to see the dancing. The shed was full of coloured lights, bright and confusing for a moment after the pale flicker of the candles in the outside darkness, but dim enough thereafter to leave shadows along the walls and in the corners.

The racket of the band seemed more robust and likeable than most dance music, with vigorous, complicated rhythms which the dancers followed energetically. After some moments, I saw Ben. He was dancing with Louisa, the girl I had collected from the London train. They were moving in the same spasmodic fashion as the rest, but kept closer together than most of them, not letting go each other's hands or even parting as far as their arms' length.

As I watched, they drew closer still, so that the girl's face was almost against Ben's shoulder, and her hair very close to his cheek. I leaned my head against the wall behind me and felt for a moment as if the whole company were illusory, a film, or an early-morning dream after a wakeful, sweating night. I looked again, moving to keep a sight of their heads as they went to the far end of the floor. This would not do. I could not spend the night spying after Ben's movements, sickening my own pleasure in his celebration. I looked across the room to where Bridget was making animated conversation to two girls – animated, but laborious, I thought. One of Ben's college friends – Jonathan or Charles? – made his way across a corner and asked Bridget to dance. She spoke again to the other girls, and then moved off with him, laughing and looking prettier, in her pale, diaphanous dress. One of the two remaining girls came towards the door to talk to her parents; the other, who seemed younger, looked at the ceiling and then at her feet.

I walked round the edge of the floor and asked her to dance. She looked up with unguarded relief.

'Oh, yes. Thank you.'

'I'm afraid I'm not much good at this kind of dancing.'

'Oh, that's all right.'

'You'll have to show me how.'

We did achieve a compromise, though a fairly sedate one, between the dancing around us and my partial memories of foxtrot and quickstep, and we even managed some conversation meanwhile. She told me, in answer to my unoriginal questions, that her name was Sarah, and that she was the younger sister of a schoolfriend of Bridget's. 'I don't know very many people here,' she added, with a little defiance, explaining to me, and even to herself, why she had been left without a partner. I said that I liked her dress, and she smiled with real sweetness and said that she and her mother had made it together.

The music stopped, and the dancers shuffled, then waited. I could see no young man without a partner. Someone called out from above the heads of the band; there was a shout of laughter, and the lights began to turn on and off in bewildering alternations of colour. Still standing beside my partner, I heard Ben laughing behind me, and his voice saying, 'Marky and his lights!'

'How do you think the lights work?' I asked Sarah, and looked round.

Ben and Louisa were talking with the young man who had been on the London train. The music started, and I turned to dance with Sarah again. Ben was walking away, and Geoffrey (unless it was Jeremy?) began to dance with Louisa. The music was getting faster. Sarah moved back to arm's length, holding my hands, and began a quick, twisting step; I copied it as well as I could. The speed increased; people began to shout and stamp and spin. We swung round, leaning back from each other, to the last roll of drums, and ended dizzy and laughing and short of breath as everyone clapped the band.

Mark had been working the lights, and might therefore be without a partner. He could not be far from Sarah in age. I took her to find a drink, and then to the archway of the great door at the far end of the shed, where Mark was sitting on a stepladder beside a tangle of wires and switches. He said, after I had introduced them, that he had known Sarah at the pony club. They began to talk about this with adequate fluency, and I drained my glass and went back to the table to refill it. I met a friend from the New University there, and we had talked for some little time before I looked back towards the archway, and saw Sarah standing by it on her own, fingering the ends of her hair.

David came up to the table with an empty glass and I filled it for him.

'Thank you so much.'

'I wonder if I could ask you to do something for me?'

'Anything, of course.'

'Would you have a dance with a young girl who doesn't seem to have a partner?'

He looked into his glass. 'By all means.'

We went over together, and talked until the band began the next piece, when David asked Sarah, with an admirable air of spontaneity, if she would like to dance. I smiled my gratitude over her shoulder as they moved away, and he winked in reply, then looked concerned for a moment, I thought, before bending to hear what Sarah had said.

I saw Julian standing within the thickness of the arch. 'It's not fair,' he said, laughing at me.

'What isn't fair?'

'Landing poor David with a schoolgirl.'

'I don't suppose he minded. She's a nice girl, and a good dancer.'

'He didn't have a great deal of choice.'

'People must be prepared to dance now and then, if they come to a dance.'

'You wouldn't find it "more rational if conversation instead of dancing made the order of the day"?'

'"Much more rational, I dare say, but it would not be near so much like a ball."'

'Right,' he said. 'I hope you've had plenty of nice partners? Or rational ones?'

'What about you?'

'Oh, I'm a technician – a backroom boy. Mark's showing me how to work the lights.'

'Supper,' said James, stopping by us for a moment. 'Supper in the house. Will you tell people, Alan? – er – Julian? Bring your partners along. Marky, can you look after that young Billington girl? The lights will look after themselves for half an hour.'

I went in to supper with the Doctor's wife and the university librarian. James was carving a ham in the dining-room, and Ruth and Mrs Lee, her cleaning lady, were filling plates with salads and cold chicken. Ben and David were taking round the wine. We found chairs in the drawing-room; some of the young sat by us on the floor; others spread into the passage and up the stairs, or out into the yard, where I could see the lighted doorways of two or three rooms – Ben's among them – which had been arranged for sitting out.

After the first course, I went to help Bridget collect empty plates and distribute clean ones, and we took round large dishes of trifle and cold soufflé. By the time we had finished, a neighbour had taken my chair, and I was able to go back into the dining-room and then up between the couples on the stairs. Ben did not seem to be anywhere in the house. I found my overcoat in the spare bedroom and transferred the Sonnets to the pocket of my dinner jacket. It is not a large edition: only a narrow white edge showed above the edge of the cloth.

I went downstairs, and out into the cool dark, and walked up and down. I had begun to feel the cold through my jacket by the time I heard music starting again. The band and some of their friends were having supper in the packing shed, and Bridget and a young man were putting records on a gramophone. Ruth came in with a tray, and I had a dance with her; the music was more familiar, and the floor was less full; we did a creditable quick waltz, and Bridget and her friend clapped us, laughing, as we finished. Ruth made them a mock-curtsey. 'Your turn now, and we'll watch you. Thank you, Alan, that was splendid. I didn't know you were a dancer.'

'Only if we can change the record. OK, Bridget?'

'It's a wonderful party, Ruth,' I said, as they span away. 'Ben must be feeling magnificently celebrated.'

'Oh, good. I do hope so. Do you think the band will want second helpings? Have you seen Ben, by the way?'

'Not since supper. I don't think he's in the house.'

'If I take them the dish, they can help themselves. If you do see him, Alan, ask him what he's done with the kitchen corkscrew.'

Thus provided, I went out again, and round to the front of the house, where a couple of cars were already manoeuvring as the younger or more distant families began to leave. The stairs were empty, apart from one or two girls and boys coming down in wraps and overcoats. Mrs Lee was wiping the kitchen table, a few of the young were still with their elders in the supper-rooms, and several more were making their way along the candlelit path to the packing shed. Ben was not among them.

The rooms in the yard remained. The door of Ben's room was closed. Before I opened it, I looked through the window and saw a couple, half-reclined on the bed, embracing. I thought they were Geoffrey and Louisa, and left them undisturbed.

There was a smell of cigarette smoke from the next room. It was the outhouse where the sacks and seed-trays were usually kept, I thought. The window at the side was open, and half-drawn curtains were blowing through it.

A voice said, 'I'm not sure it's yours, either. He's seventeen, after all.'

I stopped near the window.

'He's fourteen,' said a second voice. It was Ben's.

Standing in the shadow, I looked through the fluttering, shifting curtains, and saw Julian and Mark sitting, smoking, among some cushions against the whitewashed wall. There was a chess-board under the lamp between them. Mark coughed over his cigarette, and Julian took it from him, knocked the ash off, and gave it back.

Ben moved into the light, and within my view. 'Will you go and do those lights, or do you want to spoil the end of the party for everyone?'

'All right, all *right*,' said Mark. He got up from the floor with deliberate leisureliness. 'I said I would.'

I moved back as he came out through the door and shut it behind him. He hesitated, then dropped his cigarette, trod it out, and ran off towards the packing shed.

There was a pause, and I went nearer to the window again.

'You're being silly, Ben,' said Julian.

'I wish I was.'

'Do you? I think you're rather enjoying it.'

'*Enjoying* – what?'

There was another pause, then Julian said, 'I think you'd better come and sit down.'

'I'd rather stay here.'

'Oh, come off it, Ben. Stop being a hero. We've obviously got to talk about this, and you're giving me a crick in the neck. Come on. Come over here and sit down.'

Ben crossed the floor slowly and sat down on the far side of the heap of cushions.

'Cigarette?'

'I'm not Marky.'

'No.' Julian lit his own cigarette and waved out the match. 'Though you'd sometimes like me to think so.'

'What the hell are you talking about?

'Ben, look. It was probably very sweet at his age. But you're grown up now; you'll have to think of something else.' Julian leaned his arms on his bent knees.

'All right. What do you think you were playing at with Marky?'

'Nothing very serious. It's a nice age, when you'll do anything for anyone who'll take you seriously. Or even take you for seventeen.'

'You *dare* –'

'Now, Ben. Don't start manning the barricades before I've finished my sentence.'

'All right then,' said Ben after a moment. 'Go on.'

'He's very like you, you know. Well, he's dark, not fair, and perhaps he's not quite so thin-skinned and full of high-minded scruples.' Julian smiled. 'But he moves like you, and he's quick and confiding. And prone to hero-worship. He's really just a pocket-edition.' He looked at Ben. 'So there really isn't much for you to worry about – either way.'

'There's only one way, as far as I know.'

'Are you sure?'

Ben glanced up, then looked down at the chessboard. 'Whatever sort of game were you playing?'

'Fox and geese. He was teaching me.'

'Was he?'

'That was the idea. You haven't answered my question. Are you sure there was only one thing that was worrying you?'

Ben started to rearrange the chess pieces. 'I don't know what you're on about.'

'That's dishonest.'

Julian leaned further forward and put his hands over Ben's wrists, lifting them a little way above the board.

'What are you doing? Stop it. *Let go*.'

Ben still held one of the chessmen – a knight, I thought – in his hand, and Julian lowered that hand to the board.

'Put it down.'

Ben set it down, then jerked back and tried to pull free. 'Let go, damn you.'

'I'll let go when you've promised to answer my questions.'

They twisted their wrists this way and that, knocking over most of the chessmen.

'Truthfully,' Julian added.

Ben moved his wrists together, then sharply apart, trying to spring Julian's grasp. Julian held on.

After a time, Ben said, 'All right.'

'Promise?'

'I suppose I promise.'

Julian let go, and Ben rubbed his wrists, pressing his lips together and looking down.

Julian waited a minute; then he said, 'What did you really feel about my making friends with Mark?'

Ben breathed deeply and shakily, and said, 'I didn't believe it.'

'Didn't believe it? Then you heard about it from someone else?'

'I... well...'

'Not Marky?'

'No. No, I don't think he knows what's going on, altogether.'

'Nor do I. Who was it, then?'

Ben was silent.

'You've promised to –'

'Not if it means breaking promises to other people. I'll answer anything you like about myself.'

'Right. I'll keep you to that, and David can probably fill in the gaps.'

'Julian, no.'

'We're going back in the same car.'

'Leave David alone.'

'We'll see.' Julian shifted and settled back. 'So, you were worried about Mark?' he said in the end.

'Eventually – when I saw what was going on – yes. Very worried.'

'I think your view of what was going on may have been unnecessarily melodramatic. However. So you felt all the proper fraternal anxieties?'

'Yes.'

'And plenty of righteous indignation?'

'If that's what you want to call it. Yes.'

'And what else?'

'What else? Well, I suppose I felt – disappointed.'

'Disappointed. And then?'

Ben did not answer.

'Supplanted?'

'I don't know. I really don't know. Honestly.'

'"Honestly"? Well, think about it: you've known for some time that there was something – that I felt something. You've known that – you know you have – ever since the party at Michael's.'

'That was just terrifying. Not you, so much, but after you'd gone – the others –'

'Well, I'm afraid... Yes. They could be fairly crass, that lot.'

'And you dropped me in that – just left me there. And when I had to get out – get away – that let me in for the worst twelve hours of my life.'

'Poor Ben! What a shame! But later on, at Cambridge, over *Richard II* and all the rest of it. By then, you knew all right. And I don't think you were terrified.'

'I was – . I knew – . Well, I suppose I knew after a bit you were – . I realised there'd been something with David; and that he was having hell, and you weren't being any help.'

'And that was why you were so reluctant to make friends?'

'I suppose so, mainly. I was so bloody sorry for him. And sometimes you seemed to be making things worse for him on purpose.'

'I didn't mean my behaviour to David – or his version of it. I meant my general proclivity.'

'Oh. No. No, I don't think that worried me very much. David's one of my greatest friends, after all. It was more the way you were treating him.'

I leaned my arm and forehead against the brick of the wall.

Julian said, 'And yet you were prepared to share my room.'

'Yes, well – . There wasn't anywhere else, very much. You can't get away with sharing in college; and most people's landladies – . Anyway, I knew you a bit better by then; I thought maybe – I hadn't heard your side of the story. And then David stopped caring, anyway – '

'He stopped caring, did he?'

'In the end, thank heavens.'

'Are you sure?'

'Quite sure.'

'Quite sure. I see. Then I take it he's transferred his allegiance?'

Ben said nothing.

'Not to you?'

'No, of course it's not to me. Don't be so bloody ridiculous.'

'There is someone, then.'

'I didn't say that.'

'And you're not going to? All right. I'll let you off. It's some way to London.'

'Oh, *Julian,* for Christ's sake – '

'All right. Calm down.' He held out a handkerchief. Ben shook his head.

'Do you want a drink?'

'No, thanks.'

'You'd better.' Julian took two glasses from behind him.

'Have you been giving Marky whisky?'

'About the strength of lemonade. You'd better have mine.' He tasted one glass. 'It's this one.'

Ben took it suspiciously, and drank from the other side – a little at first, then more.

'Anyway, that's a side issue,' said Julian.

'For you.'

'We were actually discussing your attitude to me.'

'Discussing?'

'Cross-examining, if you'd rather. So: you knew what my preferences were. You were prepared to give me the benefit of the doubt – some of it, anyway – about David. You accepted my

247

invitation to come and sleep on my floor. What did you imagine I felt about you?'

'I wasn't really sure,' said Ben, slowly. 'I mean, you seemed to like me. Well, I thought you must, in a way, or else why had you –? But then – I mean, obviously I wasn't going to be as well read as you, or as clever – you must have known. I knew, all right. And you're a lot older than me. I know I seemed silly, sometimes – boring – juvenile. I know I did. Well, you let me know. But then why – ? It was great for me, obviously, in a lot of ways, but I couldn't really see what was in it for you.'

'Did you come to any conclusion?'

Ben picked up his glass and tilted it from side to side, letting the remaining whisky swing round it.

'Sometimes. Sometimes I thought you did like me, but you liked bullying people, too. Me, anyway.'

'Only for your own good,' said Julian, smiling. 'But you're underrating yourself, Ben, as usual. You'd better stop playing with that whisky and drink it.'

Ben emptied the glass, gulped, and put it down.

'Good,' said Julian, and then, after a moment, 'There was more to it than that, though, wasn't there?'

'Than what?'

'You knew I felt more for you than that.'

'Well...'

'Well, what?'

'I suppose I thought – sometimes – you might feel a bit more.'

'Go on.'

'That you were – oh – I don't know.'

'You do know. Still, I suppose I can say it for you, if it makes it easier. Did you think I was attracted to you?'

'All right, yes, sometimes. I thought you might be. I wasn't sure.'

'And how did you react to that?'

'In the end, I moved out.'

'So you were lying. You told me that was to get more work done.'

'I wasn't lying. It was true.'

'Just not the whole truth?'

'I suppose not.'

'Will you tell me the whole truth now?'

'I think I have.'

'I don't. I don't think you've told it to yourself yet.'

Ben was silent.

'Ben: look at me.'

Ben looked up.

'Was it only my feelings you were frightened of? Or your own as well?'

'My own?'

'Yes. Were you as frightened of falling for me as you were that I might be falling for you?'

Ben's shoulders jerked; he looked down and shook his head.

Julian put his hand under Ben's chin, raising it. 'No. Hold still. And tell me I'm wrong: you've never felt anything like that about me – excitement, attraction? Hope? Give me your word.'

Neither of them moved.

'All right,' said Julian, after a time. 'You can stop trying, now. It's not worth it,' he went on, almost sadly. 'You can't go on fighting it indefinitely, or dodging it, or even trying to keep it at arm's length.'

He moved his free hand round behind Ben's back, resting it between his shoulders.

Ben raised his bent arm between them, and shoved with all his force, sending Julian backwards into the cushions.

'Get off, you sodding bastard! How many people do you think you can lay in one evening? Little boys – '

'Stop it, Ben,' said Julian. 'You're not convincing anyone. Least of all yourself. You'll have to find a better ditch to die in than that. You can't really expect me to believe in all this moral outrage.'

'Can't I?'

'Not really.' Julian sat up, pushing his hair back, and picked up an overturned glass. It sounded cracked as he put it down. 'Especially if that's the only way you can express it. And if you consider who your other friends are.'

'I don't count you as one of my friends.'

'What about the others?'

'What do you mean? Hardly any of my friends are – '

'David?'

'David? That's his business. What he does with his own emotions – with the rest of him, if it comes to that – that's not the point. The point is I can trust him. I know I can trust him about anything – with anyone. He really is a friend. He'd never – try it on with children.'

'Not yet, anyway. So David's one of your greatest friends. And the others?'

'Well, who? I don't think there's anyone, apart from my own family – and Alan – as close as that, that I can trust like that.'

'And Alan?'

'What about him?'

'Ben, for pity's sake, you can't go on pretending you don't know what Alan's after.'

Ben stared at him.

'What on earth are you talking about?' he asked, after a moment.

'Would you like me to tell you?'

'I shouldn't think so. I shouldn't think I'd like you to tell me anything. Certainly not about Alan.'

'Perhaps I don't need to.'

'It's more that you wouldn't be able to. You've met him – what? – twice.'

'A dozen times, I should think, at least.'

'It probably doesn't make any difference. You could meet him fifty times, I should think, and only see what you wanted to see.'

'And you don't think the same might be true of you?'

'For God's sake, Julian. I've known Alan since I was at primary school.'

'Really? As young as that?'

Ben got up. 'It's a bad idea to judge other people by yourself. Would you go now? I don't want you in the house any more.'

There was a moment's silence. Julian put his cigarettes in his pocket.

'Give me a hand up, then.'

Ben hesitated, then took the hand that Julian held up to him, and pulled him to his feet.

'You know how much it signifies, don't you?' said Julian, not letting go of Ben's hand. 'All this sound and fury?'

He raised his other hand, and brushed something off the front of Ben's jacket, standing close to him.

'No,' said Ben.

'Do you mean that?'

'Yes, I do.'

'You're sure? You'd really prefer me to take an interest in Marky?'

Ben threw back his head and wrenched free, putting up both his hands. Julian side-stepped and walked to the door, going through it and shutting it as Ben turned to follow him.

CHAPTER 49

The door opened again, and banged shut, and Ben came out into the darkness. I stood further back into the shadow, and the light from the window reached towards him where he stood, and caught his side as he looked urgently about, trying to see where Julian had gone. He started towards the packing-shed, then put his hands to his face and turned back to the wall, leaning his head against it.

I walked to him round the corner of the building. I was shaking, and I stopped before I reached him, and took breath once or twice.

'Ben?'

'Alan!'

'Can I do anything?'

'Yes.' He turned, wiping his face with his hand. 'Marky. Please go and make sure he's OK, would you? Not – not getting into trouble – letting anyone get off with him – Julian – '

'Julian. I see. All right.'

'I would, only – like this –'

'Don't worry. It's easier for me. I'll make quite sure. I'll have a word with your father, if necessary.'

'Yes. Yes, do. Anything.'

'I won't be long. Wait here. Or, no: go down to the gate, the gate into the orchard. I'll find you there.'

I was back within ten minutes. Ben was leaning on the gate.

'Mark's all right: there's nothing to worry about. He's in the shed, packing up his lights, and your father and Bridget are both there, telling him to hurry up and get it done, and go to bed.'

'Thank God for that. You're sure he'll go?'

'I should think so. He looked pretty sleepy. And Julian's leaving for London. He came to say goodbye to your mother.'

'You didn't actually see him go?'

'Yes, I did. His friend – is it Piers? – brought the car round while I was there.'

'Oh, good,' said Ben, and started to cry, bending his head down into his arms on the top bar of the gate.

I put my arm round his shoulders. 'Come on. Come through into the orchard. There won't be anyone there, and you can take your time.'

'People will be leaving – I ought to be saying goodbye.'

'Bridget'll do that for you. She said she'd make your excuses. I told her you'd got a headache – needed some fresh air. It made you sound very dissipated.'

Ben laughed for a moment, and then started crying more wildly. I opened the gate, and took him through into the orchard. We went across through shadowy aisles of trees, and sat in the darkness, and Ben put his face against my chest and sobbed violently for several minutes.

'I'm sorry. I'm sorry,' he said eventually, gasping.

'All right. It's all right. You can stay here as long as you like.'

'Have you got a hanky?'

I gave him my clean one, and he sat up and wiped his face and blew his nose.

'Do you want it back?'

'I don't suppose it's good for much more, is it?'

He laughed and put it in his pocket. 'Oh, Alan, thank God you're here.' And then, 'I'm sorry to be such a fool.'

'Grief isn't foolish; nor is anger, or anxiety.'

He said nothing more for a time, and we sat together silently in the blurred darkness.

'Say if you're cold,' I said eventually.

'Not really. Do you think we ought to go in?'

He began to stand up, and dropped back beside me. 'Lord!'

'Are you giddy?'

I steadied him, and the slack weight of his shoulder came against mine.

'I don't know. Just weak. As if I'd had 'flu.'

'Give yourself time.'

'Yes. That's all. I'll be all right.'

After a time, he shifted his weight forward. I stretched my arm.

'Sorry. Have I given you pins and needles?'

'Not really.'

'Alan. I'm sorry. What's the matter with me?'

'You're very tired; you've had a long day; and things have gone wrong at the end of it.'

'Yes.'

'Do you want to tell me about it?'

'Aren't you cold? Do you want to go in?'

'Are you?'

'A bit. I don't want to go back yet.'

'Then let's stay here.'

After a minute or two, he said, 'We could walk down to the far end.'

'All right. Take it slowly then. All right?'

'Yes. I think so. Fine.'

We started through the trees towards the middle of the orchard.

'There should be a tap here somewhere.'

'There?'

'Yes.'

He ran water from the standpipe into his hands, and splashed it in his face again and again.

'Christ! It's cold.'

He turned the water to a trickle, and lapped it from his cupped hands, stooping.

'Don't chill yourself.'

'No, it's lovely.'

He came back to me, shaking his hands, and wiping his mouth and forehead on the sleeve of his jacket.

'Do you feel like walking? If we get through the hedge, there's a path down to the river.'

'Right. Good.'

When we had dropped down from the bank into a sunken grass lane, we walked a little way in silence. Then Ben said, 'It's lovely now. I don't know why I got so worked up.'

I waited.

'Julian – I couldn't believe it.'

'No, it's hard to believe. Especially of a friend.'

'The bloody, unspeakable cunt.'

I said nothing.

'Sorry.'

'I've heard worse in the army – not to speak of Chaucer.'

'Still. But – Marky! Alan, he's *fourteen*.'

'Yes. That's abominable.'

'You don't think it'll have done him any harm?'

'Marky? I shouldn't think so. It didn't actually come to – physical assault, did it?'

'No. Oh no, I'm sure it didn't. But I meant more, in his mind.'

'I really doubt it, Ben. You know Marky better than I do, but he's very young, and Julian certainly isn't stupid or impulsive – or short of practice, I should judge. He'd be very circumspect to start with. I don't suppose Marky noticed anything very much. One of your Cambridge friends was being nice to him, teasing him, making him feel grown-up. I expect he felt pleased – a bit flattered – no more than that.'

'Nothing permanent?'

'Heavens, no. It would take more than that to set Marky's permanent direction – or anybody's.'

After a pause, he said, 'You think I needn't have got in such a state about it?'

'No, I think you were absolutely right.'

'I threw Julian out, in the end. I mean, I told him to go.'

'That was right, too.'

'I should never have asked him, only, – would you have known? Would you have believed he could do that sort of thing?'

'I shouldn't have been certain, either way.'

'But you knew he was – queer?'

'I thought it possible.'

We walked on for some minutes without speaking. The night had begun to seem quite light, though there was no moon. Then Ben said, 'Can you tell?'

'Can you tell – ?'

'Whether someone's queer or not?'

'Well, it's not very difficult, if he starts making advances to small boys.'

'But I mean, anyway. Even if it's not with small boys. If someone's just queer. Can you tell?'

'Well, it depends, I suppose. Some people make it more obvious than others.'

'Yes.'

The banks began to fall away, and the path merged with the fields on either side. Ben cast about for a track across the plough; we found it, and turned with it, under the expanse of the cold sky.

Ben brushed his hand through some grasses at the side of the track as we went, with his face turned to watch his hand, and said, 'Julian thought I was.'

'Thought you were – of the same inclination?'

'Yes. Or said he did.'

'I see.'

After a moment, Ben said, 'Alan – ,' and then, 'He must have known it wasn't true, though?'

'I don't suppose Julian distinguishes very carefully between what's true, and what would suit him.'

'No. No, I'm sure he doesn't. Still.'

He walked on in silence for some moments. Then he said, 'Alan – if I was – you'd know, wouldn't you? You could tell?'

I could find no immediate answer. He stood still in the path, half-turned towards me.

'I must know. Alan, please. You must tell me.'

I strained for words, for a voice, to answer the long strain of anxiety and misery rising through his voice and breaking it. I opened my mouth, drawing the air into my dry throat.

'You dislike the idea very much?' I said at last.

'I think I – I'd – . Oh, Alan – . I'd – . Yes, I do.'

'Then – it doesn't seem very likely, does it?'

'No. No, I suppose not.'

'I don't think you should worry.'

'I know. I know. I don't really.'

256

We walked on together in silence, going uphill now. Then Ben said, 'It's just – '

'Yes?'

'The trouble is, I sometimes did feel, occasionally – I felt – '

I waited, but he did not go on.

'You felt something that worried you?'

'Mm.'

'And still does?'

'Well, on and off. Quite a lot, really.'

'Can I be any help?'

'Yes, but let's go on walking.' I had not realised I was slowing my pace.

Ben took in a long breath and spoke fast. 'Sometimes I think I do feel – I have felt – well, I do still feel sometimes – that other people – some people are attractive. I mean to me.'

'And – it's an unorthodox kind of attraction?'

'Yes.'

I waited, and then asked, 'As it might be to a boy, or a man?'

'Yes.'

'I see.'

'A bit – not much. Not often.'

'Yes. I see.'

'You don't think – ? Alan, you don't think, do you, that means – ?' The pitch of his voice was rising. We had stopped walking again.

'It doesn't mean that you must be homosexual, if that's what's worrying you,' I said, looking at his hands, and at mine.

'Not really?'

'No, of course it doesn't. A lot of people have felt like that at one time or another.'

'A *lot* of people?'

'I should think so.'

'And not been...?'

'And not been fundamentally homosexual. These things aren't nearly as clear-cut as people sometimes make out, you know. You don't feel nothing at all for twenty-odd years, and then suddenly fall in love. It's a very gradual business.' We began to walk on. 'There are all kinds of different stages – particularly when you're growing up; different kinds of attraction, of love. Different people to love, come to that. Most of us – most people – go through a good many of them. Some people find their real, fundamental direction quite late.'

'Later than – older than me?'

'Good lord, yes.'

'You really, honestly think that?'

'Yes. Yes, I do.'

He was silent for a moment.

'Have – Alan, have you ever felt like that?'

'Have I? Well –' Must I lie to him? Would even a half-truth endanger his trust in me, my ability to comfort him?

'Well, I suppose people vary in that way, as in so many others. But people I've known – school-friends, college-friends: I think a good many of them went through a stage like that.'

'But it never – well – took over?'

'I'm not sure what that would mean.'

'Never got so that they were – like that – for the rest of their lives?'

'Not as far as I know.'

'Mm.' After a moment, he let out a long breath. 'God!'

'You've been worrying – a good deal.'

'It's been pretty fair hell, really. All this time.'

'Is it all right now?'

'It's – oh – a *relief*. I can't tell you.'

'Good.' After a moment I said, 'Don't worry as long as that again. Tell someone before it becomes such hell. You can always tell me.'

'I thought you might be shocked.'

'My dear Ben!'

'And then I suppose I – well, I didn't really want to – '

'To admit it was even a possibility?'

'Mm.'

'I think it's usually better to tackle these things, in the end.'

'Yes.'

'But I know the feeling. Anyway, I'm there. I'm there if ever you want me. And I'm never shocked...'

'I know. I should have known. As long as you're there. Oh, Alan, I don't know what I'd do without you.'

After a minute or two he said, 'There's the river.'

I looked ahead into the darkness. 'Where?'

'There.'

I looked along his arm as he pointed, and saw the faint lines of light along the water.

'There ought to be a way round here, if I can find it in the dark,' he said.

We left the track, and went in single file along a furrow dividing two crops in the broad field. At the headland, Ben held down the barbed wire in the fence for me to cross, and I did the same for him, watching narrowly to make sure his new suit was not caught and torn. We crossed a ditch thick with nettles, and walked unevenly down steep, untilled ground towards the sound of water.

'Watch out for rabbit-holes,' said Ben. 'It's laced with them.'

At the edge, which was some way above the water, we stopped and sat down side by side. The river was running fast.

'Very full,' said Ben.

'We've had a lot of rain.'

'I suppose we have. It was pretty dry in Wales.'

'You were lucky.'

'Yes.'

We sat still; the water seemed to run louder as we listened.

'Just up there's where we used to swim,' Ben said after some time.

'Up that way?'

'Yes. There's a pool. You can dive.'

'It'd be a bit cold tonight.'

'Gosh, yes. I didn't mean now. But it's great in the summer. There's a shallow bit, too. I always thought I'd bring my children there when they were small.'

'You'd like to have children?'

'Don't you think it'd be great?'

'Yes – well, yes. In some ways I suppose I do. Sometimes, anyway:
"When lofty trees I see barren of leaves
Which erst from heat did canopy the herd –"'
'How does it go on?'
'"And summer's green all girded up in sheaves
Borne on the bier with white and bristly beard –"'
'Lovely stuff.'

I laid the flat of my hand against the book within my pocket. Was it too late now? Would it put all his trust at risk? I closed my fingers round the thick paper, remembering the care with which I had wrapped it. The risk would be no more than imaginary, if the trust was real; and if it was justified. I took the book out of my pocket and laid it on Ben's knee, pale against the dark cloth.

'This for me?'
'Many happy returns. I meant to give it to you earlier.'
He picked it up, turning towards me.
'Happier returns, perhaps,' I said.
'No. It's been terrific.'
'Not spoilt for you?'
'Not in the end. Better. Better than it's been for – oh – for months.'
'I'm very glad.'

Now it was too late to take it back. He looked at the paper, reading what I had written, then folded it back at each end, and each side, and took the book into his hand. He said nothing, turned it to read the spine, then opened it gently and evenly between his two hands.

'Oh!'

He turned two or three pages and was putting it down into the paper. Looking away, I felt his arm along my shoulders.

'Oh, Alan!'

His hair for a moment touched my neck. He said, 'You're cold?'

'Not really.'

He let me go and sat back, shaking his head. 'Such a present.'
'I thought you'd like to have a copy.'

'A copy? *A* copy! Whatever date is it?'

'Mid-eighteenth century. Just after the middle, in fact.'

'My God! I thought there hardly were any, outside museums and things.'

'As late as that, one can sometimes find one.'

'You must have had a terrific hunt, though. And spent – Alan, you shouldn't have.'

'You like it?'

'I didn't know I could be so pleased with a present. Oh, it's been a lovely day.' He smiled at me, picking up the book again, and I returned his smile.

'Where's the one about the glorious morning?'

'That's thirty-three, isn't it, or thirty-four?'

He turned over the pages. 'Here we are:

Full many a glorious morning have I seen
Flatter the mountain tops with sovereign eye –'

'Go on.'

He read the rest of the sonnet, just as it should be read, bending his head to the page in the faint light. Then he said, 'The next one's lovely, too,' and handed me the book.

I began to read:

'Why didst thou promise such a beauteous day,
And make me travel forth without my cloak –

I'm sorry, Ben. I can't see the print.'

'I don't believe you need the print.'

I made no answer.

'It doesn't matter.' He took the book from my hand. 'I must find the Lion – the one you put on the postcard.' He found it, and read it to himself, chuckling.

'So it was a fore-runner, the parody.'

'In a way. Yes.'

'I never guessed,' he said, and then, after a moment, 'You wouldn't read me another one? One of your favourites?'

'Ben – I will, another time.'

'Yes. All right. Are you tired? Should we be going home?'

'Perhaps we should. It's pretty late.'

He wrapped the book carefully in the paper again, and put it into his pocket, and we got to our feet.

The way back seemed shorter. It was more familiar now, and we walked briskly, as the night was colder. Before we came to the orchard fence, we turned past the barns to reach the gate to the yard.

Someone in the shadow of the more distant barn said, 'Ben?'

'David. Good God. What are you doing here?'

David came out onto the path, brushing hay from his dinner jacket.

'I thought you'd gone back to London,' Ben said.

'I couldn't stand it. Not with Julian. I told Piers to go without me.'

'You been sleeping in the barn?'

'A bit, I suppose. Trying to.'

'We've been down to the river. It was lovely. For a bit of fresh air.'

'Yes.'

'Come on, then. There'll be a mattress somewhere.'

We walked together towards the gate. When Ben went a little ahead to open it, David said to me quietly, 'Ben all right?'

'I think so, yes – now.'

'He was upset before?'

'Well – .'

'I know.'

'Do you think – ? Would you – ?'

'Don't worry. I'll keep an eye on him. Fend off the questions. Coming, Ben.'

We parted in the yard. I said goodnight, and thanked Ben for the party.

'Alan, goodnight. Safe home. And thank you. Thank you for everything.'

CHAPTER 50

I woke to a morning, a house, a room so empty that I was afraid of moving. I lay in bed, hearing my breath travel out into the space beyond me. Even lying down, I was shivering and unsteady; I could not believe the bed was firm on the floor. I tried to fix my mind on the furniture, the floor, the walls, the garden, but I could imagine only space, limitless and hollow, in which I felt myself sickeningly float and sway.

I tried to think of times instead – breakfast, work, the next section of the Cycle – and the little fixed points were lost in the expanse which spread round me without boundary or purpose or end. I said to myself that if I worked in the afternoon, I could walk over to the Graysons after tea to help with the clearing up. With that thought, a grief so painful overtook me that I cried out, and held the sides of the mattress with my hands. It did not slacken, but intensified, until I hunched my body over my bent knees. Then it receded enough for me to sit up, sick and shaky, and put my legs over the side of the bed.

I dared not move further, for fear of setting off another tide of pain. I did not know how I could endure it, and yet I thought it had been more tolerable than the previous void. I sat there for some indefinite time, trying to keep myself suspended, touching neither thought – which would be thought of Ben – nor the desert of the external world.

Eventually, when I was very cold, I noticed an inch of light penetrating the crevice between the curtains. Motes were moving in it. I fixed my eyes and my mind on that and moved slowly to pull a loose blanket round my shoulders, and then later to grope for my dressing gown. When that was on, and tied round me, I stood up and felt my way across the room and down the passage to the bathroom.

I cleaned my teeth and drank a little water, then went downstairs and made some coffee. It was lukewarm by the time I had drunk any of it. But the normality of the taste and the action penetrated my numbness a little. I added some hot water and managed to finish it. When I had dressed, without shaving, and pulled my bed together, I went down to my desk, found my place in the copy, opened my notebooks, and sat in front of them. I did no work until about half an hour before lunchtime, when I made a small emendation to one of the notes I had made long ago, yesterday.

At lunchtime, I ate some bread and cheese, against my inclination, and brought it all up half an hour later. I went back to the table and sat still for a time, and then, beginning to feel light-headed, I drank two cups of coffee, putting a good deal of sugar in them. Then I put on a coat and went out and walked fast for a considerable way, turning back only when the light began to fade. I felt hungry when I got home, and had a glass of whisky and tried to drink some soup. Eventually I drank two more glasses of whisky and went to bed.

My headache next morning was not much more than I should have expected. Lying in bed did not dispel it, and left too much leisure for thought. I took some aspirin and went downstairs. There were letters inside the door, and lying under one of them a piece of paper which I must have overlooked last night, returning in the dark.

Alan,
Came round to see you, but you were out. Hope that means
you've recovered from last night! Come to lunch tomorrow
(Mon.) and help finish up the leftovers,
Ben & David (here till Tuesday)

It was Ben's writing. I could not go. I stood with the paper in my hand and wanted to cry. I remembered Hopkins writing that it is not the weight or the stress of sorrow by themselves that can move us, but a touch 'Striking sideways and unlooked for' which undoes resistance and makes the edge of the blade of grief break the skin. I pressed the bit of paper between my hands, and then against my face. If I started to cry, I did not know when I would stop. I drew in a breath, and threw up my head, and yawned. As a small boy, teased at school, I had found that yawning would keep back tears for a time. I read the words on the back of the paper:

'Insul. tape. Cream. Safety pins. M's shoes. Petrol.'

They were written in a column, also in Ben's hand, and all except 'Petrol' were crossed through.

I walked backwards and forwards in the sitting-room. Work was the only real defence. I must ring up and refuse the invitation to lunch, and I must have some breakfast, but both of these could wait. I found my list of possible Norse borrowings and began checking it against Olsen's *Handbook*. When that was done, I made some coffee and a piece of toast, and took them back to the desk, and worked at the next passage of the Cycle until the middle of the morning. Then I rang the Graysons.

It was Mark, to my relief, who answered. He was unusually gruff, and took so long to reply to my apology that I was driven to a more specific excuse. I said that I had an engagement at the university in the afternoon, and had arranged to lunch there first. He said he would tell his mother.

As soon as I had rung off, I was overborne by a weight of longing to see Ben. Like the weight of water in a weir, it drove me down, almost submerging me. It would have been a relief, even a refreshment, to abandon myself to it, to go under, if the clear sense of loss had not been muddied with unease and vexation about the lie I had sent him.

I could drive to Harchester now and make the lie at least partly true. But when I thought of the car, I thought of the savage griefs which had ringed me round as I drove home – griefs kept at bay only by exhaustion and incredulity and the absolute necessity of getting home before they should close in. I felt that they would still be waiting for me, and I no longer had any of those defences.

I went back to the work on my desk, but my concentration was broken by nervousness. Every small sound seemed to be Ben or one of his family arriving to find me at home, my excuse false and my refusal inexplicable. In the end, I made some lunch early, and managed to eat some of it, then I made a list and bicycled into Bramston to get the week's shopping done. It would put the time to some use, at least, and there was little risk of meeting any of the Graysons, if they were still well-provided from the party.

Many of the food shops were shut. I realised with surprise that it was still only Monday. It had begun to rain, and I wandered between the shops in a chilly daze. I found some tins, and some expensive and stale-looking vegetables, and stocked up with folders and file paper. I remember someone – in the stationer's, I think – asking how I was, if I was all right, and my haste to get out of the shop as I made some inappropriate, standard reply.

I came home wet and cold, and when I went to run a hot bath there was no hot water, because I had forgotten to fill the Aga. I cleared it out and lit it again before I changed, and then sat by it, shivering and waiting for the kettle to boil, eating biscuits from a packet. When I heard Ben's voice at the door, the jolt was so great that all continuity was broken: I had no idea what I had been doing or thinking a moment before.

'Alan? You there?'

He opened the kitchen door before I could speak.

'I've come to say goodbye.'

'Goodbye?'

'I'm off to London tomorrow with David.'

'Oh. Oh yes.'

'You recovered from our late night?' He looked at me. 'You don't look all that great, actually.'

'I'm just cold – and cross. I let the Aga go out. I'm afraid you may have to wait a bit for tea.'

'Don't worry about tea – I mean, unless you want some. I had some at home.'

'What's the time?'

'About quarter-to-six.' I looked confusedly at my watch. 'Alan, you are all right?'

'Yes, of course I'm all right. If it's six o'clock, we'd better have a drink. What would you like?'

'Sherry?'

I went to the cupboard. 'I seem to be out of sherry. Whisky?'

'Um… yes, all right.'

'You don't like whisky?'

'I do quite. Just not too strong.'

'Water be all right?'

'Yes, of course. Fine.'

I poured out two glasses, and added some water to his from the tap.

'Thanks.' He tasted it. 'Actually, do you mind if I have a drop more?'

'Just as you like.'

He ran a good deal more water into his glass, and brought it over and leaned against the Aga. After a minute or two he said, 'I really wanted to thank you for the other night.' He stopped. 'Only – '

'You've thanked me already.'

'But I mean, properly.'

'Yes.'

'Not really. Only I don't know how – . I – . As long as you know. As long as you know what you've done for me, or even some of it.'

'Some of it I think I know.'

He smiled. 'Drink up, you're still cold.' He raised his glass, drank a little, grimaced without meaning to, and laughed.

'And when you got home?' I asked. 'It was all right? Not too many questions?'

'Yes, it was fine. Everyone was asleep – or too sleepy to ask questions, anyway. I did manage to get my mother alone, next morning, and say I was sorry I'd run out on the end of the party, and it wasn't that it hadn't been marvellous or I hadn't enjoyed it or anything. Sort of half-explained.'

'And she half-understood?'

'A bit more than half, I think, probably. And everyone thought it had been a fantastic party. Lots of people said how marvellous you'd been, chauffeuring people, and taking supper round, and being nice to the wallflowers and everything.'

I laughed.

'Mum said you even went to hunt for me, in case I'd gone off with the kitchen corkscrew.'

'Did I? I suppose I did. And had you?'

'It was in my pocket. I found it next morning.'

We both laughed.

Ben said, 'That must have been when you found me, then.'

'I suppose so. Yes.'

He turned and warmed his hands, palm down, on the lid of the hot plate.

'When you did find me: did you – had you heard much? Before, I mean, in the seed-shed; with Julian.'

'I heard something. I came past the window.'

He glanced round at me.

I drank some more whisky, and said, 'I heard you tell Julian to leave the house.'

'That was all?'

'I don't think very much more was said after that, was it? Why?'

'I just wondered.'

I looked at him sceptically, and he blushed. It was not fair. I certainly had no right to accuse him, even silently, of prevaricating; and he, after all, had not sunk to actual deceit. But there seemed no other way to deflect him before I had either to lie outright, or to tell him how much I had really overheard that evening, and by what means. That must damage the trust on which, for both of us, so much now depended. And besides, in spite of all the justifications I could produce, I was ashamed of my eavesdropping; and to Ben, few of the justifications could be made. But the advantage thus unfairly gained was damaging, too: Ben remained silent, looking down. Eventually, we both started to speak.

'Sorry,' I said.

'No, go on.'

'Just that it seems to be raining harder than ever.'

'It does, doesn't it?'

I refilled my glass. Ben's was still more than half full.

'I'm glad David could stay.'

'Yes, he was great. Next morning, too. Carting Marky off to take the glasses back, jollying him along.'

'He needed some jollying?'

'He was a bit grumpy. But I think it was mostly just staying up too late.'

'I expect so.'

'He was sorry he missed you.'

'Marky?'

'David. When we came round.'

'Oh, yes. Of course.'

'He said to say goodbye. Sent you his love.'

'Would you do the same for me?'

'Of course.'

We could hear the rain against the roof. Ben looked at his watch.

'I said I'd be back for supper.'

'I'll run you back. Unless you've got the car.'

'No, but I'll be all right.'

'It's a filthy night.'

'Never mind, I'd like the walk.'

He took his glass over to the sink, drinking a mouthful more on the way, and put it down on the draining-board.

'You'll be soaked.'

'Not badly.'

'Look, Ben: don't be silly. It won't take me twenty minutes.'

'I'd rather not, honestly.'

'But why not?'

'I'd just rather not.' He began to do up his jacket. We looked at each other.

'You weren't enjoying that whisky much, were you?' I said.

'I'm sorry. I seem to have gone off it rather.'

'Next time I shan't waste it on you.'

'I said I was sorry. And anyway – '

'Anyway what?'

'Oh, never mind.'

'Don't start saying something if you're not prepared to finish it.'

'Look, I'm going to be late.' He crossed towards the door.

'What were you going to say?'

'If you don't know, it's not much good my telling you. I *must* go.'

He went through the door quickly and banged it shut. I remained standing by the Aga in a daze of regret and exasperation, present confusion and imminent loss. Some minutes later, the door opened and Ben came in again, just beyond the threshold, with rain on the shoulders of his jacket and in his hair.

'Alan, look. I really came to thank you, and to say goodbye. I don't want to say anything else; not to quarrel with you...'

He came to stand in front of me. 'I may not see you again till next term.'

He took my hand, and we said goodbye without further explanation.

When he had gone for the second time, I found that I had begun to cry, and I leaned over the Aga and cried for a long time.

CHAPTER 51

I passed the following days in a haze of fatigue and loss. I felt as if a limb had been amputated. Sometimes it was the pain of severance which took hold of me again; more often I directed my mind to a familiar movement, towards or a desired or consoling destination – to no effect: the movement remained unachieved; the destination had vanished; my purpose was at an end before it had begun.

There seemed no reason to do anything. The little prospects of hope towards which each part of the day had proceeded – the post which could include a letter, the walk which could produce a meeting, the evening which might bring a telephone call; and the coming events of the day ahead, the coming plans for the week, all constantly, half-consciously scanned for occasions of hope to be found or engineered – these were all laid waste, a rubble of broken possibilities which could hold no real significance, no hope or purpose, even if they were to be built up again, laboriously, into the outward forms which before had contained so much promise.

I had said once to Ben that even in desolation I had assumed that life had to go on. My body still seemed to make this assumption: I ate and slept – not well, but with some kind of regularity. I had also said that one should resolve, in good time, not to despair: to hold on, to endure while one had to. I had supposed – with the easy certainty of inexperience – that in saying this I had made such a resolution. To keep it, however, was less natural than to keep the needs of physical life supplied. The only conscious purpose remaining to me was an intellectual one: the Cycle had to be completed. Aristotle says that intellect without desire moves nothing. I should have to see if this was true.

My sleep usually became less broken and less shallow towards morning. Waking late, I would sit for some time at the kitchen table, drinking several cups of coffee, and resting my face in my hands to prevent myself from reading the newspaper, or – after I had looked at the handwriting on the envelopes – from opening the post, until my headache was dispelled. When I could read without strain, I would clear up, and try to get some work, at least, done on the Cycle before the end of the morning. Everything took longer than before. I was constantly distracted by thoughts of Ben: by recollections of his presence in the room; by conjectures of what he was doing at that moment; what he would say to me if he came in now, through the door; what he would think; what I should say to him. I held interminable, futile inquisitions on our past conversations, in case there was anything I could have done or said to alter their outcome. I went over and over each part of the night of the dance.

I achieved so little every day, and with so many inaccuracies, that I knew I ought to start working by result instead of by time: to establish a quota of lines, and go on working straight through the day until they were done and properly checked. But I could not find the strength – either of purpose or of intellect. I was constantly tired: everything I did seemed to be uphill, against the heavy, ceaseless drag of its own weight of purposelessness.

One morning, almost a week after I had calculated that Ben must be back at Cambridge, Ruth came in to offer me a ticket for the concert of the local Choral Society. It was a little before eleven, and she found me sitting still unshaven at the kitchen table.

'Oh, good. I was afraid you'd be working.'

'No. No, I'm having some coffee.'

I poured her out a cup, and moved the marmalade to a less obtrusive place.

'I wouldn't have disturbed you in the morning, Alan; only if you would like the ticket there'd hardly be time to send it. And I was going past your turn – '

'No, that's all right. Very kind of you. On Saturday, you said?'

We completed the transaction: I took the ticket because I could not think of a way to refuse it. I gave Ruth some more coffee, and tried to find an opening to general conversation which would lead naturally to enquiries for Ben. I thought of saying,

'Term's started, I suppose?' but the words would not leave my mouth.

'We heard from Ben,' said Ruth. 'A letter, yesterday.'

'How is he?'

'Fine, I think. Working hard. He said to give you his love.'

Such love was a substitute for a letter, as well as for anything more. I nodded, as gratefully as I could.

'His tripos must be fairly soon?' I said then.

'About six weeks to go, I think.'

Her voice had changed.

'Is he worried?'

'I don't think badly. He'd like to get a two-one. I suppose I worry for him, really, more than he does.'

'He'll get a two-one?'

'I hope so. He's a bit on the borderline, he thinks.'

I nodded again, then we both looked up at once and felt together, for a moment, the possible misery of Ben's disappointment.

'He should be all right,' I said.

'I think he should. He's working very hard. He said to tell you, he may not have much time to write. But he sent lots of love and hopes the Cycle's going well.'

'Not too badly. Give him my love, when you're writing.'

'I will.' She got up. 'Unless you want to write yourself, Alan? I'm sure he'd love a letter, if you've time. Only you may not get an answer very soon.'

I wrote late that evening, as soon as I had finished a respectable number of lines.

I made at least two rough drafts of that letter, though I do not seem to have kept them. I said that I did not expect an answer, as I knew he was working hard, and I think I gave him some advice – perhaps superfluously – about limiting his working hours and taking some time off every day. I know I also made some sort of apology for my ill temper at our last meeting, and thanked him for the generosity which had prevented us from parting on bad terms. My news I confined to work and the garden and the weather: I remember I found a little joke in Pope about a topiarist who advertised 'A Quick-set Hog shot up into a Porcupine, by its being forgot a week in rainy weather'. And I told him of the prospect of the concert.

I could say almost nothing of what I really wanted to say: even to say what I did cost me a great deal more effort than ever before in writing to Ben, and then so much of it was stiff or dull. But it gave me comfort, nevertheless, to write it and post it.

For some days afterwards I achieved a reasonable amount of work, and I was thankful for that when I heard from Douglas about a week later. He had discovered that he might be able to take a sabbatical year, starting as soon as the summer term was over. He wanted to spend most of it abroad, and he asked if I thought we could get the text of the Cycle finished by July. I looked at the work that remained, with anxiety and not a little guilt. But at least it was not impossible now, and my uneasiness did not hold my mind long, for in the same post was a letter from Ben. I opened it last. He had written on a postcard – right across, leaving no room for the stamp or the address – and sent it in an envelope.

Wed.

Dear Alan, very many thanks for your letter. I'm sorry you shd. have been worrying about that last visit. I think we were both a bit edgy after the recent stress & strain. It didn't matter; please forget about it. Work is going OK – quite a grind, but I go running w. David most afternoons (you'll be glad to hear), or sometimes play squash (badly). Glad the Cycle's going well. Don't worry abt. the garden: I'll come & help you weed before it's actually over your head. Yes, Cambr. is looking lovely – almost as good as overleaf. (But then they have gardeners!) When are you coming over? Doesn't the dictionary need you? Lots of love,

Ben

I held my face against the card, with unreasonable joy swooping through me. It could do no good: no more could come of it; but he wanted to see me; he was the same as he had always

274

been, his candour and affection unchanged. And he had forgiven me so wholly that he pretended there was nothing to forgive. Perhaps it was enough that he should exist, and continue ever the same to me. Perhaps it was unnecessary, as well as unprofitable, to hope for more.

I felt this again, though not continuously, as I worked through the days leading to the next meeting of the Dictionary Committee. My meeting with Ben must be short, I decided, for several reasons, including the two I gave him: that I must not interrupt his work, or my own, for too long. But the prospect lightened the surrounding days as a dog-rose lightens a hedge.

We met on the Backs just after mid-day, for a picnic lunch. Ben brought bread and cheese and cold sausages; I brought fruit and, after some indecision, a bottle of wine.

Ben looked well, though he admitted he was tired, and I could feel a certain caution in his attitude to me – an anxiety that things should go well, a carefulness to say nothing I might not like. It saddened me that my bad temper should still be having this effect, and it produced an answering anxiety in myself. But I thought it could not outlast many longer meetings, and when we had refilled our glasses, and gathered up the remains of the food, and Ben had lain back against the bank and fallen asleep in the sun, I felt our mutual trust still intact.

I sat and watched him, across some dictionary entries laid on my knee, and reminded myself that I must take my happiness as I found it, not reaching after permanence or completeness.

A little before it was time for me to go, David came over a bridge to join us.

'Ben said I'd find you both here,' he called, crossing the grass. Then, lowering his voice, 'He's asleep? I should think he needs it. How are you?'

'How are you? Have some wine. Do you mind using Ben's glass?'

We sat and talked in the sun. David seemed more than usually ebullient, almost excited. He confirmed that Ben was working very hard, but could usually be persuaded to take an hour or two off in the afternoon.

'You must have exams yourself?'

'Well, yes: the same as Ben. But – well – '

'You're not letting them worry you?'

He looked at me, and smiled. 'I'm not such a worrier, really – about that sort of thing, anyway.'

'Very sensible. And lucky for Ben.'

'About music I worry; and people, sometimes.'

'How is the music?'

He looked up, and I recognised the source of his excitement. 'Pretty good, actually.'

'I think Ben said you'd had some more solos?'

'Yes. And I'm thinking – I don't know – it's a long shot – but I might try for one of the music colleges next year.'

'To study singing?'

'Yes.'

'How exciting. Why not?'

'Well – the only thing is, if I do all right in finals, it would be instead of research.'

'Yes.'

'You don't think that would be a mistake? A – waste?'

'*I* don't think so?' He made no answer. 'You mean I might be biased in favour of my own trade?' I laughed. 'Well, but good heavens, I'm hardly as biased as that.'

'But research – I mean – your morality plays for instance ...'

'Mystery plays.'

'Mystery plays, sorry. It's taking years, isn't it, editing them? Years of hard work?'

'And singing won't be hard work?'

'Yes. Yes, of course it will. And I may not get in, anyway. But some people, my father – I just wondered – '

I hesitated, uncertain quite what he was asking me.

'What matters is the music, surely, in the end – or the plays, the poetry: making them available, conveying them to other people. I don't see why my footnotes should convey more than your singing – than your solo last Christmas, for example.'

David shook his head, smiling. I looked at my watch.

'I ought to go. Were you going to wake Ben?'

276

'It seems a shame.' He looked down. 'I'll wait for him. He's getting fresh air, after all.'

'Yes. All right. Say goodbye to him for me.'

'I will.'

I left them in the sun: David with two or three history books beside him, taken from Ben's bag, and a score open in his hand; Ben lying, still asleep, against the bank.

26th May, '64

Dear Alan,

Many thanks for your letter, and many more for saying you'll do your damnedest to get it all finished by July. I don't see why we shouldn't make it, if all goes well. The plays arrived a couple of days later. Good to think that's the penultimate batch. I hope you've got mine by now. I enclose a list of queries – sorry there seem to be rather more than usual...

Don't we usually put MS folio numbers (and give recto or verso) for each reference, except where ibid will do?

I've been reckoning to use England and Pollard verbatim for comparisons, unless otherwise stated. Who are you using for Lazarus *ll. 135-137?*

Have you had time to sort out the confusion about 'wele'?...

Almost every one of Douglas's long list of queries was my fault. Only his scrupulous, dependable scholarship had prevented my mistakes from getting into print.

Alarm, relief and chagrin confused my mind. I could not decide whether to sit down immediately to the correction of everything on the list, or to get the day's section done first, and clear the decks. In the end, I wrote Douglas a postcard before starting the work already planned for the day.

Thanks for your letter and parcel, both received this morning. Forgive an abominably careless piece of work. Corrections to follow.

A.P.   *27.v.1964*

I took this to the post after lunch, and then worked on through the afternoon, finishing the day's stint shortly after supper. I went to bed early and set my alarm clock for before six. In the wet, grey light and undistracted silence of the hours before breakfast, I went through my mistakes, considering, correcting and double-checking each of them with a clear head and sober and unshakeable exactness. When I had finished, I felt better than I had felt for several weeks – for almost the whole stretch of time since the night of the dance. I felt again a sense of capacity, ready to be used and directed. I made a good breakfast, started the day's work, and fell asleep with my head on the notebooks. I dreamt of Ben. What we had said or done, I could not recall when I woke, but he had been there, and I was filled with joy.

His exams began the following week. I thought of him when I woke, and often throughout each day, willing him calm and speed and favourable questions, sending him support and love, in a way which I could not defend as rational, but I could not eschew, either, as there was now no other way to help him. It was fine weather. I hoped he was not too hot.

The evening his exams ended, the weather broke; and in the middle of a thunderstorm, the telephone rang: it was Ben, ringing from a callbox. The line was crackling so much I could hear only occasional words. I shouted conventional questions into the whirr and splutter of noise: 'How did it all go?' 'Are you celebrating tonight?' In the end, I managed to take down his number and ring back. The line was slightly better.

'Alan?'

'Ben? Is that better? Can you hear all right?'

'Yes. Yes, I can. Much better. Have you been having this storm?'

'It's going over a bit now. How is it with you?'

'Almost finished.'

'And the exams?'

'Well – .' There was a pause. 'Alan – . Oh God, I do hate telephones.'

'I know. What is it? You didn't like the papers?'

'They weren't bad, actually. But then...'

'You ran out of time?' The crackling had begun again.

'Sorry?'

'Did you run out of time?'

'No. I thought I'd fitted everything in pretty well. And some of the questions were really nice. But I seem to have messed them up, somehow. Badly.'

'Maybe not as badly as you think?'

'Sorry. What?'

'Maybe not as badly as you think?'

He was silent.

'Look, telephones are so unsatisfactory. Would you like to talk about this properly? We could meet – .'

'Could we? Would you mind? I could get the bus.'

'Or I could come over in the car.'

'No, no. I'll come. You're busy. Anyway, I'd like to get out of Cambridge for a bit.'

'That would be all right, would it? You wouldn't be cutting term or anything?'

'I shouldn't think so. Oh, that'd be really great.'

Through more crackling we managed to arrange that he would come in time for lunch, the day after next.

'And you'll be all right till then? You won't be worrying?'

'No, I'll be all right.'

'I should get some sleep.'

'Yes. Yes, I will.'

'Good. All right then.'

'See you then.'

I held the receiver a moment longer before putting it down. Ben must have done the same, for I heard him say, 'No thanks. No, I need some sleep. I'm going – ' before he rang off.

CHAPTER 52

He arrived in the sun, knocking rainwater from the bushes that overhung the path. I went to the door as he reached it, and he put an arm round my shoulders and hugged me, and then stood back, uncertain how to go on after such a greeting, waiting for me to ask him in.

I gave him sherry, and asked questions about the time of the bus and the state of the traffic. The sun had gone in, and before I refilled his glass the rain had started.

'Look at that,' said Ben. 'The weather really has broken.'

'It was fine here yesterday.'

'It was in Cambridge, too, I suppose.'

'You were busy recovering?'

'Sleeping! Yes, and celebrating. There were some parties – '

'You're feeling a bit better about it all, now?'

'I suppose so. Yes, a bit.'

'I expect it was partly a reaction after all the strain. Mainly a reaction, even.'

'Yes, and – people said – oh, I don't know.'

We drank a little more of our sherry.

'D'you think I could show you the papers?'

'I'd like to see them. Bring them into the kitchen while I have a look at the potatoes.'

'You haven't gone making things specially, have you?' Ben said, as I shifted the saucepan and put in some salt. 'I feel bad about taking up your time as it is.'

'No, of course not. I've got to eat something myself, after all. Have you got the papers with you?'

He took them out of his pocket, and I studied one of them, leaning against the stove.

'Which questions did you do?'

'On the general paper? Number four, I think, and – wait a minute – '

'Fifteen?'

'No. I marked that, but in the end I did eighteen instead. And then twenty-one – that was fairly straightforward.'

'Eighteen looks rather fun.'

'Yes; and I thought I'd done it all right. I was comparing the two revolutions, the Russian one and the Grand Rebellion: there was quite a lot. But apparently that wasn't what they were asking for at all: you were supposed to talk about something quite different.'

'It sounds perfectly sensible to me. One question, anyway, on one paper. What about this paper?'

'Well, it was a bit like that, too. I thought I'd done OK. I did – that one, and that one, and – let's see – number twelve. And then it turned out I'd done that all wrong. I should have –'

'How do you know?'

'I found out afterwards: someone told me.'

'Who told you?'

'It was Julian.'

I was silent. The saucepan lid rattled, and I moved the pan further over and tilted the lid.

'What the hell does Julian know about it?' I said.

Ben looked startled, then considerably happier. I was exhilarated by anger and relief.

'You think he was wrong?'

'Wrong? I don't think he had any interest in being right.'

'But – then why – ?'

'How should I understand Julian's motives? And why did you listen to him? That's not easy to understand, either.'

'No, I suppose not. I suppose it was stupid. I needn't have bothered you.'

'Oh Ben, of course I didn't mean that. Of course you must always come if something's worrying you. You know I'm always – glad to see you. I only meant that you should have some sense of self-preservation.'

'Yes.'

'I can't imagine why – . Well. If you do see Julian, at least you needn't believe everything he tells you.'

'No. No, I know. I haven't been seeing him, actually. I'd steered clear of him the whole term. It was just, after the exams. There were a whole lot of us; someone had brought some champagne. And he came and joined in – it was on the Backs – and I couldn't very well tell him to go away; and I didn't see why I should have to go. And anyway, it was all sort of – we were all celebrating; nothing mattered much any more. And I ended up next to him, and he started asking me how it had gone – you know – '

'I can imagine.'

'And then it all got too much, and I couldn't think what to do, and in the end, I rang you.'

'I'm very glad you did. Have some more sherry.'

'No, thanks.' He sighed at length. 'God, I am an idiot.'

'Not most of the time.'

He smiled and shook his head. I looked at him, smiling myself.

'But I do think it's about time you learnt how far Julian's to be trusted. You've known him – what? – nearly two years, haven't you?'

'More like three. Shall I do that?'

He drained the potatoes for me into the sink, and brought them back. I put some butter on them, and chopped in some mint.

'Three?'

'He'd been at my school. Robin – one of my friends – had a brother in his form. That was how – . Do you remember that party? At the University, just after I'd done A-Levels?'

He knew I remembered it: the blood came into his cheeks. I bent to the oven door.

'I think this must be hot by now.'

While I was getting out the casserole, I said, 'Yes, I remember it. So that was where you met Julian?'

'I'd met him vaguely before – with Robin and his brother, a couple of times. But that was where I first really talked to him.'

'I see.'

I filled our plates, and Ben carried them to the table while I poured out cider.

'I suppose I should have known, really, even then,' he said, as we sat down.

'Known?'

'What a – what Julian's like.'

'You weren't very old.'

'No. And it wasn't all that obvious. Gosh, this is good. He was very nice to start with – talking about plays, filling up my glass – '

'Yes, yes.'

'And when it did begin to get a bit ropey – some of his friends – you know – we'd gone on to someone's rooms – I didn't know any of them really, except him. And when it got – when I really didn't know how to cope, it turned out he wasn't there – he'd gone off somewhere: said he'd be back, but he wasn't. So I never really knew how much he'd had to do with it all – whether I could blame him. And I suppose – I gave him the benefit of the doubt.'

'So, what did you do then? How did you – cope?'

'I got out.'

'And drove here?'

'Yes.'

'I see. Yes, I see.'

There was a silence.

'I wish I'd known that,' I said, at last.

'I suppose I should have told you. It would have saved trouble.'

'Saved you trouble, chiefly, I'm afraid.'

'You were still right, actually. You said I took the risk of killing someone. And nothing's really a good enough reason for that. Not even – nearly getting – '

'A fate worse than death?'

'More or less.'

'Maybe. But still, I wish I'd known. I should have known – tried to find out – before – '

'Actually, I could have rung my parents,' he said after a moment. 'That's what I should have done. I suppose I thought it wouldn't be grown up. And I didn't know where to find a telephone.'

I nodded.

'I didn't tell my parents I was coming over, by the way. Today, I mean.'

'You'd rather I didn't mention it either?'

'Well, perhaps – if you didn't mind. There didn't seem to be very much point in worrying them.'

'Or indeed very much to worry about.'

He smiled and shook his hair out of his eyes. His plate was empty.

'Have some more?'

'May I? It's terribly good. And the new potatoes. Leave enough for yourself, though.'

'There's plenty.'

I filled his glass, too, and then paused with the bottle in my hand.

'And when I propose to drive after too much whisky,' I said, 'you get the rough end of that, too.'

He did not answer.

'Why didn't you tell me?'

'Well – '

'Yes, that's unfair. I made it impossible.'

'No; if it had really come to the crunch, I think I'd have told you. Though it would have taken some doing.'

I was silent.

'You were worried about something: you said in your letter. And I knew, anyway.'

'Did you?'

'Of course I did. And I know you still are, though not so much.'

I looked up.

'You would say, Alan, wouldn't you, if there was anything I could do?'

I nodded, and got up abruptly.

Ben joined me at the larder door. 'Alan. Stop *minding*.'

'I thought I'd just get the next course out.'

'Everyone does something stupid now and then – drinks too much, loses their temper. Goodness knows, you've put up with it from me often enough. It's got to be my turn sometimes.'

I felt a sudden, joyful irresponsibility, and rashly put an arm round him.

'You are a magnanimous friend, Ben. Don't let your food get cold. I'll bring the strawberries.'

We ate strawberries and cream with the abandon of mutual admissions made and understandings reached.

Afterwards, drinking coffee in the sitting-room, eating the peppermint chocolates that Ben had brought, we talked again, and more cheerfully, about the history course. The rain fell steadily, and I lit the fire, and stood the coffee-pot in the hearth. At a pause in the conversation, I said tentatively, 'So that was your objection to Cambridge. Or one of your objections.'

Ben nodded. 'Quite a lot of them were there, or going on there next year, like Julian.'

'And you couldn't tell me?'

He shook his head. 'I couldn't begin. I hardly even knew what words to use – even to my father. Least of all my father.'

I hesitated, and then asked, 'And it was the same later on, in the Lake District?'

'Yes – well – by that time I hardly knew what my real reasons were, any more. That evening, after the party, had sort of coloured everything – everything about Cambridge. And you'd done such a lot to help me get in. And you were so pleased when I did. I really dreaded telling you. I kept putting it off. And then Marky dropped me in it. And I still didn't know how to talk about it, and my foot was hurting – .' He broke off.

'So I imposed my authority unfairly again. And again on inadequate evidence.'

'Still, it was in the right direction.'

'Was it?'

'Of *course* it was. To have missed Cambridge – my God! If it hadn't been for you – .'

'I'm glad. And your fears – didn't come to anything?'

'Not really. Though – no thanks to Julian, I suppose.'

'No, you don't owe Julian much. Except a little experience, perhaps.'

Ben shook his head, laughing, and I asked him about the end-of-term festivities, which he said he could now properly enjoy. He wasn't going to a May Ball, but he was going to see Charles and Joanna in the Footlights, and David was singing in a concert in the college garden, and Jim and some friends were giving a party on the river, in punts.

'Jim plays rugger?'

'That's right. Lived across the landing my first year. And I borrowed his room for a bit last autumn.'

I nodded.

'Some of his friends are rather thick, but he's great. He was terrific when I was looking for somewhere in the autumn – when I was moving out of Julian's. Julian was being sort of – difficult about it, and Jim was furious. "Typical bloody queer," he said. "Shifty, devious".'

'Do you think he was right?'

'Well, he was right about Julian, as I found out later on.'

'But about such behaviour being typical – typical of – such people.'

Ben stretched back in his chair, considering.

'I wouldn't have thought it could be, all the time, could it? I mean, I don't think things are ever as tidy as that: "If you're like this, you're always like that." It's nonsense. It's like racism or something. And anyway, I know people – someone ... What do you think?'

'I think ... Well, I think that people sometimes put too much emphasis on that aspect of one's choice: is the beloved a man or a woman? Or, for that matter, old or young? rich or poor? a compatriot or a foreigner? Any of those things may seem important. But what matters in the end, surely, is simply who the beloved person *is*.'

'Just *as* a person?'

'Yes.'

We were both silent, and then I went on slowly, 'There could be someone – I think there are some people, a few, who seem so admirable in themselves, so delightful, that one must love them, quite irrespective of age, or sex, or anything else. So – *excellent* that those things, and one's own tendencies – preferences – in the ordinary way seem to be mere accidents, irrelevances.'

Ben looked up without speaking, and then turned to stare into the fire.

'I can imagine that,' he said eventually, 'though it must be quite rare.'

'People like that are rare.'

'Yes.'

'"My love is of a birth as rare
As 'tis for object strange and high:
It was begotten by Despair
Upon Impossibility."'

'Who said that?'

'Andrew Marvell.'

'Poor man.'

'Yes. But now and then – . Beatrice was nine years old when Dante first saw her.'

'And fell in love with her?'

'And wrote in his memory "*Incipit Vita Nova*".'

'Nine! How old was he?'

'Nearly ten.'

He smiled and shook his head.

'Think of Marky at that age.'

'Or any of you.'

'Mm.'

A piece of wood, burning, fell into the hearth, and he picked it up in the tongs and threw it back onto the fire. He shook his hand.

'Phew! That's hot!'

I stood up. 'What about a cup of tea?'

'Lovely.'

We set the tray together. It pleased me, as always, that he should know his way so well about the kitchen, and yet, as always, avoid assuming charge.

'What are you doing in the vacation?' I asked as I was pouring out the tea.

'We want to go to Greece in July – David and me. We haven't really fixed it yet, but that's the plan.'

'Greece? How marvellous. Do you want to borrow an *Odyssey*? Or some Plato? I'll see what translations I've got.'

'Come too,' he said suddenly.

I sat still, without answering, and then put down the teapot. He looked at me.

'Ben. I'd love to. But I think I'd better not.'

'Oh. Why not?'

'Well, various reasons. David, for instance.'

'David?'

'Might he not mind? Shouldn't you consult him?'

'*Mind*? Alan – No, of course he wouldn't mind.'

'And anyway, no; I'm afraid it's impossible. I've got to get the whole of the Cycle finished by the end of July. And I'm fairly seriously behind with it already.'

'And David can't manage later. You couldn't bring it with you?'

'It's my only copy – I daren't risk it travelling. And besides, one loses time. There's no substitute for regular hours, at home, with no distractions.'

'Mightn't some distractions be worth it? Delphi – ? Sounion – ?'

'Oh, Ben, do stop it! Of course they would – more than worth it – if I hadn't got to meet this deadline. Douglas is relying on it, and I've promised.'

'All right, of course you must. I'll stop tempting you. I'm sorry.'

I smiled. 'Have some more tea?'

'Yes, please. I mustn't be too long. What's the time?'

He had not asked my other reasons.

'About four minutes to five.'

'To five? Help! Can I make the five o'clock bus, possibly?'

'From the main road? No.'

'I'd no idea – '

'When's the next one?'

'Not for hours: gets in about midnight.'

'I can give you supper.'

'It's not that – that would be lovely – if you're sure it's not a bore – but Graham locks up at eleven-thirty.'

'Can you ring him?'

'Yes, I suppose I could. It's just – '

'What?'

'Well, I'd have to explain. And he's quite a strict landlord, and I'm not *absolutely* sure – '

I looked at him. 'Ben. You said you weren't cutting term.'

'I think I only said I wasn't sure. And actually, I'm still not sure. I bet my tutor would have given me permission, if I'd asked him.'

'Which is why you took good care not to ask him?'

'All right. Only it seems so silly, when there's no more work or anything. And I really did want to see you.'

I shook my head. 'You should plan your crimes a bit more carefully. Would you like me to drive you back?'

'No. No, of course not. I'll ring Graham. I can tell him something – say I've been consulting you on academic matters. Well, it's true.'

'In part. All right. You ring him, and I'll go and organise some supper. I think there's enough of the casserole left.'

'No, that's for your lunch tomorrow. At least I'm not going to make extra cooking for you. Let's have whatever you were going to have: bread and cheese.'

Roskoff didn't let him off immediately. While I was looking through my stores in the larder, I could see Ben standing first on one foot and then on the other, and playing with the flex as he talked. By the time he joined me, he looked relieved, though his face was rather hot.

'It's OK. He wasn't very cross, and he's going to leave the side door open for me. He sent you his regards. And said he looked forward to hearing about our academic discussion.'

'Perhaps we'd better have one.'

'Actually, I'm worried about taking up your working time.'

'One evening won't make much difference.'

He looked sceptical. 'When you're so pushed for time?'

I didn't know what to say.

'I could get the supper.'

'All right. That would be a help. Thank you. And when you've finished, I'll show you the play I'm doing at the moment. That can count as checking.'

I got quite a lot done while he cooked and laid the table; and when he had finished he came in quietly and sat down by the fire, and read the paper and one of the books by my chair – Isaac Rosenberg, I think, or Wilfred Owen – until I put down my pen. My happiness in his company, unexpectedly prolonged, and in his serious concern for my work, which I found very touching though not always convenient, seemed to be a force for concentration, and not for distraction. I was not many lines short for the day when I stopped writing and brought the pages over to the fire. We had some sherry and read the play, taking parts, with considerable enjoyment and some laughter. I noted a few corrections as we went, and while Ben was dishing up I put them into the text.

He had made thick onion soup and grated a lot of the cheese to put on top of it, and there were baked apples in the oven. While we were eating, I asked him about the places he and David hoped to see in Greece; and when he told me of David's interest in ancient Athens, and especially in Plato, I brought the Penguin translation of the *Symposium* to the table and read him one of my favourite passages, where Aristophanes describes the first human beings, with their double nature – a man and a woman, or two men, or two women – joined into a single person: ever since the gods divided them, each pair has been trying to join up again, and become complete once more.

Ben smiled as I put the book down. 'It's a great idea. And then you'd know when you'd found the right person: they'd be your other half, the one who'd been right for you all along. You couldn't do anything wrong, really.'

'About who to choose, who to love? Perhaps not. Though there would still be better and worse ways of treating each other. I don't think Plato would say that anyone, of any inclination, could claim exemption from all the rules.'

'Are there rules?'

'Well, yes. Don't you think so?'

'Like what?'

'Oh, just the ordinary things that apply to everyone: not amusing yourself at other people's expense; not making commitments you don't intend to keep; not taking advantage of someone who's younger or less experienced – those are the ones Plato mentions specifically, I think.' I hesitated. 'Honesty – as far as possible; integrity – keeping your own and not – not trying to – distort anyone else's – .' I stopped.

After a moment, Ben said, 'I wish you could tell me what's wrong.'

I still did not speak. He put down his spoon and said, without looking at me, 'Not if you can't, of course. But you do know, don't you, I wouldn't let it go any further?'

'I know.'

There was a long silence.

'All right,' he said, and then, 'I won't ask any more.'

I seemed to be struggling on every front at once.

'You mustn't let it worry you,' I said eventually.

'You're not ill?'

'No, I'm not ill. It's just – something that comes over me, now and then. Something – I'm sorry it had to be while you're here.'

He shook his head.

A lie seemed necessary to get us back from the precarious edge of truth.

'It's no-one – nothing to do with anyone you know,' I said.

He nodded, and leant across the corner of the table and put his hand over mine. I sat quite still, steadying my other hand against my knee, and the contact with Ben sent comfort flowing into me, beyond all speech. Then I turned my hand under his, holding palm to palm for a moment, before withdrawing it.

'You mustn't miss the second bus. I'll start the coffee. I think we've got time for some, if I run you to the main road.'

Driving back, clearing up the supper, waking next morning, I felt a broad pit of dissatisfaction lying below all the happiness of Ben's visit.

He had turned to me, spontaneously, immediately, in his anxiety; and by his choice we had spent most of a day alone together. There was matter for happiness, too, in much that he had said. There was no longer any special reason for concern about his performance in the exams (though I reminded myself that there had not been any very strong reason for confidence, either), and he seemed to have shaken finally and consciously free of Julian's dubious ascendancy. He was enjoying Cambridge, beyond all doubt: there, at least, I had been right to exert some force of persuasion, or so he thought.

He had wanted me to go with him and David to Greece, and my reason for refusing had not only convinced him without offence or the appearance of ingratitude but, being true, had saved me from some of the pain of that decision, and from all the danger of the opposite one. We had even touched on homosexuality, and Ben seemed to be feeling his way towards a general opinion which was not illiberal. And I had been able to suggest a distinction between a disregard for that particular aspect of traditional morality, and a general disrespect for right and wrong in matters of human relationship. I could not help feeling that that put Julian and myself very clearly on opposite sides of one line, at least – and I thought Ben knew it. And I had been able to speak for a uniqueness of love which could arise from the uniqueness of the beloved, overriding, occasionally, all lesser issues. Here, too, I thought I had convinced him that I spoke truly, and even perhaps that I spoke from experience.

Then he had confided in me, much more completely than ever before, about his earlier fears and difficulties; and had matched my increase of sympathy for him with his ready forgiveness of my previous obtuseness.

Above all, there had been Ben's tenderness to my feelings – his quick-eyed penetration of my misery, and his touching balance of reticence and concern.

Besides all this, there had been our simple happiness together – working and reading without distraction in the same room, reading aloud and laughing, taking turns to produce a meal. There had been enjoyment even in Ben's breaking of bounds – a sense of complicity in an offence so mild, and so gratifying in origin, that only a very little teasing was proper, to remind him, and me, that we should not take such complicity quite for granted. And he had laid his hand over mine, and consolation and even love, of a kind, had run from him into me until I thought I could contain it no more.

What more could I want? Only that it should be what it seemed – our honesty with each other, our trust, our quick concern, our readiness to forgive, our domestic tranquillity: that it should all be founded on something more durable than the chance of a day, the concealment of everything I felt most strongly, of nine parts of my love, and all my anguish. It meant nothing, it led nowhere, it could not stand. Without love – love declared and accepted, love reciprocated – it could be, and would be, 'with Time's injurious hand crushed and o'erworn'.

And what was it that was standing between us and that revelation, that consummation?

I remembered Ben's uncertain voice in the hall, the lamp flame shrinking and stretching, the 'sort of funny voice' which had asked him, 'Are you all by yourself in the house?' And then, later, his wretchedness under my unrelenting anger, his inability to tell me, even in his own defence, why he 'had to get away then – couldn't wait'. I thought of Julian's serene satisfaction in his power to attract younger men – to enjoy their admiration, to make use of them, to make them suffer now and then.

Somewhere there, surely, Ben's terror that he might himself be homosexual had been engendered – or, at the least, some seed, sown earlier, had been quickened into growth? He had not allowed that fear and horror to spread to all homosexuals: he resisted illiberal generalisations, refusing to believe that 'things are ever as tidy as that: if you're like this, you're always like that. It's nonsense.' And David was his close and valued friend, the friend that Ben knew he could trust.

But it would take more than Ben's kindly, liberal common sense, more even than David's friendship, to eradicate a horror so deeply rooted, or exorcise the demons called into being by those early encounters with unscrupulous and predatory homosexuals.

And so the greater the happiness of that day, the warmer and more open the affection, the nearer we had approached to the truth that still lay hidden, then the more painful the irony was that it was not, and could never be true, that the joy in which, for the moment, we had been living, was not our life, and could not for long be even a little part of it.

Two months ago, such evidences of Ben's closeness and affection would have given me days of bright exultation. Now, while I took note of them and felt gratitude – for without them, how much more empty still everything would have been – I cried hopelessly over the sink as I washed up the breakfast. It was all such a waste, such a waste, such a waste.

I tried to find strategies for dealing with this state of mind. I dragged myself through the next stretches of the Cycle with little rewards, as for a reluctant child: an extra biscuit with my coffee; ten minutes in the garden, tying up a rose and thinking about Ben; a glass of sherry with the last twenty lines before supper; or, when the sherry ran out, a glass of whisky. I was aware now of the danger of drinking more whisky than I intended when I was in low spirits, and of the effect it could have both on my behaviour and on my judgement. I kept strict count of my consumption, but there were still evenings when I felt a strong pull beyond the limit I set, and once or twice I did find some excuse for another half-glass.

I told myself that I was paying for the exaltation of our day together with a corresponding depression – with a 'low' after a 'high', as my students would have said. I could not really expect one without the other: it was part of the human condition, and I must not repine. I should work my way out of it, and return eventually to the level plain.

But what was there to look for or to hope for on the plain?

CHAPTER 53

A week or two after Ben's visit, I saw him on the far side of Market Square. He turned, as I watched him, and saw me, and put down one of the bags he was carrying and waved strenuously. I waved in return, and pushed through the confusion of vans and cardboard boxes, and between the ends of the market stalls, to join him on the pavement. His face and shoulders were in the sun, and the wind was blowing his hair about.

'Alan! I rang you. You must have left before I did.'

'I was quite early this morning.' I waited a moment and then asked, 'What was it?'

'I got a two-one.'

'Ben! My dear Ben!' I put my hands on his shoulders, and we looked at each other in delight. 'I am so glad.'

'Only just, but I did.'

'Tremendous!'

He put his second bag down, leaning it against his leg, and put his hands on my shoulders reciprocally.

'And I was so worried.'

'And you needn't have been.'

'I would have been, though, without you, – right up till now. It would have ruined the end of term. And all the time – '

'And all the time there was nothing to worry about – apart from a little credulity, perhaps.'

He laughed rather ruefully; then, as I joined in, more hilariously, and we leaned back, laughing, against each other's grasp.

'You really earned it, Ben,' I said then. 'You really did work. You should be proud of that.'

'Oh, I am,' he said, still laughing, and shifted a little, and one of his shopping bags toppled sideways by our feet. 'Oh, Lord!'

We crouched to pick up oranges and tins of soup which were rolling across the pavement, Ben working one-handedly as he steadied the other bag.

'Is the olive oil OK?'

'As far as I can see. This seems to be leaking, though.'

'Is it cream or yoghurt?'

'Cream.'

'Would be. Can we wedge it? Have one of these: they won't go back in the packet.' We ate chocolate biscuits and carried the bags up the street in the sun and stowed them in his family car.

'Where are you going now?' I asked.

'Only the library, then home.'

'Have you got to get back straight away? Shall we go and have a drink somewhere? We ought to celebrate.'

'I'm not in a rush. I'd love to. As long as I get back before the cream goes sour. What's left of it.'

We spent half an hour in the library together. Ben returned his family's books, and made some reservations for things on his reading list. He lent me a ticket – since mine were at home – for the new biography of Wyatt, which I found among the recent acquisitions. It is an enterprising little library, with nearly half a shelf of Middle English literature, and an obliging readiness to order slightly more obscure books from central stock.

Then we drove out by the valley road, and stopped at the Eight Bells just as it opened. We were the only people in the bar. Consulting Ben, I bought a bottle of their best red wine, which was not bad, and we took a couple of glasses and went across the lawn to the edge of the river and sat in the sun. Ben bought some potato crisps in a bag, so that we shouldn't be drinking on empty stomachs – he said that chocolate biscuits didn't count – and we drank his health, and talked unhurriedly and intermittently, and skimmed stones on the water until we saw a water-vole swimming at the further edge, and left him in peace. I gave Ben the remains of the bottle to take back with him. He was leaving for Greece in four or five days.

Alan,

It really is all as terrific as this. Not the town, which is gritty and noisy and dingy-modern, but the Acropolis & the Parthenon, which are beyond words (let alone words which wd. fit on here). Esp. when D made us get up at 5 (!) so we saw it all clear and clean and just getting gold in the sun, and with the breeze cool. Plato is perfect for it all, & I'll take good care of it. On to Delphi at the end of the week, then some of the islands if we can find a passage. Wish you were with us. Much love, B [secunda manu] and David

Regret, jagged and bitter, spread through me like heartburn as I read. Why had I refused to go with them? Could the Cycle, could anything, be important enough to compare with such an expedition in such company? To climb the Acropolis together and see the sun rise, to read the *Symposium*, to take boats between the islands. How much greater joy could there have been? And how much hope?

I beat my head against my hands. Why had I allowed Douglas to pre-empt my time again? Wasn't it enough to have cut short the trip in Spain last year, almost before it had begun? 'Next time it will be your turn to interrupt my idyll,' he had written then. 'Idyll'! He had a whole year, more, to do as he liked, and he wouldn't postpone his plans for a single month, a fortnight, for my convenience, my happiness, my sole, irrevocable possibility. I had not asked him. But why hadn't he asked me? Why should he assume I was at his beck and call for all twelve months of the year? Because my time was my own, and his was not. Just because his time was not always his own – and anyway, it precisely *was* his own for his sabbatical year. So I raged, swerving violently round any inconvenient, rational answers to my questions.

Anger and disappointment invaded my work. Baffled by a reference mislaid, I broke off the search before the middle of the morning, left my desk, and spent the rest of that day and all the next on telephone calls and trivial jobs in the house which I pretended to myself were necessary – punishing Douglas, by disregarding his deadline, for his expectation that I would keep to a commitment, freely given.

By the second evening, when I realised what I had been doing, it seemed alarmingly irrevocable. I was now a couple of hundred lines behind, and it was less than three weeks to the end of the month. Worse than that – worse even than the petulance and dishonesty with which I had tried to put the blame for my own decision (when I began to dislike it) on Douglas – was the fact that I had allowed distress and frustration about Ben to affect my work so greatly. If work was not impregnable against the tides of longing and misery and loss, against even the occasional rush and swirl of hope, then who knew how far the encroaching sea might break and spread – or what a salt, marshy, barren waste it might leave?

It might have been possible to recover the time lost, then and earlier, if I had been working well. But I was working very badly. I lost concentration so often that I made very numerous mistakes, and did not always discover them even in checking. Once, I started thirty lines back from the point I had reached the day before, and did not notice until I had nearly finished that I was working over the same ground.

I cancelled a series of seminars for the summer school at the New University – at short notice, and to their considerable inconvenience; I did not go shopping until there were no more tins left in the store cupboard; I left each morning's newspaper and post by the door, unexamined, until bedtime. And still, by the last week of the month, I had to ring up Douglas and tell him that I could not have the work done in time.

He was brisk and pragmatic about it, commendably concealing most of his annoyance, and even, by the end of our conversation, telling me to cheer up: distinguished writers were notorious for missing their deadlines.

I tried to laugh.

We arranged, to my chagrin, that we should split the remaining work, and that Douglas should postpone his journey until it was done.

'It's perfectly fair,' he said generously. 'I'm leaving you a hell of a lot of work on all the fiddly bits, once the text is done. No reason I shouldn't take a hand in the last few lines.'

But I still hated having to surrender any part of what had been for so long my half of the text.

In the end, we finished nearly halfway through August. Neither of us, I think, felt the triumph we had long expected to feel: rather, a weary and irritable relief. But Douglas brought me his work, on his way south, and stayed a couple of nights. I did not entertain him well. The house was dusty and disorganised, with dead lightbulbs not replaced and piles of newspapers on the chairs; the weeds in the garden were tall, and dying now, like some of the plants, from drought; and I had not bought anything special to eat, let alone cooked it. But it was good to see him, and when we had checked each other's final sections, we dined in the pub and drank to the Cycle completed. Douglas has a stronger head than I have, and neither my thoughts nor my speech were quite steady by the time we left, though the night air sobered me, and I slept better than I had for many weeks.

Before he left we planned what was still to be done: there were three or four appendices to write; the glossary to compile from the completed text – that would be the longest job; then the bibliography to make from the notes and our own working lists; and finally, a full introduction to write, covering all the aspects of the Cycle which we felt were of special interest: date, origin, analogues, dialect, prosody, dramatic structure and so on. Work on some of the appendices was fairly self-contained, and needed no more books than would fit in a suitcase. Douglas undertook these, and I was to do all the rest.

'But don't start straight away, Alan,' he said. 'You need a holiday.'

I sighed and shrugged my shoulders.

'I'm serious. I know I've rushed you, and I'm sorry.'

'It's for me to be sorry.'

'Well, well. It's done now. Sam was glad of a few more weeks at home, anyway. And they've been having strikes in Hamburg, so I haven't missed much. But you're not under that kind of pressure any more. If I know you, you'll go on working twelve hours a day out of sheer force of habit, or to kick yourself for getting a couple of days late with the text, or whatever. But it's just foolishness: if you don't give yourself a break first, you won't even do it very well; and in the end you'll make yourself sick. Take some time off: catch up on all the odds and ends,' (I thought he just prevented a glance round the room), 'and then have a holiday. Find a friend – go back to Spain or something.' After a moment he added, 'And you know you're as welcome as possible to visit me in Hamburg.'

Ben and David span their money out into the first week of August, when David had to come back for a choir-tour in the West Country. He came down to see me, rather to my surprise, a few days after Douglas had left. I had taken Douglas's advice and stopped work for a time: I was sleeping late, and spending the morning catching up on letters, or setting the house to rights, with a dismal, pernickety kind of satisfaction. It was still very hot.

David had telephoned the day before, but he got a lift for part of the way from the station, and arrived earlier than I expected, just before midday, while I was standing in a flower-bed, trying to tighten the screw of a window-catch. I was wearing no shirt. David was rather tidily dressed, his shirtsleeves folded square above his elbows. He came and held the catch for me while I turned the screw ineffectively in the soft wood. After a few minutes we gave up, and had a drink, sitting in the garden.

He told me about their trip, and my envy was softened by vicarious delight. He brought me Ben's love, and the promise of a letter before he came home, (he had stopped on the way back to visit the family in France with whom he had stayed some years before), and a packet of photographs that they had taken in Greece. Ben had thought there were some I might like, he said, and asked him to get some copies made for me. Ben was no expert with David's camera, and the ones he took are not very clearly focussed and have some incongruous objects in the foreground. But David's were taken with some skill and precision, and a feeling for light and shadow, and half a dozen of them include Ben.

I had never possessed a photograph of Ben before. It seemed extraordinary that I had never thought of trying to get hold of one – extraordinary, but sensible. I valued these so dearly, and did not know what to do with them. To leave them visible would be to break the fixed rule of discretion which I had obeyed instinctively and strictly ever since I recognised the state of my own heart, and perhaps for some time before.

Ben's letters were in a locked drawer with other letters, his presents dispersed about the house in places proper to their kind. I could think of no such unsuspicious place for a photograph of a young man sitting by a rock, with sand on his legs and sun and black shadow across his shoulders, even though the ostensible subject of the photograph, the temple of Poseidon, stood against the sky above him.

I thanked David, admired his photography, and asked him about the places in which he appeared.

After I had taken him to the six o'clock train, I wandered about the house, searching for a hiding place for the photographs which was neither too easily accessible nor so carefully concealed as to be suspect. In the end, I decided to leave them, as if not much regarded, in the yellow folder provided by the developers, and keep them near the bottom of a small drawer in my desk which I half-filled with postcards, newspaper cuttings, passport photographs and paperclips: a collection which I hoped looked as random as it was in fact deliberate. Then I felt free to take the photographs into the garden, with a drink, and look at them for a long time.

I held each picture of Ben, successively, in the hollow of my hand, and studied each shadow and line, each turn and stretch of muscle or skin, with the longing intensity of Pygmalion, but without Pygmalion's success. I thought, as I had thought before, though with less immediate cause, that the Commandment against idolatry was the one I should always find it easiest to keep. These images, seeming to hold so much of the grace and life of the original, called up so much of my habitual response to everything about him – and met it with an unresponsive blank, a patterned square of glossy paper which would not smile or turn or even stir in acknowledgement or reply.

I studied the pictures Ben had taken, too – seeing Greece, perhaps, through his eyes, albeit a little muzzily. Where David appeared – usually foreshortened behind his own feet – he looked exceptionally happy. There was no doubt those two enjoyed each other's company: there was none of the strain, the rather disconsolate hopefulness I was used to seeing in David's face, and had seen again today at the station as he said goodbye.

Next morning, I took Ben's print of Jumièges to be framed. My anxiety about the safe and secret keeping of my keepsakes had reminded me of the errand, postponed since Christmas – first by hope and then by despair – though I had got as far as enquiring prices at the stationer's shop, which advertised a framing service.

I discussed widths and materials with the proprietor, who was, as usual, helpful and knowledgeable, and whose taste, as usual, was better than his appearance would have suggested.

We agreed on narrow brown wood, with one groove and, in spite of the extra expense, a gilded line on the inner edge.

'I think you'll find you're pleased with that, sir, when you see it finished. You'll think it was worth the extra.' He held the sample right-angle of wood to the corner of the mount again. 'Beautiful effect the gold has, doesn't it? Seems to bring out the light in the picture. And such a nice piece: you don't want to spoil it for a ha'penny worth of tar – or a ha'penny worth of gilding!'

I laughed appropriately.

'France, is it?' He took up the print and looked more closely, then turned it over. He stopped talking for a moment while he read the dealer's label on the back, and Ben's inscription. Then he looked up at me in rather more intent enquiry.

'Yes, France,' I said. 'Jumièges, in Normandy. A very fine old abbey.'

'In Normandy: is it really? Well, well. Beautiful.' He turned the print over again. 'And if you wouldn't mind giving me your name and address?'

Ben's letter arrived a few days later, but told me little that I had not gathered from his various postcards; and most of that little was unwelcome. His hosts in France had asked him to delay his return until the *rentrée* at the beginning of September, so that he could go with them for a couple of weeks to their holiday cottage on the west coast. There would be swimming and boating. It sounded great, and he had accepted.

My disappointment was sharpened by concern for his work. Would the rest of September and the first ten days of October be enough for all the reading he ought to get done before the second part of his Tripos began? I did not have much faith in the 'quite a bit of time for reading' he said he foresaw by the sea.

And what was I to do with myself meanwhile? I had to admit that Douglas had been right: I did need a holiday. Soon after I had stopped work, I had begun to realise how tired I was. At first, it had been a kind of dull luxury simply not to work – to lie in late and have breakfast slowly; to weed the garden and water it (only a few plants were irrevocably lost, I thought), and to go into Bramston for whatever I needed as soon as I needed it; to attend to all the various repairs and replacements and reorganisations which had snagged ineffectively at my domestic conscience in the past months, so that life became more convenient and more orderly; to fall asleep without calculating the lines and the hours that remained. But these small aims and negative pleasures would not for much longer generate the energy to counteract a weariness which seemed to have soaked me through. Now Ben would not be back till the fourth or fifth of September – later, if he stopped in London to see David. I could not take two or three more weeks weeding the path and unblocking the outside drains, but I knew that I was not yet in a condition when it would be sensible to start work on the glossary.

I tried to read. I had got some post-war plays from the library, to alleviate my ignorance and perhaps to give me another kind of comparison – or even of illumination – for the Cycle. But I could not settle to dialogue which seemed so flat and formless, and concerns which seemed trivial where they were not obscene. (I have learned better since about some of them.) There was no savour left in the ordinary actions of the day, and for the first time the cottage became oppressive – each room full of cluttering objects, and yet barren of occupation and enjoyment. When I walked in the afternoons, the sun made my head ache, and I turned back restlessly before I had achieved any distance or disposed of any appreciable time. When I pushed on against my inclination, one afternoon, and did the long round out beyond the

Harchester road, I came home exhausted, and so sickened with headache that I had to go to bed.

A day or two later I looked at my bank balance and telephoned a bed-and-breakfast place on the coast in Suffolk. Ben would not be back for ten days at least. I would take ten days' holiday, and just before it ended I would find a reason to ring up his parents. If he was still away, I would make it a fortnight.

My heart, as always, lifted when I saw the sea. But the little exaltation did not last. I was conscious of being alone, and uneasy about it as I had never been before. No-one was alone on the shore, except an occasional mother, mercifully abandoned by sand-castling children to sleep in her deckchair. In the little town along the road there was sometimes a single boy propping himself and his bicycle against the corner, wary and aimless, but he was alone only until his friends joined him in a whooping, wheeling pack, or, if he was a little older, until his girl arrived.

I swam each morning, and took some pleasure in it when the first shock of the cold was gone; going out against the choppy little waves produced a vigour I had not felt for some time. I could not stay in for long, though: when I was dressed again, and glowing, I would sit a little time and listen to the sound of the water running up the shingle and retreating, and try to read whatever I had brought with me. But the wind and the people and the dogs too easily distracted me, and though the sky was mostly grey, the light glared from the water and the stretch of the beach. More often than not I gave up, and wandered along the shore, or into the main street of the town, where I would browse unprofitably in the bookshop, or buy a postcard to write while I drank coffee and ate shortbread in the tearoom. Swimming restored my appetite, at least.

I drove dutifully, in the afternoons, to look at local churches and a castle, but I could take no more than a perfunctory interest in their architecture, or even in their history. The contrast with last year was too close – with the expeditions together, the exchange of curiosity or admiration, the shared content, the jokes. Could I have delayed this little holiday, and asked Ben to come with me? I thought not. Not only discretion was against it; he should not curtail his brief reading-time any further. So I strayed up the naves of echoing wool-churches, and gaped at the roofs, and read the noticeboards, assailed, if anyone else was there or even approaching, by the unaccustomed prickling of self-consciousness. In the evenings I read, or tried to read, except when I could no longer politely resist my landlady's invitation to watch television with her family. I slept uneasily in my close, clean little room.

I did have one good afternoon, out on the sea-marshes, quite alone, watching birds, under a sky full of great moving clouds. And the last evening but one I went up to Aldeburgh for a concert and heard, among other things, a piece for viola by Holst, which was so extraordinarily moving, within its restraint, that I found myself close to tears.

Next day I telephoned the Graysons and asked them if everything was all right at the cottage, to which I had left them the key; and if the firewood had been delivered as arranged and left under cover; and what news they had of the children. Bridget had written cheerfully more than once from her summer course at Compostela; Mark and a friend were bicycling in Devon; and Ben was expected home on Tuesday. With relief as well as expectation, I decided that my holiday was over, paid my bill, and drove home next day.

It was not long before Ben came to see me. His face and arms were so brown that his hair, paled by the sun, looked nearly white. He was in good spirits, but there was a new assurance in his manner, almost a toughness, which gave me some misgiving. I thought perhaps it came, at least in part, from his time in France: from having coped successfully in an *ambience* where he had felt isolated and unsuccessful when he was younger. But when he began to talk of Greece, all his gentle, unpremeditated openness returned. He told me about taking boats between the islands, at night, sleeping on deck with goats and chickens (except once, when the captain offered them two berths in his cabin, explaining first that he was a man of honour). They had gone to Delphi, and run the length of the stadium, and seen the view from the Phaedriades at twilight; and they had swum from the rocks below the point at Sounion.

He had brought me a present, 'to make up for not coming': a small bowl of olive-wood, absurdly and engagingly carved with two of Athene's owls at the rim. I keep brown sugar in it, or nuts in the winter. I wished I had thought of bringing him something from my Suffolk holiday (though I don't know what I could have found for him, except a shell-encrusted pipe-rack), but I could have given no such convincing reason.

'So you're here for the rest of the vacation,' I said, as he stood up to go.

'Just about. In the week, anyway. I've got a job in Bramston, at the bakery.'

'A job?'

'Why not a job?' he asked, and added, 'Only in the mornings, anyway', showing that he knew why not.

'Well...'

'I've got to pay for Greece somehow.'

'Yes. Of course you have.'

'Well, then...'

'Well then, what?'

'Stop disapproving.'

'I didn't say I was disapproving.'

'You didn't *say*. You didn't have to say.'

'What I think is not altogether within my control – or yours.'

There was a short silence. Then Ben said, 'OK. But I'm going to do masses of reading in the rest of the day, and there'll probably be times in the morning, too, especially if I'm on the van.'

'Good.'

'Oh, *Alan*! No, all right. You're being very restrained. I just know you too well. I probably should've left a bit more time: come back from France earlier or something. In fact, of course I should. Or not had so long in Greece. But my God, it was worth it.'

'Good,' I said again – this time with less reservation. 'And thank you for the photographs, by the way.'

'The photographs?'

'The ones David brought down, from you. I meant to thank you earlier.'

'Oh, he did bring some down in the end? Don't you think he's a good photographer? Did he show you the ones he took at Mycenae?'

'Mycenae? I'm not sure. Let's see: they must be about somewhere.'

Ben's fairly pardonable improvidence with time and money in the first part of his vacation limited our meetings for the rest of it. I saw him once or twice at the bakery, where he brought batches of loaves into the shop or loaded them into the van in the yard. When the stationer's telephoned to say that the print was ready, I decided to pick it up before I bought my bread.

The framing had been very neatly done, and the shopkeeper showed it to me with almost proprietorial pride.

'That's very nice,' I said. 'They've done it beautifully.'

'Lovely job, isn't it? And when you think how reasonable – . Look beautiful up on the wall.'

He held it against a space on the wall behind him.

'Very nice indeed.'

'Makes a nice way to remember a trip. I think you said it's somewhere you've been?'

'I was there last year.'

'On holiday, were you?'

'Yes, a summer holiday; with friends. On our way south.'

'Lovely.'

'And how much do I owe you?'

Wrapping up the picture while I wrote a cheque, he said, 'I was reading a book from the library the other day by someone of that name. I wonder if it would be any relation?'

'What was the book?'

'It was historical, really. From the radio. Like an old-time religious play.'

I acknowledged my part as an editor (while disclaiming authorship), and asked if he was interested in early plays. He said he had known nothing about them before, though a friend of his took an interest in the theatre; he had picked up the book quite by chance. But he had found the plays interesting, if rather difficult, and he would like to know more. I recommended one or two of the better popular selections – Crawley's *Everyman* edition, and so on – and told him about the modern translation of the Cycle we were hoping to bring out. He noted the names in his diary, to our common satisfaction.

Ben was out on a round when I got to the bakery. I took the print home and spent the afternoon re-arranging my pictures, so that it could hang over my desk. Then I rang up and asked him to tea.

We had tea together two or three times before he returned to Cambridge. Once, it was at his house, where Mark had just got back from Devon. He spread out his maps on the table after tea, and showed us where he had gone in enthusiastic detail – confirmed or corrected by his otherwise entirely silent friend.

When Ben came to me, he did not stay very long. He was in earnest, a little defensively, about his reading, and looked at his watch and left soon after five o'clock. I had not yet started to work full time again myself, but I could hardly discourage him. I was glad, though, that he was reading with real interest, and finding things he was eager to discuss. The English Seventeenth Century was to be his special period, and we talked for much of the time about the politics of the age, and now and then about the literature. Pepys had been inexplicably left off his reading list, and I offered to lend him my copy. He was reluctant to borrow such a good edition, explaining that he would have little time to read it, except in the bath. In the end, I found a second-rate Edwardian abridgement, which he could use or misuse as he liked, and put his name in it. It was hardly a present – certainly not worth the thanks he gave me – but I said I would try to find him a better edition later on, when it would be less at risk, and he laughed and thanked me again. He was very pleased to see the print framed so handsomely, and hung.

CHAPTER 54

When Ben had gone back to Cambridge, it was time to start working properly again. I had been making some notes for the glossary in the mornings; now I began to go through the completed text word by word, adding a card to my index for every new word I found, with its context, reference, and all its possible variations of meaning. There was not space enough on my desk: I worked at the kitchen table, with the text in front of me, a dwindling stack of clean index-cards on my left, and a growing line of written ones filed alphabetically in a shoebox on my right. Several handbooks and dictionaries, none of them above reproach, were spread about, open, on the table and the various other flat surfaces of the kitchen.

As time went on, more and more of the words I encountered had already been entered: I need only check the card and add the reference, any variation in the spelling, and anything that was new about this particular usage. There was some interest in seeing unexpected connections of context: once or twice I found a mainly heroic or courtly word being used ironically. But such revelations were few: on the whole, the work was humdrum, and nearly mechanical, demanding much less original thought than the editing proper, and for this I was thankful. I was still held back by a fatigue I could neither shake off nor wholly account for. However, I was working fairly steadily, if not quickly, and I was able to report respectable progress to Douglas.

I went to Oxford for two nights to discuss the layout of the plays with Brian Robson, and I visited Bridget in her room at Lady Margaret Hall. It seemed circumspect to spread my attention rather more evenly among the family; and besides, she is a nice girl and I was glad to see her. She made coffee for me, and told me about her course, which she was enjoying enormously; and we walked across the Parks in the hazy sunshine, and watched an admirably frivolous game of football in which a friend of hers was playing, before she went on to a tutorial, and I went on to Blackwells.

When I got home, there was a letter from Ben waiting for me.

2nd Nov.

Dear Alan,

This is a begging letter, and if you disapprove of it – or just can't do anything about it – please say so straight away (and then forget about it, if possible).

Can you lend me £15 to pay my rent for the second half of term? I hate asking to borrow money, and especially from you, and I hope I'll never do it again. I'm only doing it now because there aren't many alternatives, and they're all worse.

The thing is, David's been offered singing lessons by a really good teacher (Enzo Shvableson [sic]. I think he's quite well known.) He's got to pay in advance, but he was a bit overdrawn already, & his parents are abroad; he can't get hold of them till after the end of term. He can't turn it down – it's his great chance – & he's been absolutely desperate about what to do. Most of our friends are fairly broke, too; (there is Julian, who isn't, but we thought there might be strings attached). I still had a bit in the bank, and I lent him £25. Then I needed a bit more for things I hadn't thought of (last term's Heffer's account and library fines and so on, and then my shoes wore out), so I overdrew a bit, and reckoned to live pretty cheaply for the rest of term; and then I suddenly realised I hadn't paid the rest of the rent. (Graham likes it in two halves.) There's no-one here I can really borrow from (see above); I'd ask my father, but the apples have been terrible. So in the end I thought I'd ask you and just hope you wouldn't think it was unpardonable, and would feel free to say no if you wanted to. My father always says 'neither a borrower nor a lender be', but you do know, don't you, that I really wouldn't do it except as a last resort in a fairly dire necessity? I should be able to pay you back straight after Christmas, when David's parents have got home.

I'm well and everything else is fine. I'll write a proper letter soon. I didn't want to mix my news up with all this.

With much love and very many apologies,

Ben

p.s. I haven't told David I'm writing. He thinks I'm OK for money till he pays me back.
B

6.xi.1964

My dear Ben,

I enclose a cheque for £25. Of course I don't mind your asking me about this. You know, I hope, that I should always want to help as far as I could with anything which was as important to you – on a friend's behalf or on your own – as this chance of David's. You must always feel able to ask for my help in such a case; if I have no money available, I can always say no.

I think I ought to say now that you did this the wrong way round. However generously you want to help a friend, you should in principle first make sure that the money you lend him is yours to lend. (I mean 'yours' in the practical sense that it is not already irredeemably committed to someone else. I don't think you seriously contemplated leaving Cambridge, or sleeping on the pavement for the second half of term, did you?) I did, in fact, have enough in the bank to lend you what you asked without difficulty (or rather, a little more than you asked: it sounds to me as if your financial state will not be altogether straightforward even when you have paid your rent). But if I had not had the money to spare, you can see, I think, what a difficult position you would have put yourself in – and not only yourself: your landlord, and David (who would surely have discovered the real state of affairs before very long), and me. 'Feeling free' to refuse is easier said than done, when you tell me that the debt is already incurred, and that my help is a last resort in a dire necessity.

You did not mean to force my hand, I know. (On the contrary, you could not have written more fairly and directly.) But you did let circumstances do it for you, by acting first and doing your accounts afterwards. I've never thought much of Polonius's precepts (let alone his practice): borrowing and lending seem to me to be sensible and sometimes necessary transactions between friends. But you must work out exactly where you stand first (and that includes, for example, the state of your Heffer's account). Things of this kind – money, lodgings, professional careers – are too serious just to shut your eyes and jump.

There is no hurry about paying me back. I can easily wait until Christmas – or beyond, if there is any further difficulty about David's fees. You can repay me a little at a time, if that is easier – or if you are very hard up, you may like to wait until next year, when you are earning: that would be perfectly all right, too.

I will not mention any of this to David – or to your parents, unless they ask me and you have told me I may. But do congratulate David for me. Schwäbelssohn is certainly well spoken of, and I'm so glad he's giving David this chance.

I agree with you that news should be kept apart from business, so I will only say that I expect to be in Cambridge on the 21st, and hope to see you then. Perhaps you could let me know when you are likely to be free.

With love,
Yours affectionately,
Alan.

8th Nov.

Dear Alan,

Thank you very much indeed for the cheque for £25. I enclose a receipt. Thank you for your letter, too. You are right – I shouldn't have been so feckless, and I'm sorry, and very grateful to you for rescuing me more promptly and much more generously than I deserved. The extra £10 – though I didn't mean to ask for it – will make all the difference to the rest of term, which was looking fairly bleak without cinemas or, probably, coffee. I hope I can believe you that you really could spare the money without difficulty. I'll pay it back the moment David can let me have it.

It will be great to see you on the 21st. Would you like to come and have tea, if your committee is over by then? About half-past four? I might see if David's free, too.

Work is going pretty well. I'm going to Dr. Wilson for the C17. Everyone says she's really good, and she's certainly interesting so far. We've been doing the Putney Debates. Did you know this, that Col. Rainsborough said? 'The poorest he that is in England hath a life to live as the greatest he.' How could anyone help being a Roundhead after that – an Independent, indeed – in spite of Ely Lady Chapel, etc.?

We are running to Ely in the sixth week (David and me and various other people) in aid of handicapped children. So we've been taking it a bit more seriously – running before breakfast again and so on – to get into training. It should be good, if it doesn't rain. I love that fen country late in the year.

And D. has been in on starting a College opera society, which is going to do An Italian Straw Hat some time next term. (Starting unambitious and working up to Figaro is the idea.) I've said I'll be in the Chorus, as I don't actually sing out of tune and they promise it won't be more than one rehearsal a week. (Well, they always say that. But it can't be much more, till the last week anyway: we only have a couple of songs.)

Time for hall. I wish I could say more adequately what I felt when I got your letter. I hope some time soon I'll be able to do something towards repaying it – not just the money, but your generosity, and your kindness – and your honesty – in everything you do for me.

Till then, all I can do is send you my very grateful thanks, and much love,

Ben

I got alpha query on my college exams.

My pleasure in this reply was compounded with relief. My own letter had been written with considerable difficulty, and when I could delay it no longer, I was still worried that Ben might justifiably resent at least some parts of it. And yet I did not know what else

I could have written. The letter – and the cheque – represented a compromise between impulses too strongly opposed to be easily or satisfactorily reconciled. Thinking of Ben in difficulties, I ached to help him – to rescue him immediately and completely from his debt and anxiety and embarrassment, to reassure him that he had done nothing to be ashamed of, and nothing that could not be easily set right. I would gladly have given him the twenty-five pounds – or even fifty – though it had been less easy to spare even the loan than I had made him believe. I honoured his precipitate generosity and the candour of his letter, and I rejoiced that I was the friend to whom he had turned, in whom he had confided.

But I knew I could not act on such feelings alone. He had been irresponsible, and it was not for me to take on all the consequences of that irresponsibility, even though I might mitigate them. It was proper to assume that he would repay what I sent as soon as he could (and indeed, to suggest that I needed no repayment – however it might have gratified me – would have given him more embarrassment than asking me in the first place: much more than he deserved, or than I was prepared to inflict). Nor could I let that irresponsibility pass uncensured. For his good, and perhaps to salve my conscience for the indulgence of the half-lie about my own finances, I had to tell him where he had been at fault.

But had I, after all, been unfair? Though I had acquitted his intentions, I had blamed his impetuous action for forcing my hand – for making it almost impossible to refuse his request. How could I expect him to realise how urgently such a request would affect me? How could he know, unless I told him, as I could never tell him, 'My purse, my person, my extremest means / Lie all unlocked to your occasions'?

I was afraid, at times, that I had been too hard on him. And I knew that this was the more possible because of a strand in my feeling for him which I did my best to ignore: a lurking satisfaction in seeing his youth and energy stoop, voluntarily and with such vulnerable, uncalculating readiness and so much inadvertent grace, to admit itself in the wrong, to submit to the greater weight of my authority. The submission was willing, and the authority would never be imposed, I hoped, except in his interest, or in the cause of right behaviour or common sense. Nevertheless, it was a suspect emotion – another reason for signing my name with an unaccustomed demonstration of affection, and another cause of uneasiness in the days immediately after I had posted my letter.

But Ben had answered by return of post and, characteristically, had taken all I had said in good part. I could accept his invitation to tea with a lighter heart, on a postcard.

I arrived tired, after a difficult meeting. Ben was very welcoming, and I felt that any lack of immediate ease between us was my fault. He had kept his last year's rooms – now more glorious, if rather more cramped, with a large gramophone which had been his parents' birthday present. There was a stack of crumpets on a plate in the hearth, and the kettle was coming to the boil. He asked after the Dictionary, and I found that I could tell him freely about the gaps which Peter Thorsen had pointed out in two of my more important definitions. He listened with attention and unanxious sympathy, and in the end with a kind of humorous, partisan pugnacity.

'I bet that made his day. Just because he never has any good ideas of his own – . Everyone always says he's a pedantic moron.'

I was not deceived, but I was comforted.

'What about some tea?' he asked then.

'We're not waiting for David?'

'I think we may as well start: he wasn't quite sure – . We took a bit longer than we meant to this morning, running.'

'It's next week you run to Ely?'

'This Saturday. Hope to goodness the wind's dropped by then.'

'I'm not quite clear how it is that you'll be benefitting handicapped children?'

He explained the irrational but laudable principles of a 'sponsored run', insisting first that he would not accept any money from me. 'Unless there's another one next term; if we're all square by then.

It was nearly half-past six when I got up to go, and thanked him for his restorative hospitality. 'Sorry not to see David.'

'Yes, well, I thought he might not make it. He was a bit – '

The evasiveness in his voice made me say, 'A bit what?'

'Sort of – . He heard something.'

I waited, and Ben went on. 'He knows you lent me the money for him.'

'I see. But how did that happen? I didn't tell him, and nor, I imagine, did you.'

'Someone – someone else – saw a letter. And told him.'

'Someone's been reading your letters?'

'Not exactly. It was in the paper-basket. I'd run out of matches; they took it to light a cigarette.'

After a moment, I said, 'So he saw what I'd written.'

'It wasn't your letter. Not in the paper-basket. It was just – it was actually a rough copy. It was pretty difficult writing that letter, the first one.'

I laughed with more than one kind of relief. 'It wasn't the only difficult letter in that correspondence – or the only rough draft.'

I wondered, as I spoke, what complications this would add to the already complicated intentions and effects of my letter. But to Ben it was simply a relinquishment of superior certainty, an unexpected admission of equal diffidence and fallibility, which delighted and amused him. He laughed too, perching on the back of his chair.

'What was David's reaction?'

'He was pretty upset. And furious.'

'With – ?'

'With me. Said he'd told me not to ask you. Well, he hadn't. It was just once, earlier on, when I suggested writing to you himself. He absolutely wouldn't hear of it: said he didn't know you nearly well enough, and – and so on. But he never said I wasn't to. Still, it was the same in a way, I suppose. Now he said, what on earth would you think? I'd messed up any – any friendship – any respect you might have for him.'

'But that's not reasonable: he didn't even know you were writing.'

'David is unreasonable. When it comes to people, sometimes.'

'I couldn't have thought him to blame in any way. Not even as much as you.'

'I know.'

'Which was not so very much.'

He smiled, looking down.

'But still, he feels he's been put in the wrong?'

'Very much.'

'And by you?'

'Yes.'

'Oh, dear.'

We were silent, considering the problem together. I looked at my watch.

'I'm due in hall in ten minutes. How can we put this right? Should I go and see him?'

'You could, I suppose. He might be fairly embarrassed.'

'Perhaps I should write.'

The letter kept me up for some little time in my room in Maurice Wakeford's College, after hall. It also provided a reason to see Ben before I left next morning.

I gave him the letter to read, and asked for the address of David's lodgings. While I put it on the envelope, he wrote it in the back pages of my diary, saying as he finished, 'Or I could take it for you. Or perhaps not.'

'Perhaps better not. I've got a stamp.'

The uneasiness of the day before had gone: we were together, without reserve or embarrassment, in conspiring for David's reassurance. I stayed only ten or fifteen minutes more, drinking a mug of coffee while Ben kept an eye on my ill-parked car through the bedroom window, but I left elated with a sharp, unstable joy.

CHAPTER 55

It became clear that the Cycle would not be ready for the Press by Christmas. Douglas wrote forbearingly from Hamburg: though his own appendices were done, there was no immutable deadline; January, or even February, would be all right.

David was to spend Christmas with the Graysons, since his own family were abroad until the New Year, and he and Ben arrived at my window early one afternoon, a week or so after the end of their term.

I opened the door to them, welcomed them in, and took their coats, which were bloomed with mist. While we spread them on chairs in the kitchen, Ben said, 'We came – ' and stopped, and let David go on.

'We wanted to thank you.'

'I got your letter,' I said to David. 'Thank you for that.'

'Yes, but after I'd written – I wrote straight away – afterwards it made everything all right.'

'It really did,' said Ben. 'I mean, for both of us. We came to tell you – to thank you.'

As I hesitated for a reply, he added, 'We would have come to see you anyway, I mean – '

We took the opportunity to laugh, and Ben put the kettle on while I found coffee and cups and spoons.

By the fire in the living room they told me of their plan to go carol-singing, and asked me to join them.

'For a good cause,' David said.

'We haven't decided which yet,' said Ben. 'The handicapped children, or the church roof, or something.'

'Or half and half.'

'Very classy singing, anyway. David's going to get some of the church choir and do descants and parts and things.'

'I don't know that I'm quite up to that standard.'

'Oh, there'll be plenty of ordinary mortals doing the tune. Please come.'

I said I would.

There were twenty of us, or more, when we gathered in the Graysons' hall. The door was left open, and people came in in their overcoats. Some were carrying torches, some had brought carol-books, and there were several more books in a variegated stack on the shelf by the door. I arrived fairly early, and watched as Ben consulted one of his mother's friends over a list of neighbours, and David collected half a dozen people to sit on the stairs and run through some of the music, humming parts in an undertone.

Getting another carol-book, for a late arrival, from the bottom of the stack, I saw a pile of letters, ready for the post, lying beyond it on the shelf. The top one was addressed in Ben's handwriting to 'Mlle. M-M. Moreau', at an address in France. It was thicker than the others: too thick, I thought, for a Christmas card, or even for a short letter. I handed the book across the intervening shoulders, and leaned against the wall. Probable and improbable conjectures flared up out of control in my mind, scorching the innocent, festive expectancy of the evening, fouling every prospect with fumes of apprehension and misery.

A little later Mark was in front of me, saying something.

'Sorry?'

'Ben says, did you bring a torch?'

I pulled it out of my pocket and showed it to him, and he nodded.

The hall door was opened wider, and cold air came in as people began to go out. I was one of the last to leave, and Ben saw me on the doorstep and came back to me.

'We're going down to the Ellises first. Can you take that lot there with your torch? And keep an eye on Andrew and Linda: they'll get lost if you give them half a chance.'

Walking from house to house, lighting the road ahead for the half-dozen people round me, keeping the two children within the beam of the torch as far as I could, singing automatically, and probably more inaccurately than usual, and walking on again, I struggled with a bitter, endlessly revolving cycle of ideas. Ben was writing to a girl in France. Perhaps it was only a Christmas card.

Not when it was as thick as that. But it might be only a friendly letter – a reply to hers. Why should he reply at such length? Perhaps she had written at such length. But then, might not her letter, too, have been a reply? Had Ben started the correspondence, earlier? Had they been writing to each other all the term (while I counted down the days until I could expect three sides from Cambridge?). There had been Ben's new toughness, his conscious, even self-conscious, confidence of manner, which I had noticed on his return. Had he made a conquest? Or at least had the satisfaction of some sort of orthodox love affair? Had he – could he have been to bed with the girl? Was he in love with her? It was no good letting that appall me. He was bound to fall in love in the end, with someone. And if it was now, with this girl, I should rejoice in the end to his loneliness and anxiety. I should let him tell me about it, listen to her praises, give him good advice without bias. But why had he not told me about it already? We had been busy. There had not been many occasions for the slow approaches, the tentative openings, of intimate confidences. I must make occasions: I must find out how important it was, how he really felt. I must let him know that I was there, to hear anything he might want to tell me, give him any help he might need. It might be no more, of course, than a holiday flirtation, or even an ordinary acquaintance, a little prolonged. Or not prolonged: perhaps the letter was only a Christmas card. Not when it was as thick as that.

The last group of houses where we were to sing was some little way off, along the road home, and up a farm-track which ran over the shoulder of the hill. The other singers in my group had fallen behind, talking among themselves as we walked; only the two children, less elusive now, trudged beside me, breaking forward occasionally into the circle of torchlight in front of us on the road. One of them asked me the time, and was impressed and delighted when I said that it was after ten. Ben was ahead, carrying a larger torch for David and his singers. I could not make him out from among them.

If he was having a love affair, there was no reason for him to tell me about it unless he chose. He was grown-up now – an adult among adults; he must be granted the privacy of his emotions.

But his readiness to confide those emotions was the one thing that remained to me. If that was to go ... And of course it was to go.

We turned from the road onto the earth of the track, under the close darkness of the hedges. Or at least, I thought, it was not to continue undiminished. Only a child could have no reservations. No one else could tell everything, even to a close friend, even to a beloved. There were things, most evidently, that I could not tell Ben. His confidence was a privilege; I could not expect it all the time. I could only hope for it still, perhaps, from time to time. Some of our intimacy must necessarily be forfeited, as he grew older, to other friendships, other loves. Perhaps, if I did not try too hard to keep it, I need not forfeit it all. The final danger was not in his independence, but in my inordinate longing.

We were coming out into the raw, misty air on the side of the hill. The houses, with their lights, were below us and a little ahead; the trees among them, mostly elms, reached their branches some way above our path. There was enough light in the sky to see the twigs against it, and the figures before them coming up into a crowd, then turning singly to make their way down the slope. Just before I reached the waiting group, I saw Ben's silhouette for a moment, crossing the shapes of the branches. I lighted my party down the steep, uneven way, one by one, the children scrambling and slipping, and followed them myself.

In the hollow where we stood, Ben was quite near me, holding his torch over the shoulders of David's choir to light the pages of their music. The singing began, and I tried to hold my mind to the moment – the music, the trees above us, the faint light, and the faint frost hanging with our breath in the air – full of the expectancy of more, like the children's intimations of Christmas.

At the end of the carol, Ben looked round, and met my glance, drawn to his movement. He smiled, in accord, and even I thought in agreement, with what I had just been feeling.

It was reassurance enough: if we could feel such a moment alike, could convey and understand that feeling reciprocally in a glance, making the delight mutual, and thus endlessly re-doubling it, then nothing that mattered was lost, or, I thought, could be lost. The next carol, 'The Holly and the Ivy', seemed to hold my exaltation at a height that was almost painful: the clarity and sharp air of joy hurt my lungs and throat, and stung my eyes.

There was a moment of silence in the near dark, then light came out from the door, and welcoming exclamations, and praise of the singing, and offers of soup and mince pies. I closed my hand over the beam of Ben's torch for a moment, to attract his notice, and told him I would go home from here – the nearest point of our round. We said goodnight and I walked back over the fields.

Christmas was three or four days later. I arrived in good time for lunch, carrying presents, and we sat by the fire drinking Madeira. Ben and David were in high spirits, teasing each other, and sometimes the rest of us, until they went to help carry in the goose and all its accompaniments.

We opened all the presents after tea. To my surprise, and momentary confusion, there was a packet for me from David; I turned it in my hands, unopened, trying to remember whether I had provided anything for him. I had bought a paperback edition of Mozart's letters, at the last minute, in the University bookshop in Harchester. I pulled the paper apart with relief, and took out a book (photographs of the Greek Islands? parallel text of a modern Greek poet? I can't remember.) David was standing nearby, and while I thanked him I watched over his shoulder until Ben should come to my parcel, at the bottom of his pile. It was a pleasant, early nineteenth-century edition of *The Merchant of Venice*. Mark crossed my view to stand beyond Ben and clear a space on top of the piano for the presents he had unwrapped; he put down a pile of wrapping paper, and several Christmas cards fluttered flat, two or three of them falling to the floor. Ben was beginning to open my present. I went over and picked up the cards; a separate, folded leaf of flimsy paper had drifted apart from one of them. Considering where to replace it, I read the handwriting inside: '*à Ben: joyeux Noel, chéri, et bonne Année! a bientot*? M-M.'

Ben was thanking me and giving me something; Donald was offering me a drink. I answered with what relevance I could. All the bitterness of the carol-singing night returned at once and began to turn again through my mind, but this time without the ensuing exaltation.

CHAPTER 56

The second part of that winter was very long. I no longer knew what to·do about Ben. Sometimes I thought that it was enough that he should exist, and our friendship continue; sometimes I raged with despair against the impermanence and inadequacy of such makeshift futility; sometimes I indulged in impossible plans of confronting him with my love, changing his horror to acceptance, to reciprocation, by the mere truth and heat of my feeling. The various impossible possibilities, between them, gave me little rest.

I saw him alone only once that vacation, and then the visit was spoilt by his embarrassment. He had walked over on his own, just after the New Year, to tell me that David had had a difficult telephone conversation with his parents the night before, on their return to London. His father had refused (Ben could not say why) to pay for David's singing lessons. It would be some time, therefore, before Ben could repay me what I had lent him.

I said that it did not matter at all; I accepted his apologetic offer of three pounds a month as unconcernedly as I could, and turned the conversation to David's difficulties. But Ben's consciousness of the debt – and perhaps his suspicion that it would inconvenience me more than I admitted – restricted the rest of our conversation to trivia, and made him find an early excuse to leave.

We said an unsatisfactory goodbye some days later, standing in the wind outside the Bramston cinema, where I had seen a film with him and David and some of the family.

I finished work on the Cycle about the middle of February. When the last part of the introduction had been written, and checked, and read through again, and sent off by registered post to Hamburg in the middle of a Monday afternoon, the occasion seemed to demand more than a mere sense of relief. But I spent the following day or two in an ineffective daze; I did very little beyond putting together my papers for the next Dictionary Committee, and discovering that Ben would be busy the evening I was in Cambridge, but could give me coffee before his supervision next morning. I thought I would wait till then to tell him what I had achieved, and see what chance there was of our celebrating it together.

At the meeting, Paul Ettlinger, who had recently joined the Committee, asked me to dine with him in hall, and we sat up after dinner, drinking vodka in his room. I mentioned my cause for celebration, and he made it a reason for filling our glasses several times, and eventually opening a new bottle. We discussed his recent work on emblems in the *Canterbury Tales* with some heat and (on my part) some scepticism (he took what seemed to me an unwarrantably reductive view); and by the time he showed me over to the guest room, we had both drunk a good deal.

I woke next morning forty minutes after I was due at Ben's lodgings. Shaving and dressing as fast as I could, struggling against the fairly severe *malaise* and inefficiency left by the vodka, forgetting to leave my thanks in a note at the porter's lodge – in place of those I should have made to Paul Ettlinger in person – I reached the house as Ben was leaving it. Apologies on both sides were made with some impatience: he had waited long enough to be late already for his supervision; I could say nothing of what I had hoped to say if he could not stay even another ten minutes. We could find no other time in the day to meet: I was engaged for lunch; he was going to a party in the evening.

'I'm really sorry,' he said.

'It doesn't matter.'

'I could ask if I can bring you to the party?'

'No. Don't bother.'

'Only I hate not seeing you properly.'

'It was my fault.'

'It's just bad luck – '

'I was up rather late last night.'

'You do work too hard.'

I did not answer.

'I really must go. Ridley'll skin me. When are you coming over again?'

'I don't know.'

'Write. Write and tell me. Christ, it's five past.'

We called goodbye as he ran.

I spent the morning in bookshops, looking at a rather bad new edition of *Havelok* and an execrable American book on the *Morte D'Arthur*. My headache grew worse and I did not enjoy the lunch party. Driving home afterwards, I went round again by Ben's lodgings, and stopped the car, and waited in it for some time before driving on again.

At home, at least there were things to do. But it was hard to start anything, and harder still to finish it. I worked at my correspondence, the chores in the house, the next entries for the Dictionary, with an insurmountable lethargy. With no more urgent business to cut them short, trivial last reconsiderations and rearrangements dragged on almost to exhaustion; deciding when to stop – to count the job done, to ignore the last unnecessary necessities – was the only thing that seemed even more exhausting, even more impossibly difficult, than doing them.

I would hear from the Press eventually, and there would be alterations to consider and, later, proofs to correct. But I could not be sure how soon this would be, and it could not, therefore, provide the deadline for which I was beginning to long. I found a spurious, short-lived energy and decisiveness, sometimes, after a glass of whisky.

A generous, amusing letter from Douglas, with a few suggestions (tactfully few, I thought) about my introduction, produced some cheerfulness and a little real work for a day or two, but not for much longer. When the next Dictionary meeting was postponed, I wrote to Ben, and shaped the rest of the week round the expectation of his reply.

3rd March

Dear Alan,

Hurray! Hurrah! How fabulous that you have really finished the Cycle – odds and ends and all. You must be over the moon! So that's what you wanted to tell me the other day. I was sorry I had to rush off like that, but Ridley was quite scathing enough as it was. Still, if I'd known about the Cycle, I'd have ditched him altogether, and taken you off and stood you champagne for elevenses or something. Which brings me to the main point of this letter. What are you doing to celebrate? Are you coming to The Italian Straw Hat (week after next)? Could we have dinner afterwards? I'm not very well off at the moment (as you know) but I could stand you a drink at least: it's not every day you finish five years' work (or more?). What about Friday? The first night will probably be terrible, and there'll be all sorts of family there on Thursday. But Friday would be good, and I'm not doing anything on Saturday morning...

There was a card enclosed with the letter: an absurd picture of an elephant in academic dress, with 'Congratulations on your academic achievement!' printed below it, and 'Lots of love, Ben' written inside.

The opera was rather good. David sang the lead with considerable grace, and without strain, and his little orchestra played well. The production was simple enough to avoid a good many of the theatrical inefficiencies of amateurs; there were one or two other fairly good voices; and Ben and the rest of the chorus sang adequately, and with more than adequate charm and vigour.

He was still in high spirits when he came round to find me afterwards, his face glowing though his remaining streaks of make-up, and his gestures quick and extravagant. We walked through the cool streets, and out some way along the Madingley road, under a high, half-lit sky. Ben whistled one of the choruses, and I felt a moment's ungenerous disheartenment that his exhilaration in such a peripheral affair should be greater than his – or mine – in the occasion we were to celebrate. But he had taken trouble in choosing a restaurant: a friend's recommendation proved well-judged, the table was ready, and we ate well.

Ben bought the wine: he wanted to have champagne, but I said – with truth as well as prudence – that I preferred hock, and was rewarded by his relief – and his attempt to disguise it – when

326

he looked at the wine list. We talked for some of the time, I think, about the English idea of Italy, and I was distracted into a *non-sequitur*, once, when he stooped his head towards the light, over his glass.

It was late by the time the coffee was finished and the bill paid; even in the middle of the town, the streets were emptying. At the gate of Ben's college, where he had booked me a guest room, we said goodnight, each thanking the other for his share in our feast.

'You said you were free tomorrow?' I asked.

'Some of it, anyway. Shall we do something in the morning?'

'If you've really got time?'

'Yes. Sure. What would you like to do?'

'Well – '

'It's too late for plans,' said Ben, after a moment. 'Why don't you come round to me when you're up, and we'll think then?'

'Yes. All right. About nine?'

'Could you make it ten?'

'Certainly.'

'Sorry, only I'm rather short of sleep.'

'Of course.'

We had forgotten to arrange whether we should breakfast together. I arrived, very hungry, a few minutes before ten, to find Ben drinking coffee with a young man and a girl, over a table covered with plates and crumbs.

'Alan. Great. Come in.'

'I'm glad I'm not too early.'

'No, not a bit. You know Joanna? And Piers?'

'I don't think we have met,' I said to the young man. He said 'Hello' from where he sat. Joanna nodded and smiled, and asked if I would like some coffee.

'Thank you. I'd love some.'

Ben put a clean cup in his own place; and moved to sit on a corner of the table. Joanna poured out coffee, and Piers shifted his chair slightly to accommodate Ben, and said, 'But if he's directing the Marlowe thing next term, he'll never have the time to get all this together, too.'

For over three-quarters of an hour they discussed undergraduate theatrical business: casting, personalities, intrigues, and occasionally plays. Now and then Ben tried to explain a reference or a joke to me. I drank my coffee slowly, and eventually asked for a second cup.

'You have had some breakfast?' Joanna asked.

'Not yet.'

'Oh God!' said Ben. 'Sorry. I thought you would have.'

'I thought you were to sleep in till ten.'

'Till *ten*?' said Piers, and Ben blushed.

'Well, I did need some sleep. But they woke me up.'

'You said we hadn't,' said Joanna.

'I was being polite,' said Ben crossly. 'Anyway, you must have some breakfast, Alan.' He looked round the table. 'Cornflakes be all right? Hang on, Piers. That's the last of the milk.'

'It doesn't matter,' I said.

'Oh, damn,' said Ben. 'I'll see if I can borrow some from Graham.'

There was another long delay, inadequately punctuated by Joanna, who made attempts at general conversation, unencouraged. She had started to clear things from the table by the time Ben returned with a jug of milk.

I began to eat the cereal – reluctantly, as I was beyond hunger by now – and Piers and Joanna took their dilatory leave.

There was silence after they had shut the door.

'Sorry about that,' said Ben.

'That's all right.'

'I thought you'd have had breakfast.'

'Clearly.'

'You have it so early, usually. They just dropped in. I didn't know they were coming.'

'It's quite all right.'

'Do stop being fed up, then.'

'That's hardly how I'd describe my feelings for the last hour.'

He did not laugh. 'I couldn't help it, Alan.'

'I didn't say you could.'

'Oh!' he said with emphasis, turning from the table.

He walked to the window, and then walked back and sat down. 'Look, I'm sorry: I let you starve, and then there wasn't enough milk.'

'*That* wasn't wholly your fault.'

'Piers is revolting.' He stopped and laughed. 'He can be terribly funny, though: the thing about the stage manager and the green tights?'

'I don't remember it.'

He looked at me.

'Come on, Alan, it's not *that* bad. Just because they were still here when you came. I wasn't expecting them.'

'I never suggested you were.'

'I'd have said come earlier if I'd known.'

'But since you didn't know, you preferred to sleep.'

'Well, but I'd rather have slept than seen them, too. Only they didn't ask, that's all. They just woke me up.'

'Perhaps you'd like to go back to sleep now?'

'No, of course I wouldn't. I couldn't, anyway. Look, for heaven's sake, Alan, what is the matter?'

I took a deep breath, and said, 'I don't know.'

'Have some more coffee?'

'Thank you.'

He poured out two cups, and we sat and drank together in silence for some moments. Then Ben said, 'You don't *mind* my having friends here when you're coming?'

'Of course I don't. What possible reason would I have to mind? Or right?'

He frowned at his saucer. 'Then?'

'I suppose you're not always obliged to ask them to stay to the next meal.'

'I didn't. At least, not really. I offered them coffee, and they said they hadn't had breakfast.'

'Ah.'

'Well, why didn't *you* say so?'

I did not know what to answer.

'Unless you just wanted me to feel bad about it?'

'If we can't keep the discussion above that level...'

'What level?'

'That sort of childish petulance.'

He shut his mouth tightly, then he said, 'All right, if we can't – then what?'

'Then there's not much point in going on. Or indeed in my staying here.'

He glared at me still; then the angry blank of his face broke up confusedly. 'But we were going to spend the morning together.'

'We've accounted for a good deal of it already.'

'Oh, Alan – '

I made no answer. I was suddenly unable to understand what was wrong; I could feel only disapproving curiosity about my own behaviour, though I could not retract it.

Ben's head was bent over the table. He looked up and reached his hand towards me.

'Let's stop. This is silly.' After a moment he went on, 'It was my fault. I let them go on about the May Week production, and you were left out. I should have thrown them out, or shut them up anyway, and looked after you better. At least found out you hadn't eaten.'

I was still silent, shame and respect gaining a little ground from the unaccountable extent of my exasperation. Ben watched my face.

'There's half the morning left,' he said. 'Shall we start across Christ's Pieces? I wouldn't mind going to Heffer's.'

He turned his head at a slight noise from the door and got up with mock reluctance.

'Come on in then, bother you.'

A small tabby cat slid in between the door and the jamb. Ben bent to tickle its head.

'Come to reclaim stolen milk, I'm afraid,' I said.

Ben let his relieved glance cross mine as he scooped the little cat onto his shoulder.

'He can spare it.'

'Is this one of the last batch?'

'Last but one. Polynices. He's a year-and-a-bit.'

I poured some milk into my saucer. 'Come on then, now you've tracked it down.'

Ben stooped to put the cat down, rubbing his face against its side and avoiding my eye as I held out the saucer. Then he turned out the fire and fetched my coat and his own.

'We can leave him here if we don't shut the door.'

We walked quickly over Christ's Pieces, between the trees; it was difficult to get warm.

'Beastly chilly wind,' said Ben.

'It is, isn't it.'

'Heffer's first?'

'All right.'

'Or Bowes and Bowes?'

'I don't mind. Whichever you like.'

Heffer's had the book Ben was looking for, but it cost more than he could afford. The two I had ordered had not yet come in. We wandered round the tables and stacks. Archie Tanner had published some refurbished lectures and reviews as *An Introduction to Mediaeval Thought*. I stopped to look at it (it was no more adequate to its title than I expected), and then picked up a new collection of Civil War poetry. It was scholarly and rather entertaining. I took it with me in search of Ben. He was at a table near the cash desk, reading a book of cartoons, which he shut when he saw me.

'Do you know these?' I showed him the page of Levellers' songs, which I had kept marked with my finger.

'Oh. No. What fun.' He read them through – his attention undermined by embarrassment at his own choice of reading – and handed the book back to me. I had thought of asking if he would like it for his birthday next week. I went back across the shop to replace it, and he followed me.

'You've finished here?' I asked.

'I think so.'

'You said you were busy this afternoon?'

'Not to start with. Come back and have some lunch.'

'I don't want to take up your time.'

'No, honestly. Anyway, I owe you a proper meal.'

We laughed duly. On the way back, Ben bought bread and butter and sliced ham and tomatoes, and some apples, and a pint of milk. His room was cold when we reached it. The little cat had gone, leaving the sticky saucer on the floor. I lit the fire, and Ben wiped the table and washed some knives and plates, then put out the food.

We started eating.

'How's the work?' I asked eventually.

'Oh, all right.' After a moment he added, 'I didn't get as much done as I meant to, actually, this last couple of weeks.'

'That was the opera, I suppose?'

'Mainly. Still, there's the vac.'

'You'll be at home?'

'Yes. There's masses of reading to do, still, before Part Two.'

'Mostly revision, I imagine.'

'Well – mostly.' He cut some more bread.

'And after the Tripos?'

'I'm not even thinking about that.'

I laughed. 'That's a mistake. Thinking about it – the day when it's all over – it's usually a help. Even remembering there will *be* a day when it's all over.'

'Yes, I suppose so. Life after Finals.' He smiled. 'I thought you meant – you know – when I've gone down. What am I going to *do*, properly.'

'I suppose I did mean that, too.'

He frowned.

'Well?'

'Oh, God, I don't *know*.'

'What sort of thing are you thinking of?'

'Well, as I said: I really haven't started thinking at all.'

'You must have some idea, though?'

He didn't answer.

'Even if it's only an idea of what you don't want to do.'

'Well, all right. I don't want to go into advertising. And I don't want to join the army.'

I nodded, smiling. 'No.'

He laughed.

'And more positively?'

He shook his head.

'Would you like to teach, do you think? Or there's publishing. Or is there any chance of staying on to do research?'

'Not unless I get a first. Which I certainly won't. And anyway – .' He stopped, and went on after a moment: 'I did have one idea.'

'Yes?'

'I thought, perhaps – . Perhaps it sounds silly. But I'd really like to, if I could. If I could earn enough first. Just travel a bit. Go to America or something.'

'To America.'

'Yes.'

'For how long? How long would you go?'

'Oh, a year, I suppose. Two. Something like that.'

I was silent.

'I really would like to. And I don't see why not.' He looked across the table. 'Do you?'

'No. No – '

'But what?'

'I can't see any real reason why not – any reason at all, if you can afford it. But it wouldn't solve the problem, would it? It would only shelve it till you came back.'

'I just thought it might be easier to decide, when I'd had time – wandered around a bit.'

'You didn't find you had enough time in the vacations? Or in the terms, indeed?'

'Well, I know. I know there's lots. But there are always people around – and things – and all the reading. And all the revising, now.'

'If it is all revising.'

He glanced at me.

'Anyway, I thought if I got away a bit – '

'And you don't think that's just putting off the decision?'

'Of course it's putting off the decision. But not "just"; at least, I don't think so. I really would like to see a bit more of the world. And – well – you know – find out a bit more about myself, too. Discover what I really want to do.'

'Find yourself? It sounds the right sort of thing to be doing in America, anyway.'

He ducked his head. 'Whatever you call it: isn't it quite a sensible thing to do? Don't most people have to, at some stage?'

'How many people do you suppose have the chance?'

'Didn't you?'

'I had to go into the army.'

'Oh, all right, all right. We young people nowadays...'

'That's not what I was going to say,' I said, with increased irritation, untruthfully.

'Well, you sounded like it. Anyway, you still haven't told me what's wrong with it.'

'With what?'

'Not making up my mind the minute I go down; travelling a bit first.'

'I didn't say there was anything wrong with it. I just don't see what you hope to gain from it – apart from putting off a decision which will have to be made anyway, sooner or later.'

'Then why not later?'

'It rather depends how much later. What makes you think it will be so much easier twelve months from now? Or two years? Why shouldn't you put it off indefinitely, once you've started wandering round the world at your father's expense.'

'It won't *be* at my father's expense. I said: I won't go unless I can earn the money first. And if I have to, I'll earn some more on the way.'

'If you can. Have you thought about work permits? Or currency restrictions? Have you really thought about it at all? Above the level of the Boys' Own Paper?'

'I've thought about paying you back. I was going to earn that before I did anything else, if that's what's worrying you.'

'I think that's undeserved.'

'Yes. It was. I'm sorry. But then, Alan – why are you being so – ? Why are you so against it?'

Because I could not tell him, yet could not control my despair at the idea either, I tried hard to sound reasonable, and became still angrier and more ungenerous.

'I'm not against it, altogether. And your debt to me has nothing to do with it, as I should have expected you to know.'

I waited, and then went on, 'I'm simply concerned about it, at this stage, when you should be taking every chance – '

'Wouldn't this be a chance?'

'I mean a chance to start some work – do something worth doing.'

'And if I think this is worth doing – ?'

'If you honestly think that: if it's really the best use you can find for the next two years of your life, and a university education – a decent degree – '

'All right. But it's my degree and it's my life.'

'I realise that.'

'I sometimes wonder if you do.'

There was a cold, alarming silence. I looked at Ben, and he did not drop his gaze.

After the silence had continued for some time, I said, 'Could you explain that?'

Still staring at me, though he looked frightened, Ben said, 'All right. I don't think you always realise I've grown up. I'm nearly twenty-two, after all. You can't go on arranging my life for me for ever.'

I said nothing, and he went on, more anxiously, 'However much I need your advice – and I do, often – and value your judgement, and like having you as a friend, as a great friend – '

'I'd rather you said what you want to say. I don't need to be bought off.'

'I'm not trying to buy you off, God damn it; I'm trying to tell you what I meant. I'm just saying that you're – that it's – it's all very well, but sometimes I wish to God you'd leave me alone.'

I stared at him, and he said, 'I didn't mean that.'

'You did, I think.'

I stood up. I was shaking, and I hoped he could not see it. 'It might have been better if you'd managed to say it before.'

'I – '

'But I suppose I couldn't expect that – '

'Well, you do – '

'Whatever I do, it's usually safe to assume that you'll take the easy way out: deal with anything you don't like the look of by running away from it; leave any difficult decisions to somebody else.'

He swallowed, then he pushed back his chair with a clatter, and stood up.

'All right: I do run away – I have – sometimes. And how the hell do you expect me to do anything else – get up my own courage – make my own decisions – if you're always there doing it for me? Telling me what I ought to do, what I did wrong, how I've got to put it right. Whether I've asked you or not. What do you want me to be – a sort of moral hanger-on for the rest of my life? A satellite to your conscience? How can I be anything else, if you don't lay off? When are you ever going to leave me alone, let me run my own life?'

I stood quite still.

'Almost immediately,' I said eventually, 'if that's what you would prefer.'

I picked up my coat and left the room.

CHAPTER 57

That is really all there is to say. There are few other events worth recording in the history of my acquaintance with Ben – few other events, at least, that I have the heart to record. If only my typescript had arrived from the States, I should have good reason to end this account here, before it reaches that eventless waste, and I have to record a time which I am reluctant even to try to remember – a time of which I am still scaldingly ashamed. It was a time of distress, too – painful even in memory. And I have said that I would write this account as if Ben were going to read it: that would make both shame and distress incalculably greater.

And yet to lie – even by omission, even to an ideal reader only – might be more shameful, and indeed more dangerous. If this work, which has cost me so many weeks now, is to have any worth, it must be true and it must be complete. If it has no worth, I have, for the moment, no purpose – and that I am afraid to allow.

Early in the summer, when I started writing this, I was expecting every day to find the typescript of *Mediaeval Narrative Technique* in the post, with the comments from Brian Robson which would enable me to get it into final form. It was not until three or four weeks later, when I had finished every conceivable chore that could save working time later on, and had begun to use the first part of the evening for writing as well as the morning, that a letter arrived – not from Brian, but from his secretary. He had been taken ill quite seriously in New York, and might not be home before Christmas. He would get the typescript back to me as soon as he could, but he did not want to risk it in the post, for fear it was the only copy of my work (as it certainly – though rather less importantly – was of his notes). He would send it by the first reliable friend he could find who was coming to London, but he did not know how soon that would be.

I deferred my exasperation long enough to write to Brian, wishing him a good recovery, and telling him that I was in no hurry for the typescript. After some hesitation, I added a postscript, offering to lend him what I could, if he was in any difficulty about paying his American medical bills.

Then I began to reconsider my own plans, and found that my impatience had evaporated. I was content to postpone preliminary work on the Italian influence before Chaucer – for the moment at least, and perhaps even until next summer, when I could take the working holiday in Florence which I had planned for this year. What I wanted to do immediately was to go on with this account. I had reached my holiday with the Graysons in the Lake District, and I was finding the work very different from anything I had ever done: more difficult, in many ways; more internal, less verifiable, more – much more – vulnerable to changes of mood and confidence; and yet equally requiring exactness and a scrupulous, objective adherence to fact – even to the facts of subjective feeling. It had become a little easier by then. I was writing more fluently than when I started, and with the extra time between tea and supper as well, I was covering considerably more ground in a day. As I had hoped – perhaps even better than I had hoped – it had steadied and clarified my thoughts of Ben – directed them into an honest and manageable corpus of memory which I did not feel to be ruinously inadequate to its subject – though to that subject it owes any merit it may have:

The argument all bare is of more worth
Than when it hath my added praise beside.

I still feel this to be true. The whole summer has been a happy one, though not with the happiness I had expected. The last few days have been less happy, and the coming weeks will be worse still, if I go on with this account, as I suppose I must. I would give a good deal to avoid recording the next stretch of time. However, that is the point I have reached.

I can still remember the stairs, as I went down them from Ben's lodging to the street, but I cannot remember how I got home from Cambridge. I think I was probably lucky not to have an accident. The quarrel had left my whole mind hot and stiff and raw with resentment – raw as exposed flesh to the flick of guilt, to the touch of any smallest sense that I had been to blame. Only Ben's culpability – his trivial, squandering fecklessness, his ingratitude, above all his bad faith – lay between me and this repeated and intolerable pain. To meet my concern, my love, my long and hard restraint with such accusations, was not merely savage, self-regarding injustice, it was open acknowledgement of previous cowardice and deceit – of a duplicity undermining any trust or delight we had had, hollowing out the foundations of our friendship so that it all lay, now, in retrospective ruin. Reiterating every passage of our quarrel in my mind, scanning it again and again for evidence of my own moderation and good faith, and of his unfairness and treachery, I found ample material for defence against the worst pains of self-reproach and the terrors of loss. Or I would use it instead for attack, recasting and refining my answers to cut more painfully and lastingly – in retrospect, or, if necessary, in the future.

At home, my anger gave me no rest. Wherever I distracted my mind – and I did make an effort, after a time, to distract it – it would turn back, at my first moment of unwariness, evade the consideration of work or housekeeping, attempts at leisure or attempts to sleep, and begin to grind again through the same self-justifying revolutions, over and over the same bitter ground. As much from weariness of my own undischarged indignation, as from a desire to subject him to it more completely, I wrote my anger, after a week or so, in a long letter to Ben (later, thank God, destroyed and therefore impossible to copy here). I addressed the envelope and stamped it ready for the postman, but put it aside next morning, as I heard the van arrive, on the grounds that there might be, still, some communication from Ben. The letter waited on my desk, as each morning's post brought nothing of any account.

After ten or twelve days, my sense of injury burned less fiercely, and began to cool and harden. I began to think that the quarrel had made the break, quickly and finally, which had to be made in any case, eventually, and which must otherwise have cost me so much more of a struggle, so much more misery still – in coming to a resolution, and carrying it through, in imposing it both on myself and on Ben. It would be a relief, soon – it was really one already – to know that nothing of that whole burden of concerns need be carried any further. How much of my feeling I could let Ben see; what form, if any, the great remainder could be given; what opportunities could be devised, without suspicion, for meeting and talking alone; what hopes these could hold of intimacy and confidence; how long such a friendship could continue, without damage to itself, or to either of its participants: none of this needed an answer any more. The whole back-breaking load could be laid aside, and all the ingenuity and energy and time it had exacted could be released for the rest of my life.

I could not be sure that Ben would feel the same. I could be sure, indeed, that he would not. His side of our relationship had been burdened with no such ambiguities, no such inadmissible difficulties or unmanageable hopes. When he began to regret his part in the quarrel (as well he might) he might very probably look for a renewal of our friendship. I thought he would. He would be disappointed – and not lightly or for a short time – to be met with an unqualified refusal. He would not be easily convinced that neither apology (not even the full apology he owed me), nor affection, nor time would bring any hope of a reconciliation. It would grieve him very much for a time. But would it not spare us both much greater grief, in the end? I could not persuade myself that his affections were callous, but they were young, and they must be resilient. His cheerfulness would be restored before I had wiped out the last traces of my own regret. And meanwhile, it would do him no harm to contemplate the damage he had done. He had to learn, in good time and for his own good, that irresponsibility can have irrevocable results.

In order to enjoy the satisfactions of my liberty, I walked out beyond the Harchester Road one afternoon, going fast. I stopped at a pub on the way back, and eventually drank a good deal there.

Next morning I slept through the hour or more before the postman came. I was not even downstairs to take the letters from him at the door, but heard the clatter of the letterbox while I was dressing, and found a letter from Ben on the mat.

Thursday

Dear Alan,

Can I come and see you? Please. I'll be at home next week.
Please let me know there.

Ben

I was shivering, as I opened the envelope, with distress and fear and unspecified anticipation, as well as from the chill of the morning through my half-open shirt. Reading the half-sheet of Ben's writing, turning the envelope to see the postmark – he had written from London – I felt hope and anger begin to emerge together, and in opposition, from my formless expectancy. It was safer that anger should prevail, as well as more honourably consistent.

I had determined to make this breach the beginning of our necessary, permanent division – to take advantage of the pain already suffered, already fading, in order to save us both from longer and more degrading misery. I could not, with self-respect, go back on that determination at the first ache of hope. Besides, I could not see that Ben deserved a favourable answer – or any answer at all. He sent no word of apology or even of regret. He wanted to see me, that was all – even, under the guise of good manners, demanded to see me: his letter could be read as peremptory.

I was not going to answer it. I thought that I should tear it up immediately, but found I could not do so. Some weak desire to hedge my bets – to insure the future, when I might need even this flimsy consolation – made me throw it into a drawer with other letters.

My anger did not prevent me from working out the earliest date when Ben could be expected home. As this approached, and passed, I found it more and more necessary to drink whisky in the evenings if I was to sleep at night. Nor could I prevent myself from starting urgently when the telephone rang, though once I had reached it, I could hardly pick it up. By the fourth day of the following week, I was looking at my watch repeatedly, while I tried to write letters after tea, to know how long it would be until I could have a drink.

I was pouring it out when I heard Ben's voice at the door, calling my name as he knocked.

'Alan?'

My arm jerked, and sent whisky over the table. I brushed at it with my sleeve, drank down all that was in the glass, and went to the door.

Ben had waited on the step.

'Alan.'

'Yes.'

'Alan – did you get my letter?'

'I got it, yes.'

'You didn't answer it.'

'No.'

'I wanted to talk to you.'

'So you said.'

There was a pause; then he said, more slowly, 'May I come in?'

I did not reply for some moments. Then I said, 'If you think it would be of any use.'

'But it would. Wouldn't it?'

I remained standing, silent, with my hand on the door.

'Don't you think it would?' he asked.

'I doubt it.'

He said nothing and I went on.

'I think it would be more likely to cause us both some distress.'

'But I need to talk to you. Really, Alan. Please. I want to... I want your advice.'

'My advice?' I said eventually. He flushed. 'Are you sure? I should have thought that was the last thing you wanted.'

'Look, I know. It was silly. I shouldn't have – '

'Surely that settles it. If you're in any danger of asking my advice, you'd certainly better not come in.'

Nothing more was said, but I stayed in the doorway until Ben lowered his head and turned away, and walked slowly down the path to the gate.

Two days later the comments on the Cycle arrived from the Press. For the next few weeks I worked on them very carefully indeed for most of every day, considering, checking and, where necessary, disputing their suggestions with unremitting attention. Relief at having work to do provided a good deal of the energy for this – relief, and determination that personal concerns should not again affect my accuracy. I knew that the unassailable impersonality of work was my only certain defence; I think, too, that indifference, in this one area of my life, to the ravages of Ben's accusations seemed to me another weapon against him, even another form of revenge. I should have liked him to know how well I was working.

I took an hour off after lunch. Otherwise I worked straight through the day, and did not drink until I had finished. I still consumed a good deal of whisky in the last part of the evening, but not enough to affect my work next day. This limit, however, was not as narrow as I had expected, and seemed to be getting wider. By the beginning of May I had sent my notes off to Douglas; it was some weeks longer before his reached me. This gave me a certain amount of satisfaction, but left me too long to think.

Ben would soon be taking his finals. Might he be in need again of the help and reassurance he had asked from me last year? Or even of more? He had no great confidence in his own ability, and we both knew that he was on the borderline, only, of a respectable degree. Would he take Part II more seriously – still more seriously – than he had taken Part I? And how would his present state of mind stand up to the strains of extra work and anxiety, fatigue and hope? I thought of his face as he had turned from the door. I could not convince myself – I did not really try – that he would yet have recovered completely from that meeting, or from the one before. And then if Julian decided to amuse himself again – . But I could not let myself follow that train of thought. I would not complicate the issue with a jealousy that was now not only irrelevant, but meaningless. I had given Ben enough good advice about Julian – too much, he would say now, presumably. He had wanted to fight his own battles: he must do so. If he got hurt, he could learn from that without my help. I hoped, though, that the process of learning would not include a bad degree, and I found it hard not to turn to the University News as soon as the paper arrived.

Douglas did not have much to add to my notes (and I was inadmissably gratified to find that he had missed several of my points). We settled our remaining differences in a telephone call from Hamburg: he seemed amused by the minuteness of one or two of my corrections, and by the vigour with which I defended them. I accused him of collaborating with the Press in their attempt to present the Cycle as a musical comedy; he accused me of obsessive and hair-splitting pedantry, and we ended in high good humour. As I put the telephone down, still laughing, I thought for a moment of taking up his invitation to Hamburg. I missed him, and I needed a holiday; I did not think a solitary one would be more successful than it had been last year. We could correct the proofs together, when they came. But when I took out my most recent bank-statement, I found that I had been spending rather more than I expected. In spite of Ben's three pounds a month, paid in by banker's order, the journey would leave me very little in reserve; and an undefined sense of emergency made me reluctant to diminish my resources so far. Once the final text was agreed, therefore, and ready for printing – the Press accepted most of our points with surprisingly little discussion – there was nothing to do but to wait for the proofs.

This wait was both longer and more difficult than the one before. I had neither heart nor inspiration to start any new work, and the days seemed hot and heavy. When I saw in the newspaper that Ben had got a two-two, I felt a sharp ache of guilt which I could find no way to assuage. It was exacerbated, absurdly, when I read a review of P. J. Kendall's *Sonnets and Sonnet Form*, and realised that I had done nothing about Ben's birthday in March. He was now twenty-two.

I began to want a drink, and sometimes to have one, before lunch, as well as in the evening. Near the end of July, I spent part of a hot morning trying, without enthusiasm or success, to plan the students' edition of *The Cycle*. I had owed Brian Robson a letter about it for some weeks, and had heard from him again that morning. I tried for an hour or two to make a start, but allowed myself to be side-tracked into sorting out papers. Even for this my resolution was inadequate: to be really methodical seemed too much trouble; indecisiveness increased the confusion and prolonged the work through the afternoon. In the end I started drinking well before six, on the grounds that the heat, and the dust from the papers, were making me too thirsty to concentrate. The first drink was diluted, in accordance with this pretext, but the second was as strong as usual, and the next stronger than that. The shapeless tangle of the day receded far enough to seem a tolerably useful part of a larger scheme. Grievances and justifications began to slacken their guard as the looming, vigilant shapes of grief and terror withdrew a little in their perpetual siege of my consciousness.

I had started a fourth or fifth glass, and carried the next toppling load of folders upstairs to stack on the spare shelves in the bedroom, when I heard a car in the lane. The pile spilled across the floor; from the window I saw the Graysons' car slowing and turning beyond the gate. I stood, looking about irresolutely, and caught sight of my face in the glass. There was dust across my forehead and on my neck, and my hands left more there when I tried to wipe it away; the grime on the neck of my shirt was of longer duration. My face was unevenly red, and greasy with sweat; I had not shaved for two or three days.

Through the window, I saw that Ben was standing by the car, pocketing the key. I left the room and ran along the passage and down the stairs. As I reached the kitchen, I heard him knock at the front door. The back door was locked: the key was in the sitting-room. I made for the kitchen window, opened the lower part and clambered through and down onto the rough grass below, landing unevenly and turning my ankle. Then I ran, lurching and stumbling, across the space of ground, along the hedge and into the shed at the far end. I never locked the front door of the house by day, but as long as he had waited there a minute or two – as I thought he would – he could not have seen me. I pulled the door of the shed to behind me, and stood pressed up awkwardly against the garden tools. I leaned my head on my arm against the wall, and drew breath shakily and painfully into my chest. As the urgency of flight became less immediate, the other aspects of my state grew clearer: disgust and shame and fear of discovery closed

345

in, fleering and jabbing, leaving no gap for escape, like a ring of bullies at school. I twisted my head to and fro on my arm, praying that Ben would leave without looking for me, or, if he looked for me, that he would not notice the kitchen window, swinging unlatched.

Even after I thought I had heard the car go, I waited a long time – as much as an hour – before I dared to assume that he was certainly gone. Then I went slowly back to the house, and into the kitchen to shut the window. There I saw a note on the table, written on a page torn from his diary.

Alan. I came to tell you I got a II.ii, and also to see you. But I think you may not want to see me, so I won't come again unless you ask me. Ben.

He had accepted my intention: there was nothing left for me to do.

CHAPTER 58

I spent the next day in a kind of stupefaction at the prospect of absolute blankness before me, continuing not only as far as I could see or imagine, but as far as I knew that, for me, in principle, time could extend. The lifelessness of this expanse seemed to deaden my mind, so that I thought and felt very little. Later I was surprised by the mechanical efficiency with which I must have put away the remaining papers, cleared up the kitchen, and tidied my desk. But after another night, feeling began to return as sharply as heat to frozen fingers. I woke early and lay, turning my mind about, and my body, this way and that, to find, even for a moment, some posture of relief from the cramping grip of wretchedness. I had no success: the grip tightened and my sense of it increased as the light broadened. Only my will remained numb. By mid-morning I had begun to drink, and I spent the next three or four days in almost continuous drunkenness.

I finished the whisky fairly early one morning, thank heavens, when I was still just sober enough to know that I must not drive. I washed my face and changed my shirt, and walked over the fields to the pub, and bought as many more bottles as I thought I could carry. I realised how bad my judgement was on the way home, when I had to rest every few hundred yards. But I thought that perhaps I had simply failed to allow for the effect of the last few days on my physical stamina. Neither explanation was gratifying, and nor was my recollection of the landlord's face: I was not used to looks of that kind – of concern, and incipient disapproval, and even pity – nor to solicitousness about how I should get my load home.

The sun came out when I was halfway back, and the deeper draughts of air which the exercise enforced dispersed some of my nausea, and made my head a little clearer. By the time I met the post-van in the lane, I had recovered enough to wonder why there was a second delivery, and then to sign my name with tolerable regularity for several registered parcels, handed through the window.

They were the parcels of proofs. Walking on up the lane, I wondered how I would correct them at all, let alone properly. It would be simpler to abandon them immediately. I could rely on Douglas's accuracy without a double check. And if he did not agree, I thought for a moment, it would not matter: there was no reason, any longer, why anything should matter more than anything else; and nothing else mattered at all.

But long habits of intellectual thrift were too much for me. Even now, I could not finally disregard the years which had gone to making fast and seaworthy every plank and joint and dowel of this work. I could not really bear to let the whole ship founder, in the launching, for want of this last, negligible scrap of tar. But looking at the bottles in the basket, wedged apart by the thick envelopes of proofs, I did not know how I could ignore them until I was fit to begin the work – still less until I had completed it.

I put down the basket, panting, when I reached the gate. Two blackbirds flew down from a tree just inside the garden, one above the other, fluttering and fighting; they were both black and bright, both cocks. When I had got my breath, I went into the house and poured all the whisky from the bottles into the sink.

The proofs did not really take very long, though for the first few days they seemed interminable. After a better night's rest, quantities of coffee, and an afternoon walking over to the river and swimming, my head seemed clear enough, and my hand steady enough, to start.

I saw almost no-one in those next weeks, and I did not go into the town. I was afraid of another opportunity to start drinking. I lived from the store cupboard, and when that was finished – even the last delicacies, kept against an unexpected feast: the preserved ginger, the little jar of pâté de foie gras – I bought bread and meat-paste from the milkman, and eggs from the farm, and stewed the windfall apples.

Douglas was due in Edinburgh before the start of his term. I sent the corrected proofs to await him, and started looking through our Glossary for words and uses of words to be added to the Dictionary. I had been aware for a year that this should be done eventually, and the knowledge that Peter Thorsen would find some of the uses surprising, and even incredible, did not make the work less satisfactory.

Douglas soon telephoned from Edinburgh. He was too busy with a new syllabus to pay me the visit he had hoped for, but he was delighted that I had done with the proofs, and hoped to get them back to the Press soon after the beginning of term. His time in Hamburg had been very profitable; Sam had thriven with his sister's family in Perthshire; and they were both in good spirits. We planned to meet at Christmas, and I settled down to some undemanding work on the students' edition.

*

[hand-written]

CHANGE OF ADDRESS

From 11th October:

Ben Grayson and David Williams

Flat b, 138 Lillie Road,

London, SW5.

Telephone (8.30am–5pm) FUL 8891 (ext. 125)

(Thames Water Authority, Filing Dept.)

*

Printing started in October, and at Christmas I spent three weeks in Edinburgh. I had not done much of the students' edition – a preliminary plan, the texts of a couple of plays – but I felt as tired as if I had been working at full stretch since the summer. It was an extraordinary relief to have an alternative to work which was not solitary leisure. Edinburgh was very cold, but beautiful, in snow, and we walked about the streets, and sat talking over the fire, and visited Douglas's friends, and went to the excellent National Gallery. Christmas itself was a little muted, in the Scottish tradition, but Hogmanay was festive, and on the morning of New Year's Eve I had a card, forwarded by the Post Office with the rest of my post – a Nativity from a fourteenth century Book of Hours:

WITH ALL GOOD WISHES FOR
A MERRY CHRISTMAS
AND PROSPERITY IN THE
NEW YEAR.

Ben

Next morning I walked alone to the top of Arthur's Seat, and looked out over the city and all its snow and granite, glittering in the sun, and wondered what I had been doing and what could be done. I had started out late, after the celebrations of the night before; I ate something on the way back, and the early dusk had begun before I was home.

CHAPTER 59

The Cycle came out at the end of February. The reviews were very good. Even Archie Tanner wrote favourably, and almost without captiousness, in *The Spectator*. Douglas rang from Edinburgh with elation, and the Press reported that the first sales more than justified the alarming price they had put on the two volumes. We both had a good many letters about it: dealing with the post provided an almost regular reason for putting aside the students' edition until mid-morning. Among my letters was one addressed in Ben's handwriting. I thought for a moment, when I had opened the envelope, that it was empty, but there was a small rectangle of newsprint near the bottom to qualify my disappointment. It was a review of the Cycle, enthusiastic though not well written, from the Book Page of the *South West London Performing Arts Gazette*. Ben had put an exclamation mark in the margin against a particularly incongruous mixed metaphor, and had written 'B.', with the date, at the end. It seemed illogical, as I answered that day's letters, to leave him, alone, unthanked. I sent a postcard to his London address:

Thank you for sending me the cutting. I was glad to see the review. A.P.

21.iii.1966

I spent the next few days in a state of excitement I could neither ignore nor justify; only as it began to fade, in the following week, did I realise that its source had been simply my own acknowledgement of Ben's message, the sense that mutual contact, however sparely, had been renewed. He did not write again, however, and as the spring came in my little savour of hope began to be sour and flat, to make me feel a fool for having relished it.

Work lagged, as the days grew longer and clearer; and sunny parts of April, with the blossom coming out on the apple trees, seemed a reward I had not earned, and could not take. There were mornings worth playing truant for, to rejoice in 'proud pied April, dress'd in all his trim'. I did play truant, but from so little other purpose that I could not rejoice.

Then Ben came to see me. On the way from my desk to make yet another cup of coffee, I went through the door of the sitting room and found him in the hall. Thought stopped, with breath and movement, as if all current had been cut off. I stood with the cup in my hand.

'I did knock,' he said. 'I don't think you heard.'

'No, I didn't hear.'

'I said I wouldn't come, I know. But you did write.'

'Yes.'

'I thought you wouldn't mind. I mean my coming at all – perhaps. But I wouldn't have come in, only you didn't hear.'

'That's all right.'

'I just came – '

'Won't you come in and sit down?'

I turned and pushed the sitting-room door open.

'Yes. May I?'

'Would you like some coffee?'

'No thanks. Don't bother. Really.'

We sat down opposite each other, by the fireplace.

'They've done the Cycle,' said Ben after a moment. 'I saw it in the Charing Cross Road. In the Press bookshop. It looks great.'

'Yes. Did you? We're pleased with it.'

'It got good reviews.'

'On the whole.' He shifted, and I added, 'Thank you for sending the cutting, by the way.'

'Oh. Well. I thought you might not have seen it.'

'No.'

'I thought you might not take the *Performing Arts Gazette*.'

He had tried to say it as a joke, but neither of us managed to laugh. Then he said, 'I just thought I'd come – I must come – if you didn't mind – '

'No. No, that's quite all right.'

' – come to say goodbye.'

'You're going?'

'Yes.'

'Where are you going?'

'I'm going –' he looked down and then up, ' – going to America.'

'Yes.'

'It'll be – ' the same hesitation, 'it'll be for a couple of years. Two. Or possibly three.'

I said nothing.

'I've got a sort of job,' he went on more quickly, 'in a children's summer camp. And I've saved quite a lot of what I earned at the Water Board. And I think I can get a job after the summer, delivering cars across to the other side. So that should give me long enough to look round – find something…' He looked at me, his voice tailing off.

'Yes. That all sounds – workable.' After a moment I added, 'Interesting. It was what you wanted to do.'

'Well – it was really.'

'When do you go?'

'On Monday.'

'Monday. From Gatwick?'

'Heathrow. I'll stay the night in London. I've had this flat, with David.'

'Yes.'

'Of course. You knew. He's having to find someone else. It's easy for Heathrow, anyway. You can just walk up to the air terminal. From us, I mean. I can.'

'Yes. Well. That makes it easy. So you leave here tomorrow?'

'Yes. That's why I came now. I hoped you wouldn't be working. I did want – I wanted to say goodbye.'

'No, I wasn't working, really. Are you sure you wouldn't like some coffee?'

'No, really, thanks. I ought to be going.'

'You must have a lot to do.'

'Yes. An awful lot still.'

We both paused.

'And my packing,' Ben went on. 'It's chaos, really.'

He stood up, and so did I.

'It was good of you to spare the time.'

'I wanted to. I wanted to come, just to say goodbye.'

I said nothing, and for a moment I could not look at him. Then we both said, almost together, 'Well, goodbye.'

I put out my hand. Ben, turning away, saw it and turned back and took it. We shook hands, and parted hands again.

'Goodbye. Alan...'

'Goodbye. I hope it all goes well.'

'Goodbye.'

As he left, I said, 'I'm glad you came,' but I did not know if he heard me.

I could have told him that he had been right to come – that I was grateful. I could have wished him well more warmly. It had taken courage to come, and I had let the conversation die so soon, let him go. I had not asked him about his job in London, or his flat, or David. About his plans, I had heard only what he had volunteered. If he had stayed – if we had talked even a little longer – we might have come to talk of his degree. I had never said anything about that; perhaps he thought I saw it as a disgrace.

I had hardly seen him for over a year: why had I said none of this – said nothing but the dry necessities of acquaintance, of the mere negation of hostility? I thought of him in his room, packing, among piles of books and shirts and litter from his table. He would take down his posters. I could have given him a book. I could find one now and walk over there, and look in. His family would be there, keeping out of his way, trying not to dread his departure, ready with last-minute assistance and a farewell supper. I had hardly seen them, either, in all this time. They must be aware of that, and have guessed, at least, some part of the reason. If I could say nothing of consequence here, to Ben alone, what could I say in their presence?

Waking next morning, I thought that I could telephone. Then, at least, I could talk to him singly again; I could say something, anyway, if not everything I should have liked to say: give some signal, at least, of goodwill renewed and continuing. I could start by saying that I had meant to give him a book: I'd send it after him, if he could let me have an address; it might take some time by surface-mail...

I began to look along the shelves, and thought then of a better opening – more immediate, more plausible, and perhaps more useful: I would give him the address of Saul and Marcia Heyman, tell him to look them up, say I'd be writing to them. I found my address book in growing haste, and went to the telephone. The number was engaged. I tried again, and then again. I brought in the milk and tried again; took off the kettle and tried again. I tried every few minutes as I got the breakfast. I asked a dilatory operator if there was a fault on the line, and she answered eventually that the line was good; the number was engaged in conversation.

At some indistinguishable hour of the morning, I got through and Ruth answered. She told me that Ben had left for London and that his flat there had no telephone.

'There's no way of getting in touch with him then, really?'

'Not really, before he goes. Is there anything... something I can do?'

'It doesn't matter.'

'There's a *poste restante* address in New York; and – wait a minute – I've got the summer camp address somewhere. He'll be going there in June.'

'Don't worry. Thank you, anyway. It doesn't matter.'

'It's nice to hear you, Alan. Do come round and see us some time.'

'I will. Thank you.'

'You're sure – you're sure it wasn't important?'

'Not important at all.'

It was not important. It would have made no difference. I knew that, in fact. However long we had talked, we could not have penetrated the strain and unreality, the impossibility of talking about what most concerned us, could not have set going any real current of communication. We could never have found the old, live contact we had had once. The contact, I knew, was dead. I had known that since yesterday.

355

CHAPTER 60

The next seven-and-a-half months were the worst I have ever spent. I cannot, thank heaven, remember them very clearly. What I can remember is appalling enough. Drinking, alone, could blunt the jagged edges of final loss and regret, unsheathed at last, bright and hard and newly whetted, from all pretence of disregard. But the price of this partial anodyne was an almost perpetual nausea and a constant uneasy confusion of my surroundings with the hot, ungovernable shapes of nightmare.

As I slept later and later – or at least lay in bed, postponing the queasy, lurching pains of getting up – my day shifted further and further from the rule of the clock or the sun. The next night there would be longer still to wait, and to drink, before I could sleep; the following day, the beating of my head and the heaving of my stomach would go on still later and more violently into the morning, and yet with still less effect in the struggle in which they had been incurred. Before the fumes of last night's drinking had cleared, the outlines of misery and punishing isolation would begin to shoulder through them again, like prison guards, to be baffled and blotted out only when I began once more to drink. This was not quite immediately: always, before I started, I went through the motions of work; and I would put off the moment of settling to work with trivial jobs about the house – straightening the books on the table, sorting out the coats behind the door. And what I produced then was little enough, often nothing at all, and it began to seem hardly more than a clearing of the decks before the real business of the day.

Nevertheless, absurdly perhaps, and often unproductively, I would sit at my desk for an hour, or as nearly an hour as I could keep to, staring at the next few lines of the students' edition, writing half a dozen footnotes and crossing out half of them, confusing references and losing pieces of paper. I did have rather more success with the verse translation. It wasn't easy: to let my thoughts lie open to different possibilities of rhyme or metre or alliteration, different equivalents for an idiom or a proverb, was to let them lie open, too, to memory and regret, and futile and agonizing hope, and thence, very soon, to the need for a drink. But in occasional bursts of inspiration I did manage to produce a few hundred lines, though I wasn't sure what Douglas would think of some of my less conventional solutions to the various difficulties of translating poetic drama.

Before long, however, I realised that I was incapable of giving a lecture or conducting a seminar, and I used the small space of relative sobriety in the morning to cancel my various engagements on the implausible ground of too much work. I missed both the Dictionary meetings of the summer term – one of them without notice – and when I tried to put together my next set of definitions for the post, I found them so confused and incomplete that I had not the face to send them.

A postcard from Ben, one morning in high summer, parted the miasma for an hour with a direct sense of his presence.

The Grand Canyon really is astonishing (colours over not as fake as they look). More like a whole landscape – till you look out to the horizon & see, not more mountains, but the flat line of the far rim. Walked to the bottom – from pinewoods and squirrels to desert & rattlesnakes, with climate changing to match – & up again: took all day, and 6pts. of water, each way (the provident book mules 6 months ahead). Making for the W. Coast, then back to N.Y. where there seems some chance of a job. [I will send – deleted]

Everyone v. friendly & weather great.

Ben

Feeling, for the first time for many months, what it had been like to have him in the room, to hear the intonations of his voice, to watch the repose and movement of his hands, the lights and hollows of his skin, I was taken up, for a short moment or two, in a single, complete delight, unmixed with any other concern. I looked at the picture, and read again what he had written, and turned back to the picture again. I saw the improbable purples of shadowed rocks, the path between the crested humps, and found that I was in tears.

I cried at first easily, feeling tears relieve the lowering, humid weight of grief unexpressed, and cool and clear the climate of my mind. Then thinking with love of what I had lost, I realised more and more clearly how utterly I had lost it. The months when I had thought myself so desolate, when, after Ben's party, I knew my love could not be declared, seemed now an unacknowledged province of the country of my heart's desire. I had still seen him, often, and when we parted I had known it was not for long. He had come to visit me, saved up jokes for me, brought me presents, brought me his news and his anxieties. And whatever we talked of, whatever we said, our communication was real and direct. On my side it might not be without reserve – nor, perhaps, on his. No matter. Where our minds met, the contact was true, the energy of thought and feeling could run straight through, both ways, unchecked. Now all that was gone, with all the concomitant delight. All that remained was a determination – stronger, characteristically, on his side – to bury our friendship decently, with the proper forms of respect, and to commemorate it, for a time at least, with the ritual duties of acquaintance: the polite interest, the farewell visit, the occasional postcard.

I began to rage against the maudlin self-pity that had left so much good unrecognised. For a moment I felt that the misery of the present was no more than the just desert of such ingratitude. Then I thought that not many things could really deserve misery of this degree and duration: no just God or fate, however rigorous, could inflict it for ingratitude alone. But – even supposing some evidence that fate had ever been just – why should I pretend that ingratitude had been the whole of my offence? Was it not I, as well as Ben, who had abandoned this last region of paradise, walled it up, and left it to wither? I was crying now hotly and despairingly, and finally with a violence which shook me, and left me sick and light-headed. I went to sleep and woke craving for a drink.

Some vestigial sense of pride or privacy made me try to keep my drunkenness hidden from my acquaintance. I visited no-one, refused all invitations (including one for Bridget's twenty-first birthday), and kept the front door locked, unlocking it only to take in the milk. I went into Bramston to buy food and drink when I had to, before the morning's drinking started, and having first had a bath, shaved, and drunk several cups of coffee. On a fine day, I went by bicycle, and then I sometimes managed to last until the evening without a drink.

It was on one of these occasions that I decided to buy some more blocks of paper. This was a gesture of intention, rather than a necessity: I had several blocks still unused at home. But it gave me some slight, spurious sense of action, and perhaps a reason for staying a little longer in the town.

I could afford small, unnecessary purchases now, without calculation. If the payment for completion of the Cycle, and the first royalties, had not been so good, if I had had no money for whisky – if I had even had to work full-time in order to survive – would that have stopped my drinking perforce? Sometimes I hoped so, though it said little for the autonomy of my decisions. Sometimes I thought that I should merely have found some still more degrading alternative.

At the stationer's, the shop-keeper was almost effusive, searching remote shelves for blocks of the size I preferred, and asking after my health.

'Long time since you've been in, sir. Been keeping well, have you?'

'Yes, thank you. Yes, quite well.'

'We mustn't grumble, must we? I thought perhaps you'd been away.'

'No. No, not recently. I've been rather busy.'

'Of course. You must have been, of course.'

He looked at the blocks in his hand – the first I had bought for several months.

'I was meaning to say, sir: I'm sure we could give you a wholesale price on these, if you'd be interested.'

I accepted the offer with embarrassment, taking reluctant advantage of some undeclared concern (that I was taking my custom elsewhere? that I could not afford the paper I needed?).

'That would be very useful. Thank you. I... expect to be doing quite a lot more writing now. There have been other things recently: proof-correcting and so on; lecturing.'

'That would be in connection with the new book, I suppose, sir?'

Having stretched the truth so far already, I could only continue.

'Well, yes. Mainly.'

'I expect you've seen this? Came out some months ago.'

He took a folder from below the counter and handed me a page of the local newspaper; it was folded back to either side of an article headed 'Local author's success. Ten years work after "Mystery" find'.

'No, I hadn't. Thank you.' I read it quickly. Besides quoting from other reviews, it told me only that I was a well-known figure in Bramston, and that I had been unavailable for comment. 'Very interesting. Thank you so much.'

I handed the paper back to him. He looked it over with satisfaction, and put it away.

While he was replacing the folder, he said, 'I've been meaning to ask you, sir. I don't know whether you'd ever have the time, but we have meetings every month, at the Dramatic and Literary Guild. We like to get interesting speakers...' He waited a moment, and then added, 'Not quite the learned audience you'd be used to, I'm afraid, but I know everyone would be very interested. And with your living locally and so on...'

I agreed in the end because there seemed to be no good way to refuse.

My permanent reluctance to reduce scholarship to anecdotes and after-dinner jokes, and my more recent misgivings about speaking in public at all, were a little alleviated by the prospect of immediate and necessary work. The hour in the morning became two, and sometimes even more, as I drafted a mildly light-hearted account of Douglas's discovery and our various problems with the manuscript, and then described the development of mystery plays from the early tropes to the Corpus Christi processions. It was all absurdly over-simplified, of course, but at least I was able to give Douglas his due (as the misjudged local loyalty of the Bramston paper had failed to do), and I said nothing for which there was not good evidence from primary sources.

My audience might not be receptive to fine points of textual criticism, but I reflected that they were, after all, closer kin than I to the people to whom the plays had originally belonged. Market-town shopkeepers, minor professional men, craftsmen and tradesmen like them would not only have been among the first audiences of the Cycle; they would have provided the actors, the technicians, very likely the author. It was they, and not the scholars of the universities, who had first made it and first enjoyed it. I wondered whether I could make this point without condescension.

It remained only to find some of the best passages for reading aloud, translate them into Modern English where it seemed absolutely necessary, and string them together in an account of the Cycle's more obvious merits.

Harold Byford, my friend from the stationer's, was the secretary of the Guild, and when he and the treasurer met me at the door of the Old Corn Exchange, I realised that he had taken trouble over the evening. Such illustrations as I had been able to provide had been neatly arranged in the hall, with copies of some of my books and a small poster from the library. More heroically, he had raised a respectable audience of thirty or forty people, whose faces, when I saw them from the platform, suggested that they had been persuaded to come more by his importunity than by spontaneous interest in the subject. My original nervousness returned. I had not had a drink all day, and though I did not think my outward appearance gave much away, I felt inwardly inadequate. I had not spoken in public for over a year, and I had very little idea of the expectations and capacities of this audience; my concentration was troubled by nausea and diffused by impatience to start drinking.

The audience were adequately attentive, however, through the chairman's polite and inaccurate introduction, and when I began to speak I found that even the outline of our enterprise – the excitement, the work, the reverses and discoveries, the final achievement – brought with it its own energy and clarity. My listeners began to stir and laugh more readily; my account of the Corpus Christi pageants diverged from my notes to become less formal and more particular. I drew a parallel with their own Guild and their town, asking them to imagine a cart drawn up by the War Memorial on Market Square, draped with cloth from Winch and Webber, decorated with paints provided by Mr Byford, and with their chairman, perhaps, playing God, for two shillings, or Noah in his new four-penny mittens.

By the time I began to read from our own Cycle, they were ready to approve of it. They listened to the dialogue of Abraham and Isaac in real suspense, and laughed almost uproariously once or twice in the comedies of Noah and of the Shepherds. At the end of the final passage, from the Crucifixion, there was the moment of silence which is a truer and much less common tribute than any amount of immediate applause. The applause after that was loud, however, and of some length; and when Harold Byford proposed the vote of thanks, relief and surprise and proprietary pride were expressed almost as clearly as official gratitude.

My elation was prolonged by the congratulations of the committee, and by members of the audience, many of them with faces familiar from the shops, who came up to tell me how much they had enjoyed the talk. The fork supper with the committee afterwards had something of the air of a small triumph: for them, because speaker and audience had done them more credit than they had feared; and for me, because the Cycle had shown its enduring vitality and power among the people for whom it had first been made. My own work and self-restraint had also contributed to its present success. I had earned a drink.

Whisky was not provided, but there was a good deal of cheap, red wine. Harold Byford filled our glasses, and introduced me to most of the company. I talked to a friend of his who worked for the Rural District Council, to the two women (the draper's wife, I think, and the Church organist) who had provided the supper, to a history teacher from the secondary school, a naval officer's widow, and the Baptist Minister. Conversation continued to flow more easily than I had expected: the wine was still going round after the food had been finished, a few people left, and the rest became more convivial.

The local government clerk had heard some of the plays when they were broadcast, and I thought his tentative comparisons showed a genuine feeling for drama, as well as considerable ignorance. He admitted to an obsession with the theatre and, after more wine, to past ambitions – unsatisfied, but not, I thought, quite discarded – to act or to direct. He told me of a moment of glory as Brutus, ten years ago, at school, and quoted, not quite accurately, from the farewell to Cassius. I supplied the answering lines and, looking up, shared for an instant his sense of excitement in their tragic reticence.

It was the first time for many months that I had felt this pulse of mutual communication, this sudden exchange of understanding, unspoken. The feeling might not be altogether creditable – the excitement was tinged, perhaps, with *schwärmerei* and self-indulgence – but the mutual shock of recognition was nonetheless strong, and, after so long, was very welcome. I offered to lend the young man a book on Shakespearean acting, and when the rest of the party began to leave, he asked if he might show me a play he had bought recently from a second-hand stall in the market. It seemed very old, but he could not make much of it out – he thought perhaps I might be able to tell him – might even be interested – he did not live far away.

By the time I had said my goodbyes, and we were going down the steps into the street, I began to wonder if the book was something of a pretext for further acquaintance. But I had drunk enough wine to be glad of an opportunity for delay before driving home, and when he said that he hoped I would have time for 'a night-cap, or a coffee or something,' I justified my decision by choosing the coffee.

After the inevitable moments of awkwardness, when our separation from the company made conversation more necessary and therefore more difficult, my companion began to talk rapidly. He told me his name (which I shall not record here) and explained that he had often heard about me from Harold Byford. I expressed the usual facetious hope – with more than facetious intent – that what he had heard was not to my discredit, and he assured me of his friend's admiration.

'He's always been wanting me to meet you, as a matter of fact. He's said so often, I really ought to meet you: I'd be so interested, all the things you've done. He knew how interested I was in the radio plays. And then writing books, travelling...'

'Well...'

'I said, well, yes; but I said, why should *you* be interested? And he said, I'd be surprised.' He paused.

'Really?'

'Never mind that, he said. Take an interest in anything, anybody. I'd be surprised.'

I began to be embarrassed, and a little sceptical. I turned the conversation to local opportunities for acting.

His rooms were above a wireless shop in East Street. He hung up my coat and put the kettle on before showing me the book. It was an early eighteenth-century Wycherley, without binding or title page. His bewilderment – in so far as it was genuine – could be accounted for only by the unfamiliar spelling and the long s's. I found what I could of interest and admiration to say about it. Fortunately, his historical sense was too vague to appreciate its distance from my own period, even when I had told him the date.

He brought our coffee, and with it two glasses of brandy, and asked if I liked John Galsworthy. He had seen a recent production of *Strife* in London. He showed me the programme, signed by one of the actors, and wondered if I had met him: he sometimes worked for the BBC. His other recent discovery was Flecker's *Hassan*: he longed for the local dramatic society to put it on (with himself as Rafi), though he knew, he said, that they would ruin it. He fetched the book and read one of the more florid speeches, with a mixture of vulgarity and sensitivity which was in some ways rather touching. Then he gave me the book, still open, and asked if I would show him how it should really be read.

Declining as civilly as I could, I felt nevertheless that I had snubbed him. His shelf had few other plays that I knew, but I took down an anthology of poetry and, looking through it – a very clean copy, a school prize, with signs of wear only in a small section of the late nineteenth century – I found some of Donne's dramatic monologues. They seemed a good antidote to Flecker's artificial sultriness. I began to read *The Damp*; the satirical astringency delighted me, and also, I thought, the young man. At 'First kill th'enormous giant, your Disdain', I looked up and he caught my eye and laughed. But I had forgotten – as one can with Donne – how the poem ends. I reached the last lines before I could find a convincing place to stop:

> '...do you but try
> Your passive valour, and you shall find then,
> Naked you have odds enough of any man.'

As I put the book down, the young man caught my eye again and smiled, and put his hand on my knee.

Must I remember? I did not move, and I did not prevent him. The brandy in my glass had been finished and twice replaced; I was tired, and not yet at the end of my excitement, and for the first time for many months I was pleased with myself. This new encounter seemed to offer some hope of rapport, some small passage out of the perpetual, circling self-containment of unhappiness and the flight from unhappiness.

He was young, and his enthusiasm, though self-conscious and ill-directed, had still something genuine in it; so, perhaps, did his admiration. These are all reasons, though not excuses. There was a kind of consolation, confused with distaste, in his proximity. As I sat still, he leaned nearer, letting his side rest against mine, and moved his hand along my leg. I did not withdraw, as he increased his embraces. His youth and commonplace good looks did not retain their slight, general attractiveness at close quarters, but in the end a tawdry and impersonal sexual excitement took its place for me. What he felt, I cannot say. We fondled each other, below the waist as well as above, and I took in the end as active a part as he did. There was hope of pleasure in it, but little actual pleasure, beyond a destructive and puerile kind of enjoyment in the breaking of bonds – not least, perhaps, of some of my bonds to Ben.

We came fairly near to consummating this abuse of feeling and misdirection of appetite. A little – very little – before that point, my disgust, both inward and outward, at the degraded and unmeaning simulation of intimacy grew strong enough to make me break away and pull my clothes together.

I could hardly answer his protests, still less his questions. In the wrong I had done us both, and let him do (and though he had been the instigator, I was by many years the elder), I had reached a position which could not be retrieved without further wrong of one kind or another. I made some random apology, and fled. As I drove home, I thought for part of the time about driving the car through the railings of the bridge and onto the railway far below, but I had not quite enough irresponsibility to do it, nor, I think, quite enough physical courage.

CHAPTER 61

Drunkenness was no longer enough. My guilt and self-loathing still kept before me, however much whisky I drank, what I had done with all the good that had remained to me. My love for Ben, however painful, however stiflingly unexpressed, however outwardly restricted through his fault and, of course, through my own, had still been love and nothing else. (I looked, now, straight through the pretence of the last eighteen months, that I could discard such love, could 'get over' it.) It had remained clear and whole and unalloyed, in accordance with his worth, beneath all that anger and self-deception could do to obscure it. Now it was cracked and crazed from within: its clarity (seen again only as it shattered) flawed across and across by my betrayal.

I could not think of Ben, now, without obtruding thoughts of the other young man. The highest joy remaining to me had been to forget, for a brief moment, the impossibility of my constant hope – to stay, now and then, for an instant, before the correspondingly steeper and sharper return to hopelessness, in the imagined possibility of love mutually accepted. Now the apex of that precarious joy could no longer be the physical expression of our love. Ben's form, before the senses of my mind, had sometimes been shadowy – faded, sometimes, disconcertingly, to an outline, a silhouette, the touch of hair or skin – but it had always been himself, unblurred, undistorted. Now my hand on his hand, his body, became my hand moving along my other companion's thigh. The tepid, self-seeking hunger of that kissing took over Ben's face and mouth and throat; the approach to the most secret places of our bodily love was slubbered with greed and guilt and knowing contempt.

I cannot write much more of this time. It went on longer than I can bear even to record.

Sometimes I told myself that what I had done was irrelevant to anything of importance: I had not reached the point where faith is unarguably broken, and, in any case, I had had no faith to break. Besides, there was much evidence in literature – recent literature especially – that such things have no greater significance than we assign to them. If every husband – every plighted lover – had come to such despair when he had kissed a pretty girl – or a pretty boy – behind a door, how many marriages, how many human lives, indeed, would have remained intact? But it was of no use. I knew that I had thrown a pearl away, richer than all his tribe, and that no more of any worth was left to me.

There was another, minor cause of wretchedness – a fear, fairly remote, and relatively trivial, but strong enough against my debility when, now and then, the floodtide of desolation seemed to recede. This was the fear of exposure, or even of blackmail. I thought that neither could add very much to my distress. The young man was of age: I was not sure how far, if at all, we had broken the law, and in any case I thought that prosecution was unlikely. As to loss of reputation, 'my own domestic criticism', as Keats once called it in a very different context, had given me pain without comparison beyond what public ignominy (such as it would be) could possibly inflict. The idea of blackmail was repulsive, particularly in the continuing association with the blackmailer, but the idea of having less money did not much alarm me; and the demands, if they became exorbitant, might give the signal and the last impulse for an end to my grief.

I knew how gravely I had underestimated the risks only when a brown envelope arrived in the post, addressed to me, incorrectly, and marked 'Rural District Council'. I put it down quickly, and looked at it, and thought that a scandal would not mean general ignominy only. It would be local news, which the Graysons would hear and, ultimately, Ben. Then he would learn of my proclivity, not from me, as one part of my affection for him, left out of count for his sake, but from gossip, or even from a newspaper report, as the whole motive of my friendship, cynically concealed in the interests of pursuit, coldly and squalidly indulged when his absence made it safe.

To give in to blackmail, if that was what the letter demanded, could only postpone the payment of this ultimate penalty. If I was to forestall this, it would be better not to open the letter: the temptation to retreat, to compromise, would diminish what courage I had. I did think seriously then of ending my life. My considerations of the means are better left unspecified. While they were going on, I cleared my desk, and addressed a packet of recent work to Douglas. I did not drink all morning. It did not seem necessary, now that I had so clear an objective.

In the afternoon I took the packet to the postbox, and then walked across the fields to the river. I spent a long time looking at the water. But the river was not the place. I would go home before it was dark.

Returning, I found a sudden, extraordinary width of time. Because I could end it when I chose, there seemed also to be no end to it, and nothing to fill it, that I did not choose. I took a book from the shelves and read poetry, at random and with keen, strenuous pleasure. After a time, I came on one of Hopkins' terrible sonnets. I began to read it as the expression of my own desolation; then, as I read, I saw further into despair than I had ever seen before. By the end I felt not kinship, but shame: that was what his suffering had been, and he had continued to live, and to work. Nothing I had felt could equal that.

A huge relaxation came over my limbs, in the wake of pity and horror: a lassitude which I had no means, and no reason, to resist. The last strand of my resolve, the sense of the stature of my own suffering, was gone. I sprawled over the desk, with my head in my arms, letting go of all decision, all effort, like a swimmer abandoning himself to drift or drown.

When I woke, it was after three in the morning and very cold. I went upstairs and fell asleep again in my clothes.

The next day was a kind of limbo. I seemed to move in a wide space, luminous and empty, without restrictions or obligations. The air was clear of craving and of hope and of self-respect. I could take my life or leave it: nothing could make any difference. I spent some time in the garden, in the morning, and in the afternoon, I opened the envelope.

It contained nothing but the notes for my lecture. The threat, withdrawing, shook me, as a subsidence of rock shakes a whole region, drawing the sea into its vacuum and tilting and cracking the land. I felt my old griefs rush in across the distance, that had seemed infinite, of the last thirty hours. I began again to struggle, to crave, to be afraid of drowning, to know that I would go down. I longed for a drink, but in the moments before I went to find the whisky, I looked again at the half-educated handwriting on the envelope, and wondered what the writer had felt. Had the aftermath of our meeting been for him at all what it had been for me? I thought it unlikely.

Nevertheless, I had shown him little kindness in my actions, and less in my thoughts; and he had deserved more credit than my suspicions had allowed him. It was not impossible that he had suffered something, if only temporary disappointment. I could, at least, acknowledge his courtesy in returning my notes, and I would do it before I started drinking.

I wrote briefly, thanking him for sending on the notes, and then apologising, in general terms, for giving rise to expectations which, in the end, I had felt bound to disappoint.

I ended:

'I think you will agree that it would be better if we did not meet again, but I wanted to send you my thanks, and my apologies, and to wish you well, especially in your interest in the theatre.
Yours sincerely,

Alan Pearce

p.s. The book I recommended is F. S. Roberts, Merely Players, Methuen, 1959'

As I signed my name, I realised that it could furnish further material for blackmail, but this no longer seemed a real danger.

Walking back from the post, I thought again of the encounter in the room in East Street, and then of Ben. I saw the streaks of sky, grey-black and blue, behind the bank's pale crest of grass and seed-heads, and I remembered lying side by side in the roof above

David's room, and talking together about despair. I had counselled early resolution to endure, and he had said, 'I don't think everyone could manage that, not alone, anyway,' and then, later, 'You'd have to go to a friend or someone.' I thought that I would ring Douglas when I got home.

Douglas was out, and I decided, with some relief, that I could write instead. I was not sure that I could steer my voice between a false insouciance, negating the purpose of the call, and shameful and incoherent breakdown.

I managed to finish the letter before starting to drink again, and I then drank more, more quickly, than I had ever drunk before.

It seemed to be about three days later, in the evening, that I heard a car door slam. I got the front door unlocked and went out onto the step. It was dark and wet, and I could feel the cold air, through my pullover, on the sweat in my shirt. I saw the lights of a car turning away into the road at the bottom of the hill, but there was no light showing in the lane. Then Douglas's voice, not far away, said 'Alan?' and I moved back against the door, swinging it further open, and throwing light, with my shadow, over the step.

Douglas's dark form came into the light from the darkness beyond.

'Alan: you're there.'

'I'm here, yes. Come in. You got my letter.'

'I got your work.'

In the light of the hall, he took my shoulders in his hands and looked at me. Then he steered me into the sitting-room. I felt an increasing dizziness, and sat down. Douglas looked round the room, then at me again, and said, 'What's the matter?'

I can remember only a little of what I said then. I offered him a drink, and he refused, and collected the various sticky glasses and bottles, half-full and empty, and took them out to the kitchen. When he came back I was more or less incoherent, and he sat by me for a long time, listening as if I were talking sense, and saying very little except in invitation to go on.

In the end he brought me a large glass of water. Then he made some coffee, and later on he found some food. When I had eaten what I could, he cleared out the hearth, asking my advice but declining my help, and laid the fire and lit it, and we tended it together until it burnt up well.

'How did you get away?' I asked, when he had sat down again. My voice seemed level enough, now, and my mind clear enough, for standard hospitable conversation.

'There was no difficulty. Term's well over. I left Sam with my nephew.'

'It's December?'

'Yes.'

'Good God! You came straightaway, then?'

'More or less. I got the early train. The work came yesterday in the second post.'

'Not the letter?'

'I didn't get a letter.'

'Then – ? You came – ?'

'I could see things weren't right. Ring me up, another time. And don't leave it so long.'

'Yes. I should have. I did try, a few days ago.'

'It looks to me as if you should have tried a good deal sooner than that.'

'Yes.'

He took my cup and gave me some more coffee. Then he said, 'So you're in love.'

'Is that what I said?'

'Well – what you gave me to understand.'

'All right.'

'Is it a man or a woman?'

I looked up.

'It's all right. I'm not asking his name. Or hers. I'm not asking anything, in fact, that you don't choose to tell me.'

After a long pause I said, 'It's a boy. A man.'

'And you're worried about the law?'

'Not primarily.'

'Well, it looks as if that won't be a concern for much longer, anyway. Unless he's under age?'

'No.'

'Then he won't have you? Or he – one of you – doesn't think it would be right?'

'Both. Neither. He doesn't know. But it was his great dread – that he might be homosexual. When he finally told me that, he'd been worrying about it for months.'

'He told you about it?'

'Yes. Just in time. Just before I told him.'

'Oh, Alan.'

'So in this case it would be wrong for me – and I suppose for him. I wouldn't say in all cases – or would you?'

'My dear Alan, for heaven's sake: where would the arts and sciences be? What about A – ? or B – ? or C – ?'

'And the sciences?'

'I'm not so sure about the sciences. Maybe – . Or maybe they're just not such gossips.'

We laughed a good deal, and I spilt coffee into my saucer.

'But then – ' Douglas went on, '– you must say when you want to stop talking about this – but then you're still friends, as far as he knows?'

'Not really.'

'Something happened?'

'It was a quarrel.'

'I see. I see. Well, well. You love him, and he's alive. It's enough to be going on with. If you'll only come to your friends for help, when you need it.'

'One should be able to manage.'

'Maybe. But if you can't, friends are better than whisky.'

'Yes.'

'You need some sleep, and so do I. What do you generally do about the fire?'

He stayed with me for some weeks, nursing me as I needed it, but never too much. He gave me sleeping pills that night, and each night until I could sleep without them, gradually reducing the dose. He told me he had carried them since he had had trouble with a painful knee; he kept them now locked in his suitcase.

After a day or two of utter idleness, with meals on trays by the fire and a great deal of music, Douglas started to clean the house, and I, perforce, to tidy it. When that was done, we tackled some long overdue household repairs. It was dull, steadying, companionable work; we did it without talking very much, and in the afternoons we cut back the brambles in the hedge or walked into Bramston for groceries.

I still had hours blasted and desolate with loss, especially late in the evening, but I slept better, and I tried to drink less. When I offered Douglas a drink, he refused. When I took one, he noticed and said nothing.

One morning at breakfast I looked up from a letter I had opened, and Douglas said, 'What's wrong?'

'It's just an invitation, for Christmas Day. From the Graysons.'

'You can make me an excuse if you'd rather not go.'

I put the letter down and said, 'You know – you've known – how did you know?'

'I'm sorry, Alan. I didn't mean to let on.'

'Oh, what does it matter? If I make it so obvious...'

'No, no. You don't. You're a model of reticence about that, as about everything else. But I do know you very well, and I've known you a long time.'

'How long have you known this?'

'For an absolute certainty, not till now, I suppose. But as a probability – well, for some time.'

'How long?'

'Longer than you have, I daresay.'

I felt violently angry. I got up and refilled the kettle and put it on, and then stood by the sink, looking out of the window.

After some time, Douglas said, 'Nothing of what you've felt, of course, or very little. Or said, or done. Only the bare identity. And that should be no such great surprise, should it? He's an endearing boy, after all.'

My irrelevant indignation melted. I sat down at the table and began to talk about Ben. Douglas listened, hardly interrupting, nodding now and then in endorsement of my praise, or understanding of my longing. He made more coffee, and at twelve o'clock we were still sitting at the table, and I was still not dressed. (Douglas usually had the breakfast ready by the time I woke up, and I had fallen into the disorderly habit of breakfasting in my dressing gown.)

I told him a good deal after that morning, and he listened with unfailing attentiveness and accurate sympathy. My only considered omission was the encounter with the young clerk. I held back from telling him anything of that – from shame, and also, I suppose, from a feeling that I should not try to absolve myself too lightly.

One day, in the week before Christmas, Douglas said he would show me how to make flapjacks: it was his solution to the problem of finding presents for the Graysons. We walked into Bramston in a high wind for the ingredients, and after tea we became rather childish and hilarious, measuring and mixing large quantities of butter and brown sugar and oatmeal. I dropped one of the pans, getting it out of the oven, and there was nothing to be done with the irregular remains but to eat them. While the rest were cooling, Douglas produced a bottle of Madeira he had bought surreptitiously while I was in the grocer's, and poured us each a glass. The relaxation of unspoken restraints was even more effective than the mild, unfamiliar glow of the drink.

We began to talk of the Cycle, and I told Douglas of its minor triumph, and mine, with the Bramston Dramatic and Literary Guild. Then I went on to tell him about my visit to the young man's room in East Street. He listened without comment, asking questions only as my account began to falter. There was silence when I had finished.

I said, inadequately, 'Now – I feel such a fool.'

Douglas said, after a pause, 'You feel more than that, though.'

I told him, as far as I could, what I had felt, and – in answer to his questions – what I had done about it. I did not tell him of my approach to suicide. I thought it might not surprise him, but it would be an unjustifiable addition to the large burdens of friendship already so uncomplainingly undertaken.

In another silence, I asked, 'Is it always indefensible, do you think? That sort of – carrying on? Or can it ever be excusable? Or justified even?'

He took time to reply.

'What the young would call a 'one-night stand'? I think it must depend on the people concerned, mustn't it? For some, it might be no more than rash and unprofitable. For you, I imagine, it was very wrong, and I imagine you knew that at the time.'

I could not say anything for a time, feeling as if I were winded.

'How can I undo it?' I said eventually.

'You can't undo it.'

'I know.'

'You can put things right with the young man, as far as possible,' he went on. 'You've seen to that already – '

'And then?'

'Well – what is there to do, beyond accepting that that's what you've done, and you wish you hadn't?' He looked at me. 'Alan, stop punishing yourself.'

I shook my head, in some hopeless, general refusal.

'It does no good,' he said, 'and it makes no sense. You're not the first person to fall badly short of your own standards; and if it's the first time for you – well, it probably won't be the last. You'll have to get used to the idea.'

'It's a rather defeatist point of view,' I said, without looking at him, 'especially for a son of the Kirk.'

'As a son of the Kirk – a son of the Manse, indeed – I know quite a bit about the ninety-and-nine just persons which need no repentance.'

'And the alternative – as of course you know – is to be on your own, in the wilderness, and lost.'

'But not for ever.'

'I think that depends on where you've gone.'

'And on how much you want to come back.' He put down his glass. 'If you go on like this, you'll destroy yourself. And that would be the real rejection, the real betrayal: then there really would be nothing left.'

'How much do you think is left now?'

'You still love Ben. That's still there; nothing you've done has destroyed that.'

'I sometimes wish it had.'

'Yes. It's a great deal to bear. I know that. But if you can stand it, it's worth preserving – for your own sake. And for its own, because it's good in itself. And for your work's sake. And for Ben's.'

'For his?'

'Of course. No matter what he does about it – or doesn't do – or doesn't know. It's a power of good, for him – directed towards him. If you destroy it, you'll deprive him very greatly.'

I was silent.

'And if you're going to preserve it, you'll have to preserve yourself.'

'How?'

'Forgive yourself.'

'You've said that nothing could be undone.'

'It's not the same thing. If you could undo it, you wouldn't need to forgive it. As it is, there's no alternative, except destruction. If you can't bear the idea that you've done such a thing, you'll have to try to blot it out as if it hadn't happened – cut it off by sheer willpower – cancel it out by what you do to yourself: in the end, destroy yourself. If you're going to let yourself have any sort of life, then you'll have to reckon to live with what you've done – including the things you disapprove of.'

' "I acknowledge my transgressions: and my sin is ever before me." ?'

'The Psalmist didn't know everything: I think the two are really alternatives. If it's not the one, it'll be the other: you'll never stop seeing it in front of you, and hating it, and punishing it. Until you acknowledge what you've done, you won't be able to forgive yourself. And until you forgive yourself, you won't be able to forgive anyone else. And when you can't take any more, you'll start in on the whisky.'

I said nothing.

'I'm sorry, Alan. I'm speaking out of turn.'

'Not altogether. Would you mind cutting up the rest of these? I need some fresh air.'

'No, of course. You'll be all right?'

'I'll be perfectly all right. Leave some of the clearing up for me.'

In the windy darkness, I put on my jacket and buttoned it to the neck, walking fast. I wondered how far Douglas was right. I had, after all, looked at my own behaviour that evening in Bramston as squarely as I could, and it was not only the shame, but the bitter sense of wanton destruction – past and to come – constantly and inescapably recurring with that contemplation, which had driven me beyond drinking to the possibility of ending my life. And I had, in any case, started drinking – had become a drunkard – well over a year before that disgrace.

I stopped where the road forked, wondering whether to go on, or turn and take the quicker way home by the side road. I stood quite still on the little grass plot where the roads met, leaning against the signpost in the darkness, and my mind seemed to empty itself so that I thought of nothing: I was conscious only of the wind starting up again, or perhaps still dying down, in a distant field, and the cold, and the December sky. Then I remembered driving home from Bramston late in the evening, and seeing the railway line, far below, through the railings of the bridge. And I remembered Ben walking slowly away towards the gate, with his head down. And I thought of Lear, as he began to realise at last what he had done to Cordelia – and cried out, 'Oh, most small fault.'

After some time, I moved, stumbling, with stiff legs, and took the side road home, swinging my arms and slapping my sides to bring the blood back into my hands.

Douglas had made some supper and kept mine hot for me; and though I felt his scrutiny when I came in, he asked me nothing, and talked only of practical, immediate matters.

The rest of the week was unusually festive, since Douglas insisted that he didn't want to miss any of our pagan rites, as he called them, while he was south of the Border. So we joined in the carols round the Christmas tree on Market Square, and watched an endearing and enthusiastic Nativity play at the primary school; and one afternoon we walked over to the wood to cut holly and ivy, and spent the evening decorating the cottage.

On Christmas Eve we went to the midnight service, walking in the dark to the little church over the fields. It was chiefly for Douglas's benefit, since the Kirk provided no such ceremony in

Edinburgh, but I found benefit myself, more, and more consolingly, than I had expected, after so long an absence and out of such a continuing lack of conviction.

I thought of Ben – at the carol service three years ago, and now thousands of miles away. With friends? On his own? When would he come back? Would he come back? What had he done to me? What had I done to him? I tried to fix my mind on him with a love which was without reference to myself.

Next morning at breakfast there was a gaudily wrapped parcel from Douglas by my place: a new anthology of parodies (and an excellent one, as I discovered later when we read some of it aloud, to our great diversion). Moving the bright paper, I saw that there was an air-mail envelope beneath it. I broke off my thanks, forgot the page I was turning, the book in my hand, to open the envelope gently, and the card in haste:

Meilleurs Voeux
Felices Fiestas
С Рождеством
Frohe Festage
~~Season's Greetings~~
[hand-written:]
Happy Christmas
and love,
Ben

I smiled and looked up.

'Sorry, I was saying – . It's from Ben.'

'Yes. I hoped you wouldn't mind. I kept it for you.'

I was too touched, for a moment, to reply. I looked back at the card. The front had an unusually good modern design of doves and stars, attributed overleaf (in five languages) to a Finnish painter. On the back was a further message in Ben's handwriting.

Hope your Christmas is good (partly with my family?). It's odd in N.Y. – properly snowy & busy & bright, but too many tatty Father Christmasses everywhere. and poinsettia (?) isn't the same

*as holly. I'm staying w. friends of friends and looking for a job:
legal ones aren't easy to find, but there may be a chance of some
teaching. Happy New Year. B.*

I read it again, and then, after a moment's hesitation, handed it to
Douglas. I had never before shown anything Ben had written me
to anyone. It seemed the best reply, and acknowledgement, I could
make; and besides, I wanted his opinion. I watched him read it
through and smile; then I asked, 'What does he mean, '*legal* ones
aren't easy to find'?'

'That he hasn't got a work permit, I should think.'

'You think that's all?'

'What else would it be? Come on, Alan: you don't really think
he's going to get mixed up in crime. At the very worst, he's doing
some unofficial washing-up in a café, and if he gets caught he'll
lose his visa. And have to come home.'

'Yes. All right.'

'It's a lovely card.' He gave it back, and I stood it on the table
beside me.

'Yes, of course. You must open my present.'

We walked over to the Graysons before dusk. I had realised from
time to time, and particularly as we approached the house, that it
would be an awkward meeting; but I thought James and Ruth went
out of their way to make us both welcome. And Douglas's presence
helped, both to account for the formality of the first minutes, and
then to provide a point of private understanding and reassurance
within the company. While we were all distributing presents (the
flapjacks were received, and tasted, with due enthusiasm) there was a
telephone call for Bridget. She went out to take it in the kitchen.

'Don't be ages,' Mark called after her.

'Ben rang last night,' said Ruth.

'That's your elder son? The one in America?' Douglas asked.

'So expensive for him,' said Ruth, smiling.

'How was he?'

'He was fine, Alan. He's found somewhere to stay – he's in
New York – and he thinks he may be able to get some work,
teaching: part-time, anyway.'

'That's good. It's very difficult, I believe, unless he's got a work permit.'

'Perhaps he'll come home,' said Mark.

'I don't think there's any chance of that. I mean of a permit,' said James. 'It's almost impossible for a foreigner.'

'Yes.'

Bridget came back into the room, looking flushed and pretty.

The last presents were unwrapped, and Mark turned out most of the lights, and started lighting the candles on the tree. James was talking to Douglas, and Ruth and Bridget were consulting an engagement book. I lit a spill at the fire; and went to help Mark.

'You having a good holiday?' I asked, unenterprisingly.

'OK,' he said. 'Fine, really. A bit too much work.' He laughed, also conventionally.

'This is – let me see – your last year at school?'

'Second last. A-levels in a year-and-a-half.'

'Oh, yes. I see.'

'I'm doing biology,' he went on, laboriously. And then, 'Ben's sent me a great book, about flying. Flight, I mean: how birds do it and everything. Amazing pictures. And you can make models – see how it really works. It only got here yesterday: just in time.'

I looked at him, and saw his face change.

'It's quite a time for Ben to be away,' I said.

'He's never been so long before. No-one has. I mean Cambridge isn't all that far really. And even Oxford. And that's only in the term, anyway. I wish we knew when he was coming back.'

'Yes.'

We both stopped a moment, the spills burning their little flames along towards our hands.

'New York's not so very far,' I said. 'He rang up the other night, didn't he?'

'Yes. Yes, he rang. But it's not the same. It's always been all of us. It's not really the same.'

'No. No, I can imagine that.'

Douglas had to get back for the start of term a little after the New Year. Before he left we planned the remaining, peripheral work on the students' edition of the Cycle, dividing it between us in detail; and then we spent some good evenings on the verse translation. (Douglas did not mention the attempts I had sent him before Christmas, and as I recalled some of the lines I had written then, I was grateful for that.) The book of parodies provided some entertaining examples of verse-forms, as Douglas admitted he had hoped it might.

I knew that he was not wholly easy about leaving me alone. Indeed, he suggested that I should return with him to Edinburgh for a working visit: it would, after all, make collaboration much simpler. But I felt that such complete and anxious avoidance of solitude would be an admission of a weakness I could not afford, or even of defeat. It would also improvidently use up my last reassuring possibility, my last reserve of support. I said that I would visit him at Easter, unless I found that my plans had changed, and agreed that we should write regularly. I also discussed with him the idea of getting someone to come in and clean the cottage once a week or so. I thought I could afford it, and there would be various benefits – besides a little extra time for work – of which we were both aware, and which neither of us mentioned.

The evening before he left, I put a pile of long-overdue library books in the hall, and found a letter between two of them. It was addressed to Douglas, just legibly, in my own handwriting. I took it to him in the sitting-room.

'I never posted this.'

After a moment, examining the envelope, he said, 'Shall I read it?'

'If you like.'

He opened it, and read it through, and held it out to me, interrogatively. I nodded towards the fire.

'It wouldn't have told you much, would it, even then?'

'It would have told me to come. You're sure?'

I nodded again, and he leaned forward and pushed the letter into the heart of the fire, where it glowed, then flamed and fell into flakes.

When I had taken him to the station next morning, I came home and wrote a long letter of thanks to await him in Edinburgh.

CHAPTER 62

Douglas had told me that he would come again, at a day's notice, at any time I needed him, adding with almost convincing firmness that he was sure it would not be necessary. My most immediate consideration now was how to ensure that he was right: that when I next asked for his advice or his company, it would be for work or in the beaten way of friendship. The decrease in my drinking while he was with me had reassured me that I had not yet become an alcoholic (a prospect which, before his arrival, had merely contributed to my despair, and thus to its own approach). But I realised with a good deal of apprehension the dangers of being alone again. Going into Bramston shortly after Christmas, I had put the remaining bottles of whisky into the car, and Douglas, at my briefest suggestion, had taken them back to the wine-merchants as the residue of an unspecified party.

Now I must decide how to spend my time: how to fill it, indeed, since it was evidently safest to leave as little as possible unaccounted for. Work on the students' edition would not be enough to fill the day for very long, and I was still doubtful about my ability to work without distraction on the verse translation; but I was not ready yet for any new work on a large scale. No subject had occurred to me yet in which I could feel that live germ of excitement, of conviction and discovery and argumentativeness, which alone could sustain the long labour of growth. Nor could I afford the fallow time, after the last scattered gleanings of the Cycle had been finally garnered, in which such an idea would be most likely to germinate.

I decided, therefore, to work on the Cycle in the morning only – a long morning, with a short break in the middle. (Knowing that I was to get up fairly early was one way of ensuring that I would get to bed in good time.) After tea I would work on the dictionary – first revising all my recent definitions, and then getting ahead as far and as comprehensively as I could with the next set: I should have to write for these to Peter Thorsen, who had sent nothing since I missed the two meetings in the summer.

When I had brought this up-to-date, I would use the early evening for reading. For the past year I had opened hardly any of the learned journals: there was a small stack of them, still in their wrappers, by my desk; and now Douglas had told me of several recent books on Middle English subjects – all necessary to read, and some worth reading. Then there were the gaps in my general reading, which could no longer be excused by the priority of work: several authors I wanted to know better – particularly some of the Russians (in translation) and some Spanish poets; and several more I knew I ought to know better – or, in many cases, to know at all: mainly modern American and European playwrights. I drew up a list, following each obligatory author with a re-reading of Shakespeare or a Middle English writer by way of reward, and copied the list out fair, like an undergraduate postponing his revision.

That would leave the afternoon for the household chores, shopping and gardening, and the evening after supper for writing letters and mending. If any free time remained, I would walk (in the daylight) or read what I chose, or listen to music (in the evening). I intended to be very tired by ten-thirty, and to go to bed then, even if it meant stopping in the middle of a movement or a chapter.

It was a great deal less easy than it sounds. Less even than I had expected, though my expectations had not been sanguine. The active work of editing made the mornings pass tolerably, and I did work hard each afternoon, first indoors, then out of doors, and felt well exercised by tea-time. After the last frosts, when the pruning was done and the weeds had not yet started, I had some long walks over the early spring fields. But my mind too often took advantage of its freedom, while my body was active, to set me again on the treadmill of my own thoughts. This, and the drowsiness of recent exercise, made the hours after tea the most difficult – a test of resolution that I often failed.

To stay awake, and to mark my serious intention, I would sit at my desk, rather than by the fire, and open the current volume of

Brecht or Genet. Half a dozen pages on, my eyes would begin to slide to the foot of the page; re-reading the slack, awkward, self-conscious dialogue, trying to concentrate on the characters, so crudely or so inadequately differentiated, I would find myself concentrating instead on my own effort of concentration, or on how many pages were left to the end of the scene. I would begin to think that I should be able to read properly if I could have one, just one, glass of whisky. I knew how much this thought was worth, but I know that if there had been any whisky in the house I'd have drunk it.

I would look up from the page for a moment to clear my mind and gather my will, and my thoughts would return to Ben: his existence and my longing; his remoteness and my guilt. I would shake my head and rub my arm to and fro on the edge of the desk; I would get up and walk about the room, or sit down, half-turned, in the armchair, with my face against its back, and weep. Or I would keep such distress at bay with fantasies: a letter in the post tomorrow, a car stopping in the lane, a conference in New York. Sometimes I would construct long dialogues, in which we somehow negated our final quarrel, or invent emergencies in which I rescued Ben with improbable heroism. Sometimes I simply imagined him coming through the door. But the picture was always false – false as well as imaginary – always a little awry. The image of Ben, conjured to appease my longing, was never quite true. Though I knew it, and longed for it, I could not properly recreate, in imagination, his direct and gentle unexpectedness, his lovely candour.

The only barrier, as I gradually discovered, to such a complete abandonment of intention – and of a whole evening's work – was to decide in good time to move on, after all, to another more familiar and beloved book on the list. For some time, I avoided the Sonnets – avoided even seeing my copy on the shelf. But one evening in March, after a day of sun and wind, I found the book in my hand as I made room to replace *Richard III*. I opened it and began to read, with the dangerous but irresistible desire to return to the intensity of past grief. But I found the grief lifted from me, no longer gripping and burdening, but standing separately, resting its weight unshakeably in the firmness and completeness of the lines. Everything I felt was there: betrayal and remorse, longing and despair; but so were expectancy, trust and delight, and so was forgiveness; and while I read, the different states were held in counterpoise, no one outweighing another. The dragging grip of grief would soon return, and not long after I had stopped reading. But to know that it had been so shifted, and that the poems were there, was a continuing source of consolation.

There was another consolation in the Sonnets, of which I became more gradually aware: the poet's splendid arrogance, his confidence in the worth of his own work:

So long as men can breathe, or eyes can see,
So long lives this and this gives life to thee.

It would be more than arrogance to claim any such glory of immortality. But there was nevertheless something in his assurance which called to a small, private, answering certainty in myself. My work might be ancillary, and the work it served must, in such company (though not in many others') be counted, unarguably, minor. But it was true poetry and true drama, and it would live – with my help – beyond my loss and longing. Whatever else must fail, and fall to decay, this need not:

And thou in this shalt find thy monument,
When tyrants' crests and tombs of brass are spent.

My monument, and (more consistently with Shakespeare's meaning) Ben's: his worth had long been, perhaps – and might now be, more consciously – the foundation of my work. Ever since the Fourth Passus of *Piers Plowman,* he had been present in my mind as the type of excellence, of what was most worthy of love. My work on the Cycle should be – was already – dedicated to him in spirit (though not, alas, in any sense in the letter. Even his initials below the title would have brought too grave a risk: I could hardly hope that Ben would be as lucky as Mr W.H. in evading nearly four centuries of scurrilous gossip and academic curiosity.). The Sonnets were more and more often the book I chose to read, when there was time, at the end of the day.

Even the Sonnets were not a panacea. There were weeks when I came very near to capitulation – when I was within a few hours of ringing Douglas for help. It was worse when I began to spin out work on the students' edition by alternating it with the verse translation. Sometimes even the modicum of invention required for translation deserted me. After two or three mornings writing nothing, or a few lines so inept that I could hardly bear to leave them visible under my deletion, I would surrender even before midday to fantasy; and, gathering momentum through the longer stretch of time, my desires would demand more and more violent stimulus, stronger and stronger, and ever more unobtainable, satisfaction; my imaginings would become more and more grossly distorted, less and less true to Ben's own truth and reticence. By the evening, I would be sickened by the accumulation of my own thoughts, and not less ashamed because I knew that such contamination of what had been most whole and clear had its source in my own behaviour: the betrayal of my own sense of the excellence of love, however much regretted, however suffered for, was still exacting its price.

One evening, when the damage seemed intolerable, an incurable corruption of everything that had been good, I drove to a pub five miles away on the Harchester Road, and brought back several bottles of whisky, and drank myself asleep. I did it quickly, knowing that if I stopped I should begin to find my obligation to ring Douglas unavoidable; and feeling by the second glass a resurgent craving which was a powerful motive in itself for continuing undissuaded.

I woke next morning feeling very ill, and very frightened indeed. I had broken every resolution I had made; and I knew of no others which would be any more durable to stand between me and the final destruction of my work and myself. I could write to Douglas now, or telephone, but I was unwilling to ask, in failure, for the help so generously and hopefully offered in resistance; and there seemed in my physical wretchedness and near-despair no reason, anyway, why that help should be any more permanently effective than it had been before. If I was not to depend more and more helplessly on Douglas – in the end, to lose my autonomy, and at his expense – I must find for myself a sure way to prevent this happening again: an unbreakable sanction, before anything else, against such drinking.

Weights drummed and shifted in my head; a prickly, creeping sweat of nausea ran over my body; my mouth was foul and dry; my throat burned. Looking at my watch, I made out with difficulty that it was a little after eight o'clock. I determined to drink nothing – neither alcohol, nor coffee, nor water, nor anything else – until after four o'clock that afternoon. By the time the eight hours had passed, though I had done no work at all – had barely, indeed, managed to dress and shave and make my bed – I felt that I needed no further resolve to avoid alcohol. The memory of that day – a physical memory, in eyes and throat and stomach, as much as a mental one – made it painful to think of tasting whisky, let alone to contemplate such an excess, and such an aftermath.

Standing at the kitchen tap in the afternoon, gulping glass after glass of water, I felt only the quenching of thirst and the achievement of my intention. Later, I thought that the physical discipline had not been all – had not been even the main thing. It was no more than a symbol, perhaps an indispensable one, of other things, which I owed mainly to other people: of a determination, which Douglas had retrieved for me, to preserve my mind and my work; and of their value, which – as Douglas had suggested – rested ultimately on my love for Ben.

After that day, I found things a little easier. I could not confine the vagaries of my imagination all at once, nor find any such drastic way to prevent them. I struggled for some time to keep my thoughts away from Ben altogether; but the mind is a great deal more elusive than the body: even to determine not to think of something is to be thinking of it already; to set and undergo a penalty for thought's deviation is to beat a moment's straying into a trodden path. Besides, he was the air I breathed, and a man is never more conscious of air than when he thinks he is indefinitely deprived of it.

So many skirmishes ended in defeat, and every small defeat made a discouraging breach, an easier opening for the next attack. In the end, I had to admit that such a position was untenable, at least without far greater strength of mind than mine; I had to retreat to a kind of strategic and limited leniency. I would let myself think about Ben at certain times of day, as long as I had kept my mind at other times on the work in hand, honestly and immediately dismissing the thought of him whenever it arose unbidden. This was just possible, on some days – and on more, as the days went by; the power to concentrate on other things slowly extended; and within the quarter- or even half-hour of grace, things rank and gross (whether natural or not) had less chance to choke the true, small shoots of memory and love.

So, slowly, with many lapses, with difficulty, and not without pain, the present pattern of my life was laid down. Some things were still beyond my control: migraines returned with a force I could neither avoid nor ignore, and cost me, at one point, as much as two or three days in a month. But after the fury of the first few hours was past, I would grant myself the convalescent's luxury of unrestricted thought. Lying for the rest of the day in the dark, not seriously tempted then, for some reason, to the grosser distortions of fantasy, I would write long letters to Ben in my head, sending him the trivia of an imaginary intimacy, telling him what I had been doing, and what I was thinking, and how much I missed him, and how greatly and for how long I had loved him. I was afraid, sometimes, that it was the sweetness of such days which suborned my body so soon into another migraine. But, as I seemed to recover no more quickly and to succumb again as soon if I directed my mind elsewhere, I let this indulgence, in the end, go unrevoked.

I never had to go too long without the ease of company, to slacken my pre-occupations and diffuse my focus. The Graysons knew, I thought, that there was, or had been, something wrong which solitude might aggravate, and they were generous with invitations to meals. My legitimate interest in Ben was so far acknowledged that I could gradually lose my self-consciousness, and my fear of what it might betray, about mentioning his name and asking his news. His life in New York was interesting so far, it seemed, if not very productive, financially or otherwise. I noticed that Ruth was quick to counter any mild concern of James's about where it was all likely to lead. She would produce some firmly general and reassuring term for what he was doing – 'branching out', 'looking round', 'trying his hand at all sorts of things'

– usually adding 'while he has the time'. Then she would move on to an episode in his most recent letter with a briskness which suggested that she was not without anxieties of her own. Occasionally she would fetch the letter itself from her writing-desk, after supper, to read the account to me in Ben's own words. Once she left it on the arm of my chair, where it lay for the rest of the evening against my arm.

He was living, it appeared, on his savings, and on what he could earn by teaching English to families attached to the United Nations. For this, it seemed, he did not need a work permit. I thought he would be a good teacher, and he wrote entertainingly of his various pupils and their families, with their diverse attitudes to him and to the language: the camaraderie of one family, and the ceremonious arrogance of another, who insisted that he should use the servants' lavatory, and wait in the kitchen with their bare-footed maid-of-all-work until his pupil was ready. 'The maid was shy and giggly, but made me a cup of coffee, and smiled and raised an eyebrow when the *senora* called me.' His Japanese pupils would never admit, by so much as a blink, that they could not understand; the Indian parents took their children through every lesson again, as soon as he had gone home; the French family were not convinced that it was necessary to learn the language at all. Left inadvertently one evening in charge of five very small, very wakeful children from Senegal, he had given up the attempt to keep them in bed, and let them dance to the radio: 'Anything more enchanting you never saw: none of them higher than the back of the sofa, each dancing independently, in complicated rhythms, with serious delight. The one who was too young to stand sat on the floor or on my knee and danced from the waist up. Luckily Dr and Mrs O. didn't seem particularly surprised – let alone cross – when they got back from the reception about midnight.'

He was sharing an 'apartment', which seemed to consist of about a room and a half, with two students from the City College of New York. It was not clear, from the parts of his news that I heard, whether they were young men or young women, or even one of each. (Their undistinguishing American forenames – Wynne and Bernie, I think – gave nothing away.) I tried to frame idly conversational questions which would lead to an informative pronoun, but without success. Something Bridget said later in the year, however, about their having 'made it up' made me think that there was some kind of love-affair between them; a relief in the short term, at least, though not, perhaps, without awkwardness for Ben.

I guessed that any disappointments or anxieties he had would be given little weight in his letters home; but much of his cheerfulness and eager amusement seemed genuine. Sometimes this happiness would communicate itself to me, beyond the expected happiness of any such contact. Sometimes it would start a pang of loneliness and regret which would cut more sharply as I left the lighted house and went home, and become almost intolerable before I could get to sleep.

It was Ruth, I thought, who came closest to divining the form my trouble had taken, or perhaps who had simply taken the most interest in it. She was the quickest and the least curious in accepting my vaguely medical excuses for drinking no wine, and it was she, next time, who asked me to draw the curtains in the dining-room, and then rapidly gave the wine glasses to Mark to take back to the kitchen.

Ruth also offered me her freezer, for a very small sum, when she bought a larger one; and she took a good deal of trouble to find someone to clean the cottage for me. She warned me that unless I was much more strong-minded and less sociable than herself, I would spend at least half the time saved on house-work in talking over tea at the kitchen table. However, she pursued the matter with an energy which suggested some of Douglas's extra, unspoken reasons for approval, and by April we had arranged that Mrs. Weaver should come in for half a day every week. It is her singing as much as our conversation (more than our conversation, at the beginning) which curtails my work on Wednesdays, but the regular presence of another human being in the cottage – an incongruous presence, in some ways, but an interesting, kindly, and courageous one – has become surprisingly important to me: almost as important, perhaps, as the saving of time and thought on the minutiae of housekeeping, and certainly much more so than the mild, though increasing, pleasure of the bloom and neatness of the rooms: the stacked, sheer edges of the piles of periodicals, and of the towels in the linen-cupboard; the clear flat surfaces, pleasantly catching the light; and the reform of matters I had assumed to be irremediable – the state of the curtains and the inside of the oven.

Both as a reinforcement, and as a reward, of my renewed determination, I had rung Douglas on the second evening after my final bout of drinking. He sounded unsurprised to hear me, and I made no reference to my recent crisis of resolve; a crux in the translation gave me a fairly plausible reason for telephoning. But about a week later he rang me, with a question which could still more obviously have been dealt with by letter; and when he had rung again the following week, I began to feel an obligation to share the cost by forestalling him next time. So we gradually established our habit of discussing work, regularly, and sometimes other things, on the telephone – a habit continued for many reasons, professional and sociable, but originating, I think, in Douglas's quick ear and undeceivable sympathy. There are still plenty of problems, of course, whenever we are collaborating, which are better discussed by post.

It was not many weeks after his first call that I paid Douglas my promised visit at Easter. I was afraid that it would be necessary, when we were face to face, to tell him of my near-defeat – (at the very least, I should have to explain my avoidance of alcohol); and I spent much of the journey north considering, with increasing anxiety, how I could do this without implying that I had rejected his standing offer of help. But before I had found the words, or the opportunity – while we were still drinking coffee after our first meal together – he asked, 'So you managed all right?'

'Yes. Well, in the end.'

'Mhm.' He nodded. 'I thought so. I thought you'd manage, in the end. Though I didn't suppose it would be entirely straightforward.'

'No. I'd have rung you if I had to. I came near to it.'

'I can imagine.'

'Knowing you were there – that I could ring you if necessary – that was what made it possible, I think. Although I didn't.'

'Of course. That was just as I hoped. Just what I had in mind, indeed: to become unnecessary.'

'Not in any other sense,' I said, and we laughed, with a feeling of equilibrium restored.

It was a good holiday. We worked together in the mornings, and walked in the afternoons, exploring the little ancient wynds and lands of the city, or driving out to walk with Sam by the Firth, or on the Pentland Hills, in the first, gleaming, chilly spring days. I extended my visit a week or two into the University term, to our common satisfaction, and I thought that Douglas's regret, when I left, was free from the undeclared anxiety of our last parting.

CHAPTER 63

The cottage seemed unexpectedly welcoming at my return. The Aga was alight, and Mrs Weaver had left milk in the fridge, and a jar of narcissi and a shepherd's pie on the kitchen table. I began to feel again the old delight in solitude, and a little of the old eagerness for the next piece of work. I did not yet know what this would be, but next day, when I had put in order the papers I had brought from Scotland, I began after tea to plan a serious re-reading of the Middle English Romances, and their French counterparts.

The evening's reading, in the following weeks, started to gather speed and purpose. Distractions fell away, at least some of the time, or were drawn into the train of my thought, lending it their extraneous energy. I began to see much further than I had seen before into the strange, anomalous doctrines of courtly love. Its excesses and absurdities, I started to realise, were more than a convention carried to preposterous lengths, more than the self-regarding posturings of lover and lady, or the perverse indulgence of thwarted emotion. They were only the extreme instances of something much more serious: a representation, a re-affirmation, of an essential part of the reality of love. Not, thank God, the only part (though the Romance writers, I must admit, sometimes write as if it were). Love can, and does, do many other things, most of them happier. But the suffering of the courtly lover is, surely, what all love must be ready for, if it may properly be called love: true love must be prepared – though it may not be required – to feel, for the beloved, the pain of loving without requital, and without outward acknowledgement of the suffering, or even – more than a little – of the love. I was surprised and excited to find how much of the literature of the *amour courtois* was illuminated for me by this idea. The focus of my plans began to narrow promisingly.

There were still certain practical difficulties to deal with – the ragged ends of past failure. Starting some notes on my reading one Saturday evening, I discovered that I had almost used up my last block of paper. The shops would be shut before I could get to Harchester, and there was nowhere to buy it in Bramston except the stationer's, which I had avoided since the autumn. After two days of using scrap paper, and wasting time and concentration by confusing my notes with old rough copies of other work, and mislaying the small pages under the large ones, I drove to Bramston. I looked through the window of the stationer's shop before I opened the door, and saw Harold Byford, alone, rearranging cards on a shelf. I stood still for a moment, then went back to the car and drove to Harchester, and bought enough paper to last for several months, trying to mitigate my sense of cowardice, and even of treachery, with considerations of prudence.

In the early summer I took the rare opportunity of seeing a film by Vittorio di Sica, at the Bramston cinema. It was shown after the main, American film, and coming out afterwards, with the small audience, into the mild night, I heard someone behind me say, 'Enjoy the film, sir?' It was Harold Byford. As I turned, he went over the kerb, to unlock the chain round the wheel of his bicycle.

'Yes, thank you,' I said, walking on. Then I turned back. 'Very much. I hope you did?'

'Very much indeed, sir. Beautiful, I thought, the photography.'

'It was, wasn't it?'

He freed the chain, and began to tug at his pocket.

'It's often the black-and-white films, oddly enough, that have the best photography,' I said. 'Or so I find.'

'Do you, sir? Do you find that? You find they're more artistic?'

'Well. In a sense. I suppose the photographer has to take more trouble – take more interest in the patterns he can make.'

'Whereas with the technicolour, I suppose, it's just anything goes. You saw the main feature? Before this one?'

'Just the end of it.'

'Dreadful.' He began to fix a lamp to the handlebars. 'And call that acting!'

'I thought the Italian actors were very good,' I said.

'Marvellous. The old man. Sad, though, wasn't it?'

'Very sad.'

'I thought it was a mistake he didn't go back, in the end. I don't know why he didn't.'

'No. Just, I suppose – everyone makes mistakes.'

'It's true. Everyone makes mistakes – their own mistakes; and it's not for anyone else to tell them different. Got the car, sir, have you?'

'Just down the road.'

We started together in that direction; he wheeled his bicycle beside me.

'There it is, though, isn't it?' he went on after a moment. 'If we all make mistakes, we all have to make allowances.'

I smiled, and he smiled in return.

'If they'd only made more allowances for the old man,' I said. 'But then it wouldn't have been such a good film, I suppose.'

'That's true, sir. Isn't it this one? Your car?'

We stopped, and I felt for my key.

'Goodnight, sir,' he said, as I got in.

'Goodnight. Very nice to see you.'

I found some needs, real and imaginary, to supply from his shop on the following Thursday, and he greeted me with the same unintrusive friendliness and dignity which have made it possible, and indeed enjoyable, to deal with him ever since.

We finished the students' edition in July, while Douglas was staying with me. We were pleased with ourselves on the whole: it was a compromise, but an honest one, between real scholarship and the needs of the unlearned. Almost all the critical apparatus had had to be omitted, of course, and every slightly idiomatic phrase given a modern equivalent in the glossary; but the spurious air of certainty which this gave to the whole was qualified by an introduction referring the reader very emphatically to the main edition.

'Only students never read the introduction,' I said.

'Of course they do,' said Douglas. 'How else do you think they write their essays?'

The text itself, being the one established for the main edition, was as good as we could make it.

The verse translation was well under way, too, and on the whole it was going successfully. There was a good deal still to be done, but we felt disinclined to take up Brian Robson's offer of finding a university poet to complete it for us. There were none, in any case, who could really be trusted to respect the subtlety and precision of the original, even where they were aware of them. We decided, since the Press was not in a hurry, that we should work on it only as inclination or inspiration suggested, and feel at liberty to take up other projects.

Then Douglas insisted that we should have a holiday, and we spent three weeks, walking, near Derwentwater. Good weather and company, and strenuous exercise on hills which seemed to have grown steeper, made it a better holiday than my last, solitary one on the Suffolk coast, three years before. But the choice of place was a mistake: there were too many views and smells and sounds which sharpened memory beyond nostalgia to a pain so acute that it cut my breath. I knew that Douglas had taken the holiday more for my sake than for his own, or even for Sam's, but it was difficult, even by the last week, to produce more than occasionally the greater ease and high spirits I felt him looking for.

I returned to the cottage, nevertheless, sounder in wind, and better able to sleep, than I had been for some time, and settled with a good will to serious consideration of my next major piece of work.

I spent some time organising my recent notes on the Romances, and began to draft the first chapter of a book on Courtly Love. But I found that it was not really possible. To do more than a routine survey of the ground (a record of history and influence, a discussion of other critics' views, a reply to Lewis's *Allegory of Love*), to expound the discovery which had made me want to write the book, would be to expose a part, and far too great a part, of what was most private to me. I did not altogether recognise this at the time: I only knew that for that aspect of my subject there seemed to be no words which were not either embarrassing or inadequate.

In the end, I put the notes away and began to look again at the various attitudes to love in Chaucer – particularly in the Marriage Group of the *Canterbury Tales*, which, of course, transcend the restrictions of any single tradition. There was plenty of material, and I had as much time as I liked to work on it. It had become an unfamiliar pleasure to be working hard and regularly, without a deadline or more than an occasional distraction.

Listening to the wireless one evening in October, while I was mending the edge of the carpet, I heard a programme of Renaissance music in which David Williams was one of the singers. His voice seemed to me to have developed impressively since I last heard him sing, and his two or three solo pieces were both accomplished and movingly direct. I sent him a postcard of congratulation, and in his reply he asked if he might pay me a visit.

I felt a surprising and increasing trepidation as the agreed weekend approached. No-one but Douglas had stayed with me in the cottage for nearly three years, and though my recent dread at the prospect of any more public view had slackened enough for me to accept Mrs Weaver, it had not yet apparently lost all its power. And it was a year and a half since Ben, or any of his family, had come beyond the end of the lane: I feared the renewal of that contact, at only one remove, with the private region of my life.

David made it easier than I had expected. He had grown up considerably since he had left Cambridge, losing much of his eager diffidence, and gaining a kind of solidity of purpose and confidence. He spent some hours each day in singing practice, having first asked my permission. (I said it would not disturb me, and managed to finish most of Saturday's work early on Sunday morning.) We picked walnuts, and walked, and drove into Harchester for a brave attempt by the repertory company at *The Playboy of the Western World*. He told me about the course at his college of music, where he was starting his third year. It was going well, and in the summer term he had won a major prize, which had finally persuaded his father of his talent and his determination.

'So he's paying my fees for this year, which is great.'

'How did you manage before?'

'Partly a scholarship, partly working.'

'In the vacation?'

'And in the term: evenings when I had classes; mornings when I had rehearsals.'

'That sounds pretty exhausting.'

'Sometimes. And boring, even more. No time for anything else – except practice.'

'It's come at the right moment, then, your father's help: you must need the extra time for your finals.'

'Well – finals among other things,' he said, smiling, and then, 'I still have to pay for my lessons with Enzo Schwäbelssohn. But that's not such a problem. I can do that out of the scholarship.'

'He teaches at the college?'

'No, he's private. But he's incredible. I couldn't give him up. I was afraid my father was going to make that a condition, actually.'

'And you'd have had to accept it?'

He shook his head. 'I'd have turned down the whole thing.'

'Yes. I see. It's not singing, in general, then, that your father disapproves of? Or a singing career?'

'No. Well, it is. But he's come round a bit on that. But Enzo – it's more – it's a personal thing, really.'

'I see.'

'Such – such rubbish. He's an utterly *professional* person. He'd – . It's singing he cares about. That's what matters to him, first, last and in between.'

'And to you?'

'And to me. First and last. Though I suppose – well – there are other things. One or two – in between!' He was laughing.

He asked me about my work, about how I spent my days, and his tone changed as we talked, losing a faint strain of friendly impudence – a challenge to gravity, about his own affairs – and taking on a warmth of concern about mine that seemed genuine as well as polite.

He did not mention Ben until after lunch on Sunday. My longing for any news he might have had, for any link he could make, even for the chance to hear Ben's name and to use it, had been kept silent by the fear of what my voice might reveal. I did not think David was imperceptive.

But as I poured the coffee out, he asked, 'You heard anything from Ben?'

'Not recently. I had a card at Christmas.'

He nodded.

I asked, 'Have you?'

'Once or twice. It's my turn, actually. I'm a bad correspondent.'

He paused again, and I said, 'How was he?'

'Oh, fine. I think he likes New York.'

'Yes.'

'And he had a marvellous summer, taking someone's car over to California.'

'Splendid.'

'He came back by New Mexico: he said it was terrific. The letter was mostly about that.'

'Very interesting.' And if it was about anything else, I thought, it was not something that David was prepared to tell me.

He looked up, stirring his coffee; then he said, 'I'm hoping to see him after Christmas.'

'He's coming over?'

'No, I'm going out there. We've got a tour – the chamber choir, the one you heard.'

'You should be a great success. Where will you be singing?'

'Boston, I think – or Cambridge, Mass. – and Washington. I'm not sure about the rest; it hasn't all been settled. But probably New York, anyway.'

'I see.'

'So I'll probably see Ben.'

'Yes.'

'Unless he's off to Mexico with his friends, or something.'

'He has – he's been there some time, hasn't he? – he has made friends?'

'Oh, I think so. Anyway, I shall go and sleep on his floor, and he can take me up the Empire State Building. I *must* write to him, actually. May I put your cup down, or would you like some more coffee?'

I was to take him to the train after breakfast on Monday. On Sunday evening we listened to a recital he wanted to hear. At the end, he got up and switched the wireless off as the applause began; then he said, 'Sorry. Do you mind?'

'No, of course.'

He came back to his chair, and sat down, looking at the fire.

'Oh, my God, I wish I could sing like that.'

'Do you think you might, one day?'

'I don't know. Sometimes. And then sometimes I wonder what the hell I'm doing, messing about, when I know I'll never be good.'

'I should have said you were good already.'

'I mean really good.'

We were both silent.

'What does your teacher think – Schwäbelssohn?'

'He doesn't say much. I think he thinks I'm *some* good. Well, he wouldn't take me otherwise. And he did once say I could be a real singer.'

'That would mean a good deal, I imagine, from him?'

'Yes. But only that I *could*. 'You could be a singer, David, a *real* singer, but only provided that you would concentrate.' He's Austrian, mainly.'

'Don't you concentrate?'

'I do when I'm singing. I can't do anything else. But I think he means more – in the rest of my life: be *dedicated*; go to bed early; don't go to parties; don't – don't fall in love.'

'And that's a degree of dedication you're not prepared for?'

'Well. I suppose I am in a way. In principle. But can anybody be like that *all* the time? *Never* let up? Could you?'

'How can anyone answer that for someone else?'

He said nothing, holding out his hand to the fire. Then he said, 'But other things do matter, don't they?'

'Yes. Of course they do.'

He took up the tongs, as the fire settled, and moved the logs together.

'There's this boy,' he said, 'in the first year. I think I've fallen in love with him.'

401

'I see.'

I let him tell me about it, listening with a sharp, recurrent pain of recognition, trying to convey by my silence and occasional questions that I was not shocked (which, indeed, he did not seem to expect), and that he could tell me anything he liked; trying to show enough of my sympathy, without showing too much.

'It's the first time you've felt like this?' I asked, when he seemed to have come to an end.

'Yes,' he said, and then, 'No. It's always been – I mean, it's never been a girl. But this is the first time – till now it's always been someone older.'

I nodded.

'I suppose really I was looking for a father-figure or something.' He laughed, for the first time a little artificially.

'Perhaps you were.'

I did give him a little advice, in the end: not to assume that his affections would always be homosexual; not to put himself on the wrong side of the law.

'An adult love affair is no longer illegal, thank God. But it's still forbidden for anyone under twenty-one. And I suspect that's going to be rigorously enforced. How old is he?'

'Eighteen. Nearly nineteen.'

'Do be careful, won't you?'

'Oh – that's the least of it.'

'I daresay. But it wouldn't do your career any good.'

'I know. Of course. But that's the whole thing: do you think it could hurt it in other ways – in important ways?'

'Going to prison would not be unimportant. But you mean, in some more internal way? Could this be damaging your actual singing?'

He nodded.

'If it stops you working, doesn't leave you enough time to practise, then I suppose it might.'

'If only he didn't live in Finchley. I seem to spend most of my time on the Northern Line.'

'Well, you'll have to work that out for yourself. But otherwise, as long as you're doing enough work – and getting enough sleep – then I don't see how this could hurt your singing. On the contrary, I should imagine it would be doing it good.'

'Really?'

'I think so, in the end. I think it's probably one of the conditions of achievement – real achievement.'

'A love affair?'

'To have felt with that intensity; to have loved. Not necessarily to have been loved.'

'That's all right, then,' he said; and then, without irony, 'It's certainly intense.'

'I know.' We were silent. I looked into the fire and felt him looking at me.

'There is something else,' I said, eventually. 'I know this will sound unsympathetic, and I know it's not easy, but do think of him, too.'

'When do you suppose I think of anything else?'

'I mean, of his side of it: how far it's fair to involve him, while he's still so young. I don't pretend to know the answer – for you, let alone for him. But don't forget that he still has a lot of his life to live – more of it, even, than you have.'

He started to say something in reply, then stopped and took a breath. After a moment he said, 'Yes. You're right. But I do think of him, Alan. He's so – ' He broke off and laughed. 'Don't start me off again. It's after midnight and you're tired. And I've got packing to do.'

We said goodnight. I was tired, but I did not sleep well. Parallels and ironies, impossibilities and possibilities made wakeful patterns through my thoughts and my shallow dreams.

David thanked me for the weekend as we stood by the car outside the station.

'Don't wait. I know you've got lots to do. And I kept you up too late last night.'

'That was all right.'

'It was great, being able to talk; it's always been... I wish I could tell you. But I'm sorry I went on so, about my own affairs – my problems. I do know, really, they aren't the only ones in the world.'

'No. But they feel like it, don't they, at the time? Always.'

'You must come up to London,' he said. 'Come to a concert. Would you do that?'

'I'd like to very much. It's ten past. I think you should go.'

He put down his bag to shake hands. 'I'll let you know. And I'll tell Ben when I write – '

'If you're writing – '

'Tell him I've seen you.'

'If you would.'

'Give him your love.'

CHAPTER 64

It is almost November. I have spent the whole summer in writing, and a good deal of the autumn, and there really is very little more to say now. Ben had been in the United States for a year-and-a-half, when David came to spend the weekend here. Since then, two more years have passed without any significant change in the pattern of my life, with very few events worth recording that are even tenuously connected with Ben. I have got a good deal of work done, as one can by keeping regular hours. My re-reading of Chaucer soon began to suggest interesting parallels with some of his contemporaries, and, eventually, a view of the mediaeval way of telling a story which differs radically, in some respects, from received opinion. I wrote *Mediaeval Narrative Technique* – with a certain amount of missionary zeal, as Douglas called it – in not much more than a year. It is really only an outline of my position: a brief challenge to the view (too widely accepted) of Middle English narrative as a haphazard cobbling together of existing themes. One day, perhaps, Douglas and I may combine on a book more nearly commensurate with the subject. It would be good to be working together again on that scale. But *French and Italian Influences before Chaucer* must be finished first.

It cannot be long now before I can start on the final revision of *Narrative Technique*. Brian Robson is out of hospital, and staying with friends in Maine; he seems to be recovering well, and still hopes to be home before Christmas.

Even if he has raised an unusual number of problems, it is unlikely to take me more than three or four weeks to deal with them. A few may have to be discussed on the telephone, or even by a visit to the Press. But it can hardly be far into the New Year before it is all in final form, before I can settle again, every day, to a full morning's writing in the still, sunny room.

I see David from time to time. Some weeks after his visit, he sent me a ticket for a concert at his college. I gave him supper afterwards, and met the boy he had spoken of, who seemed to me to be beginning to reciprocate his feelings. A year or so later, when David had finished his course, and was starting to get a few professional engagements, they took a flat together. I sometimes have lunch with David when I am in London, or meet them both for a concert at the Festival Hall, (always finding a reason, however, to decline their offer of a room for the night).

Ben has sent a card each Christmas, with a little news, mainly duplicating what I have heard from his parents. At the moment, I imagine, he is still teaching English, either 'to well-heeled diplomats' children', as he put it, or 'to very badly-heeled immigrants' children, for a change'. Such communications, once so longingly anticipated, so closely treasured, have come to mean less, as it becomes more and more unavoidably evident how little they imply, and how much less they promise.

I still keep them, however – and a picture postcard of Manhattan at night, which he and David sent me together – in the drawer with his other letters, and the photographs from Greece, and the rough drafts of letters I wrote to him. I used to keep these locked up, but I need the drawer that locks, now, for these notebooks; and the drawer below, with a top layer of miscellaneous letters and receipts, seems after all security enough for our correspondence. I suppose Mrs Weaver's undistinguishing attitude to 'papers' gives me a sense of privacy.

Last summer Douglas and I read papers at a colloquium on Mediaeval Drama, at Lund, and took a fortnight afterwards driving among the Norwegian fjords. I enjoyed it very much at the time. Soon after our return, I discovered, when I met James in the bank, that Ben had been home for nearly a month to visit them, leaving five days before we got back. For some hours I was knocked off balance. I did not know what to do with myself, and I could neither work nor rest. I rang Douglas in the evening, however, and after talking for an extravagant length of time, I was able to withstand his immediate offer of company (either here or in Edinburgh), and to go to bed and even, towards morning, to sleep. (I was still keeping no alcohol in the house unless I had visitors.) By the middle of the next morning I was able to work again, and within a week to work well.

This negative event – this occurrence of nothing happening – marked, perhaps appropriately, the last possibility of any real contact with Ben; and I feel some confidence now in my ability to cope with similar reversals in the future. Some I suppose there must be, but they will surely become less frequent. I still have not freed my thoughts from the unremitting pull, the constant undertow in one direction, towards one point. But I can hardly believe that the force will not slacken, in the next few years – at least while there is work of a kind and in a quantity to maintain an adequate counter-current.

Already there are moments when I think that my susceptibility to this power is partly self-induced: that I need a destination for my longing, a subject for hope; and that if love for Ben did not supply me with these – and with an ever-available reward of day-to-day intentions undefeated, a constant, secret possibility of delight – I should have manufactured some other feeling in its place. Obsession has a way of making itself indispensable, long after its motive force is depleted, or dried up. But it is not so often, now, that I find myself measuring all the trivial actions of an evening – the letter being written to a colleague, the record I have put on, the very fastening off of a thread – against his imagined reaction. Still more rarely do I set up experiments and auguries to predict – in defiance of all reason – the prospect of my hopes or the state of Ben's affections. It must be several months since I counted the alternations of the traffic-light at the crossing with the coast-road outside Harchester.

It is here, then, that this account must end. It has taken longer, and been more difficult – more dangerous, even – than I had foreseen. When I began it, I did not know how serious a labour I was undertaking, or how nearly, sometimes, it would threaten my self-possession. Recalling my grief and my guilt, recounting the slow stages of unfolding hope and the process by which it was laid waste, delineating the emptiness by which I am still surrounded, I have come near, several times, to renewed despair.

There have been mornings when I thought I did not dare to go on, and evenings when the prospect of the next day's work seemed impossible. But to leave it unfinished was impossible too. Work on this account was, after all, work, and, properly done, could still define the day's purpose, and hold back the shallow, spreading tides of misery.

And recollection was not always unhappy. I could remember serenity, now and then, and some times of unbroken intimacy and confidence, and a few, clear moments of joy, with an immediacy which overcame the sharpness of present loss. Even grief, remembered across a long enough space of time, known and completed, holding no new points of anguish in reserve, can become an accepted form in the pattern of what has taken place, a point of rest, perhaps almost of consolation.

Above all, no pain I felt was at variance with my subject, to distract from work or stifle inspiration. Writing this account might intensify the sense of my loss, but that sense, though it might make me reluctant to go on, could never undermine the work of writing, to leave me without my last defence.

> How can my Muse want subject to invent
> While thou dost breathe...?

I have written without delay, though not without remorse, straight on, 'obedient to the stream', to reach this haven of present calm. And I can keep within that haven, I think, for the few weeks remaining, before I embark on the next main enterprise. Several smaller undertakings, accumulated in recent months, will give me employment and direction and ballast enough: the Press has sent me two long books for review (both on Middle English dramatic verse: one good, I think, and one very bad); Peter Thorsen has just asked me to draft a set of principles for grammatical consistency in the Dictionary (which should, of course, have been done long ago); and in the evenings, recently, and walking in the afternoons, I have begun to turn over ideas for the verse translation again, and even to grapple successfully with some crucial lines.

All this should bring me within a week or two of Christmas, when I can take some evenings – perhaps even some mornings – in preparations: some more cooking, some shopping. (I cannot imagine what to get for Mrs Weaver. Last year she gave me a card and some strongly scented and very expensive lotion to use after shaving. I had to pour a little away each week, to diminish it at a convincing rate, and even, on Wednesdays, to use some on my face.) I shall have to get in some wine – some sherry, too – if I am to ask George and Barbara Frewin over from Harchester while Douglas is here. The cottage is still fairly tidy, but I could take a little time – and some pleasure, too – in making it festive. There are the candlesticks from the back of the cupboard to be polished. (I believe Harold Byford sells coloured candles). I might have a fine afternoon getting bay and holly from the wood, and I should clear some space for Christmas cards. I must write some, too.

Tomorrow is Sunday. I think I can take one day of complete idleness to celebrate the finishing of this account. I shall sleep late, and spend the morning with the Sunday papers, or something equally undemanding, while the chicken is cooking. In the afternoon, if it is still fine, I shall have a really long walk – to the river, perhaps, and some miles along the bank, and home the long way. I should ring David after supper: if I am to be in London on Tuesday to have a look at these new manuscripts, we might meet for a concert in the evening. Or shall I suggest the new *Twelfth Night* at the Old Vic? Would we get tickets at such short notice?

Why am I putting down these petty ruminations? What have they to do with the subject of this account? Very little, really; or nothing at all.

I suppose, after so many months, it is simply difficult to stop: to leave the work I have been constructing for so long, so carefully – with such pains, such moments of recovered joy, and, ultimately, with some solid satisfaction. To acknowledge it completed, to turn away and leave it standing behind me, to rely on its mere existence, at my back, for that defence which its creation has provided against the terrors of vacancy, to shut the notebook and turn to other work – it is harder than I expected.

And what other work is there in which I can celebrate my love, and the object of my love? None, of course, in which I can do it so clearly or so directly. But there is plenty of other work that is worth doing, and that may perhaps build, ultimately, on the same foundation. And if it is to be done, I must end this account here, now that it is not adequate, but complete: as near as I can make it to the worth of its subject, written with the full rigour of my faculties, as truthfully, as exactly as if I could show it to Ben, now that it is finished.

3rd November, 1969

11th May, 1970

I have opened this notebook again to add a last, small incident, connected only remotely with my subject, but giving me, partly through that connection, extraordinary delight.

About four months ago, soon after the end of Douglas's Christmas visit, I was trying one evening to trace a reference, which Brian Robson had questioned, in *Mediaeval Narrative Technique*. Brian's list of queries, which arrived with the typescript a few days before Christmas, had been short and uncomplicated, and I had dealt with most of it in a couple of days. If I could find this reference, and make one or two more minor emendations, I should be able to finish the whole thing before supper, and get it to the Press before the end of the week.

An interruption was, therefore, rather more than usually unwelcome. After nearly five years, the hopes which stirred and tightened at every unidentified approach – the post, the telephone, the car in the lane – had dwindled almost to atrophy. Hearing a knock, I made a note of yet another book which had not provided the missing reference, wrote down one more possibility which had occurred to me, and went, fairly irritably, to open the door.

It was Mark, with a cardboard box in his hands.

'Hello,' he said, after a moment, then seemed about to add my name, then stopped.

'Hello, Mark. Come in.'

'I don't want to disturb you.'

'Not in the least.'

I thought he was about as tall as Ben now. 'Won't you come in? It's nice to see you.'

'Well – . It's really just – . It's nice to see you. I brought you this.' He held the box out. 'David asked me to.'

'David?'

'Yes, when I saw him. In Cambridge, before Christmas.'

'You're up at – Bristol?'

'Mm. But there was a dance. My – a friend of mine asked me. And I saw David: he was doing a concert we went to, and we had a drink together afterwards. And we talked and everything, and in the end he said, if I was coming over to Cambridge again after Christmas, which I was, could I pick this up and bring it over.'

'I see. How very kind. What is it, do you know?'

'You'd better open it. But not out here, probably.'

'You'll have to come in then, and help me, and have a glass of sherry.'

He set the box on the floor in the living-room, and then his glass beside it, and untied the string. We turned back the edges of the box, and found hay below. Mark sat back on his heels, smiling, and I worked my hand through the hay until my fingers encountered fur, and then the whole hand touched warmth beneath. I held some of the hay back with the other hand, and lifted out, sprawling on the flat of my palm, looking about with puzzled, unpractised vision, a little cat, very young, with fur ruffled.

I looked up, and found Mark looking from my face to the kitten, and then back again with enquiry. 'Well?'

'*David* sent this?'

'It's from Graham Rostov. In Cambridge. A granddaughter of Jocasta's. He thought you'd like it; David did, I mean. He asked me to bring one as soon as it was old enough to leave its mother. Actually, I meant to ask you first: David said to. But when I got there, I realised I hadn't, and by then it was all sort of fixed up – it was a bit late – '

'Yes, I see.'

'I can easily take her back, if you like. I mean, if you don't want a cat, or they give you hay-fever or anything.'

I looked at the kitten, now held in my two hands.

'I did pick the one I thought you'd like best. If you do like them. It's a pretty colour.'

'Very pretty.'

'And she's got a sort of nice look. I thought I'd come straight here, so she wouldn't have too many changes. But I can always take her back.'

I held the little animal against me while I pulled some hay from the box, then I set her down in it, on the floor. She turned about in a circle as she lay, sniffing at the stalks of hay, searching and beginning to mew.

'Should it have some food?'

'If you had any milk – ?'

The kitten was asleep before I brought it. I put the saucer down near the hay, and we finished our sherry, sitting by the fire. She lay on her side, the streaked fur, a dark, tabby ginger, rising and falling very quickly with her breath.

Mark drained his glass and went over to crouch down by the kitten. He put his hand round her side, and said, 'I'll take her back, shall I?' and then, 'It's no problem.'

'She seems at home. I think you should leave her. But you'll have to tell me about looking after her.'

She woke sometime after Mark had gone, and drank most of the milk when I had warmed it again. I broke back the sides of the box to make it shallower, and shook up the hay, and took her upstairs in it when I went to bed. She woke only once in the night, stirring and rustling, and crying once or twice. But very early in the morning, soon after five, she woke again and cried in earnest, and would not be cajoled to sleep. I went downstairs and warmed some more milk for her, but she seemed unable to find it, or to know what it was for, turning her head aside and wailing without consolation.

The room was very cold. I put the saucer on the bedside table, and took up the little cat, and sat down on the bed. I dipped my finger in the milk, then, and wetted her nose with it, and watched her tongue come out to wipe it off. Next time, she licked it from my finger, too, and went on licking, searching for more, her eyes beginning to close, her cries diminishing. After three or four more

412

fingerfuls, she fell asleep on my knee. I drew the top blanket round her, and pulled my dressing gown over my shoulders, and woke, rather cold, more than two hours later.

The little cat was still asleep. I looked at the quickly, gently moving fur, the large, pointed ears, pink within, the small legs, symmetrically barred, and the weight of her head, resting between her forelegs. I felt a kind of tenderness run through me, and rise, and grow to extraordinary strength. I laid my hand over her warm side and the finer, pale fur of her stomach, the small rib-cage expanding and contracting against my palm. I was alarmed, even ashamed, to be so nearly overwhelmed by such a feeling.

I looked up at the windows – the nearer one still dark, with the curtains across it; the further one letting in the bright, chilly light from an early sky. No tenderness, surely – no benevolence of any kind – was shameful. She stretched, pressing down her chin and extending her claws, and fell back into sleep. I realised with a shock what it was that I was feeling: this sharp, half-amused, half-frightened responding to the little animal – to her extreme vulnerability, her absurd inefficiency, her entire, confident reliance on my goodwill – this brimming, stinging affection, was a single stray eddy of the most persistent and inexorable of all the ancient tides of human feeling. What I felt now, consciously, for the first time, and for something so peripheral to my life, so delightfully unnecessary as this little cat, was an emotion without which no human kind – no species of mammal or bird, indeed – would have survived: something more dependable, less mutable, than any of the forms of erotic love. It was a feeling I was never likely to know in its full force, but as it was quickened now by this small creature, I began to recognise it as having had some part, from the beginning, in the most central of all my affections.

The past few months have not been uncomplicated delight. The little cat – who seemed only barely ready to have left her mother – had needs which were not altogether easily reconciled with mine. She has begun to sleep through some nights now, and occasionally, with the admirable self-sufficiency of her kind, even to find her own way down to the kitchen for a drink, if she wakes thirsty before it is light. If I lift her onto the draining board, she can go out through the lower half of the kitchen window, and she calls at the back door when she is ready to come in. When she can't go outside, she uses the tray of ashes, more often than not: I should not have to clean up after her for many weeks more. I think she is an intelligent little thing.

Her liking for company was greater than mine, and a good deal more compatible with the business of her life. The first stages of *French and Italian Influences* were much interrupted by her sociable inclinations. At one point, indeed, I gave up two or three mornings to letter-writing, and other less concentrated work, hoping that if she was free for a time to sit on my knee, jumping down and returning whenever she liked, she might begin to understand that I would not go away, and might therefore be willing to sit by the Aga, or to wander in the garden, while I was working. But she saw it otherwise.

I managed to ignore her pleas outside the door – or at least to refuse them – for the first part of the morning when I started to do real work again. At eleven o'clock there could be a respite for both of us: milk and a little company for her; silence and coffee for me. But I had reckoned without her joy in my reappearance. Before I was through the sitting-room door she had jumped straight up almost to my waist, then she scrambled to my shoulder, holding my jacket with her claws, butting her round head under my chin, uttering an astonishingly voluminous purr, interrupted with short, monosyllabic mews. I could not bear to dislodge her immediately; I poured out the milk and made the coffee with one hand. And in the end, when I went back to work, I left the sitting-room door ajar.

So now I am learning to work with her on my lap. She is less restless than she was, but it is the necessity to leave the door open, as much as her coming and going, which deflects my concentration. And I begin to think that I might miss her warm weight on my knee, the occasional heave of her head under the desk-flap, if she were to be gone for too long.

Sometimes her presence seems even to benefit the work. When my mind begins to skirt round an arid stretch of one of the minor romances, or a word evades me, or a sentence refuses to shake itself out into clarity, I can run my hand through her fur, or rub her jawbone just below the ear, to make her purr; and my thoughts, released for a moment without being too far diverted, may return quite soon to the problem before me, with greater tenacity, and sometimes with a solution. Now and then, I even talk to her. I cannot pretend that I have got more work done since she arrived. But the urgency is not great: I am not badly off at the moment (the royalties from the Cycle are still very good), and the Press have accepted this next book in principle, without giving me a deadline. And it is over a month now since I have had a migraine.

I spent a whole evening, while I was mending some books, trying to decide on her name. I was inclined to continue Rostov's tradition, and give her a name from Sophocles, but I could think of none that were not comically inappropriate. I watched her dance and scuttle after a scrap of bark from the firewood, then stand to reach her forepaws into the wastepaper basket, until it overbalanced and engulfed her. She wriggled out backwards. Antigone? Electra? I widened my search to the other tragedians (Hecuba?) and then to Greek literature in general: the heroines of Aristophanes or the nymphs and shepherd girls of Theocritus might supply something.

After a time, she came to lie by the hearth, near my feet, and groom and lick her ruffled fur until it lay sleek again. Wasn't there some nymph who was sleek? I could not think what the word might be in Greek, but there was no translation I knew as well as I knew that phrase, except Pope's (and it was not Pope). She would hardly stay sleek, in any case, when she started playing again. 'Sleek Panope, with all her sisters, played.' It was *Lycidas*. When I first met the poem, as a boy of twelve, I imagined Panope to be a seal: it was 'on the level brine', after all, that she had played.

I looked again at my small cat. There was something seal-like about her: her blunt head, her intelligence, her freedom to move in three dimensions. More properly, I thought she was acquiring, as she grew, some of the fluid, light-hearted waywardness of a water-nymph. She should be Panope, and Panope she is, though Mrs Weaver abbreviates her, confusingly, to Pan.

It is Mrs Weaver, however, who has solved my only serious remaining perplexity, by offering to come out to the cottage and feed Panope if I have to be away for the night.

'Or when you want to take your holiday, just let me know, and I'll be up every day. Or I could stay over the time, if that would suit you: be on the spot, and my husband could go to one of my daughter's. You've only to say.' I thought I heard a note of hope in her voice: her husband is no easier, I am afraid. And there is mutual approval between her and Panope.

I wrote to Rostov, and to David, and sent Mark a postcard, a couple of weeks after Panope had settled in – or rather, once I had acknowledged that there was no question of my sending her back. Rostov invited me to dine with him next time I was in Cambridge, and David telephoned in reply and has been down for a weekend. He brought as a present a copy of T.S. Eliot's *Practical Cats*, which I had not known before. Eliot certainly understood cats – better, perhaps, than he understood the Middle Ages.

4th September, 1970

I hope Panope will be all right. This is the first time I have had to leave her for more than a single night. Mrs Weaver is coming out to the cottage, declaring herself delighted to stay there, and to have the opportunity for a 'good sort round'. And she says that she and Panope will be great company for each other. I expect she is right, but I wish Panope knew that I was coming back, and when. I really don't think I should miss this conference. It just seems perverse to make us all travel as far as Wales to discuss a language and a literature that was neither spoken nor written there at any relevant time. There is some interest, perhaps, and some room for research, in the mutual influence of the Celtic languages and Middle English, but it can be overstated, particularly by Celticists.

13th September

Mrs Weaver was right, of course. Panope is in fine form, and welcomed me on the doorstep. There has been nothing in my home-coming to offset the rewards of the conference.

The two big flowerbeds have been weeded, all the windows are clean, and the larder is newly whitewashed, with bright paper lining the shelves. Mrs Weaver had a high tea ready in the kitchen; I managed to notice most of the work she's done and, more readily, Panope's excellent state of health. (We agreed that she's grown perceptibly within the week.) I had even remembered to buy a present, at the last minute, from a shop near Cardiff station: a scarf, printed with 'Welsh folk designs' of no great authenticity. We had a very convivial high tea, all together, and now that Mrs Weaver has gone home, Panope has come to sit on my knee at the desk while I sort out my papers from the conference.

I was well advised to go. In the last three-and-a-half years, I have been recovering – thanks to Douglas, and a little, I must admit, to Peter Thorsen – some of the ground lost in the two years before that. The Dictionary Committee have asked me to oversee the appendix on stress and pronunciation (having accepted the draft of grammatical principles almost unaltered). *Mediaeval Narrative Technique* has provoked some disagreement: several reviewers called it 'controversial'. But, as Douglas says, controversy does no harm, if one is defending a good cause, on good grounds; and on the whole the reviews were favourable. The Press have written enthusiastically to both of us about the verse translation (finished at last, after a concerted effort in the Easter vacation, and another in July); and they hope to have it in print before the end of the year. I have begun to lecture again, now and then, at the New University, and there is some suggestion of a seminar there next term – probably on Middle English verse. For all this, I was unprepared for my reception at Cardiff. I suppose I have not been to anything of the kind in this country for some years.

It is the Cycle, of course, for which Douglas and I are chiefly known, and he has consolidated that reputation far better and more thoroughly than I. But my three papers on three aspects of Mediaeval Religious Drama (European Analogues, Dramatic Prosody, and Sacred and Profane Love), written at speed and almost without a break (except where Panope interrupted me), were received with far greater interest – and even acclaim – than I had supposed possible. Each produced a discussion of unusual length and value, which continued informally – over meals and in chance meetings – for much of the week. I had various invitations to speak, later in the year, and one to collaborate in a new anthology of early poetry. And late on the last evening a suggestion was made 'off the record' (so I had better not record the details here) that I should let my name go forward for a chair of Mediaeval Literature. I still find it hard to know what I feel about this – except, of course, for a good deal of satisfaction at the compliment. I want to discuss it with Douglas; and now that I have heard about his prospective move – equally flattering, and a good deal more certain – there should be no awkwardness in talking about it when he is here next week.

14th September

Perhaps I should set down, before I put this away, a curious little encounter I had on the journey home from the conference. Its connection with the main events of this account is close enough, I think, to make it worth recording for the sake of completeness.

I came home from Cardiff by way of Cambridge. I had left the car there, near the station, and I was to spend the night with Maurice Wakeford and drive home next day, after a Dictionary meeting. On the long, cross-country journey, there was, as so often, over an hour to wait at Bletchley. It was a chilly evening. There was no fire in the waiting room, but I wrapped my overcoat round my knees, and began making notes on the Romance I had been reading on the train. After ten minutes or so another passenger came in, holding a book in his hand. I realised with regret that he would have to sit opposite me by the empty fireplace: the light was not strong enough for reading anywhere else.

'Alan Pearce?' he said.

'Yes.'

'Julian Foster. Do you mind if I sit here?'

When I looked up, I recognised him.

'I think you'll have to, if you want to read.'

He sat down and turned through his book to find the place.

'God, it's cold. You'd think they'd have a fire.'

'Not at Bletchley,' I said, checking a line reference.

He laughed. 'Do you suppose there's any coal in that bucket?'

'I don't know.'

He went to look himself; then, still in the silence I had intended to suggest, he opened his briefcase, found a notebook, and tore out the last three or four pages. I could not help looking up to see if they were unwritten. I am superstitiously reluctant to use even blank pages of work paper for anything but work: to destroy any part of a draft, or a set of notes, in manuscript, until it has been checked through, and copied where necessary, and checked again, would be appalling. But he had crumpled the paper too quickly for me to be sure.

He put it in the grate and shook a little coal over it from the bucket. Then he felt in his pockets, produced an empty matchbox, and looked up at me from where he was squatting. I looked down at my work. After a moment he got up and went out, taking the bucket with him. When he returned, he put down the bucket, which sounded full now, in the hearth, and struck a match. Light began to flicker over my page and, without looking up, I could see the paper flare, and soft, bright blue flames begin to fill the chinks between the small lumps of coal. Julian remained, squatting by the hearth in silence, adding pieces of coal at intervals, until a brassy, brownish glow and a strong, steady heat were coming into the room.

'That's better,' he said at last, and I felt obliged to answer, 'Yes.' He laughed again, sat down quietly, and began to read.

Some time later, finishing a section of notes, I shifted in my chair and held a hand out to the fire.

'I hope you don't mind if I say how much I enjoyed your papers,' said Julian.

'You were at the conference?'

'Yes.'

'I didn't see you, I think.'

'I don't expect you did. But I came to all your papers, and I thought they were some of the best things I've heard.'

'Thank you.'

'The first one, particularly: on the Analogues.'

'Really?'

'Superb. I expect the others were just as good, but that's rather more my field.'

Academic justice and good manners, not yet quite forfeited, made me search my memory of recent publications.

'You've been doing work on the literature of the Auld Alliance.'

He nodded.

'I've heard very well of it. I'm afraid I haven't read it yet, myself.'

'No.' He smiled. 'I shouldn't expect it.' Then he added, nodding at the work in my hand, 'I imagine you'll be expanding your work on the analogues.'

'This isn't drama.'

'No, so I see. But in other departments. The Breton lays, the Romances? Isn't there room for some comparative analysis there?'

'Very probably.'

'I mean, what has there been, recently? Apart from Archie Tanner?'

'Tanner? What's he done?'

'Only that thing that came out last year: 'Early European Gnomic Verse'. You must have seen it.'

'I don't think I have.' There was a pause. 'Is it any good?'

'Of course it's not: it's quite as bad as you'd expect. I suppose it does cover the ground... But such a small area – and such an uninteresting one, characteristically. That's why your paper was so exciting. There's so much to be done, still: almost all the rest of that field. And with your approach – and your knowledge, obviously. I don't know who else could do it.'

I did not take up his lead, and after a moment he added, with mock hesitancy, catching my eye, 'Besides, that was the gossip at Cardiff.'

'I see.' I could not refrain altogether from smiling.

'Perhaps it was wrong.'

'Not entirely. I had been considering something along those lines.'

'And now – ?'

'The work seems to be changing tack.'

420

'In what direction? Unless you'd rather not discuss it: if it's too early …'

I was silent for a moment, then I said, 'I think it will be a study of Courtly Love.'

'Really?'

'I shall be able to use a good deal of the same material.'

'Of course.' He may have seen my sudden elation. 'And then the work for your last paper – . Every bit as necessary as the Analogues. More so, in some ways. A marvellous subject. And the right person to do it. We ought to drink to it.'

He looked round the dim room and found a glass and a cup on the windowsill.

'Just a minute.' He took them through the internal door into the cloak-room and returned with both of them wet and clean. 'There's a tap in there. Do you like water with it?' He was rummaging in his briefcase.

'Whisky?'

'Yes.'

'Just a little.'

He left his undiluted, and put the half-bottle between us, by the hearth. He raised the thick, white cup to me as he sat down.

'Courtly Love.'

I acknowledged the toast, and we drank for a little time in silence.

'I saw Ben in New York.'

I held everything as still as I could – my glass, my breathing, my hand, my eyes on the glass.

'What were you doing in New York?'

Without looking up, I felt him smile, or heard it, perhaps, in his voice.

'Oh, an exchange thing at Columbia.'

'Very interesting.'

'Yes. Ben was very well.'

'Good.'

'I thought you'd be glad to know. Unless you've heard more recently?'

'When were you there?'

'In May.'

'No.'

'You don't write?'

I did not answer.

'I thought perhaps you didn't, any more; though – '

I had looked up, after all, as he delayed. 'What?'

'Oh, just that – you never know. Things change.'

'You mean Ben has – something has changed for Ben?'

'For him, among others.'

'In what way?'

'Various ways, really.'

'Is he all right?' I did not even try to keep the anxiety out of my voice.

'He's *all right*,' said Julian, laughing. 'In fact, he's fine.'

'But – ?'

'But – oh, nothing very much; nothing to worry about for either of us.'

'Either of us?'

'It's the same for both of us, isn't it?' he said, as if in reply. 'For you and me. We're in the same position.'

'Are we?'

'Only in one respect,' he said, as if apologetically.

'In *what* respect?'

'I could hardly have meant, professionally.'

He waited, but I did not answer.

'I mean, simply with respect to Ben.'

After a moment, I said, 'I was not really asking about your position, or my own. I was asking how you found Ben.'

'Yes, though I think the two are related.'

I did not reply.

'All right: Ben was all right. There's nothing at all to worry about.'

'Is that true?'

'Yes.'

I drank some whisky, and he watched me. 'As true as what I said before,' he added.

'How true is that?'

'You can probably tell me that.'

'What can I tell you?'

'Whether we're both in the same boat.'

'Very possibly, in one way or another. Should we go out on the platform?' I looked at my watch. 'It should be in in a few minutes.'

'You're going to Cambridge, too, I take it?'

'Yes. I'd like to get a seat. I've got some work to finish.'

'Right.' He nodded in acknowledgement, rose to his feet, and picked up the whisky bottle. 'A little more?'

'I think we should go.'

'We've got ten minutes.' I looked at my watch again. 'Nearly.'

'Five,' I said. 'No, thank you.'

But my voice was submerged by the loud-speaker, announcing a delay: our train was expected to be forty-five minutes late; our inconvenience was regretted.

We looked at each other, and sat down. Julian leaned across and poured more whisky into the glass I was still holding.

'I really don't want any more.'

He smiled and shook his head. 'It's not as easy as all that, is it? At Bletchley, anyway.'

I thought of tipping the whisky into the fire. Then I went into the cloakroom and added a good deal of water to it. I drank a little before I returned. We sat by the fire for some time before either of us spoke.

'How much of that conversation did you hear?' Julian asked.

'What conversation?'

'The conversation I had with Ben, in the seed shed.' I did not reply. 'On his birthday.'

'It wasn't his birthday.'

'You're right. How much did you hear?'

I had cut off my simplest retreat. 'Not very much.'

'Enough, though?'

'Enough for what?'

'Enough to know what I wanted from Ben.'

'And not only from Ben.'

'Oh – that wasn't serious.'

'For you.'

'For anyone. It was only for Ben's benefit. He'd been annoyed with me about something.'

'So I gathered.'

'About David – '

'I suppose that wasn't serious, either?'

He was silent.

'I did overhear more than was necessary,' I said eventually. 'More than I should have. I owe you an apology for that. I can't pretend that my own position is very strong. But I've been wanting for some time to say that I found your behaviour that evening wholly contemptible.'

After a silence of some length he said, 'Yes.'

'To play with other people's feelings in that way – particularly the feelings of the very young – is grossly irresponsible. To make use of them for your own ends, knowingly, calculatingly, and causing distress as you did, was a great deal worse than irresponsible. It was iniquitous.'

'Yes,' he said again. 'I know.'

'Do you?'

'I know that's what you felt – what you've been wanting to say.'

'You would disagree?'

'In the main, no.'

There was another, longer silence. Then, against my better judgement, I asked, 'How did you know? That that was what I felt – that I knew – ?'

'By your face, when I was saying goodbye to Ben's mother. You'd come to cover up for Ben. I knew as soon as you saw me.'

'I see.'

I hoped it was true. There seemed to be nothing further to say. There were still thirty-five minutes to wait, by the waiting-room clock, and it was probably fast. After a little, I opened my notebook.

'I've been avoiding you ever since,' said Julian.

'Have you?'

'I think so, really. It was a mistake, though. I shouldn't have let it go for – whatever it's been – six years. There were several things I needed to consult you about: Gower's French Sources, Northumbrian forms in the Repton Cycle ...' He waited.

I did not answer.

'I'd have done it before now, with almost anyone else. But as it was, with you...'

'What difference did that make?'

'Not much, in principle, perhaps. But in practice – well: I still saw you partly through Ben's eyes, I suppose. And then you'd behaved so well – so much better than I had – in the same situation. I felt the more discredited.'

'The same situation?'

'I don't think that's quite fair. I've let you know my side of it – advertently and inadvertently. You know what I mean.'

I was silent.

'We both wanted – we were both – pursuing Ben; and we were both rejected.'

I said nothing.

'That was the case, wasn't it? For you as well as for me?'

'Not entirely.'

'You mean – you weren't rejected?'

'There was nothing to reject, or to accept.'

'I don't think you can ask me to believe that. I've known since – oh, since you came to look for him in my room in the Kite – how you felt about Ben.'

'Have you, indeed?'

'In essentials. And I don't think it's changed. And I don't think, in honesty, you can deny it.'

'I didn't deny it; or confirm it.'

'You said there was nothing to reject.'

'Or to accept. The question never arose.'

'You didn't ask him?'

I made no answer.

'You didn't tell him? In all those years. My dear Alan. Why not?'

'It's not something I'm prepared to discuss any further.'

'You mean I wouldn't understand if you did tell me.' He bent forward, putting his cup down in the hearth, and said, only just audibly, 'But I might, you know – I might.'

We sat for a time in silence. Julian kept his eyes on his hands, which he held between his knees.

'I could, if you liked,' he said slowly, at last. 'I could tell him for you – what you feel.'

'If you dare do anything of the kind...' I stopped.

'If I do – ?' He smiled. 'All right. You don't need any sanctions. Besides, he might not believe me.'

'That's very possible.'

'He didn't last time. As I think you know.'

I felt suddenly weak. I could say nothing further. The glass in my hand blurred.

Julian held the whisky out to me. I nodded, and he refilled my glass, this time without any challenge or insistence; it seemed rather a gesture of goodwill. We sat together, sipping our whisky and watching the fire. A little before the train was due, he took up the book he had been reading, from where it had slipped down beside him in the chair.

'I'd be interested to know your view of this. If you wouldn't mind?'

I took the book from him. 'Simone Brouwer: *Chaucer as Polemicist*? I've only seen the reviews. What's it like?'

'Very convincing, so far. But then, I'm not hard to convince in that field. What are the arguments on the other side?'

We talked about it until the train came in, and then, finding an almost empty carriage, for the rest of the journey. I had forgotten how quick he was to take a point and develop it, how well-equipped to produce analogies from other literature. We argued with increasing warmth and increasing enjoyment, reaching laughter and substantial agreement before we got to Cambridge.

On the way from the station (I gave him a lift), he told me something of his own work. He had a research fellowship at a university in the North Country, and he had become interested in the links between Mediaeval Scotland and France while he was turning his thesis into a book.

'Not until then?'

'Not seriously.'

'Beckett wasn't serious?'

'Beckett?'

'His connection with – Dunbar? Or was it Henryson?'

'Ah! That wasn't allowed, thank God. They knew a pretentious idea when they saw one.' He laughed. 'Beckett indeed!'

Now that he had seen *John Barbour and the Auld Alliance* through the press, he was hoping to do an edition of Michael Scot, if he could find a collaborator. For a moment I felt, and for half a moment considered, an unspoken suggestion that I might undertake it with him. But I let it pass, which was right, I am sure, for many reasons.

16th September

Waking this morning a little before I had to get up, I began to consider why this meeting with Julian seems so oddly important – why it is still so disproportionately unsettling my spirits.

To tell him at last, unequivocally, of my long-held anger and disgust was a release which shook me at the time, the more so as it necessarily involved admitting my own dereliction. But now that it is done, I feel relieved of a weight of bitterness greater than I had known I was carrying. It was a weight, moreover, that I could not have discharged so completely if he had not accepted it. His apology was characteristically wary and oblique, but I thought it was nonetheless genuine.

What is it I feel, then, beyond relief and serenity and a certain gratitude? Exposure, I suppose: for all his candour and, later, sympathy, Julian would not rest until he had extracted from me a tacit admission of the nature of my feelings for Ben. This, too, was characteristic, and less admirably, though I believe he was telling the truth when he said that he would not give me away.

But there is more than this: there is an ambiguity, an uncertainty which goes deeper – and may, perhaps, reach further ahead as well.

He has seen Ben, and something has changed, and he won't tell me what it is. That is the source of my hope, of course, of the happiness with which I woke this morning. It seems just possible that the change he refused to define – but spoke of smilingly ('He's all *right*: in fact he's fine') – is a change of affections, even, perhaps, of sexual direction. It is more likely, of course, to be nothing of the kind. If it is anything to do with the state of Ben's emotions, and not simply of his work or his finances, it is probably that he has fallen in love with a girl – perhaps decided to live with her. (Would Julian assume that this would shock me? As well as knowing that it would hurt me? Or does he just enjoy keeping a secret – especially Ben's secret – from me?)

Nevertheless, there it is: a flicker of hope. And if it is, as seems most probable, no more than a marsh-light, it still takes more warmth than it is rationally entitled to from even so slight and indirect a connection with Ben – with his wellbeing, even simply with his reality: his existing in New York, being visited, having friends. I suppose I must admit that there is some comfort, too, in the knowledge (also trustworthy, I think) that Julian's pursuit of Ben has not succeeded.

But there is an ambivalent side even to these small hopes. There is something unacceptable even in the most optimistic projection I can make from them. Is it, perhaps, their origin: the fact that they have their source in Julian's information, his interpretation, his contact with Ben? Is it that this would somehow bring my own relation to Ben into parallel with his? Is it this thought which is intolerable? I have long suspected, though never altogether admitted, that my well-justified anger with Julian was violent and tenacious even beyond that justification, because I saw in his attitude to Ben a crude and humiliating parody of my own. It may even have been that implication – understood by me, whether or not it was intended by him – which added sharpness to Ben's last accusations, and bitterness to my reaction. That the single centre of my affections, of so many years' hope, of the pattern of my life, should be no more than a cast from the same mould as Julian's unscrupulous self-indulgence – that might be little more endurable than loss.

Besides, I have begun to wonder, occasionally, in the past few months, whether my hopes will remain so singly centred for ever. It has seemed possible, sometimes, that I shall throw off, one day, the long tyranny of this all-excluding, all-concentrating love. I cannot believe I could ever think of Ben without affection, but may it not become an affection which no longer dominates my thoughts (or rather, determines their form, makes up their substance), which takes its place among other affections, leaving me free to disregard it or dwell on it as I will?

I cannot really imagine such a state of mind, yet; do what I will, it leaves the world too empty. But I have felt recently, more than once, a stirring of interest and gentle excitement in an encounter with some other man. It is very far from an irresistible attraction: it is only a little more than negligible, and it has none of the sour, self-contained craving which led me to accept – to reciprocate – the approaches of the young clerk. It is rather a small, uncomplicated delight – unearned, unlooked for (so far) and, I think, innocent: a pleasure from which I can take – or, almost as easily, leave – warmth and light, as from a candle-flame; and with as little effect on anyone besides myself as a watcher has on a candle. Nor have I wished for any greater effect. I am too old to be unaware of the dangers of playing with fire; and the warmth and light, though grateful in themselves, matter more for what they seem to suggest: that the blight of my hopes has not blasted the ground for ever; that there is some life ready to stir even at such small and transient heat; that there could still be growth, burgeoning even, if it were to be touched by the sun.

There was a young man in Cardiff who read a paper on *Piers Plowman* – I took up one or two points with him later. He was wearing a very informal shirt, with a small brooch in the form of a wooden mouse where one of the buttons should have been, and he had fair, curly hair, rather low on his neck. He was eager to know my views, though he had some good ones of his own, and we smiled afterwards when we passed in the corridors. And there was the boy – much younger – helping on his father's stall in the Thursday market in Bramston, who sold me a lidded basket for Panope, and counted the change so carefully, and made a last-minute little joke about carrier-pigeons. And an older fisherman, grave and solitary and humane – unaware of me, I think, across the water, as I rested against the bank at the turn of a long walk. It was on an unusually fine day at the start of the spring. I thought of him a few days later, reading Yeats's *Fisherman*.

And with Julian, too, it is true that I have felt the same glimmer – at Bletchley, and earlier too, perhaps – though it is complicated in his case by various other emotions, and complicating them in its turn. I think both resentment and *rapprochement* glowed more keenly for it. It is not more important, in essence, than what I have felt for some others, and I have little fear of its escaping my control. It is another reason, all the same, for thinking it wise to avoid collaborating with him on an edition.

18th October, 1970

Brockenhurst

I heard from Ruth this morning. Being on a holiday – albeit a working one – I've been spending longer over breakfast with the paper; and a day or two after I arrived, I saw their name in the list of Forthcoming Marriages. It was Bridget who was engaged, and that afternoon I wrote a note to her parents. Ruth's reply came rather earlier than I had foreseen.

My dear Alan,

Thank you so much for your very nice letter. Yes, we are delighted – not just in the obligatory, conventional sense, but really. Charles was at Cambridge with Ben, and he and Bridget got to know each other better when he was doing post-graduate work at Oxford in her last year. He's a dear – humorous, intelligent, kind, and fits into the family beautifully. He and Mark get on particularly well: he teases M. about his girl-friends (a steady stream!) and I think M. confides in him. And I've never seen Bridgie so blooming and happy.

They hope to be married in the summer, when Charles knows where he'll be. He's applying for the British Council, and hopes to

430

start with them in London in the New Year, which would fit in very well with Bridgie's job with Penguin Parallel Texts. (Did you see the Twentieth Century Spanish Poetry which she and a colleague brought out this summer? Her first publication!) I hope the wedding will be while you are still at home, and not deep in some ancient and un-get-at-able European library!

I find I really rather like the idea of being a mother-in-law – and even more (privately) the idea of being a grandmother later on. But best of all is the feeling that one of the children has found the right life for herself. I know marriage – and this marriage – is right for Bridgie (indeed, I've known it for some time) – although, of course (as Mark often points out to me) there are so many other possibilities nowadays! The great thing, really, is that in the end each of them should settle into what is truly and permanently right for them, as people, and with the right other person, if it includes one. Convention, prosperity, even grandchildren come a long way after that. But that – I can't tell you how much I want it, for each of them, and how happy I am that Bridgie seems to have found it. But I think you probably understand this better than most people.

Bridgie sends her love, and many thanks for your good wishes. She hopes to see you soon when they are down for a weekend.

Ben writes cheerfully, and is delighted about the engagement, for which he claims a lot of credit! I think he's really enjoying the teaching, still, though it's hard work.

What is your news? It's too long since you've been to supper; though it is good that you are getting a bit of a holiday this year, after all. Animals are a tie, aren't they? – but I'm glad Mrs Weaver has taken to Panope – and vice versa! The New Forest must be looking lovely, now – especially if St Martin is taking his little summer as seriously for you as he is for us this year.

We hope to see you when you're back. Thanks again for your letter, and love and good wishes from us both.

Ruth

How very much more important this letter – this day – would have been six or seven years ago: a landmark, a point of calculation, a pivot for the entire fortnight. As it is – it brings me a little news of Ben (I am glad his teaching is going well, though I hope it is more than a stopgap, continued only for want of other opportunities. He might teach well, I think); but Ruth's happiness and evident goodwill are not, after all, so very much less important to me. I suppose Ben's news is just reason enough to copy the letter here, though I am not sure that I should bother if I were at home. I must do something, at the far point of a walk, if I am to sit still for long enough to take in the quietness of the forest and the balm and smoke of the air, without restlessness, and to let the ponies wander near without alarm. I have finished almost all the books I brought with me, even the serious, morning reading, in spite of the idle, holiday hours I've been keeping. And if I am to save the Provencal Lyrics for the end of the evening, there are not many alternatives, except for the paper-backs on the stand in the General Store. I was well advised, after all, to abandon customary caution and bring the current notebook with me: when I've put down here everything of even conceivable relevance, I shall have to start taking an interest either in cold war espionage, or in deep-sea diving. I wish I had brought some Jane Austen.

Enforced leisure has its merits, though, and I suppose I should make the most of them in these last few days: there will be plenty to do when I get home. Now that the Press have agreed to the new direction of this next book, I want to start writing as soon as possible. I am surprised how much material I have accumulated already: there is little more really essential new reading to be done now (though there will be a good deal of re-reading, of course, both before and in the course of writing); but getting everything into order will be hard work, and complicated. The original scheme can stand, I think, but only as a kind of substructure, to be expanded and extended into a much bigger work than I originally foresaw. There is more relevant literature, and much more to say about it, than I realised three or four years ago.

This is the main reason why I am still undecided about letting my name go forward for the Chair of Mediaeval Literature. When

Douglas came down at the end of last month, he was very keen, at first, for me to agree to it (partly, I think, because with characteristic generosity he would then feel able to rejoice even more whole-heartedly in his own appointment, now imminent). 'What fun to be brother professors,' he said: 'Two kings of Barataria' – and he began to hum a tune from *The Gondoliers*. But when we had talked it over for a day or two, and I had shown him the scheme of my work (already considerably enlarged) for *Courtly Love*, he began to realise why I was so reluctant to take on anything else till it was done.

'It's a big undertaking, Alan. You'll do it superbly, but I can see you'll need a good deal of time.'

'Three or four years, anyway – very likely more.'

'And it wouldn't be the same to take on the Chair, and reckon on six years for the book?'

'I don't want to lose the impetus: what I have to say – I feel strongly about it, at the moment.'

'Yes.'

'If I drag it out … And then the longer I take, the more chance there is of someone else getting in first. I wouldn't put it past Tanner, if he heard what I was working on – '

'Archie Tanner? I'd like to see him try! But I see what you mean.'

'I don't think it will be easy writing, either. I found that before: it was harder – more difficult simply to write, to express – than anything I'd done before.'

'I can imagine.'

'And I really ought to get something substantial done, now.'

'I'd call the Cycle substantial.'

'Of course: our great work. But what have I done since then?'

'A good deal. And you've published *Narrative Technique*.'

'Which is not much more than a monograph.'

'Don't be ridiculous. It's a good piece of work, and a useful one. A very necessary redressing of the balance. And it has the makings of more than that.'

'One day – if we can get together. But meanwhile – . And meanwhile you've produced the standard work – the definitive work – on Northern Dialects, with all your university stuff besides.'

'Everyone has fallow periods – using the term relatively. How soon do you have to decide?'

'I'm not sure. And then it would mean leaving – leaving the cottage, the garden – '

'But you'd keep it, wouldn't you? You'd come here for vacations?'

'I suppose so.'

I have heard since that my anxious deliberations – and indeed the original enquiry – were unnecessarily early; the appointment is not to be made until next summer. Perhaps by then I shall know more clearly how things stand.

The light, under the trees, is beginning to go, and I'm getting cold. If I start back soon, there will be time for a bath and a drink before supper.

If the young man is there this evening – serving in the pub, or at table – I could show him the passage in Malory we were talking about yesterday. I think it would make him laugh. I haven't seen anyone so ready to laugh for a long time. It's never unintelligent laughter: rather the overspill of energy, and an intelligent sense of the absurd. The same energy spills over when he takes things seriously – the American Civil Rights Movement, or a new Greek film, or, sometimes, what I have said. It is the first time that I have felt that small flame reflected, redoubled.

I don't think any harm will come of it – I don't intend to let it. I shall not do anything rash; and anyway, I am going away in just over three days. But I have not felt such a sense of possibility – of freedom in affection – for ten years, or perhaps a good deal longer. He is buoyant and charming, and he makes me feel amusing and kind and impressive. (Disgraceful that admiration should be so captivating!) I don't think he will take any hurt: his little quickening of liking and excitement is hardly of a kind to outlast my stay for long – certainly not beyond the end of the year, when he begins his travels.

Should I find him a book, if I go into Lyndhurst on Thursday? It might be a consolation, if any is needed, at the end of the week.

Or would that be to make too much of it? It depends on the book. If it's objective, fairly impersonal? Something appropriate to his journeying in Cyprus and Israel, or even – failing that – to his studies at University next year. (Did he say they were to include Archaeology? To both, then, with luck.) A paperback. And it depends on how I give it to him, too – how casually – before I go. His name is Stephen (Steven?). But I shouldn't inscribe it, I think.

I may be a little disconsolate myself, I suppose, but not past cure, when once I am home.

4th February, 1971

I wonder if I can write this while Mrs Weaver is in the house. It is not the weather for walking – at least until I am rid of this cold – and now that the notes for Chapter Two have fallen into place so easily and quickly, I'd like to leave them to settle – turn my mind elsewhere for a little before I start writing. I have been finding it rather easier, recently, to work through interruptions: the swinging door, even the songs, break my concentration less violently and less irreparably than they used to. Besides, Panope is asleep, and it would be a pity to disturb her. I don't know how much longer she'll fit on my knee while I'm working. She's not much more than a year old, and already her side touches the flap of the desk with the movement of her breath. I suppose I could find a lower chair.

Julian Foster has asked me to lecture to his Duns Scotus Society. I think I might accept: it's a nice letter, practical and unintrusive, and making some interesting suggestions for a subject. Douglas might have views on the choice, when I see him at lunch next week. It is a comfort having him so much nearer.

I had a postcard from Jerusalem last week (a pleasant incongruity). The signature is difficult to read, but I think it must be from Stephen. He sounds extremely well, proud of his adventures and not in the least heartbroken. The little book I gave him is 'v. useful and apropriate' [sic]. He does not give a return address.

It's nearly four. If I put the kettle on now, I can run Mrs Weaver home in good time. She shouldn't have to wait for the bus in this sleet. I might pick up some more index cards on the way back. I don't think Byford's shuts till half-past five.

I think Ben is in this country again. It may be a mistake, of course. Mrs Weaver thinks he was expected home last week – on Thursday night, or possibly on Friday morning. 'Their boy, that's been away,' she said. It may be Mark, though it's not the vacation. She has been doing some work for Ruth while Mrs Lee is ill. I don't know what to do.

5th February

I am not going to let this make any difference. There is no reason why it should. I could have communicated with Ben before now – across the Atlantic – if I had thought it would be of any use. What is the point of letters – of literacy – if two or three thousand miles of distance were all that has been keeping us apart? If he is here, I shall have to see him, I suppose – unless he is going back soon, which would, in many ways, be a relief. But we shall be no nearer in any effective sense. This excitement and restlessness are not much more than a reflex, I think; the twitching of nerves in a corpus of hope, too long retained, well after the end of any live intention or desire. That and an ill-advised habit of mind which left Ben's image as the focus of every prospect, when the true perspective of my mind and happiness was shifting elsewhere. I hope he is all right. I am not going to ring up the Graysons and find out. I shall hear his news from Ruth, sooner or later, in the ordinary course of events. There is time before supper for a first draft of the start of Chapter Two.

12th February

I have seen Ben. He did not see me. It was some distance away, across the little car park behind the Methodist Chapel. He was standing by his father's car, fitting the key into the lock, stooping a little, and steadying a paper carrier bag, with the other hand, on the bonnet of the car. I stood quite still, and waited, and in a little time he got in, reversed, and turned and drove away. It is nearly a fortnight now since he came home, I think.

13th February

Ruth rang up yesterday evening and asked me to lunch on Sunday. I have said I'll go. It's two days from now.

14th February

I wish I did not have to go to lunch with the Graysons tomorrow. It need not last long, and I know, after all, that Ben and I are capable of adequate polite conversation. But this churning of nervousness and reluctance and empty expectation is an unprofitable discomfort and distraction. The nervousness is mostly the anticipation of ordinary social awkwardness, I think, increased, as it is bound to be, by the strangeness of fitting a reality, inevitably changed, into a long-held idea. But I wish it could be over. There really isn't any way I can get out of it.

15th February

It is too late to start writing anything, but I think I shan't sleep until I have put down something of what happened this afternoon.

When I arrived, I could not see Ben's face. Even when he turned and came over to me at the doorway, I could not see it properly. I had to look up to take his hand, but I could not take in whatever I saw, though I did have the impression that he was smiling. I spoke first.

'How are you?'

'Alan. It's a very long time. How're you?'

'I'm well, thank you. Very well. You're enjoying America?'

'It's been fun. Yes. Not El Dorado, but – well, I'm glad I went.'

'New York is an extraordinary place. Extraordinarily interesting.'

'Right. And your work? You've had something else published?'

'Something: a rather minor work.'

He nodded. 'What are you working on now?'

'A book – I'm doing some work – hoping to do a book – on the *Amour Courtois*.'

'That's – Provence?'

'To start with. But a good deal of the rest of Europe, in the end.'

'A major work, then? Yours, I mean.'

'I think so. I think it may be. There's plenty of English stuff – Middle English; I can make that the centre of the book, luckily.'

He laughed. 'Right. What would you like to drink?'

He fetched me some sherry, and was called into a discussion, on the far side of the room, between Bridget and her fiancé, Charles, and Mark, home from the university for the weekend. Ben leaned across the back of the sofa to join in. I could see him now: his fair hair and an unfamiliar jacket; the familiar line of head and shoulder and arm; and his face: the lines of it were straighter, more settled; he listened and talked more definitely, with more confidence, and yet, I thought, with less expectation. When Mark said something emphatically, Ben caught Charles's eye and smiled, as he always had, with completeness, abandoning all other considerations for a moment. But his face returned to something more sober, more strained, even, than I had known. His skin was less fair than it used to be, more sallowly tanned, even so long after the end of the summer.

He came back to speak to me before we went in to lunch, and he was sitting next to me at the table. Bridget was on my other side, and I took care to ask her about her wedding plans. She seemed, indeed, as happy as her mother had said.

When I turned to Ben, I found him turning to talk to me. He told me about his work in New York. While he was teaching English to foreign diplomats' families, to earn his living, he had begun working with immigrant children, one or two afternoons a week, in a poor part of the town.

'Puerto Ricans, mostly. Lovely children: so bright, lots of them. And their families come over, and there they are in a class of thirty-something, and all this English going on over their heads, six hours a day. It's no wonder some of them start behaving badly: surprising more of them don't, really.'

'So you teach them English?'

'To start with. Other things sort of came in, of course. You've got to talk about *something*.'

'Of course you have. And you earn something for this?'

'Not at first. It was voluntary. I did get my bus fares. But then I started taking evening classes to qualify as a teacher. Over there, you can build up credits like that until you've got enough to begin the teaching practice. And just before I qualified, I saw an advertisement for a school in East Harlem – for a job there. The district I was working in already. They wanted someone to organise all the classes for the immigrant children – English, reading, math – maths – the lot. It's not as if the schools out there are all that marvellous – in Puerto Rico. 'First Generation New Yorkers' Studies Co-Ordinator' it was called.'

He was looking at me sideways. I could not altogether restrain the smile I felt him watching for, but he half-returned it, as if he knew it was not unfriendly.

'A very sensible plan, though,' I said. 'An important job.'

'Yes, and I got it. I don't know how they swung the work permit, but I got it. I think maybe they were fairly desperate: it's not a very popular area.'

'I can imagine. Did you have any – difficulties?'

'Well, they can be quite difficult by that stage – quite tough, sometimes. But – '

'What stage is it?'

'Junior High. Twelve to about fourteen.'

'I see. But – ?'

'But I knew straight away, really, that it was going to be all right. It was what I ought to be doing.'

'Ought to?'

He glanced at me again, this time more evidently defensive.

'I don't mean *morally*. At least, not in the regular sense. I mean, simply, it was the job that really suited me.' I nodded. After a moment, he added, 'I felt like a compass that's suddenly been allowed to draw circles.'

'That's the best feeling in the world, I think.'

He smiled – in agreement, in recollection, simply in relief? I don't know. But I felt with terror a shifting of foundations I had thought secure.

I drank some wine and asked, 'How much actual teaching do you do?'

'Quite a bit, in fact. It was supposed to be just organising. But once you're actually in the school, of course, you find yourself doing whatever most needs to be done. I'll do that, Charles.'

He got up to change the plates, and I asked Bridget about her work for Penguin. In the drawing-room, when Ben brought me a cup of coffee, he stood by my chair long enough to make it necessary to say something more.

'How long are you over here?'

'Oh – indefinitely.'

'You don't know yet when you're going back?'

'Or whether. If I can find a job, I'll be over here for good.'

'And otherwise?' I asked at random. There was nowhere to put my cup. I bent down and put it on the floor.

'Otherwise – wait a minute, I'll get a stool. Marky, can you – ? Otherwise, I don't know.'

'A job here. In the same field?'

'If there is one.'

'What are the chances?'

'Not too bad, I think. There are a good many immigrant children here, too, after all.'

'Yes. And – it went well, in New York? You'll have good references and so on?'

'Oh, well – .' He smiled. 'You know American references. That's no problem; at least until employers over here get wise to them.'

I nodded and smiled, too.

'You've applied already?'

'One or two places. I haven't really checked out the system yet – got it worked out.'

'But you're looking for the same sort of work?' I asked again.

'More or less,' he said, without impatience. 'I don't mind, exactly, as long as I can actually work with the children. Do some teaching. Some of the time, anyway.'

'Whereabouts are you looking?'

But he had turned to take a tray from Mark. He offered me sugar and cream, and when I shook my head, he moved on to other people.

He did not return before it was time to go. I drank my coffee and talked to various people, I suppose: to Mark about his debating society at Bristol, I think; and to James and Charles about the price of houses, and local conservation. Then I got up and said goodbye. Ben was not there. He had gone to take a telephone call in another room.

As I buttoned my coat, he came back across the hall.

'You off?'

'Yes. I ought to be going.' There was a moment's pause. 'I didn't realise how long I'd stayed,' I added, untruthfully.

'Well, very nice to see you.'

'Nice to see you back.'

There was another pause.

'I don't know if you've thought of it,' I said, 'but there is a Department of Education at Harchester – at the New University. It may not be any good, not what you want – '

'I didn't know there was one.'

'It's chiefly for the Diploma of Education, or whatever it's called now: the teachers' training course. But I think they have some research going on, too: practical projects and so on. They might have some ideas, at least.'

'Yes. Well – that might be very useful.'

'I could discover a bit more, if it would be any help. I've various friends: they'd know who you could write to.'

'That's very kind. May I think about it? I'll let you know – give you a call.'

'Of course.'

We said goodbye, and as I went out, I think he added, 'Or I could stop by.'

It was already late in the afternoon, and there were – there still are – several letters on my desk to be answered. But instead of driving home, I took the valley road, branched off across the river by the new bridge, and drove until I was in unfamiliar country.

I parked in a gateway (as one can on Sunday) and walked up a track to a wood on the crest of a hill, and through the wood, and on for some way, circling back to the car and seeing less and less of the landscape as the sun set and my thoughts circled more and more tightly.

I am not free of Ben. I have deceived myself, or perhaps been honestly deceived, by his absence, and by some of the things I have managed to do in his absence: to get my life into order again; to direct my thoughts, and even some of my affections, elsewhere; to get some work done, and not least, perhaps, this work: to consign the chief burden of memory and thought and feeling to this account, where it can stand separately, bearing its own weight, leaving me free – or so I thought. These foundations of stability and independence have been long and painful to lay down. I think they really are as strong as I can make them against internal lapse, but against an external force there has been, till now, no real occasion to test them.

I should perhaps have known that they were not impregnable. And yet, if I had known, how could I have continued? I think both speculations are unprofitable.

Ben has always been gentle – that is perhaps what I have loved most in him: gentle, in the modern sense, and with something also of the wider sense of the Mediaeval word. It seems to me now that his gentleness has really become *gentilesse*, spread and strengthened into the whole set of virtues proper to chivalry: the tenacity and courage, as well as the kindness and courtesy; the sense of fitness, and the certainty of purpose. I cannot imagine much more admirable work. I wish I had managed to tell him so.

And what did he feel when we met? No such admiration, certainly. My greatest achievements since our last meeting have been no more than the return (*hoc opus, hic labor est*) to the level at which he first knew me. Friendship of some sort remains, and at least some real communication: after the first stiffness of meeting (which he managed better than I) we did talk without the nullity, the deadness of that last, terrible conversation. There was even some warmth, though not of a kind which gave much away. Some things were said, but I felt that perhaps more were withheld. There

442

was a sort of vigilance directing the conversation, ending it when he thought fit, steering clear – apart from one moment – of confidence (though that moment was enough: indeed, far too much).

And he is here indefinitely. How can I manage? 'Here' need not be – will not be, for long – at his parents' house. He'll find work at a school in a large city – in London, or the North, or the Midlands. He'll come home, though – for Christmas, for weekends, for the school holidays, even. Was he slightly reluctant to take up my suggestion about the Department of Education? Did I press it too far?

He said he would telephone; he may have said he would come round. I mustn't count on that: I shouldn't even look forward to it. How can I help it? I must help it. He can't stay at home very much longer; he's twenty-seven (isn't he?), and he's already looking for a job. I shan't have to hold out very long. I'll make out a strenuous plan of work, and keep to it. I should do it now, before I go to bed. But I think I'd make a muddle of it: I really am very tired. I shall make the plan first thing tomorrow morning.

Is there perhaps an inexorable minimum of hope? Must I – oh, God – begin all over again?

Monday, 16th February

10.15pm

I have made out the plan, and today I've kept to it. I slept well last night. I suppose I'd walked a long way: it was nearly eight by the time I came home. And Panope's untroubled pleasure in my return, her decision to spend the night near my feet on the bed, were unreasonably reassuring.

I woke a little before the alarm, and felt for a moment a breath of past serenity, a sense of far-distant lightness and content. I was very tired last night, from the walk and from the long-anticipated shock of meeting Ben. I think that may have made me overestimate my difficulties. If I keep working, I can cope with Ben's proximity a mile or two away, with the chance of seeing him again once or twice – even with the event. He will not be here for long. The important thing is to let nothing interrupt the steady concentration of work – neither the distraction of Ben's presence nearby, nor the aching of old wounds.

I knew, after all, when I undertook this work on courtly love, how much my understanding of the subject owed to what I myself had felt. And if such feelings have not withered in me as completely as I believed, if there is still vital growth in them, here and there, ready to be renewed, then perhaps they need not be merely disruptive. Properly handled – accepted, understood, used – may they not provide fresh material for the work in hand: green wood, live and tough, to bend to my purpose? Or if such raw feeling is not to distort the whole frame of the work, must it be left to season, to dry out with time, before it is put to use? Is this as true of criticism as it is of poetry? I don't know.

If I could perhaps retrieve that early moment of serenity? There was a kind of un-acquisitive content, and a lightness, in both senses – the counteraction both of gravity and of darkness; but only the echo of a flight, the reflection of a reflection.

Thursday, 26th February

8pm

It is ten days since I wrote that last entry, and Ben has neither telephoned nor come to the cottage. He could have rung this afternoon, I suppose, or a week ago at the same time: he would hardly remember which day I usually do the shopping. But if he really wants to talk to me or to see me, he will try again – he would have tried again.

It is becoming very difficult to work. I don't think I can go straight on through Sunday; and yet last Sunday, when I didn't work, was the worst day of all. Shall I take Saturday off instead, and go into Harchester? I could look up George Frewin and discover his views about joining the Dictionary Committee. And I need some new towels. If there's time, I could see what I can find out about the Education Department: they might have a handbook or a prospectus, or something of the kind.

Saturday, 28th February

7pm

'If there's time' was disingenuous. I went to the Department first, as I had known I would. They had quite a sensible prospectus, and some leaflets on various practical enterprises and experiments they are running. The leaflets have titles like 'Career Options in Special Education' and 'Mother Tongue? Multi-Linguistic Potential in Ethnic Minorities', but I am struck by the humanity and intelligence of the contents. And some of the projects they describe seem to involve work of the kind Ben is looking for – or near enough to it, at least, to make it worth passing the leaflets on to him.

I could post them; I cannot go round. I can't go tomorrow, anyway: to visit the house on Sunday afternoon would be too close to inviting myself to Sunday lunch, or at least to suggesting that I should have liked to be invited. And there is a good deal to be done in the garden.

~~Monday~~

Tuesday, 3rd March

2.40am

I can't sleep. It doesn't matter. I have slept too much already today. But I'd rather get up and write something than lie with no defences against my thoughts.

I got nothing done in the garden after all. ~~Yesterday~~ Sunday morning's work went so badly that I had to use most of the rest of the day to finish it. Having worked on after supper, I slept uneasily, but I woke this morning knowing that I was going to take the leaflets round to Ben in the afternoon: it seemed so inevitable that there was nothing to be gained by disputing it. At least it concentrated my mind in the morning. In the last hour or so of work, I began to feel an ache of fatigue in my head and eyes, but I did not let it delay me: if I finished in good time, I could walk to

445

the Graysons, rather than driving: fresh air was probably what I needed.

I lunched early, with little appetite, and set out across the fields. It was a cold day, with a grey glare between the thicker masses of the cloud, and before I was halfway it was becoming difficult to look into the light. I took off a glove as I crossed the last field, and held my cold hand over my forehead for a moment.

As I stood at the Graysons' door, I did the same with the other hand before I knocked. It was Ruth who opened to me. She said something welcoming and unsurprised, and I said something ill-expressed about having come to see Ben, but being glad to see her. She told me that Ben was away, being interviewed for a job. She asked me in; and the chance to sit down seemed to be worth the necessity of talking.

We went into the kitchen, and Ruth offered me lunch. I realised that I must have arrived inconsiderately early, probably not long after one, though I could not bear to focus on the face of my watch. She countered my apologies with hers: would I forgive her finishing her own lunch while we drank our coffee?

She put the kettle on, and we had begun a few exchanges about Bridget and the weather when she looked up from an apple she was peeling, and said, 'Are you all right, Alan?'

'Yes, I'm all right, thank you.'

She looked unconvinced.

'I got a bit of a headache, working this morning.'

'More than a bit, isn't it, by the way you're sitting? Is coffee the right thing? Would tea be better? Milk? Would you like to lie down?'

'No, no. I'll be all right.'

But I leaned my head on my hand as I spoke, her kindness and perception undoing my resistance. Sickness and shivering ran up and over me, and bitterness came into my mouth from my throat.

'It's a migraine?'

I nodded.

'I didn't know you got those. Is there anything you usually take?'

'Just aspirin or something.'

'And that works?'

'A bit. I haven't had anything like this recently, as a matter of fact.'

'And when you did – ?'

'I'd just lie down until it went away.'

'Much the best thing, I expect. The spare room bed's made up: you can be quite quiet there, and you won't be in anyone's way.'

I tried to protest, and insist on going home, but without conviction. Speaking jolted my head. She led me upstairs, turned back the cover of a bed, and brought hot milk and a chemist's white box of pills before I had finished taking off my shoes.

'It's two at a time, I think. They're just painkillers. James had them for a tooth.'

I took them from her without argument.

'You'll be all right? I've got to go out a bit later. There's nothing else?'

'Nothing, thanks.'

'I should stay there, then. If I've gone before you leave, just slam the front door when you go. Stay there as long as you like: have a sleep if you can.' She went out, and I swallowed the pills with difficulty, drank a little of the milk, and lay down on the cool, tidy bed.

The pain returned violently after a minute or two, then slackened a little as I lay still. I remembered that this had been Ben's room when he was younger. I began to drift into sleep.

I woke out of great depths of sleep, to a darker room. There was an eiderdown and a bedspread over me, and I was evenly warm, my limbs slackened deep into the bedclothes below me, and yet drifting and weightless. The house was completely quiet. The pain was gone from my head, at least while I lay there. It was not really dark yet: there was plenty of time before I should start home. There was no more work to do today; even tomorrow could be a holiday, after a headache of this severity. There were things to do in the garden.

After a time I held my wrist out into the dim line of light that came between the curtains, and looked at my watch. It was a little before five. Perhaps I should be getting home.

I sat up gradually and felt a weight swing in my head. It swung back more heavily as I put my legs over the side of the bed, and bent to find my shoes. My skull ached and tightened, and sent a shifting pain behind my eyes. I must take more time, if the headache was not to begin again – more time, and more aspirin. Every four hours was the usual prescription. I thought it would be about three-and-a-half, and that would have to do.

I drew back one curtain, and looked about for the box of pills. The mug of milk was still by the bed, but the pills were not beside it. They were not on the chest of drawers, and the nearer top drawer was empty; the further drawer had only a cardboard box, pushed to the back. I pulled it forward: it was half-full of letters, stored on edge, the unevenly opened tops of their envelopes uppermost. In the empty space beside them, there was something, but it was only a folded handkerchief. I turned the box and saw the front of the first envelope: it was addressed to Ben in my own handwriting. The envelopes were almost all of a size. I looked through them, and found that they were all from me.

So he had kept my letters. But not in his own room. With the sense of detachment from the rules of right behaviour which illness and half-light, among other things, can bring, I opened the other drawers, each in turn. The top, long drawer was empty; the one below it was filled with clothes – mainly sweaters: the ones I could see I recognised as Ben's. I put my hand among them before I opened the bottom drawer. Half of this was neatly stacked with shirts and folded socks, also Ben's; in the other half was a miscellany of tools and papers, some maps, a camera, a clothes-brush and a torch. A cylinder of stiff papers at the back proved to be three or four posters, rolled together. There were tripos papers lying loose under the tools, several envelopes of photographs, some unwritten picture postcards from Greece, and a bundle of other cards held together by an elastic band.

I took this off: they were all cards sent to Ben for his twenty-first birthday. Mine did not seem to be among them. I looked through the pile again, opening the cards, or turning them over, to read the inscriptions – formal or affectionate or facetious – from his family and his friends. Near the bottom of the pile was a card of incongruous vulgarity: a postcard, unusually large, with a slightly unfocussed photograph of two pink roses on it; there was a drop of water, catching the light, on a petal near the camera; below this, across one corner, was written in embossed silver letters, 'To let you know I care'. On the other side, it was addressed to Ben, at the reading-party in Wales, in a literate, italic hand, and inscribed, 'Get out of that one'. It was postmarked Cambridge.

My card was not there. I had used my eyes too much: my head was beginning to ache again in earnest. I bundled the cards together, put them away, and shut the drawer. Then I went to the bathroom and groped in the medicine cabinet, with my eyes half-shut against the glare of the light. I found the pills eventually, took two more with some water, and went back to the bedroom.

Before I lay down, I looked once more at the box in the top drawer. The postcard I had sent for Ben's twenty-first birthday was standing along the side of the box, at right-angles to the letters. I took it out, and saw the Constable drawing, and the shape of the parody-sonnet on the back. I held it a moment longer in my hand, then I put it back, catching a corner in the folded handkerchief, and tipping some of the letters flat. Amoral guilt at the prospect of detection outweighed for half a minute longer the increase of pain in my head. I switched on the light and set everything straight, refolded the handkerchief, and found my own name in the corner. I shut the drawer and put off the light and lay down. The pills were taking longer, this time, to work, which was my own fault.

The handkerchief was still in my hand, beside my head, on the pillow. I did not know why it should have been among Ben's things. After some time, the pain eased again and I began to think of times I had lent him a handkerchief. I had drenched one in the stream, to bind his foot beside the gully. Hadn't he brought it back, though, next morning, dry and folded, to my room? And after the dance, when he had wept so violently. Had he kept this since then? He had not noticed it, perhaps – had thought it was one of his own. My mind was beginning to blur with sleep, but I thought that then he would have kept it with his own, not separately, not in a box with my letters.

I woke quite suddenly, in the dark, with a clear head. I was still holding the handkerchief: it was against my cheek. I sat up and put it in my pocket. Then I put on my shoes, and straightened the bed, took up the mug, and went downstairs to the hall. There was a line of light under the drawing-room door. If anyone was at home, I ought to say that I was going. I hoped it was Ruth: if it was James, I should have to explain myself. I put the mug down and ran a hand over my hair; then I knocked and went in. Ben was sitting by the fire, writing a letter.

He looked up, and said, '*Alan*? I didn't hear you.'

'I didn't know you were here. You were away: your mother said you were away.'

'I had an interview, but I got back. Obviously.' He smiled, not quite certainly.

'Obviously. How did it go?'

'Pretty well, I think. I wondered why the door wasn't locked.'

'I was just going home. Ruth had to go out. She said I should slam the door.'

'Yes, I see.' His voice implied the opposite.

'She said I might wait a little – rest a bit – before I went back.'

'You'd walked a long way?'

'Not really. I was – . I came over to see – . I saw your mother, and then I wasn't feeling very well, temporarily, and she suggested I should stay and rest a bit and let myself out. She had to go out. I thought – I didn't realise there was anyone in the house.'

'You had a headache? One of your migraines?'

'Something of the sort.'

'Is it all right now?'

'Yes.'

'You're sure?'

'Really. I've been asleep for – for hours.'

'Good. I should think you'd like a cup of tea.'

It was what I wanted above all.

'Or sherry or something?'

'Tea would be excellent. If it's not too much trouble?'

'How much trouble is a pot of tea? No, you stay there, won't you? Sit down. I won't be long.'

He switched off the bright light above his chair, and went across the glow of the fire to turn on a fainter one behind me. I sat, when he had gone out, in a kind of peaceful suspension: my body blessedly beyond the pain, but not yet fully returned to the sense of its own weight and use; my mind in a lucent, expectant vacancy.

Ben came back with a tray, put it down, and poured out a large cup of tea for me.

'Thank you so much. Oh, that's good.'

'What you needed?' He smiled.

'How was the interview?' I asked after a moment.

'It was – . Look, do you want to talk? I could put some music on. Or you could just sit and drink your tea. I've got a letter to write.'

'It's all right. Thank you, but I'll be all right. And I'd like to hear about the interview. Unless you ought to finish your letter.'

'That can wait – ' he hesitated.

'I'll let you know if it's too much.'

'As long as you do.' He filled up my cup. 'Well, it was fairly good, I think,' he said, sitting down. 'The kind of thing I'm looking for, and they were reasonably encouraging.'

'About giving you a job?'

'Quite possibly. And about my getting one somewhere, anyway.'

'Where was it?'

'Leeds.'

'Leeds. I see.' I moved my hand towards my pocket, then picked up my cup instead. 'What would you be doing?'

'Co-ordinating, mostly. Planning programmes, visiting schools in the area, that sort of thing. Sorting out problems.'

'And that's what you want?'

'More or less. Not enough teaching, that was the only thing. And they weren't very hopeful about giving me more. I suppose one has to start somewhere.'

'Have you tried anywhere else?'

'There's somewhere near Cambridge. That would be great.'

'That would be – a pleasanter part of the world, anyway.'

'Yes. Though that's not the whole thing.'

'No. Of course – '

'Or I'd apply at Eton – '

I smiled, but he did not look up.

'Near Cambridge. I didn't know there were many immigrants up there.'

'Not so many. But in some patches – over towards Bedford and Stevenage. And then the gypsies round Newmarket. It's a pretty big area. I've seen some of the schools: it would be great.'

'You'd get some teaching?'

'Three days a week. And one day going round the schools. Primary as well as secondary. I'd love it. And the fifth day planning and writing reports and so on. I'd just have to be on the telephone. I could be at home.'

'You'd be living here?'

'To start with. I'd find somewhere of my own in the end, I expect. But I could still come back for the weekend; the Friday, too, probably.'

'What's the pay like?'

'Terrible.' He laughed. 'But I don't think I'm going to get it, anyway. Too many people in for it; people with experience over here – Manchester, Brixton. Oh well.'

We were both silent, thinking of the possibility. Then he said suddenly, 'Would you give me a reference?'

'Ben – of course I would.'

'Thank you.'

'I'd always do that. You must have known – '

'I wasn't sure. But you did say, would I have good references.'

'And those American eulogies aren't enough?'

'I'll need – they ask you for someone who's known you a long time.'

'I have done that.'

'Yes.'

There was another silence. I wanted to say that I knew how well he would do such work, and that I should be glad to vouch for it. I wanted to tell him how admirable I found it. But I could find no words to do it without apparent condescension.

Ben got up and went across the room; he looked through a shelf of gramophone records, and put one on.

'That's the Double Violin Concerto?'

'I imagine you still like Bach?'

'This, especially.'

It was, after all, a relief to have stopped talking. We listened in silence. Once, at the start of the second movement, Ben shook his head with a kind of delighted disbelief that it could still be so excellent. When the last movement ended, he smiled, sat for a moment longer, thinking, and then went to take the record off. He chose another from the shelf.

'Madrigals?'

'Lovely.'

'The first three on this side are David – his group. I think they're very good.'

They were good – among the best. While we listened to the second side, Ben took up his pen and paper and went on with his letter. I sat and watched him. We had been able to work like this before – in the same room, not intruding on one another's peace. At least, I did not seem to be an intrusion on his; he was my peace, at the moment. I thought I had not been so happy for a very long time. It was almost certainly at the expense of greater unhappiness later on: I knew that, but it was beyond consideration.

By the time the last madrigal began I knew, though, that I must say something if this luminous serenity, this reflection of past peace together, were not to grow like a bubble into something too great for the present – swell out, too widely stretched, and shatter dangerously into emotion or disastrous candour. Ben folded his letter and put it into an airmail envelope, and addressed it.

'David's doing well,' I said. 'That's a recent record?'

'Fairly. He brought it over when he came to New York. He's done a couple since, but I still like these almost best. The second one, particularly.'

'The tragic one?'

'Yes. Heart-breaking.' He stamped the letter and put it down beside his chair. 'Well, I suppose that's something he knows about.'

'He – but he's all right, isn't he? He's not unhappy?'

'Not now; far from it. But before – unhappy enough. Before he made the record, I mean.' He considered for a moment, then he said, 'I think it has to be, doesn't it? It has to be over – whatever you've felt – before you can use it like that?'

'I think perhaps it does.'

'And yet for anyone else – just listening to it – it doesn't matter: it can be great – it can even help – while you're still in the thick of it.'

'Yes.'

'Funny.'

He looked slightly uneasy, as if he had taken the subject too far.

'David had to wait,' I said, 'wait some time, I think, before his love was returned?'

'Quite a time. And even before that, he wasn't sure, for a bit, he even ought to ask for it. His – the other person – was very young.'

'Quite right.'

'I suppose so. Yes. Yes, it was. But it was fairly hard. He'd done a good deal of waiting already in his life, hanging around – hoping – '

'That was for Julian Foster?'

It was unwise – as a question, as an admission – but the choice of subject was not entirely mine. Ben, too, seemed to be wanting to tread near the dangerous edge of confidence.

'Julian? Yes, but that was ages before. At Cambridge, just at the beginning. It was after that, too.'

'And before this boy in London? There was someone else?'

'Someone else?'

'Isn't that what you meant?'

'You never knew?'

'We never talked of such things. Except once, much later on. Otherwise, I really only saw him with you. And then when – and then later – there would have been no way of knowing.'

'So you never realised.'

'What?'

Had I been wrong about their friendship all along? Had David been in love with Ben? Was Ben trying to tell me this? And even that, later on, they had been lovers? But then – I looked up and found Ben looking at me. It was not the look of a lover, nor yet of a beloved, revealing a past love. It was direct, serious, surprised – even sceptical.

'I thought you must have known, in the end.'

'You mean – ? Oh, my God.'

He was silent while I tried to digest this. I shut my eyes and shook my head. When I looked at him again, his expression was rather less sceptical, though no less serious.

'Oh, my God. Poor David. And I was really as insensitive, as stupid, as that?'

'You aren't usually,' Ben said, not wholly reassuringly.

'I wish you'd told me.'

'How could I?'

'Yes. How could you? Oh dear.'

'There was nothing you could have done.'

'No, but – '

'At least, I don't think there was.' He sounded almost hopeful.

'No.'

'No,' he repeated, with a note of finality.

'But if I'd known, I suppose – '

'He was desperately careful that you shouldn't.'

'Yes, I suppose so. I suppose one usually is.'

'Yes.'

'How long did this go on?'

'Quite long. A couple of years, at least. Maybe a bit more.'

'Yes, quite long. At his age, that's quite long.'

He waited, still watching me seriously.

'Ben, I am very sorry about this. I didn't mean it to happen. But it did happen, and it must have made David very unhappy, and I think I ought to have realised. If I hadn't been so wrapped up in my own – in work – in myself – '

'Well, but you didn't hurt him intentionally.'

It was somewhere between a statement and a question.

'*Intentionally?*' I looked across at Ben, and his expression sent my indignation veering round, with hateful recollection, to myself.

We stared at each other, our faces beginning to burn.

'I do that very rarely,' I said at last. 'And when I do, I regret it: most bitterly, and permanently, and without relief.'

There was a very long silence. Then Ben said, 'I know.'

I could not look at him any longer.

'I know,' he said again, rather sadly. 'I've known for a long time – all along, perhaps – that you regretted it, what we said to each other that last time, in my room – wished you hadn't said it – wanted to take it back, but somehow you couldn't.'

If I answered, I might not be able to contain my tears.

'I should have said – '

'*You* should have said? Oh, Ben – ' I put my head into my hands.

'I know. I went through the motions. I could tell myself I'd tried. But I didn't say what would have made all the difference: that I knew you were sorry about it, too. I didn't want to get in any deeper. Because I was afraid of you, partly, of what you might still say. But more, really, because I was still angry, and I wanted to go on being angry.'

'You had cause to be.'

'No cause. Not enough.'

I was afraid that my tears would begin to run through my fingers.

I heard him get up and come over to where I was sitting.

'I shouldn't have brought it all up. Not tonight. Not when you've not been well.'

'I love you. I have loved you for nearly nine years,' I wanted to say. 'Longer: since you were a child.' But I didn't – thank heavens, I suppose. I sat bowed in my chair, and let the tears go on running into the palms of my hands, and down my wrists on the inside.

I felt Ben touch my shoulder. 'Alan. Ah, now, Alan.'

'I'm sorry,' I managed to say after a time. 'It's just – it's been on my mind for some time.'

'Yes.' He stood beside me a little longer, and then went away across the room. I struggled to stop my tears, feeling in my pocket for a handkerchief, finding the one which had been in Ben's drawer, putting it back quickly, and searching until I found another.

Ben was coming back across the room with two glasses. He handed me one. I took it from him with a moderately steady hand, and sniffed at it.

'Brandy?'

'Yes.'

'It's as bad as that?'

He smiled. 'I'm having some, too.'

He did not return to his chair, but stood where he was, looking down at me as he drank. After some time, he said, 'I shouldn't feel too badly about David, you know. He survived, and he's happy; it's all over. And he's a bloody good singer.'

'Yes.'

'And you did a lot for him. He valued your friendship very much – still does – quite apart from … . He's often said how much you've helped him – talked to him. It's not all bad, being in love.'

'Never?'

'As long as … Well, there are people who aren't worth it. Then it's not so good. But loving someone who is worth it – . Then, even if it doesn't work out – even the unhappiness – can be something one doesn't regret, I think. A net gain.'

'Maybe.'

'Isn't it in the *Symposium*? That admiration of goodness – of a good man – can inspire excellence?'

'Something like that.'

'And admiration is very close to love, surely? Have you never felt that? How attractive – I mean, actually, erotically attractive – goodness can be? Among other things – ?' He stopped. 'More brandy?'

'No thanks.'

He shook his head, smiling.

'I think you must be the only person in the world who's not in the least gratified to find that someone's been in love with you.

457

No-one else could help triumphing a *bit*, however sorry they were: gloating a little, at least.'

I laughed.

'Well, there you are then,' he said. 'How could anyone – ?' He looked at his glass, then stretched to put it down, carefully, on the mantlepiece. 'It's too long since lunch. Shall we have something to eat?'

'What about your parents? I really ought to be going.'

'They're out to dinner. There's no rush. For me, at least.'

'Nor for me, really.'

We took our glasses through into the kitchen, and laid the table there, and Ben made a large pan of scrambled egg, and toasted some bread and grilled some tomatoes to go with it. It was all very good, and we were both hungry. I had the appetite of returned well-being, and Ben had had nothing since breakfast, he said, but 'a rather dead sort of sandwich' on the train.

We talked a little more about his job, and about his travels in America, and he asked me about my work. Still avoiding too specific a description of my present subject, I mentioned the Cycle, and he told me that he had bought the verse translation in New York.

'I really ought to read it in the original, I know.'

'This isn't a bad approximation. Douglas and I did it ourselves, in the end.'

'I know, and it's very good.' He looked younger for a moment, flushing. 'I mean, I enjoyed it. As a translation, the scholarship – for that, I take you on trust.'

I laughed. 'I'm glad it reads well. And the pace is important, I think. That North-Midland dialect can be slow, if you're out of practice.'

'Or were never in. Still, I'll read it one day. Just then, I didn't have the cash.'

'It is expensive.'

'I hope it made you lots of money?'

When we had finished and cleared up, I said I must go home. 'I'll run you back.'

'No, please. I'd like the walk, the fresh air.'

After a moment's pause, he said, 'Then I'll come with you.'

We walked for a time without talking. The night was less cold than the day had promised, or perhaps I felt it less. The wind seemed quite warm.

We went round by the postbox with Ben's letter.

'One more done, at least,' he said, as we turned back towards the field-gate.

'You've had a lot to write – about the job?'

'That, yes. And various people in the States.'

'You made a good many friends over there.'

'A good many, I suppose. One or two, particularly.'

'You shared a flat with friends, I think Ruth said.'

'Yes. Though that … Oh well. But it was through them – one of them – I met quite a lot of people from City College.'

'They'd be about your own age?'

'About. Graduate students, mostly. And then there were people at PS. 97 – at the school.'

'They were congenial, too?'

'Some of them.' We turned through the gate and walked on along the headland. 'One or two. It's extraordinary, really – an extraordinary profession. They can be such a job lot, teachers, and then there'll be one or two – '

I waited.

'There was one. I've never seen anything like it. The wildest children, the most disturbed – a few of them could really be hell – and what he felt for them, what he'd *do* for them – when I'd have given up; I did, pretty well, sometimes. But he never would, ever. And the children – because of that, I suppose; because they somehow realised it – they trusted him: they'd go to him.'

'Extraordinary. And inimitable, really, I suppose.'

'Really, yes. It's not something you can *copy*, or just pick up a couple of tips on. But if you worked with him – . I worked with him some of the time, and he'd come and help me, sometimes, when things were really rough. I learned a tremendous lot from him like that.'

'About what to do?'

'About the children: what it was like being them; what we were trying to do; what it was all for. But really, I found out that to handle some of the problems, you have to *be* like that – like him. Girls of twelve thrown out for being pregnant; children mixed up with drugs; abused by their parents – sexually, sometimes. There aren't specific things to say, or even do: it's what you are – what you've been, up till then.'

'I think I can understand that. Not easy to achieve, though.'

'No.'

We were silent.

'He was – this was one of the friends in your flat?'

'Oh, no: lord, no. He was a good deal older. He was married; I don't think very happily, but – no, he was just a colleague. Though in the end, perhaps – I think he'd have said he was a friend.'

Again, I waited, and after a little time he went on. 'Whatever he was, you could always go to him. I went to him once – more than once – in a bad patch.'

'A bad patch in your teaching?'

'That anyway. But – that and other things. We were very close, in a way. I felt very close. But with him – I suppose it was a professional thing really. He'd do anything – really *anything* – for someone in trouble: stay up night after night, stop a knife-fight, take on City Hall. But there was always a bit – something separate; a bit of your life, your privacy, that you didn't let other people in on. I suppose there had to be.'

'I suppose so. Otherwise – '

'Otherwise you'd go crazy.'

'Yes.'

'I did think, once – I thought I'd got through. Once when he was shaken; he hardly ever was. And I tried to help and listen. And he said – oh, well. But then – oh well; never mind.'

We walked on, and after a few minutes Ben said more easily, 'It's all right though, now. He's still a friend. I really think he is, in a sense. I've written to him – just news. If only Americans ever wrote letters.'

'I know.'

'Well, if he doesn't, it doesn't matter so very much, now. I'll see him if I go over; he'll still be there, doing the same work. I like to think of it – of him, doing it. But I won't – I don't *mind*.'

There was a long pause. Where the headland narrowed, we went in single file for some way, Ben leading; at one point, he stumbled, and I caught his elbow to steady him.

When we had crossed the hedge at the corner, and could walk abreast again, I said, 'What you were doing – you and your friend – what you'll be doing here: I do find it very admirable. Teaching of that kind – as well as being so immensely, so extraordinarily demanding, I mean – it seems to me it's the essential – the heart of the matter – what teaching really should be. I can't tell you how much I respect it.'

'Really?' His face was turned towards me. 'You approve? Really?'

'A good deal more than approve.'

'I'm glad.'

We were nearly home, and we crossed the last field in a lighter silence. It was steeper than I expected; I thought Ben slowed his pace to mine. When we were a few yards from the hedge of the garden, there was a little shadowy movement ahead, and Panope ran over the plough to meet us. I stopped, and she put her forepaws on my foot, rubbed her head against my leg, and then sprang up, as I stooped, into my down-stretched hands.

'Hello.'

'There's a welcome,' said Ben.

'You ought to be asleep,' I said, tickling her head.

'Business of Egypt, I suppose.'

'What's that?'

'Hunting – poaching. I think it's what the gypsies call it.'

'So you've been hunting, have you?'

'Or she just wanted to see you home safe.' He turned and stroked Panope, where she lay across my shoulder. 'So this is the kitten?'

'The cat, now, very nearly. You knew, then – ?'

'Oh. Well. I think Marky mentioned it. David – . Yes, I knew. She is very pretty.'

He looked down at her again, but our eyes met on the way, and even in that shadowy light I saw that he had known before. I smiled and, looking up again, he smiled too.

We turned and walked up towards the house. At the hedge, by the elms, we stopped.

Panope dropped from my shoulder and trotted on through the gap and into the garden. For a moment I thought it might be possible to suggest that Ben should stay.

'Well,' he said, 'you've got company now. I must be getting back.'

'Yes. Of course you must. It was good of you to come so far.'

'I'm glad I did.'

'Thank you so much. And thank you for supper – for tea – brandy – '

'You're welcome. Very welcome.'

There was a pause. The trees' shadows made it darker where we stood.

'As for the other thing,' Ben said, and stopped, and then, 'As for that – what we said to each other – before I left.' He stopped again. I wanted to speak, but could find no way of doing so. At last he went on, 'For that: if you can forgive me – '

'If – . Oh, my dear Ben – '

He held out his hands, and I took them in mine. 'Ben, that's not for me to do: there's nothing for me to forgive. If you can – if you ever can – it's for you to forgive me.'

'I know. It's all right. We both know.'

The grasp of his hands closed tighter, and then of mine. Then he let go. 'It is all right?'

'Yes. Yes, I think it is.'

We stood near each other in silence.

'Alan – then – goodnight.'

'Goodnight.'

'I'm glad your headache's better.'

He turned back into the field, and I came across the garden and into the house.

Since then I have been in a state of happiness far too high for sleep. It was against this – and against hope and excitement –

that I needed defence as I lay awake. I must keep them under control: to let myself rejoice beyond the bounds of reason, to construct sequels of impossible delight, is to invite disaster. But we have talked, really talked, as we used to. Almost as we used to. There is still something guarded in what Ben says (*a fortiori* in what he doesn't say). But then he has more, now, to be guarded about.

He has felt strongly since he last told me what he felt: has been in love, I think. And if he did not want to talk of this in so many words, still he said enough – and chose to say it – to let me know something of the nature and strength of his feeling. There is cause for jealousy here, as well as for happiness, I suppose. And yet it does not disturb me very much – at the moment, anyway. I am too old to think, even in the remotest, most ridiculous fantasy, of rivalling such heroism. But I think perhaps Ben is too old – or soon will be – for such hero-worship, however well-justified, to content him. I think he was saying something of the kind: 'It doesn't matter so very much, now... I don't *mind.*'

He has told me enough of what he felt in this case; and even something of what he might later be capable of feeling. If I am right about that love (and of course I am right: his voice, in the dark, his hesitations) then has his old terror of that side of his affections – of that direction for his love – been exorcised? (Exorcised by that good man? I should like to meet him.) He was a married man; his friendship was the most Ben hoped for (could hope for) in return. What Ben's attitude might be to someone who reciprocated his own feelings is not so certain.

There was something between him and his flatmates – one of them, anyway – which made his voice more wary, for a moment almost bitter, as he changed his mind about the direction of the conversation. And before that: 'There are people who aren't worth it. Then it's not so good.' Was that another part of the strain I have seen in his face? Is he still suspicious of homosexual love, offered directly, in its own name? Is he even unaware, still, or not fully aware, of the homosexual nature of his own love? Is he capable – *Ben?* – of such self-deception? And am I capable of such arrogance? How many years did I take to acknowledge, without reservation, the nature of my feelings? And must I, anyway, subscribe to the facile modern belief that the sexual element is the 'real', the defining part of any relationship? Even my own love, which is certainly sexual, is many other things as well. Many Victorians refused to acknowledge any such feeling in their own highest loves. What mixture of presumption and prurience makes us so certain that they were always wrong, factually or morally? Ben must think what he likes about his love.

If only I knew for certain – even a little more certainly – what he would like. Was I wrong – could I have been right? – in hearing a suggestion, – an implication, very faint, – running through an earlier part of the conversation, that he might have felt something of the kind for me? He broke off once – twice? – as if the brandy, on an empty stomach, was making him say too much. But he had said already that what was admired as goodness could be erotically attractive.

Could anyone be as magnanimous as that? To have seen such goodness, to have felt such admiration in the first place, would be generous enough – far enough beyond my desert. But to remember it, to give credit for it still, after what I have done, the way I have treated him – .

And yet he has forgiven me, and given me the opportunity, the right – undeserved, and yet necessary – to forgive him. And it wasn't the easy, blanketing, unsatisfactory forgiveness of oblivion, the dutiful 'let's say no more about it', leaving resentment unresolved. He told me – he let me know – what cruelty he knew I was capable of. Though he took so much – so extravagantly much – of the shame to himself, he left me enough to pierce through to what I had done to him, to let us both see it, and see what I felt about it, without pretence, and both forgive it.

It is almost dawn. I have just drawn back one of the curtains: the line of the field is more certain against the sky.

I'm getting hungry. Perhaps I'll make some coffee. There should be some biscuits, I think. Panope is asleep by the Aga; she'll be delighted to see me in the kitchen at this hour. I suppose she can have some milk, as long as she doesn't think we're going to make a habit of it. I could probably sleep now. Breakfast might be better than coffee. I can sleep on afterwards. (Today was to be a holiday, wasn't it?)

Reading over the last few pages, I think I had certainly better stop, before I start writing even more roughly and disjointedly. I can hardly say that tonight's entry is written with the full rigour of my faculties. Time for bed, then. I haven't lain in such happiness, to wait for sleep, for a very long time. There are so many other, smaller causes for it, too, only I'm too sleepy to put them down in full. Too superstitious, too, perhaps. We have been silent together, as well as talking: we can still do that. And I have managed to tell him (however awkwardly) how much I respect his work: he was pleased about that. He may even – it's just possible he may – get a job in this area. Live at home, or somewhere nearby. (I never did give him those leaflets. Better so.) He knew about Panope. Could he have instigated the plan? Is she Ben's present – a token of – what? His affection? His concern?

And he has read the Cycle – in translation, anyway; our translation.

10.40pm

I must try not to be too happy. I slept well into the middle of the morning, had an early lunch (or a second breakfast), and spent the rest of the day in the garden. It's been a day of sun and cloud and wind. I've worked hard and got a lot done. I feel no urgent need to see Ben again. A sense of him has remained with me all day – coming back to me again and again, with memory, from different points in the garden: the path from the gate (which will soon need weeding) and the rose-bush spreading over it, too far; the first shoots from the bulbs I planted out, when they had flowered, from the pots he filled for me, and kept reminding me to water – narcissus and hyacinth, mostly, and some scyllas, and one clump of golden crocus (but he would not tell me what they were going to be: I had to wait until they came up); and the snowdrops and crocuses he found, under a tangle of grass, before a Latin lesson, while I was getting the tea.

I am comfortably sleepy, in spite of my late rising. I think I should be able to get the section on Chrétien de Troyes into shape tomorrow.

Friday, 6th March

I suppose I should wait for Ben to come and see me. I should like to see him; I want to know about the job; there are plenty of good and openly admissible reasons for walking over there. But he is not indifferent to seeing me, either. I know that now; and perhaps I should let him make the next move; perhaps I should wait. I think it's common prudence.

I ought to admit that it is also a kind of test. By coming of his own accord, he will confirm my sense of communication restored and friendship recovered – show beyond doubt that it is real and mutual, not private or illusory.

And if he doesn't come? That will be a test of another kind. I must not let myself forget – I have known all along – that this is all a bonus, an extra, uncovenanted joy, like the warmth in the air or the iris leaves coming up under the wall: something to enjoy but not to depend on. I am not going to stop working if the irises come up blind, or the spring turns cold. I must not allow my relation to Ben to determine the pattern of my life. If I let this present happiness become the basis for serious hope, or prediction, then that hope may become the basis of my life. And that must not happen. If he does not come, I must leave it there. But I think he will come, probably.

Sunday, 8th March

6.45pm

I have spent this morning, and a good part of this afternoon, writing a reference for Ben. It is extraordinarily difficult to convey enough, without conveying too much (to his prospective employer and in fact, of course, still more to him). I haven't got it right yet. But it gives me great happiness to be writing it. I'm glad I didn't start last night, when I remembered it. (And how did I come to forget it? Through that treacherous tendency to oversteer, I suppose, which comes of navigating against the current of one's instinct.) It was too late, then, to do it – or enjoy it – properly, and I left it till today: a good use of the time, if I was to take Sunday off from work – and leaving something to look forward to for the rest of Saturday evening and the beginning of the night.

So today I have been putting down, openly, definitely, in words, and for Ben's practical benefit, some, at least, of the qualities I have so long loved in him. Or I shall have put them down, when the words are right.

I should be able to finish it this evening, or tomorrow afternoon at the latest; and then I must get it to him. (I hope it's not too late? He would have telephoned, surely, if he had needed it?) It gives me a reason – an unexceptionable one, on both sides – for getting (or 'being', as Ben would say now) in touch with him again. But I won't take it round. I can send it by the last post tomorrow, at the latest. Will that perhaps seem unfriendly? Not with a covering note.

9.iii.1971

My dear Ben,

I enclose the reference I promised you. I hope it is not too late, and is the kind of thing you want. I have avoided the panegyric style (since you say you have plenty of that) – perhaps to the point of understatement.

It was good to see you last week, and I was very grateful for your hospitality and all your other kindness. I hope to see you again before too long.

With love.

Yours ever,

Alan.

(sent by 4 o'c. post.)

Thursday, 12th March

Many thanks for the reference – just what I needed, except too complimentary. Just off for two more interviews in the North.
  In haste, B

[Postcard. Received this morning.]

Thursday, 19th March

4.30pm

I don't know how much longer my resolution will hold. The weekend was tolerable: I had various things to do, and Ben's absence in the north gave me a rest both from hope and from anxiety. But Bridget and Charles came in late on Sunday afternoon, in the course of a walk, and when I enquired, over a glass of sherry, what Ben was doing, they told me that he was expected back that evening. That was four days ago, and there has been no word from him.

Since our last meeting, well over two weeks ago now, I have had nothing but his perfunctory acknowledgement of the reference. I don't know what to do – or rather, whether I can go on doing it. I wish there wasn't still most of a bottle of sherry in the house. It seems melodramatic to pour it away, as well as a waste of money; and I should have nothing to offer anyone who came in. At least there's no whisky. I am not going to drink anything – anything alcoholic – unless someone else is with me.

I'm going to make a pot of tea now. If I can't get on with the *Roman de la Rose*, I'll type up what I did last week. There isn't a great deal of it: I should get it finished by supper. It will be all right. I have managed before.

Friday, 20th March

5.30pm

Typing is a soothing, steadying activity on the whole (except when I have to put in a new ribbon). It occupies quite a lot of one's mind, much of the time, especially if there are still changes to consider. I rather wish I hadn't finished this stint.

I got to sleep in the end, last night, and woke suddenly, quite early, and thought that it is Ben's birthday very soon. On Monday, I think. The Press were as tight-fisted as usual about complimentary copies, but there should be one copy of the Cycle left. It's his, anyway – it's all really his, dedicated to him, privately but inalienably, for many years now. If I can't find that copy (it's on the landing, isn't it? – still in its packing, on the bottom shelf) or if it's not in good condition, there won't be time to send to the Press with a cheque for another one. I could look in Harchester tomorrow. But that would take a good part of the day, and might be fruitless. The real reason for my reluctance is that I am superstitiously alarmed by so close and ominous a parallel.

9.10pm

It was there, on the landing, and in perfect condition, as far as I can see. I must find a quotation for the flyleaf – of the first volume, anyway. (I can't think he'll use the volume of notes very much, except the glossary; but I'd like him to have it. I might initial it, perhaps.)

Something in *Abraham and Isaac*? – let's see – 78? Or *Magi*? 149? Or something from *Peter*? Yes – 287 – 288. That's it.

To send this by post would be absurd. I shall take it over on Monday (unless he has come here by then, or telephoned). With that prospect, the weekend's waiting should not be too difficult.

Tuesday, 24th March

I allowed a little longer for the walk, with the two heavy volumes of *The Cycle*, and reached the Graysons when it would be easy, not obligatory, for them to ask me to stay to tea.

James opened the door to me; and, when I explained the reason for my visit, he admitted that the family had celebrated Ben's birthday the day before, when Bridget and Charles could be there.

'But I know he'll be delighted to see you. And I think there's still some birthday cake left.'

I smiled. 'Any news of a job?'

'Nothing definite yet. I think he has quite a few irons in the fire. He seems to have a real feeling for it – these young tearaways: it's extraordinary.'

'Yes. He's found his calling, I think.'

'All rather depressing places they seem to do this sort of thing, though. And rather far away. Oh, well. They have to live their own lives.'

'Of course,'

'I don't know if there might be anything round Harchester: the teacher-training place? Do you see anything of the people there?'

The leaflets were still in my pocket. After a moment's indecision I gave them to James, and he looked through them.

'These are just the sort of thing, aren't they? Could Ben get hold of them somewhere?'

'I got those for him. Do keep them – give them to him.'

'Won't you?' He handed them back. 'Parents – you know. And it's more your line of country – '

Unconvinced, but unable to say so, I returned them to my pocket.

We joined Ruth and Mark as they carried tea and half a birthday cake into the drawing-room. And when Ben came in, a few moments later, I wished him many happy returns and gave him the parcel. I felt some caution mingled with his thanks – and before that, too, when he came into the room: his eyes suddenly more intent, his face setting, when he saw that I was there.

He was pleased with my present. He did not look at me as he sat down and started unwrapping the parcel, but when the standard Press binding showed through a gap in the paper he looked up, our eyes met, and for a moment I felt the full, unguarded warmth of gratitude and affection.

'Alan, it's – ?'

'It's the Cycle. You said – '

'Of course I did. But I didn't think – I didn't mean – '

'No, of course. I know.'

'That's marvellous.'

He turned each volume over in his hands, opened it and read what I had written on the flyleaf, smiling. Then he leafed through the text, reading here and there, until the tea was poured out and the cake was cut.

'No-one's seen the lead for my record player, have they?' Ben asked, as he moved some cards and a gramophone record closer together to make room for the two volumes on a side table.

'There were a couple of things,' Ruth said, '– one or two – that I couldn't fit in, in Marky's room. I don't think there were any gramophone bits. Anyway, they're in the spare room.'

'I'll have a look. It was great having it all organised – all shifted for me: that was the only thing I couldn't find, almost.'

Conversation became desultory. I asked Ben when he had got back from the north.

'Oh, a few days ago. Thanks so much for your reference, by the way.'

'That's all right. I got your card.'

'You haven't heard any more?' James asked him.

'Not yet. Except the Cambridgeshire place. I think I told you.'

'I don't think so. What did they say?'

'I was short-listed, but I didn't get it.'

'They must have thought well of you,' I said. 'How many were in for it?'

'A lot. Nearly thirty, I think.'

'That's pretty creditable, to be short-listed from as many as that.'

'Alan was saying there might be something round here,' said James.

'I know,' said Ben.

'But he's been looking into it. It's really very much the sort of thing – what you've been looking for.'

Ben was silent, looking down, looking even, for a moment – unhappy?

'Do you have those leaflets, Alan?' James asked.

'It was just on the chance. I picked them up – I happened to be in there – just in case they might be any use.'

Ben did not move when I pulled the leaflets out of my pocket. James took them from me and showed them to him.

'There's one – wait a minute – yes, this one. I thought –'

'Thanks,' said Ben, interrupting him and putting them in his own pocket. 'I'll look at them later.'

Not long after that, I said I must be going.

Monday, 30th March

I have not seen Ben since then. What has gone wrong? Was none of it true – that sense of friendship restored, our concern, our sympathy renewed? Our mutual forgiveness?

The obstacles that held us up, that blocked our way (though never for long) as we approached our former closeness and understanding – the awkwardness of first meeting after so long, the sometimes unnerving sense of the void just behind us, the occasional tactlessness and answering defensiveness – could they be enough to account for this negation of all that I thought (that, surely, we thought) we had felt since his return?

I wish we had not shown him the leaflets. I should have followed my instinct and kept them to myself, rather than giving them, or trying to give them, to James. I had known since we were saying goodbye on that first Sunday afternoon that something was making Ben wary of looking for work near here. There was even a hint, a gentle, half-humorous one, during our evening together, that he would resist any suggestion of working in a pleasanter or more affluent part of the country. Did he feel it as a criticism of the kind of work he had chosen to do? Even as a temptation to betray the kind of people he wanted to teach? Or was he simply made uneasy by what he saw as his family's attempt to keep him at home?

Any of these concerns might perhaps explain his cautious reaction at the start of my last visit. But even if his parents had already expressed such views more insistently, less tactfully than I should expect, could anyone – let alone anyone as unresentful as

Ben – take serious offence at my quite small and tentative contribution to the debate? Resent it so strongly that he would cut off all communication, indefinitely?

Surely not. So what has gone wrong? I don't know.

Wednesday, 1st April

I should not have let myself hope. If it were not for that, my state now would be little worse than it was two months ago – with work to do, and no great difficulty in doing it; the days following their regular pattern; the house in order; things coming up in the garden; Panope for company, and friends not too far away. My hopes and regrets about Ben, seasoned almost to harmlessness by the passage of time, would still be little more – not very much more – than internal material for *Courtly Love*. And Ben himself would be no less accessible than he was in New York.

Looking back to that evening when I came downstairs, and found Ben writing his letter by the fire, I feel chiefly an aching weight of nostalgia, limitless, overpoweringly heavy, holding within it all the other times of hope or even of tranquillity: the moments when Ben turned to me; when we recognised something in each other; the moments when I knew he was there; even the time before I knew he was there, the unregarded quiet and liberty.

How can I go on? Hope deferred maketh the heart sick. And if it is deferred for ever? Is there any way out? I must finish *Courtly Love*.

It was Ruth, then, who put the box of letters in the drawer. What does she think of Ben's reasons for keeping them, and keeping them separate? What do I think? Could he have put them aside, when he was sorting things out and packing, before he left? Put them aside, with the handkerchief, to *return* to me? And then lacked courage to do so? Or time? Well, the handkerchief has been taken back, anyway; pardonable larceny, I think. And, absurdly, it gives me some sort of comfort.

Panope is more comfort than anything else. It is I who seek her company now. She finds this surprising, sometimes, but usually accepts it, for a time at least, with grace and affection.

Perhaps I should go away. It is the indefinite prospect which is so hard to contemplate: to be here alone, without any change, any respite or limit in view at all – not even the little alleviation of visiting James and Ruth. And the term is over at Harchester.

I could stay with Douglas in London. I am not due for a holiday, but I could work in the British Museum in the mornings (or in his College library? I believe it's quite good). I could look up various friends; David, too, perhaps. (That would not be too near? Too rash? It's time I heard some music.)

Ben might come round, after I had gone, and find no-one here. And if I have not told him I'm going, or for how long – . But how can I tell him?

I can't tell him. That mistake, at least, I can avoid. I must not try to get in touch with Ben again. I can't afford this kind of thing.

I'd come back. He might. But how long is there now until he leaves home? And after that, how often will he be here? How much chance will there be, any more, of seeing him?

And I should have to ask Mrs Weaver about having Panope, or coming to look after her again. I'm not sure at the moment I can bear – I can really bring myself – to leave her. Somehow it seems, nonsensically, ungrateful, a rebuff, when she has given me all the consolation she knows how to give.

If he had got the job in Cambridgeshire (will it make things worse to put this down? Might it break the endless reiteration of hypothesis and dream and returning emptiness?) – if he had been appointed, he would have had three days a week to spend at home. I could have had the supper ready on Thursday evening, – laid it in the garden when the days got warmer. And then the three whole days.

Work on Friday, but together: I could put the table in the corner by the window for him; coffee together halfway through the morning. Time off in the afternoon – walking? Or working in the garden? (He knew long before I did how much there was to be done with this garden.) Or would he want to keep office hours? That would be for him to say. I could do the same, perhaps: find some work mindless enough for those sleepy hours in the afternoon. Then we could be free together after tea. All the evening for listening to music, reading aloud – (has he been reading Plato?) – talking.

He might want to sleep late on Saturday – the young need a good deal of sleep, sometimes, I think.

And the whole weekend still ahead. I could show him the best of the long walks; he probably has some of his own, too, to show me. Quite soon it will be the perfect time of year. One of them: October is very good, too. In the summer we could go over the stubble fields and swim in the river. Three whole days to spend together; and four nights.

I'd see him off on Monday morning (he wouldn't have to leave till then?), get up early and make him some breakfast. And the next Thursday evening he would come back. He would have come back.

Did I write that yesterday, or the day before? I seem to be losing count of time. I am still working but I want a drink very badly. I must not start drinking. I have got to get *Courtly Love* finished. The sherry would not do me much harm. Even two-thirds of a bottle: I should probably just be sick. No.

I wish I could go to bed. I wish I could get into bed and sleep and know no more about anything. But I can't sleep. I'm not sleeping for more than a couple of hours a night. It doesn't seem to be making work impossible yet, though it's making it very laborious, and I feel no confidence in my judgement.

I could get some sleeping pills. Might that not be as bad as drinking? Less bad in various ways, I suppose, if I did not exceed the stated dose. A certain amount of sleep is necessary for work, after all.

Tuesday, 7th April

I did sleep last night – and well on beyond the time I should get up. He certainly gave me the strong pills he promised me. A nice man: one could confide in him, up to a point, and trust him not to probe beyond that point without medical necessity. I suppose the aftermath is bound to be fairly strong, too. There is a thick taste in my mouth, and I can hardly check over yesterday's work, let alone get on with anything new. Even writing this in working hours doesn't seem to be doing much to concentrate my mind.

Still, I feel better, not least from knowing that the pills are there – I mean, so that I can be sure of some sleep, sometimes at least. If I use them on alternate nights (at most), then I should be able to work properly every second day, which is better than nothing.

I wonder if I can type with any sort of accuracy?

My griefs seem bundled and padded with a kind of woolly, waking oblivion. If I stop working (trying to work) and have a long walk to clear my head, will they cut through, clear and sharp, again? I think not, somehow. Anyway, I'll have to risk it. It's a fine, bright day, though the wind's cold. I might have lunch in a pub. No, better take sandwiches.

9.45pm

I have just had a long talk with Douglas, and I feel a good deal better. He was glad the Dictionary is so nearly done, and wondered if that would affect my decision about the Chair. I suppose if there's nothing else to keep me here – but I'm still concerned about delaying the publication of *Courtly Love* for so long. We'll have more time to talk about this when I see him. He's away for the next couple of weeks, but I'm to go to him for ten days after that. He's persuaded me not to worry about leaving Panope: he thinks she might even welcome a rest from her responsibilities. He promises me a full programme of theatres, concerts, and friends, a new exhibition at the Dulwich Picture Gallery, and walking Sam (rather less strenuously now) in Greenwich Park, as well as plenty of work: 'not a moment to call your soul your own'. Excellent friend; dear man.

I went as far as Harbourne St Jude today. I don't often get beyond the river in that direction, but I didn't want to turn home before I had to, and the new bridge past the Graysons gets one into some pleasantly bewildering lanes.

I had lunch in the lee of a haystack, and felt the warmth of the sun. As I went on, the steady stretching of my body seemed to draw off the blurry numbness from my mind and leave it to work freely, but without compulsion – turning over one or two questions in Gower, and then considering my own condition with a sort of practical, compassionate detachment, as if it were someone else's.

I thought that I should like to be somewhere where I could keep still for as long as I needed to, without the distractions of work, or hope, or housekeeping, or even the curiosity of passers-by.

A church would be out of the wind and quiet and open, and provide the right to sit still unquestioned.

It was some way to the next village, and the church was up a side road, on the slope of a hill, below a wood. I went in quietly, hoping there would be no-one cleaning the brass, but determining, in that case, to be a sightseer until I was left alone. The church was still and dusky. I shut the heavy door behind me and went to sit down in a pew near the back. There was the cold smell of stone.

The chancel arch was very early. I concentrated my mind on that, on its curve and weight and pattern of indentations, and after some time my thoughts began to fall into place, and then to become quiet and leave my mind clear, like water. After some more time had passed, another kind of perception, which was not thought – perhaps rather receptivity – began to gather, like a current, in my mind. I leaned forward and let it run through me, resting my head on my hands.

When I looked up again, I had no idea how long I had been there. My hands and feet were cold, but the rest of my body felt light. I sat for a moment in a kind of gap – a vacancy of transition – and then stood up and buttoned my jacket. I went to look at the East window, and at the archway into the Lady Chapel, later and more delicate than the chancel arch, and read the memorial plaques to local worthies on the walls. There was not a great deal more to see in the little church.

I went out, and stood for a moment in the porch, reading the notices. It was not really twilight yet, outside. I had turned to go, when the church door opened behind me, and Ben came through it into the porch. We looked at each other: he was rather white, his eyes startled and glistening, and a smear on his cheek. An urgent sense of pity overcame all my other feelings. He looked at me an instant longer, then ducked his head, went past me out of the porch, and ran down the path to the churchyard gate. I longed to follow him, but I was afraid of intruding on some desperately private grief.

I sat in the church-yard for a while, on a tombstone, to let him get ahead, and then I came home.

11th April

1.20pm

Why can't I work, now that my head is clear? And I even slept, undrugged, for a part of last night.

Determination, self-discipline are not enough. (They never are enough, I suppose, in themselves.) I have been sitting with work in front of me for four hours now, leaving my desk only twice (to let Panope in, and to make some coffee at mid-morning). And I haven't written a single sentence worth keeping. I shouldn't have written a single sentence of any kind, if I hadn't put down two or three truisms, at about twelve o'clock, by way of priming the pump. I crossed them out five minutes ago, just before I stopped work.

I suppose my subject is too near to me again – or my most urgent feelings have grown back too near to my subject. Now, again, I can keep no equilibrium in writing about these things – about *devocioun* and *loue-longynge*; I feel myself toppling, constantly, either towards the formless, dangerous marsh of undistanced feeling, or towards the flat, trodden earth of *cliché*. There seems to be no room to keep my balance in between.

This may be just a difficult stretch: I have had those before, though never one quite as baffling as this. If I keep on, I shall come through it. If I have done no more in a couple of days, I might leave the *Roman de la Rose* for the time being and move on. It should not be so difficult to make the notes for the *Vita Nuova*.

12th April

What frightens me is that this has happened before. I had to leave this subject three and a half years ago, for reasons of the same kind. But this time the reasons are much stronger and more immediate.

And I think I've gone too far, now, to turn back and start something else. If work on this book must be left unfinished, if it is all wasted, I don't know where I can find the inspiration or the energy or even the interest to begin work on another.

With such a prospect becoming steadily more likely, I realise, too, more and more clearly, how reluctant I am to put in for the Chair: how little pleasure I should take (and, very probably, how little ability I should show) in running a large department; how irreplaceably privacy and scholarship are the stuff of my life.

What would there be, then, for me to do? Is there anything, anything at all – anything possible – that I really want to do?

I should like to comfort Ben, if I knew how it could be done.

15th April

I cannot write anything about the *Vita Nuova* either. Even notes seem impossible – the choice of words vitiated.

17th April

2.05pm

I have started to index the chapters I have done. It is not an economical use of time – it would be quicker to do it for the whole book at once – but at least the only mistakes I can make are factual ones. It is a relief to be working again, and when I have written this entry, and made a cup of coffee, I think I shall work on through the afternoon. It is too windy to do much in the garden. (I ought to see if the storm brought down any tiles last night, though.) I need not hurry. I can alternate the work with writing this as I feel inclined. I don't want to finish too soon, or run out of index cards before tomorrow.

The Sonnets are still extraordinarily consoling. I read 36 last night, among others, and felt again the weight of misery lifted, given form and a separate existence and resting place:

> Let me confess that we two must be twain,
> Although our undivided loves are one:

and 116 So shall those blots that do with me remain,
Without thy help, by me be borne alone.

I might read some more before tea.

5pm

87, too, speaks astonishingly closely to my condition:

> Farewell, thou art too dear for my possessing,
> And like en

18th April

8.05am

I don't know what to do. I think Panope may be hurt, and I can't find her. I think she may even be dead.

I thought I heard her crying yesterday, early in the evening, but not at the sitting-room door. I stopped writing to listen; then I smelt something burning and went to the kitchen, and when I opened the door flames came out to meet me. But beyond them I saw – I was certain then that I saw – Panope drop down from the top window to the grass outside. I shut the door and rang the fire brigade. I couldn't get to the kitchen tap, but I found a bucket by the path, and filled it at the water butt, and went round to the back door. The fire wasn't as bad at that end of the kitchen, and I think the draught was less. I threw water on the flames and refilled the bucket several times before the fire engine arrived. I had wondered at first how long it would be before I had to abandon the fire and get the books and papers out of the sitting-room.

The firemen poured what seemed to me an unnecessary amount of water into the kitchen, but they were effective and friendly. They explained how the fire must have started, without suggesting that I was very much to blame: 'Wind like we've been having, that makes these kitchen ranges go on so, they're red-hot before you know it.' The two cloths hanging on the rail must have caught fire and lit the roller-towel on the back of the door. Then one of them fell, still burning, onto the wastepaper basket.

I made them some tea (the electric kettle was upstairs, and still working), and they insisted on my having a cup, too, and putting sugar in it, 'for shock'. They may have been right.

When they had gone, I went to see where Panope had run to. I couldn't find her. And when she didn't come to my call either, I ran back in horror and dread to the kitchen. She wasn't there, thank God. I searched every corner, every shelf. The relief was so great that I began to clear up quite cheerfully, expecting her to re-appear soon, thinking how little that really mattered had been damaged, and wondering whether the insurance would pay for the paint.

I opened the lower window and called through it now and then while I worked, and put out a saucer of milk on the inside of the sill. By the time I'd got most of the water up, and put everything that was completely charred out by the dust-bin, my unanswered voice was beginning to sound ominous. And by then it was getting dark.

I went all round the house and the garden and the lane, calling. I looked in the shed. Then I took the torch and searched the grass outside the kitchen window. Below the sill, the grass was bent, and darkened with sooty marks. I found a few more of these, fainter, making for the hedge, and near one of them a tuft of her tawny fur, singed at one edge. I am terrified that she was already on fire when she managed to get out of the top window. (Why didn't I hear her call before?) Thank God it was open anyway. Though I suppose if it hadn't been, there might have been less draught: that was why I'd shut the lower window. She may be lying somewhere, badly burned – so badly that she can't answer me? It would be hard to hear a small noise in this wind.

I searched the length of the hedge, and all round the next field, and went back to the house and got a jacket, then looked round the field on the far side of the lane. I went up to the post, and then over as far as the wood, and I looked in the wood for half the night.

I came back at about three or four in the morning, I suppose, and put out more milk, and food, and made sure that everything was still open, then went upstairs to get another sweater, and fell asleep for a few hours.

This is about the time she usually comes in for breakfast, so I'm waiting in, in case she comes in in a bad state. I meant to go on clearing up the kitchen, but it's not as bad as I thought, so I'm writing this, instead, while I wait. I do feel tired, physically, too: it may be as well to save energy for searching later. If she's not here by 9, I'll go down to Mrs Harris at the farm. If she hasn't seen her – and it's a fairly remote chance – I'll search over last night's ground again. It will be easier in the daylight.

If anything has happened to her – I mean if she is dead – I don't know what I can do. Especially if she has died in pain. I don't know what there would be, of any kind, that I could do any more.

2pm

Mrs Harris hasn't seen her. She has promised to look in the outbuildings, but thinks it's unlikely Panope would have gone there, because it's the farm cats' territory. She was very much concerned about her, and about the fire, and has offered me a bath whenever I want one, until the Aga is in order. I came back to the garden and searched there again, and in the shed and the lane and the hedge and the two fields. On the way to the wood I began to feel giddy, and realised that I had had nothing but a cup of tea since yesterday afternoon. I came back here to eat some bread and cheese, hoping – more faintly now – that she might come in at lunchtime. On my way up the garden, I thought I saw something move inside the sitting-room window. It was too high up for Panope – I saw that after a single moment of hope. It looked like someone with his back to the window, standing near the desk, stooping a little. Dazed with hunger, anxiety and the

482

lurch of hope and disappointment, I imagined for a moment that I was seeing Ben.

She wouldn't come in any later than this. I'll go down to the wood again.

She's all right. She's all right. She's all right. She's here, on my knee. We've both had tea. She came down the path to welcome me when I got back from the wood an hour ago, running unevenly, mewing. I stooped and caught her as she stood to spring. Her fur was clogged and muddy and smelt of soot. I held my face against it, and we seemed for a time to speak the same language. One place on her side is painful. She yelped when I touched it, but did not try to get down from my arms.

I wiped my eyes and took her into the house and gave her milk with warm water and a little sherry in it, and she drank most of it. Then I made a pot of tea for myself, and drank a great many cups while she sat on my knee in the armchair and let me sponge the mud off her fur with a cloth. I haven't touched the sore place again: the fur is gone there, and scorched round the edge, and the skin is blistered and suppurating a little. But it's not a very large area: the vet says it's not serious. He can dress it this evening: he'll try to fit us into his evening surgery, if we go at half past six, when it starts.

The rest of her coat is fairly clean now, and beginning to dry and get fluffy; she's washing it sleek herself, sitting on my knee at the desk while I write. I can get one more cup of tea out of the pot without disturbing her to reach the kettle.

Panope is asleep. I've been reading through these recent entries again: there's not much else within reach. How baldly I've written, sometimes.

Which is Sonnet 116? I can't remember. I can't even remember writing that reference.

'Let me not to the marriage of true minds…'? But I can hardly have meant that one. It has been one of my favourites, though, and Ben's:

'…love is not love
Which alters when it alteration finds.'

Time to go to the vet. If I get up very carefully, I may be able to get Panope into her basket without waking her. I can't get at the drawer. I don't think this will show if I put it under the index cards.

Alan,

I've read it all – this notebook, and all the other ones in the drawer. You must forgive me. (Forgive me too for writing in your notebook. Where do you keep your rough paper?) But anyway, it's all right. I love you. I've loved you for a very long time, I think – all those years when that's been the star to my wandering bark, though it took me so long to realise it. And then, more recently, when I began to understand what sort of love it was becoming, it just terrified me – I was so sure it wasn't any good: you could never feel like that about me.

So I thought I'd better just stay away: there didn't seem to be anything else I could do about it. But that was no good: it made me too miserable and I couldn't manage it – especially when I found your front door open.

You must have known how much I've always looked up to you, but just how much *I love you – how very much and with what good reason – I didn't really know until I read this last night – all night! Perhaps your height was taken, but your worth – your whole amazing worth – was unknown to me till then.*

One day, I'll tell you my side of things, to make us square. I think there'll be lots of time.

Oh, I'm so glad Panope's all right. I did hunt too, this afternoon, after I'd come back and found your early-morning entry, and discovered what had happened. But it was you she was looking for.

You'll both be tired tonight. Sleep well. I'll come round tomorrow morning. About eleven?

Love – nearly eighteen years of it, I suppose, one way and another,

Ben

CPSIA information can be obtained
at www.ICGtesting.com
Printed in the USA
BVHW070337030123
655324BV00024B/257

9 781839 758904